No Fire Escape in Hell

No Fire Escape in Hell

Kim Cayer

Winchester, UK
Washington, USA

First published by Roundfire Books, 2016
Roundfire Books is an imprint of John Hunt Publishing Ltd., Laurel House, Station Approach,
Alresford, Hants, SO24 9JH, UK
office1@jhpbooks.net
www.johnhuntpublishing.com
www.roundfire-books.com

For distributor details and how to order please visit the 'Ordering' section on our website.

Text copyright: Kim Cayer 2015

ISBN: 978 1 78535 225 6
Library of Congress Control Number: 2015946050

A CIP catalogue record for this book is available from the British Library.

Design: Stuart Davies

Printed in the USA by Edwards Brothers Malloy

We operate a distinctive and ethical publishing philosophy in all
areas of our business, from our global network of authors to
production and worldwide distribution.

Chapter One

My bags were packed. I knew this day was coming and today was the day. I was leaving my husband. For the past two weeks, I'd kept a suitcase packed with a few changes of clothes, the usual assorted socks and underwear, a couple good books. In the garage, in a black garbage bag, I had hidden a sleeping bag and pillow. And in a huge storage box that had once held a tent and camping supplies, I'd stuffed the most important tools of my trade. They absolutely had to come with me. Without the gorilla, my Madonna and Marilyn Monroe, I'd be without work as well as a home.

* * *

To outsiders, Mrs. Ben Magee had it made. Nice house, two cars in the drive, a child who was pretty decent, and a great job. I didn't work anywhere near forty hours a week yet I earned enough that I could afford to keep my husband at home. What the world did not see – what I didn't even let my closest friends or family see – was that this was one marriage that had totally unravelled.

When Ben and I first met, I had just started in my line of work. Purely by fluke, I found myself in the singing-telegram business. My best friend was an aspiring actress and had landed a role in a community play. Directed by a guy we also knew as the local Dollar Giant owner, my pal Peggy had an impressive part. On opening night, the first of their three performances, she wished that someone would send her a good-luck telegram. I tried to get her one, but time was of the essence, and I procrastinated (nothing new with me). At the last minute, and because the play was a murder mystery set among celebrities, I got dolled up as Marilyn Monroe and wrote a song wishing Peggy luck. I was

1

able to see her before the curtain went up. I did my best impression of Marilyn, sang her the telegram (and admired how I used 'Peg' to rhyme with 'Break a leg') and then left to take my seat. I figured I'd make a quick side trip to the ladies' room and wash off the fake beauty mark, remove the wig and put on less-revealing clothes.

However, I was barely out of the dressing-room door (also known as the Chem Lab at the Central Tech High School) when I almost ran into a man who strongly resembled Santa Claus. I gawked at him before I stammered, "Ooops, sorry... Wow, you look like Santa!"

"It's what I do," the stranger said. "And you look like Marilyn Monroe."

"Actually, no, I don't," I corrected him. "It's just a get-up, like a costume, you know? I gave my friend a singing-telegram kind of thing."

"Really? I've heard of that kind of thing...more in the US than here in Canada."

"Yeah, same here, that's what gave me the idea," I replied.

"Hhmm," the man mused, giving me a strange look. "I think I could use someone like you."

Before I could even inquire as to what he meant, a voice came over the school's speakers. "CURTAIN IS IN FIVE MINUTES. TAKE YOUR SEATS, PLEASE."

The man quickly reached into his breast pocket and pulled out a card. "Take this, and give me a call," he urged. "I've got to give these flowers to my wife." With that, he entered the chem lab/dressing room.

I was left wondering what he saw in me. Yes, I was dressed in a white halter dress with my breasts half-hanging out, I was wearing a lot of make-up and a sexy platinum wig...but he did mention his wife within the first thirty seconds of our meeting. I didn't think he had romance on his mind. How could he "use" me?

It was about a month later that I decided to contact him. Our chance encounter kept running through my mind while I went through the motions at work. If he had a job offer in mind, I was ready to accept it. Anything would be better than the job I was working, even though the title of Conveyor Belt Inspector held a certain eminence. But what I did was inspect the conveyor belt as it sent sheets of cookies past me. Any that were broken or misshapen were thrown away or eaten by me. Hey, it was the best job I could find after two months of looking. So much for my idea of forgoing a university education.

The brief meeting between Santa and I led me to believe that, if there were a job offer on the table, it would be distasteful. I mean, the guy caught a good eyeful of 36DDs, and that's probably what registered. If googling had been around back then, I may have assuaged my fears with a couple internet searches. But all I had to go on was his business card, which read 'Harry Goldblum Agency – I Can Supply All Your Needs' and listed his phone number. Fearing he was the owner of an escort agency is what delayed my calling him. What finally prompted the call was the batch of chocolate cookies that came through on the conveyor belt, missing the white filling. Since management didn't care what we did with the discards, I ate about eighty of them. The stomach-ache afterward was the sign I needed a new line of work.

It's funny when I remember my first call to Harry. He recalled who I was and suggested I drop in for an interview. When I asked him what he had in mind, he simply asked, "Well, how would you like to earn a few more dollars a week at a part-time job?" Ah ha! I just knew my suspicions were going to be true! Yet something made me ask for his address and we settled on a meeting for the next day.

Before we disconnected, he shouted, "Oh! Madeline! Make sure you come dressed EXACTLY like you were when I first saw you."

"That was a costume," I reminded him. "I don't really look like that."

"That's the look I want to see," he stated firmly. "OK? Noon tomorrow."

The next day, I got myself dressed up again as Marilyn Monroe. I took a lot of time getting ready, but it still felt like I was entering a Halloween Best-Dressed competition. The Harry Goldblum Agency was located in downtown Toronto and I had to park quite some distance away from his location. I felt like a fool as I parked my car, walked three blocks to the office building and waited for an elevator with twelve other people, all pretending not to look at me. I was only too happy to escape on Floor 14 and scurry down the hall to 1414, the Harry Goldblum Agency.

I opened the door and saw a sight that gave me deja vu. I swear I'd viewed this scene in some black-and-white movie, or seen it in an old comic book. Upon entering, I immediately saw rows and rows of photos. They weren't lewd photos of semi-dressed women; instead I saw images of jugglers, acrobats, magicians, fire breathers, puppeteers. I even saw a photo of a heavyset Marilyn Monroe. A voice brought me back to earth. "Hello, can I help you?"

Full of gratitude that my fears were unfounded, I beamed at the receptionist. "Yes! Hello! How are you?"

"I'm fine," she replied. She looked at me over the top of her little round John Lennon-type glasses. "Did you have an appointment?"

"Yes, I'm sup—" I did a double-take at the employee. Why, with her hair in those corn rows, and those glasses, and the fact she was black... "—supposed to see Harry Goldblum at noon." Then I stated the obvious. "Boy, do you ever look like Whoopi Goldberg!"

"No kidding, do you have a job for me?" she said. In response to my curious look, she continued. "It used to be Whoopi was so popular. What happened? Anyhow, Harry's a bit backed up. Take a seat."

And this is where the deja vu feeling continued. Whoopi pointed to a section of the room with a couple couches. There was a guy sitting there with a colourful crank box and a monkey. Obviously an organ grinder. The monkey was so lifeless, I feared it was drugged. Next to him was a man who kept clinking and clanking, what with the tambourines between his knees, cymbals at his elbows and drums at his hips. I surmised he was a one-man band. Across from them was a beautiful woman, sitting in a beaded gown, with twenty or thirty hula hoops leaning against her. I took the seat next to her and brazenly checked out the hoop dancer. Up close she wasn't as young as I'd thought; she could have been up to twenty years older! Yet her facial life lines were artfully camouflaged, and I saw the gown was reinforced with a lot of whalebone action. When I caught the hoopster's eye, I was about to speak up and ask just what the hell this place was. Harry took that moment to walk into the room.

He held out an envelope to the one-man band. "Here's the pay for your last two shows and the details for the gig this afternoon." He turned to the organ grinder. "Sandro, I told you, buddy, I would call you if I had work for you. I don't need to see your act again."

"Puh-leeze, Mr. Goldblum," the organ grinder beseeched. "Me and monkey, we got a new trick. I show it to you."

Harry looked at the animal. "That monkey looks sick."

"It's only because he no work! Me, I can paint houses. The monkey, this is all he know!" Sandro prodded his pet. "Monkey! Loop de loop time! Wake up!"

The monkey woke up, blinked two times and went back into its stupor. Harry just shook his head. "I hate to say it, but Monkey may be getting old. Isn't he the same one you started with?"

"Yes, but monkeys live a long time," Sandro explained. "Maybe I can wait until Monkey wake up."

Harry looked like he would prefer Sandro to leave but after a moment, he shrugged his shoulders. He looked over at the hula-hoop gal. "Lena, you ready? okay, go in the office. And fix your cleavage, something's off." He turned to me. "Madeline, I'm glad you made it. I'll only be a few minutes. In the meantime, can you sign this form?" He placed a piece of paper and a pen on the coffee table in front of me and walked away.

The form basically allowed me to grant all parties the right to photograph, videotape or vocally record me. I signed it and waited my turn to see Harry. I could tell he was taking photographs of Lena! The Hula Hoop Sensation! Flashes of light kept illuminating the office and Harry could be heard encouraging her. "Come on! Another one! Two more! Spin 'em, Lena! Faster!" Eventually there was a loud crash, a moment of silence and then Lena exited the office with all her hoops. Harry called me in.

A coat-stand had been knocked over, along with a large stand-up fan and a plant. Harry was putting his office back to order and offered me a seat. "I want to thank you for wearing the Marilyn look," he said, picking up his camera. "May I?"

"May you what? Take a photo of me?" I put the permission form on his desk. "Go ahead, I guess."

Harry took a couple shots and I smiled brightly. But he didn't look happy. "No, that's not right. Can you smile with your mouth wide open?" I did as he asked, but it just felt so awkward. "Try tilting your head back, it will feel more natural," Harry suggested. And what do you know? It felt much better. Harry snapped off a few more photos and then put the camera away.

"Ok, I'm going to develop those, and we can get some better ones made up later," he said. I still didn't know why I was there.

"Uh, Harry? Is this about a job of some kind?"

"Only if you're looking for a job," Harry said. "And I really think you could work out." It turned out Harry ran some kind of talent agency, where you could find acts that were off the beaten path. Unusual acts. One-of-a-kind acts. Or acts that just didn't fit into the usual categories.

"So you would want me as a Marilyn Monroe?" I asked.

"In a way," he said, pulling out a folder with a label declaring it HOLLYWOOD STARS. From that he pulled out four photographs. They were of different women, all portraying Marilyn Monroe. "Two of these girls work non-stop," he said. "They sing live, so they do all the stage shows. And this girl is pregnant, she won't be working for awhile, and my fourth Marilyn is...well, she just doesn't know how to work a crowd."

"Oh, boy, this all sounds exciting, Harry, but I can't sing," I said. "I couldn't carry a tune if it had handles."

"I heard you sing that song to your friend," he reminded me.

"Yeah, but no, but yeah, but..." and I stopped to gather my wits. Wow, he was talking showbiz to me! It can get to a girl's head, you know. "I guess I have an okay voice, but I was always better at putting on a character voice—"

Harry cut in. "Look, here is what I'm going to suggest. I need somebody to do singing telegrams. The main thing we supply for is birthdays, and do you know how many times I get people asking for somebody to sing 'Happy Birthday' the way Marilyn Monroe sang to President Kennedy? I've asked my other Marilyns to do it, but they're used to the big bucks from the stage shows. They won't condescend to singing telegrams. I told them – this ain't corporate. This is some private joe who's sending this as a gift."

"So you'd like me to do Marilyn Monroe singing telegrams?" I asked, just to get it straight in my head.

"That's it. But tell me first, what are you gonna charge me?"

I didn't know what to say. I was currently making a tiny bit more than minimum wage; so if he could beat that...? Instead, I countered with, "What were you thinking of paying me?"

Twenty years ago this was. He offered me $60 a show and I jumped on that so fast, you would have thought it was an escort agency.

Since then, I've more than doubled my rate. Though I still work for Harry, word got out about me. Other agencies found out about my services and I expanded my clientele. But back then, I didn't even know if I could pull off my first job. I expressed my doubts.

"Look, Miss Madeline, this ain't rocket science. It will be just like the thing you did for your pal. We'll get some info on the guy and you write a song about them. Then you joke around, kid around, few laughs, you sing 'Happy Birthday' just like Marilyn sang to the President, and you're outta there. Piece of cake," Harry explained.

"OK, I'll give it a shot," I decided. "And, Harry, I gotta clear up something you said when we first met. I said you looked like Santa and you said, 'that's what I do'. Do you really play Santa Claus?"

"When it's that time of year," he agreed. "Christmas time is a bonanza for me."

I laughed. "Oh! I thought you were Jewish!"

"I am, but that won't stop me from playing Santa. Not when there's so much money to be made! So just because you're not a dead movie star shouldn't stop you from pretending to be one. Give it one job, and see how you like it."

And a month after that meeting, I was giving my notice to the cookie company. That first show was nerve-wracking. I almost didn't do it. But as far as shows go, it was as simple as they get. I went into a nursing home, was led to a room with the 90-year-old birthday boy, and sang my song. The nurses watching me didn't bother me; neither did the senior citizen laying in the other bed. It was so easy, I couldn't wait for my next one. A couple days later, Harry called and he had two gigs for the same day. I sang 'Happy Birthday' to the President of a tire company and then to a lowly worker at a dry-cleaning company.

When the weekend rolled around, Harry had three more.

When it dawned on me that I could actually make a living doing this...when doing three telegrams a week basically equalled to me working 40 hours at my old job...well, Mama didn't raise a fool. Even if this job was short-lived, I didn't want to miss any potential bookings because of the cookie line.

As I said, twenty years ago. Since then, I totally expanded my repertoire of costumes. Marilyn is still my bread and butter, but I get the occasional Madonna as well. Gorilla telegrams are huge, French maids, bag ladies, cops, nuns... And I was good at what I did. By some stroke of luck, God had given me a certain bone structure to my face. I was able to very convincingly pull off Madonna and Marilyn Monroe. If needed, I could look very beatific as a nun, or quite intimidating as a cop. I always felt like I was playing make-believe, and nobody would know who was really behind the mask...even if I wasn't wearing a mask.

If you saw me as myself and not a singing-telegram performer, you wouldn't look twice. I have the blandest of all appearances. I'm not beautiful, but I'm not ugly. My height is normal, my clothes are unremarkable, my hair is almost always in a boring ponytail. But once I had a costume on, I became very funny, very engaging and flirtatious, quick with comebacks and bon mots.

I was just getting the hang of the singing-telegram business when I met Ben. It was a dark night, and his sister had booked me to sing 'Happy Birthday' to their uncle. After my act was done, Ben stepped forward and said the streetlights were out; did I want him to escort me to my car? I accepted, rather charmed, and I also gave up my phone number when he asked for it. I was single, so was he, he was also cute, and I was (in retrospect) a fool.

Ben had a pretty decent job working as a carpenter for a housing development and his weekly paycheques were cause for useless purchases. However, he never saw a person make money like I could. Mind you, even I was amazed. And because I was brought up to save money for a rainy day, perhaps even a retirement, I socked away as much as I could.

From meeting to marriage didn't take long. Within a year we had announced our engagement. Maybe deep in my heart I didn't feel quite ready, maybe I still had a few years to look around. Yes, Ben was handsome and he had a good job, but there were already things I didn't like. Mainly, he wasn't happy unless his bank account read nil and there wasn't a penny to be found in his house or pocket. But in a moment of weakness (Was I drinking? Was I stoned?), I agreed. *Oh well, I'll be engaged for a couple months*, I thought. A couple months later, I found myself pregnant. Rather than have his mother go into shock over the fact that her 28-year-old son was having sex, we decided to get married immediately.

I worked well into my seventh month of pregnancy, although Marilyn and Madonna were shelved at the five-month stage. I watched what I ate and after popping out an eight-pound girl, I was left with having only twenty pounds to lose. I played one of those heavyset Marilyns until I was back to my fighting weight of 120 pounds. Suddenly I found myself incredibly busy. Between work, nursing and breast-pumping, I was also searching for some kind of babysitter. Nobody seemed pleased with my paltry offerings.

"Well, say I have a show in Scarborough at two p.m.," I said. "I would need you at one o'clock and I'd probably be back at three."

"You need me to come from my house, to come to your your house, for two hours only?" I'd often be asked.

"Yes, but I'd pay you top dollar," I enticed them. "The going rate is, what, five bucks an hour? I'll give you $7."

The smart ones would say, "Ooohhh, wow, $14 for me to bus it over here and take care of a crying, pooping baby. Are you crazy?"

Sometimes the mother-in-law would babysit, but that was asking for a huge headache. She was forever doing math of some kind. Take her last duty as nanny.

"You knew Ben for how long before you got engaged? I dated his father for six years before we got married," Phyliss, the current Mrs. Sheaffer, said.

"Yeah, but weren't you married to a Mr. Tomlinson for four of those years?" I asked.

"But I still waited two more years to marry Ben's father," she said in her defence.

"Oh, please," I begged. "That's because Tomlinson wouldn't sign the divorce papers. You got married the day after the divorce."

She changed the subject. "And Shannon is three months old now. Look how chubby she is! You said she was born two months early – how can she be this big?"

"Maybe it was more like six weeks early." I lied, she was born full-term, but Phyliss had such contrary ideas, premarital sex being one of them, that Ben and I had to fib to her my entire pregnancy. "She's not due for another eight weeks," I'd say, though I was as big as a barn and my hospital bag was already waiting by the front door.

"Then she's far too big to be a premature baby," she decided. "I think it's your breast milk. It may be too rich for her. I heard formula is much better for babies these days."

She was easy to read. After having made this ludicrous statement, she backed up to a cupboard by the fridge. I gave her the eye and walked over.

"Don't tell me, Phyliss," I warned her. "I better not find any kind of formula in your cupboard..."

She meekly tried to block me. I stopped and picked up Shannon, who was still in her car seat. "Listen, no singing telegram is worth you messing around with my baby..."

"Don't deny me access to my grandchild!" she cried dramatically. "Fine! I won't feed her formula! But your stupid ice-cube trays of breastmilk are so time-consuming!"

I placed my child down, making it look like she'd won this battle. "Just please stick to the feeding schedule. Breastmilk only." I wanted to do something right by my child. Heaven knows I failed at having a natural childbirth. I was barely into the first contraction before I was bellowing for drugs. "I promise you, Phyliss. Before you know it, she'll be eating baby food. Then you can knock yourself out."

That brightened her, and we managed to part on a happier note. But I didn't feel happy; I felt stressed. Seems every time I had to interact with Ben's mother, it took the wind out of my sails. I'd walk into an office, or stroll into a wedding reception, dressed as Marilyn Monroe with a big phoney smile plastered on her face. I know – I saw photos people would send to the agency. I could always tell when I'd seen Phyliss before a gig. It wasn't a smile on Marilyn; rather, it looked more like a snarl.

There seemed to be only one solution – turn this new Magee family unit into a single-income operation. As it was, Ben only worked about five months a year. Blame it on his lack of seniority, rainy days, his knack of oversleeping. Being allowed to not work at all – just sleep in 'til he wanted, play his online video games, surf the net – he agreed to the idea with more enthusiasm than he'd shown on our wedding night.

Mind you, he still had a baby to look after. But how hard could that be when the working wife was often home most of the day, maybe stepping out at noon to do a quick telegram and returning at two p.m., just in time to wake Shannon up from her nap. Perhaps I may leave again at nine p.m., once Shannon was put down for the night. On the weekends, Ben had his work cut out for him. He actually had to warm up one of the many bottles I'd prepared earlier. And as the months wore on, he graduated to feeding Shannon baby food. I hope my poor baby carries no memories of having to wait for a dragon to be slain before she could get a mouthful of Pablum, and then having to wait some more while the warrior slew a gladiator before getting her next bite. Feedings could take a couple hours.

The deal was that Ben would stay home with the baby until one of two things happened – she reached full-time school age or the good times stopped rolling and Ben might have to go back to work. Yet even though we quickly found ourselves in a recession, it didn't affect my business whatsoever. On the contrary, it seemed that the more miserable people got, the less they minded spending money on something that gave them a good laugh. Ben got to stay home and chill out to his heart's content; we still dined on pizza and sushi nightly; and I worked hard those early years. While Ben had his heart set on a big-screen TV for the kitchen of the apartment we were renting, I was still managing to pinch pennies for a house. Could life get any better?

* * *

Fast forward about fifteen years. Things between Ben and I had come to a boil. Actually, we were on a steady simmer the entire marriage. Maybe we didn't know each other long enough, maybe we rushed into marriage because I was pregnant, but truth be known, my husband and I were just not meant for each other. We created an amazing kid, but I prayed she inherited just my genes.

End-of-marriage stories are so twisted. How to capsulate in one paragraph? Remember the deal? I work, Ben plays at Mr. Mom, and we wait until Shannon reaches Grade One. By then, there was a multitude of options, including the one that I'd likely be home 80 per cent of the time school let out.

Shannon was six when I started dropping subtle hints that Ben think about going back to work. She was eight when I asked him to start looking for a job. By then we were in our new house and the bills were quite substantial. When Shannon had her tenth birthday and Ben dropped her fancy ice-cream cake, I saw the light. He was so nonchalant about it, and simply asked for another 40 bucks to go get another one. It was then that I fully realized he had no concept of money and what it cost just to get by. That night, I begged him to go back to work. I pointed out that we had a lot of new expenses, things like furnaces and air conditioners. When our baby was 12, even though I was still working often, it was nothing like the 'old days'. I made it clear to Ben that I wasn't getting any younger – Barbie telegrams were going to the performers who actually looked like they were in their early twenties. I hadn't done a showgirl in over a year. Agents weren't going to be so rude as to say, "Babe, you're getting old. Can't use you as a princess anymore. You're more queenly now." No, they just start to wean you off them. It's kind of creepy anyways, when you're 38 and you're doing a showgirl for a 19-year-old. You hear the word 'cougar' more often than if you were on safari.

Back to tracking our landslide of a marriage through Shannon's years. From 14 to 16, Ben and I did nothing but argue. It dawned on me that perhaps Ben didn't want to go back to work, no matter how much I harped. In order to make ends meet, I was taking every job I could, even if it meant I had to drive across town in Friday rush-hour for a single show. Those turned ten-minute jobs into four-hour treks. And in 16 years of marriage, I know for a fact that Ben emptied the dishwasher twice and made me a meal five times and changed the bed sheets five times and never did a load of laundry. Some Mr. Mom. More like Mr. Stay At Home and Make Sure the Kid Stays Alive Until the Mother Gets Back.

It came as blessed relief when Ben said he wanted out. I wanted out pretty much 15 years ago, but did I mention nobody could procrastinate like me? What I wasn't prepared for was Ben's ultimatum. He would leave, gladly, once I paid him his "due". Say what?

"$100,000," Ben decreed. "For the years I've been married to you. I think I should get that much."

"Where am I going to get a hundred thou?" I blustered.

"You have savings," he stated. And that was true, I did have

14

some money saved up. Isn't that what all sensible women do? But there was nothing close to $100,000!

However, I was so eager to be rid of him that I agreed to the deal. "Fine, I'll give you $100,000. Of course, not all at once, but maybe over ten years or something."

And that's when any love remaining between us completely flew out the window. "I want all of it, at once, and I'll be gone for good."

"How am I going to manage that?" I cried.

"You cash in your RRSPs, your investments, your savings..."

"That still won't amount to what you want!" I retorted. "And you want to leave me penniless? Don't forget, we have a kid in high school, going to university soon. You're going to do that to us?"

"I don't care how you get me the money, just get it. I want out as much as you want me out," Ben said with a sneer.

And then came four, five months of utter hell. All Ben did was nag at me for his money. I set up a separate bank account, labelling it Ben's Escape Fund. I cashed in my savings and dumped the money into that account. I found two banks willing to give me lines of credit and with a sick stomach, I threw another thirty grand into the secret stash. I cashed in every coin jar and piggy bank we had in the house, coming up with another $250. But I still had fifty thousand to come up with, and I felt I was out of options.

Ben would wake up. "Good morning, Shannon," he'd say to the kid. To me, "Madeline, did you get me my money yet?"

Ben would lose at his World of Warcraft game. "Goddam stupid game! If you gave me my money, I'd be playing this in my own place."

Ben would take a shower while I had the dishwasher and the laundry machine running. "No hot water! If you gave me my money, I'd be in a place with all the hot water I wanted!"

Money, money, money. He didn't let up. And it was getting to me. All I would have to do is find myself in the same room as him and he'd start the same old litany. I began to take the back roads on the way home from gigs. I just wanted the peace and quiet, the lonely roads, the time spent to myself. Going to work was like getting a day-pass out of Hell. Going home just put me in the worst kind of funk.

I was in such a bad state of mind that – and I don't want to sound strange – suicide would flit across my mind. It wasn't like I was EVER a fan of suicide before all this trouble started. It was just that lately, the idea of committing suicide didn't seem scary, or even crazy. It felt more like a welcome escape from the life I was living.

There was one strong reason why I knew I would never go through with it, and that was obviously my child. Shannon was turning out way better than I could have imagined, and having the stigma of a mom who hung herself (or whatever method I would use) would surely haunt her. Plus she needed me; I was her mother.

And then one day, while driving all the way to Windsor (six-hour round-trip) to do a ten-minute French maid, the answer just slid into place. I knew where I would live! And it would be cheap, and it was a place I knew very well...

I discussed the idea with Shannon, who was completely against it. "That's crazy!" she exclaimed. "Just stay home."

"I don't know if I can," I admitted. "Your dad is making me mental. All I do is cry in this house. I'm tired of feeling like this. I need to get that last bit of money together and I need to be away from him."

"Tell me about it," she noted. "I wish you would just go to a women's shelter."

After a particularly loud shouting match once, I barricaded myself in Shannon's room and had my fifth big cry of the day. Shannon pulled out her laptop. "I'm afraid things might get worse, Mom," she said, looking concerned. "Let's see if we can find you a place where you can go and Dad can't find you."

We did find a few and I held onto that list for a couple months. One day, again after a fight that had my new neighbours all agog, I ran to my car and peeled out of the driveway. I was going to one of those shelters, I decided. A moment later, I assessed the situation. Did they accept people who would be coming and going at all hours, obviously earning enough money that they could be staying in a hotel nightly if they wanted? I just didn't feel that I would belong, that I would somehow be discriminated against. No, I couldn't live at a shelter.

"I don't like the idea of you living like that," Shannon pouted.

"Really, Shannon, don't worry about me," I soothed her. "I want to live there! I'm actually looking forward to it!"

Ben knew I couldn't take much more. Perhaps the packed suitcase gave him a clue. "Oh, you think you can leave, do you?" he jeered. "And you're leaving Shannon with me? You know that's called child abandonment, huh?"

I wasn't too concerned. In a couple years, Shannon would be an adult and could do what she wanted, even if that included living with me. "Just keep pushing me, Ben. Keep running your mouth about money. I sure could save up a lot quicker if you got a job. You know, dual income? I wouldn't even care if you didn't give me any of your paycheque, as long as I'm not paying for your games and your coffees and your lottery tickets—"

"I'm not getting a job, I told you! Just get me my money! Get me my money! GET ME MY MONEY!" And he kept shouting it at me, not six inches away from my face, spittle flying into the corner of my eye and into my mouth. He was acting like he might suffer a breakdown, which only further angered me. Yes, I know he wanted out, but how bad did he have it?

"Leave me alone!" I shouted, running from the bedroom and down the stairs. Ben followed me into the living room. It wasn't the Ben I knew though. This was some demented guy who had grown tired of using his words and was considering using some other kind of tool. "How long do I have to wait for my money?!" he screamed.

"Just go away!" I cried, running into the kitchen. He followed me, and it would have seemed childish if he didn't have the beet-red face and clenched jaw. He repeated his money-grubbing line again. I flew back up the stairs and into the bedroom. I was going to lock the door on him.

I had just clicked the lock into place when BAM! he forced the door open. I don't even think he bothered to see if it was locked; he just threw his weight against the door. "You get me my money!!!" he roared, right up in my grill again.

I backed up in fear, bumping into my suitcase. Or maybe the suitcase reached out for me, just a reminder to say, "Hey, I'm here if you need me." I placed my hand on the handle of the case and suddenly a thought came into my mind that felt as right as rain. IT WAS TIME TO GO. I didn't want to be in the house if things were going to get worse than this. As it was, I felt fearful. Maybe not that I would be killed, but afraid that I would get the shit kicked out of me.

Grabbing the suitcase, I shoved past him. "I'm leaving!" I screamed. "I'll get your stupid money, but I can't be around you anymore!"

"Go ahead and leave," he yelled. "Just get me my money!"

I ran out of the house with my purse and my suitcase. Knowing he wouldn't hear the garage door opening, I quickly grabbed the supplies I'd left there and threw them into my car. Boy, I didn't think I was taking much, but in no time at all, my car was completely full.

I walked back to the front of my house and snapped a photograph of it with my cellphone. I was ready to go. Yes, I was crying, sobbing actually, but this had to happen. I turned my back on my lovely house and walked over to my next place of residence – my 2004 Suzuki Swift.

Chapter Two

When did the idea of living in my car really start feeling like a good idea? I believe it was the day I had three gigs, all in the Richmond Hill area. A morning, late-afternoon and evening show. Instead of wasting gas going to and fro, instead of subjecting myself to more haranguing at home, I decided to while away the downtime in my car. I caught up on bookwork. I ate a delicious lunch that was far too large, and it turned into a sufficient dinner as well. I had a much-needed two-hour nap, woken only by my pre-set Blackberry alarm. I caught up with a couple girlfriends via old-fashioned telephone conversation. All while in my vehicle.

And you know, it wasn't too bad. I realized I could probably be quite comfortable residing in my car. At least it would be a respite from my exhausting, negative-energy husband. I began thinking about it on a level that probably wasn't healthy. Obsessing on it until I finally brought the subject up with Shannon. Of course the plan didn't sit well with her, even though I stressed I was surprisingly excited about the idea.

"It's just not done, Mom!" she said. "It's kind of creepy actually."

"Well, you have to admit my life at home sucks, Shannon." I stated the obvious. "And it's not like it'll be for a long time. It's just until I can get that last bit of money together for your dad. Then I'll move back in, he'll move out and life will be beautiful."

"OK, but only as a last resort," Shannon gave in. "And we'd have to keep in touch. Not just texts or phone calls, but actual meets."

The depression I thought could go no deeper found a new low. "Oh, Shannon, please don't think I'm gonna disappear for good! You know I love you beyond belief."

"Ditto," said Shannon.

"So we'll find days where we can meet, have dinner, maybe catch a movie..."

"Meet, talk, maybe no movie though. You know my schedule is all over the place," Shannon reminded me.

I gave her a hug, which I needed more than her. "My people will call your people." I laughed through my tears. "Anyhow, I barely see you as it is. But I'll need to get my mail, my cheques, my bills. You'll need to get that to me because I'm not coming back until your dad is gone, baby, gone."

Shannon had a good head on her shoulders. I know I've probably mentioned she is a super kid, but let me briefly tell you what I truly loved about my only child. Never mind the fact that she somehow managed to put her parents constant battling on a shelf and concentrate on her own personality. She currently held a school grade average of about 86% and she played on a rep baseball team, which meant they were all extraordinary athletes. She helped me clean the house, she took phone calls sensibly, she ate wisely, and she has been involved in a loving romantic relationship with the same person since she was 14.

Shannon was head over heels in love with Jody. And Jody couldn't treat Shannon any better if I'd picked out the boyfriend myself. They had each other's backs, they were loyal and when Shannon wasn't busy at her studies, her baseball or her part-time job, I knew she would be with Jody. The thing I loved the best about Shannon was that she was helping Jody with a rather mind-boggling problem. It was something you thank your lucky stars you never had to deal with.

Both Shannon and Jody were 'straight'. Shannon liked boys and Jody liked girls. The only tiny, teensy little thing was that Jody was born a girl. He (she? But from now on, he will be called 'he') didn't look like a girl, didn't act like a girl, didn't sound like a girl. He was actually a very nice-looking specimen of the male human race. Jody longed to be an actual man and after years of mental pain, as well as physical pain caused by those who just didn't understand, he began to seek treatment. Shannon was there for Jody every step of the way.

That was my 17-year-old daughter and other than a set of dysfunctional parents, she seemed to have her act together. Me? I was doomed if I stayed in that house another minute. If I didn't get out now, she'd have a dad in jail, and a mom who, were she to have a broken nose and blackened eyes, could not get work. Then where would that leave us? Mom trying to support everyone working as a Walmart shelf stocker? I had no skills other than my looks.

And if I were in a mental institution, where I felt I was heading, I wouldn't be able to support us at all.

Chapter Three

With my sight blinded by tears, I didn't want to drive far. In the past, after a particularly brutal verbal match, I would flee my house. The place I would usually go, after picking up my XL double-double Tim Horton's coffee, was the local church. It wasn't my faith, but it was a church and I always felt pacified after a visit. Sometimes, if I would communicate some of my marital problems to my mother, she would often suggest I go to church. And her advice was right on the mark. Though I wouldn't actually go inside, the parking lot always seemed to do the trick.

I backed my Suzuki Swift into its 'usual' spot, in the rear of the lot. Facing forward, because even though I live in fairly safe Mississauga, Ontario, Canada, I still wanted to see what was in front of me. I was parked under a tree, close to a chain-link fence that enclosed a lonely playground. I cracked my coffee lid open, took a big gulp, scalded my throat and renewed my crying.

Crying? Quite the understatement. This was the bawling binge of a lifetime. When I managed to stop, the enormity of my future plans caused the sobs to start all over again. Was I really planning on living in my car? Wahhhh! After a couple hours of this, my coffee was cold and I had to pee. I went back to the Tim Horton's store, used their ladies' room and decided to grab another coffee.

I recognized the lady who took my order. It was Mahatmamu. Not that we were anywhere near friends; she wore a name-tag that I saw countless times a week when she served me at the drive-through line. She was very pleasant and it didn't matter if I looked like Marilyn Monroe or a bag lady, she would always recognize me.

But not this time. She simply took my order with a vacant look in her eyes, which put a stop to my usual immature greeting, "How do you do, Mahatmamu?" She would smile, while I always got a big kick out of my own joke. So she had me wondering how I could look any worse than I did when I was an overly made-up, teeth-blackened bag lady. I decided to pay another visit to the loo, and maybe look in the mirror this time. Besides, I'd used up all my Kleenex tissues and perhaps Tim Horton's would lend me a roll?

What was staring back at me in the mirror wasn't human. My face was beyond splotchy, my eyes were swollen and puffed, my lips were chapped and dry. And the hair! Was it my own or a fright wig? Who could know that running my hands through it a hundred times in grief would cause it to stand straight up? I tried to grab a roll of toilet paper but the coffee shop had them locked down. The best I could do was unroll about a kilometre of it, knowing I was in for another crying jag.

I returned to the exact spot I had vacated minutes earlier. Getting cozy with Christ, hoping He might show me a sign that everything would be all right. With the heater running through the night, my crying jag reduced itself to those big hiccups. I managed to fall asleep for a couple hours. I kept coming to with a start, surprised by the darkness, then being completely floored by the fact I was not in my bed. Not tonight and not anytime soon.

By seven a.m., I was awake but in a daze. Thoughts of 'doing something' rolled through my mind. Gee, it was seven o'clock. I should be unloading the dishwasher...filling the laundry machine...making Shannon breakfast before she left for school... But all that would likely be left for Shannon to do, while her mother was on the lam from her father. The sniffles began again.

The church was showing some action. I wasn't really paying attention but I could see cars showing up and parking close to the front door. Not wanting to be seen by these people, I would duck low into my seat. None of the cars would stay long though, and by nine a.m., the church's lot was almost empty again. Perhaps four cars, and they were parked quite a distance away from me. I was free to howl and get the rest of my freaking tears out of my system.

Time seemed to drag by. It kept occurring to me that I should drive away, but where would I go? It appeared I would eventually drive to a gas station, since heating my car all night had almost eaten up the half-tank it had. And I suppose I should pee. But the lethargy was overwhelming.

That is, until I saw a short, middle-aged woman standing in the doorway to the church, staring at me. I quickly slunk lower in my seat and waited a couple minutes, then peeked my head over the steering wheel. Shit! She was still there and she was still looking at me! Once more I ducked, but then realized I may be acting like a criminal. Straightening up, I snuck one more look at her, only to find that she was almost at my car!

Upon closer examination, I didn't think I had any problem. She was a short, older lady with a Mother Goose-like appearance, especially with her blue apron that had teddy bears emblazoned over it. Her hair was permed in an old-fashioned way, each curl perfectly obvious. She hugged her arms to her body to keep warm and almost slipped. Foolish lady, not wearing a jacket in February, and sporting a pair of Croc shoes when it was definitely winter-boot weather. Her cherubic face held a slight countenance of worry to it. What could she want with me?

Lowering my window, I tried to smile but it was a truly lame attempt. Call it an exercise in stretching my lips. "Is something wrong?" I asked.

"I'm sorry, but you have us very concerned. We run a daycare out of the church and you've been parked here all morning and we need to let the kids out for their morning break and we see you here watching the playground..." Mrs. Goose nervously babbled on.

"WATCHING THE PLAYGROUND?" I interrupted forcefully. "What are you talking about?"

"Well, you know, in this day and age, we can't be too careful, and we even had a couple parents who saw you and wondered what you were doing here..."

"I'll tell you what I'm doing here! I'm at a church, where I always come when I need some spiritual guidance," I shouted. "My marriage is falling apart, I don't know what I'm going to do, I don't know how my kid is going to make out... I thought, maybe I'll come to God's house, maybe He can help me... BUT NO!!! You think I'm some kind of pedophile? And so you've come to kick me outta God's house?!"

"It's just that it's so suspicious," the lady offered. "And I'm real sorry to hear about your situation. You can explain that to the police, if you want to remain here. I'm sure they will understand..."

I put the car into Drive. "OK, I'm leaving," I told her. 'But now you've really done it. I will never come to this church again." And I drove off.

I peeled out of there quickly, hoping nobody had bothered to take down my license plate. The big bad child molester was leaving – you can let those sexy little toddlers out to play. I hope the daycare was happy, because now I had no home and no faith.

Chapter Four

That first full day of living in my car went from bad to worse. I didn't feel like thinking about my dilemma. After gassing up, I found a spot at South Common Mall, a local shopping centre. It was farther away from the mall that was within walking distance from my home...well, the house on which I was paying the mortgage. I felt sure that Ben would never drive out there and I didn't want to leave the Mississauga area.

After cruising around the lot for ten minutes, looking for just the right spot to grab a much-needed snooze, I decided to park right behind the big SOUTH COMMON – MISSISSAUGA'S FAVOURITE MALL sign. I don't know who gave them that moniker – I'm pretty sure they came up with it themselves. Other than the ubiquitous No-Frills and Walmart stores located at opposite ends, the rest of the place was a ghost town. Even though the sign fronted the street, I was sure nobody would notice me. The multi-worded plank completely hid my car.

Snow was coming down in gentle pellets and the sign cast a long shadow over my vehicle. With the heat on high, I instantly started to yawn. Oh, I just knew a good sleep was coming my way, and I couldn't wait. I reclined my seat...that is, I tried to lay back, but the chair would only tilt down a couple inches. I had so much stuff thrown hari-kari into my car, it was so jam-packed, that laying down became a dream in itself. I was doomed to sleep upright, but that was okay. I was so bloody tired, I could sleep standing up in a Tim Horton's line-up.

Was that an alarm clock I heard? I didn't recall setting it...and as I strove to awaken from my deep slumber, I stabbed at my Blackberry. The ringing stopped. I was just about to slip back into serious REMs when the ringing started again. As I fumbled to grab the phone (did I hit snooze instead of quit?), my eyes glanced upon the dashboard clock in the car. Three p.m.! Wow!

That had to be the most solid nap I'd ever taken.

And what was this? The phone was ringing because DUH, I had a phone call. In my amazement at this, I neglected to answer it. It went onto the missed-call list, which now numbered 15. I started to get an icy feeling, the first thought always being Shannon. Yes, ten calls were from Ben, but a quick look at my texts showed there was nothing wrong with our daughter. The other five were from Shamrock Shows.

Why would they call me five times? They were one of the many entertainment agencies I worked for. Though they were not one of my favourites, they were a source of income. If I saw ONE missed call from them, they knew I would call them back as soon as I possibly could. I mean, work paid the bills, right?

I gave them a friendly call, my voice a bit hoarse from all that howling at the moon I did the night previous. "Hey, Stan, it's Madeline. You called?"

Stan was always calm. I don't know how he got much business with that monotone of a voice. But his reply threw me for a loop. 'MADELINE WHERE THE FUCK ARE YOU?"

"Uh...at a mall?" I tried on for size.

"So you blew off your Madonna?" he spat out.

OH SHIT. In all this drama, I totally forgot about work! I was so caught up in poor poor pitiful me, I forgot that I actually had a life! Telegrams to sing, income to bring in, a daughter to raise and a husband to pay off. How could I screw up so badly on my first day of freedom?

"Oh, Stan, I totally forgot!" I exclaimed. No need to fill him in on the actual story.

"Well, listen, they don't leave the office until five, so you can still do the show, they said. But you gotta be there by 4:45 at the latest," Stan informed me. "Can you do it? I don't want to lose this client."

"Yeah, yeah, I'm on my way," I said quickly. "Thank goodness they managed to change the time! And Stan, again, I'm real sor..."

"JUST GET GOING!" he yelled, hanging up.

Taking a moment to grab my breath, I thought about the show I had to do. I knew where my Madonna costume was (buried) and had my balloons and silk roses in the usual place (but now under my suitcase). I still had to write the customized song and had no idea where I was going.

Scrolling through my saved Blackberry messages, I came upon the details of the show. Oh, great, in the heart of downtown Toronto. King and Bay, stockbroker land. Of course it couldn't be easy, like Mississauga, with its miles of free parking for every address. Or even Etobicoke or Oakville, neighbouring towns. No, this had to be smack dab in the busiest area of Toronto, with its fancy underground parking lot mazes.

I opened the attachment for the details on the song. With most telegrams, the client would supply interesting tidbits about the 'victim'. Things like his hobbies, his pet peeves, nicknames, accomplishments. I would then turn that info into a humorous song. People would feel thrilled that a ditty had been written especially about them! I groaned aloud as I looked at what they sent – it read like his biography! Even on a good day, I would be miffed at the amount of information they'd supplied. I had hopes of driving and writing this song at every stoplight I came across. That is, while I also applied my make-up. Well, screw that idea. I was just going to write my memorized stock song, one that would work for any joe. (You're handsome, you're great, you're the best, Flattery 101).

It was time to retrieve the Madonna costume. Out of all my telegram characters, she was the one I wanted to discard. Never mind the fact that the real Madonna kept changing her damn appearance, the costume had about thirty pieces, what with the bangles and corset and crucifixes. And let's not forget the long blonde ponytail and conical bra. I opened my door so I could look in the hatchback of my car for that cursed Madonna outfit.

Lo and behold, the soft snowflakes that I'd fallen asleep to had turned into quite a snowstorm. Now that was a nuisance! I wasn't worried about my driving skills; I drove a lot in my line of work and I felt I was quite adept behind the wheel. What bothered me were the other drivers. For some reason, in the greater area of Toronto, a single snowflake drifting down was the cause for 62 fender benders. This serious downfall of snow would surely add to my driving time.

Madonna wasn't buried too badly, just squished between the clown and the Grim Reaper. I threw my garment bag onto the front seat, pulled some stationery out of my agenda book (oh, gee, look, today's date? Madonna, one p.m...) and began the slippery trek downtown. I was grateful I'd chosen the south end of Mississauga to nap...it was close to the Queen Elizabeth Highway that would take me downtown. From there, the inter-section of King and Bay was a hop, skip and a jump.

You can take those directions to the bank, if the day wasn't like today. There were vehicles who, nearing the end of a Canadian winter, still didn't have their snow tires on. A traffic light would turn green and the Honda Civic or Toyota Tercel would attempt to pull forward, only to have tires not gripping. Fishtailing back and forth, often they would be the only car to make it through a green light. I cut it close on a couple late yellow lights, but I was on a mission.

Arrive late, miss doing show. Miss show, anger client. Anger client, anger my agent. Anger agent, lose his business. Shamrock Shows may only account for ten per cent of my income, but word getting around the business could do more harm. I had to arrive by 4:45 p.m.!

At every red light, I applied my stage make-up, making sure I didn't forget the slight gap in 'her' front teeth or her beauty mark. Once I hit the highway, I had the full make-up on and was ready to write the song. With every slowdown in traffic, I would eke out a few words. Then we'd slowly move forward. When I'd next write, the words would appear on a different line, or slanted. I decided to just write it in shorthand, so that I could read it and then pretend to forget to leave it. As long as I remembered to say at the end, "Happy 40th Birthday, from the gang at the office." Boy, was I gypping these people.

The song written, I was still on the highway. At this point, I'd expected to be dressed and ready to exit my car. Usually, when I found myself unable to dress or do make-up while in my car, I'd blow up the balloons. I always arrived with a silk rose and balloons. It was a cheap gift to the telegram recipient, but it served another purpose. If people saw me on the street or at a banquet hall or WHEREVER, they would, they should, assume that I was some form of entertainment or something. I mean, what with the balloons, a rose and a nicely ribboned scroll of fancy paper, surely I wasn't some kind of whacko just because I was dressed like a French maid.

Now, with every slowdown, I searched for my stash of balloons and roses. I tried to feel under the seats, to move them forward so I could reach into the back floorboard, but my car was stuffed so haphazardly that these cheap gifts remained elusive. Well, since I decided to shortchange them with the hand-delivered customized song, why stop now?

Finally the exit sign appeared for Bay Street. Seeing time slipping away, knowing I still had to get into that freaking costume, I considered my parking options. Should I try to get as close to the job as possible, and search for parking spots there? And negotiate with lousy drivers the next four blocks... OR just park in the underground garage that belonged to the Royal York Hotel? It's expensive as hell, but it's almost the first building you see once you get off the highway. I considered my choices as I idled in the line-up of cars trying to exit the freeway.

I've logged pretty close to a million kilometres doing singing-telegram jobs. At times I've been asked to travel mighty distances, but most of my shows are in the general Toronto area.

I can get anywhere faster, more accurately, than any taxi driver with his GPS. I've come to know where I can park my car for twenty minutes without fear of being towed or ticketed. Often when I get to a gig where there is nothing but pay parking, I will simply drive down the ramp that says 'Deliveries Only'. What the hell – I'm making a delivery, so I feel entitled to park there.

But hey, I work a lot in Toronto, which means you run into power trippers or people who don't understand the concept of a singing-telegram delivery. If I'm not carrying a clipboard or groaning under a heavy box, there's no admitting the dumb blonde who's standing there babbling with two balloons. Then I'm forced to enter the carpark. Now, rather than waste expensive minutes cruising through the aisles, looking for a spot, I put into effect my tried-and-true method. Ignore all signs but the ones that point down, down, down. Or up, up, up. You'll know when you're in the right place. Barely a car in sight and usually a spot right in front of the brightly lit elevators.

In this particular case, I knew the Royal York Hotel had many points in its favour. It was the closest parking lot in sight, it was heated and it led to an underground maze of shops and pathways. One of those pathways led to the office tower where I had to perform. Since the traffic was still at a standstill, that became my destination.

I tried to put on some of the costume. I quickly pulled my pants off, got one leg of Madonna's tights on, when traffic started to move. I drove into the carpark with one cold bare leg, did my parking plan and finally stopped the car. A quick glance at the car clock told me there wasn't a chance of being on time. I desperately just wanted to say "Fuck it," but there was still a small Ethel Merman inside me, reminding me "The show must go on!"

Throwing dignity to the wind, I grabbed the Madonna garment bag and threw it across the hood of my car. I saw something on the ground and thinking something had fallen out, bent to pick it up and almost tripped myself. It was the other leg of the tights and I realized I'd forgotten to finish putting them on. *Well, wall-mounted cameras, since you've seen that much, let me entertain you!*

I got dressed fast, but there was still guilt. I dispensed with three crosses. No earrings. Didn't lace the army boots. Those things didn't bother me so much as the stuff I couldn't leave out. The conical bra, for instance. Due to my rushed packing, Madonna was buried under and between many other things. No harm done, except to the bra. One boob had a big fold in it, so that it pointed sideways. I could probably fix it, if I had a couple hours. Today, Madonna was going to be a sideshow freak.

And the ponytail, the bane of that costume. If I put it on and did the show two minutes later, and didn't move too much, then I rocked the Madonna look. However, I'm physical when performing, especially as Madonna, and that ponytail had a mind of its own. The big clip that held the heavy appendage of hair would start to slide down of its own accord. Today, rather than slip to the back of my head, it decided to slide forward, a la unicorn style.

I threw the rest of my stuff in the car, including my coat. I was grateful for the warmth; it was almost cozy hot in the parking garage. Grabbing my chicken-scratched song, I made double sure to lock my car (my whole life was in there!) and hot-footed it to my awaiting audience.

* * *

The clock read 4:55 as I hurried into the high-rise offices of Innovative Investments. The walk from my car to the address was a blur. I didn't even notice if I was being made fun of or gawked at. I race-walked from Point A to Point B. I was out of breath as I tried to put my voice, and personality, into Madonna-mode. "Hey, doll," I panted. "Sorry, I'm ten minutes late..."

"Actually, it's more like four hours late," the receptionist imperiously informed me. "We expected you at one. We close in five minutes."

I was not in the mood for pleasantries, and besides, isn't Madge known for being a bit bitchy? "Well, I suggest you get Gary Polson here immediately then."

Gary was found and showed up in reception at 4:59. By then a crowd had gathered, but mainly they were just hovering by the exit, ready for the 5:00 whistle. I began my show but at five, most of them began to leave. A few more stuck around a couple minutes, hoping I might be a strip-o-gram. When they realized that my clothes would remain on my body, they caught the next elevator heading south. At the end of my act, when I read the line 'From the whole gang', there was just me, Gary and the receptionist.

"Are you done?" the receptionist asked, walking around the desk. "Happy Birthday, Gary, but I gotta lockup. It's past five and I'm going to charge you for overtime."

Could she make me feel any worse? I just wanted to get back to my car and maybe, after checking my agenda to see if I had any more shows today, schedule another big mope. Couldn't I catch a break?

Apparently not. I tried to do the quick walk back to my car, but was stopped at the MMMmuffins shop. At MMMmuffins, I knew I would turn right, walk quite a ways to London Cleaners, up a set of stairs and into the carpark. Suddenly though, there were workmen in yellow vests advising one and all to exit up the immediate stairs. Frowning, I ran up the stairs and ran down as quickly when I saw they led directly outside. I approached a fellow who seemed in charge.

"Excuse me, would it be possible for me to just scoot down this hallway?" I asked politely.

"Sure, why not you, and nobody else?" he replied. I didn't quite know how to take it.

"So...I can go then?" I asked as I tentatively started to lift a yellow caution tape.

He grabbed my arm. "Whaddaya think you're doing? Nobody goes down this hallway! Can't you see the water all over the floor?"

"But I don't have a coat on!" I wailed. He gave me a sneer as he looked me over.

"That's not my problem," he dismissed me. "Besides, who goes out in winter just wearing a bra?"

* * *

Funny how you wonder if you can catch a break, and then some Comedian Up There decides to toy with you a bit more. So I ascended those stairs, swearing at the repairman, and came out onto some street. I was all turned around. I went one minute in one direction, figured I was going the wrong way, went another way, and then realized I was right the first time. Then I wasted time looking for another entrance into the underground pathway. Finally, seeing the facade of the Royal York Hotel, I just decided to trudge through the snow using the regular streets. Now I really had people looking at me.

The only thing that kept me going was knowing I surely would eventually reach my car. I would not die on the streets of Toronto; somebody would hopefully drag me into the nearest store or restaurant to warm up. I did my best to ignore the cold; the only thing I could do for warmth was take the ponytail off and wrap it around my neck as a scarf.

And of course, because I was not allowed to return to my vehicle the way I remembered, I had to relocate it. I knew I was on the bottom level, but north south east or west? When I finally found my battered blue 2004 Suzuki Swift, I could have kissed its dusty headlights. I was home!!! I opened the door, threw the garment bag, crosses, etc. onto the floor of the parkade, and started my car. Even though the garage was warm, I needed to feel hot air blowing on me for a long time. I looked at the clock. It was little over thirty minutes since I'd left my show, yet it felt like I'd just been through a battle.

Before long, my body was back to 98.6 degrees and I shut the car off. Slowly I took Madonna off and got back into boring Maddy Magee. As I put the costume into its garment bag, I wondered where to pack it. The more I looked at my car, the more I realized how quickly I'd escaped. The way it was packed had no rhyme nor reason! Why not take this golden opportunity, in a fully heated luxurious garage, to repack my car more sensibly? Or I could leave the parkade now and drive back to Mississauga in rush hour during a snowstorm.

An hour later, my car still looked jam-packed, somehow even more so, but there was a method to my madness. Costumes were packed to the ceiling, as well as my own clothes, books, etc. But behind the driver's seat was a space that was only covered with a sleeping bag and a pillow. That was going to be my sleeping area. There was no way I'd spend another night sitting straight up. I needed to stretch out! Every square inch of that car had a purpose. All the floors had stuff on them, but the passenger seat was left empty. That would be for my purse and whatever project I had going at the time – whether it was getting ready to do a gorilla or eat my lunch or pay my bills.

And speaking of eating, when was the last time I did that? All the re-arranging made me hungry, so I ran into the Royal York and got a $19 hamburger, but at least it came with fries and a soda drink. I don't know why, but I took it 'to go' and went back to my car to eat it. With the last sip of my pop, I felt quite sated, as well as a bit weary. It had been an emotional day. A nap would do me a world of good.

It was time to test-drive this new sleeping arrangement.

* * *

I slept the sleep of the dead. All night long, I slept in that box-like space, my hands crossed over my chest. It was like sleeping in a coffin. That wasn't the usual way I slept; I liked to sleep on my stomach. Maybe I could learn a new position. The 10- or 11-hour sleep, stretched out with the back window at my head and the emergency brake at my feet, was purely restorative.

Chances were great my emotionally spent self could sleep another ten hours, but the call of nature is what woke me up. Though the bed was amazing, getting out of the arrangement was more difficult than I'd anticipated. My front seat was pushed up as close to the steering wheel as possible. Boxes and suitcases and costume bags surrounded all the doors.

Inch by inch, getting my morning exercise, I finally managed to flip the car door lock open. Laying with my head almost in the ashtray, I stretched my arm under the front seat. I managed to find the lever to slide the front seat back. As I tried to get out of the position, I realized my arm was stuck. Somehow my watch had slid onto the lever and I couldn't slide it off.

I don't want to be found like this, I thought, wrenching my arm, trying to figure out why it wouldn't slide off when it obviously slid on. Stopping to catch my breath, I considered that idea. There must be something else at play. This time, I managed to get my other arm under the seat. I felt along the lever and damn if there wasn't a gizmo attaching the lever to the floor.

My hand felt for the other hand, and crept up to the watch. I could feel some kind of spring attached to it and without further ado, I undid the strap of my watch. My enslaved wrist fell to the dusty floor. The other hand went to gently pull it out. With a final effort, I pulled myself into the driver's seat.

Okay, now I really gotta go, I thought. My mind raced to the Royal York Hotel just an elevator ride away... Would the food court be open? My eyes glanced at my wrist, but nothing was there but indentations of a watch worn all night. I could leave the parking lot and find a McDonald's or something but as I squirmed, I knew I wouldn't make it.

Maybe I can use the washroom in the lobby of the Royal York, I decided. As I searched for my toothbrush and paste and make-up remover (may as well, while I was there), I started jumping in my seat. There was no way I could wait for an elevator, take its five floors, walk past all the shops, through the wondrous chandelier-lit main foyer of the hotel and locate the washroom.

I threw my toiletries onto the passenger seat as I scrambled for the door handle. I opened it and then, quickly peeling my pants down, I took a step outside and went into a squat. I kept myself as hidden as possible behind the open front door.

Aahhh, relief! As I created a big puddle that turned into a river, following some slight incline, I kept my ears and eyes alert. I happened to look skywards when I heard the rumble of a big truck. *Uh oh, somebody might be coming, get ready to cut it short...*

And that's when I saw a security camera. Not just that one, but a few mounted here and there in the garage. Fast as a whip, that piss was terminated and without the benefit of a wipe, the pants were quickly hiked back up. I prayed some eagle-eyed guard hadn't been monitoring his camera and caught me in the act.

Now I just wanted to get out of there, and fast. Starting up the car, I squealed out of my spot and finally managed to find the exit. I was exultant that during my brief stay at the Royal York Hotel (parking garage), I'd managed to keep track of my parking stub. I also made sure I didn't spend the remaining forty bucks in my wallet, though how much could overnight parking be?

"That will be $48," the parking attendant told me. I did a double-take.

"I'm not renting a room here," I said sarcastically. "I just parked overnight."

The guy just pointed to the rate sheet. I tried to add it up... I could see I was getting a deal on overnight parking, but from the time I'd arrived (about 4:30) to the start of cheaper hours, I was paying prime rate. That was $6.50 per 20 minutes!

A big cargo van had pulled up behind me and was waiting. I jumped when it gave a short honk. "Look," I told the attendant. "I had no idea it would cost that much. I only have forty on me."

"You can use your credit card," he told me.

"I'd rather not," I said. I was trying to steer clear of going into further debt. "I'm sure I can find the money on me." I pulled my purse off the passenger floor to start digging through it.

"Please pull your car into that spot," he pointed. "We can't have you holding up the line."

The cargo van wasn't very pleased about having to back up, but he had no choice if he wanted to get out. I pulled my Swift into the spot and started looking for eight dollars. At first I was making progress...two toonies in the bottom of my purse, three loonies in my change purse, 50 cents in the slot on my car door.

"I almost have it all, I'm up to $47.50!" I called out to the attendant. "Will that do?"

"There are bank machines in the lobby of the hotel," was his answer.

Three pennies under the floormat, a few more cents under the seat. A good hour had passed; I prayed he wouldn't charge me for this extra time. Finally, feeling it was dumb but looking in the leather folds of the emergency brake's housing, I found the last nickel I was looking for.

The attendant was given the money. He didn't congratulate me; he simply raised the gate to let me out. By this time the urge to urinate had returned since the first attempt had been cut short. No problem, I'd get out of there, get on the road and find myself a coffee shop.

Emerging from the dark garage into the brilliant sunshine, I immediately realized I was in Toronto rush hour, supposedly the worst in the world. In the middle of the night, from the Royal York Hotel, I could reach the highway in one minute. In rush hour, especially in the morning, this turned into thirty minutes. I knew from years of working downtown jobs that there were no places in the vicinity where I could pull up my car, run in and use their facilities.

My damp front seat can tell you the rest of the story.

Chapter Five

For two nights, I slept in that crypt. I was still in the Suzuki but when I went to bed at night, boxes piled high on either side of me, snuggled under my sleeping bag, I was in a blissful metal cocoon.

Though the night I spent in the heated Royal York Hotel parked couldn't be matched, I still found myself quite relaxed. On the plus side, I found it fairly simple to sit up, lean forward, turn on the key and start the engine to blast some heat. I had also found a way, by slowly twisting my body, to sleep on my stomach, although the seatbelt connector bruised my ankle. On the negative side, I still couldn't get out of the car before the urge to pee overtook me. To get out of any door of my car, I had to move all sorts of articles and body-rock my way around the rest.

This morning, I wasn't too worried. I had parked in the same place the past two nights, and the locale pleased me. I was within a stone's throw of the big water tower in north Mississauga. In the corner lot of a vast industrial site, in the farthest spot that was half-hidden by trees, I parked my car mere steps from a railroad track. The occasional hypnotic sound of the odd train passing by only served to soothe me.

The sun sets early in February still. Two days ago, I was in my old 'hood, as I was to meet up with Shannon between school classes the next day. I had just picked up a bag of Wendy's junk food and was looking for a place to park and eat. I had been in the line-up, ready to take my tray and sit down, when I remembered this was one of Ben's favourite fast-food outlets. Panicked he may see me, or my car, I ordered the counter-girl to make it to go...fast! Faster!

Driving down a nearby street, I allowed three big tractor-trailers to make their way out of a driveway. I glanced to my right, saw the big water tower and quickly made a right-hand turn into that same lot. I drove as close to the behemoth structure as I could, and ate my fries and half my chicken nuggets in its shadow. A train rumbling by caused me to take note of the tracks.

After my late lunch, I decided to take a walk and check out this part of Meadowvale (a suburb of Mississauga) that I had never seen before. I found myself at a barbed-wire fence that had been completely trampled down for quite a distance. It served no use in keeping me off the tracks. I walked over the wire, down a small incline and stepped onto the rails.

I turned to the right and walked closer to the water tower. There were steps high up there, and I briefly considered finding a way to get up them. I could even see some kind of room halfway up. Oh, I could only imagine finding a way to sleep there tonight! But they probably kept it locked.

Soon I began to feel exposed, as a couple guys came out of their workplace to check out the tires on their truck. I turned around and saw a tunnel at the other end. Stepping over each railway tie, I headed in that direction. I passed out of the workmen's vision as I approached the stone wall of the tunnel.

I wondered if I should continue my walk? The only thing stopping me was that a train might come through just when I got to the middle. I didn't know if I was in any shape to outrun a train. I walked in a few steps and could see other people had also come this way. There were coffee cups, sneakers, pop bottles, paint cans.

Another few steps and I came to an abrupt halt. It seemed like I'd stepped through a magic portal, leaving Meadowvale behind for this urban art gallery. There were larger-than-life pot leafs, painted multi-neon colours, looking like they were on acid. A gorgeous rendering of a voluptuous woman with snakes coming out of her eyes, smoking a huge blunt, had a signature that I couldn't decipher. To be honest, I could barely make out any of the words written on the walls; they were too blocky, ran into each other, misshapen...but man, the images were astounding.

Taking a good hard look down the tracks to make sure I was safe, I briskly walked the length of the tunnel. I saw spots where the area widened a bit so that, if need be, I could squeeze myself in there and not become rail-kill. I imagined a few of these graffiti artists had done that but I had a weak stomach. I didn't want to put it to the test.

I cleared the tunnel and came out onto a section of land that looked difficult to navigate. Again with the long-distance look, this time even with my ear to the track like some native Indian scout, I half-ran, half-stumbled along the railroad tracks back to my car. I saw a couple more 'paintings' that had escaped me the first time – a quirky Minnie Mouse as well as an image of a diamond ring, outlined in a sparkly reflective paint.

As I walked out of the tunnel, I saw a spot where I could step over the barbed wire and get back onto the parking lot. I brushed past an overgrown pine tree that had started taking over one of the parking places. I surveyed the rest of the location and it seemed perfect! No windows at this end, no loading docks. It seemed to lay in the middle of two giant buildings so I decided to get my car and make that spot home for the night.

* * *

The next morning, at my usual 6:24 a.m., I woke up to the call of nature. Struggling out of my 'bed', I opened the door and checked my surroundings. The glorious pine tree, with its boughs scraping the ground, beckoned me. I disappeared behind the tree and saw I could have complete privacy, unless a locomotive happened by.

A few minutes later, I pulled into McDonald's and freshened up. I brought a water bottle to fill, but didn't care for the taps I'd been finding lately...no hot- or cold-water choices; just the one spigot offering its lukewarm take-it-or-leave-it. I wanted to look nice for Shannon and arrived early at a different McDonald's, this one close to her high school.

It's quite intriguing, all the conversations those hard plastic seats must witness. In the half-hour we had, the conversation got quite intense. Shannon spent her time before English class urging me to move back home, to reconsider my options. She may have won first prize in last year's debate event but today she was wasting her breath.

I was all business as I explained her place in this new arrangement – she was to tell her dad she was in charge of the mail. All cheques and bills were to be held for me until we met again. Ben was welcome to his online-poker mail and monthly reminders to come back to Netflix. I gave her a wad of cash for incidentals, things a mother should provide for (tampons, bus fare, new mittens as she hadn't worn any). Shannon tried to give it back but I refused.

"It's not a lot, Shannon," I said ruefully. "Besides, please, I'm your mom. I want you to have it."

"I have a job," she reminded me. "Three, actually. So I'm not hurting for money." She pushed the envelope of cash back at me. I pushed it right back her way.

"Take it or we leave it for the guy who wipes the tables," I threatened. "Besides, I want you saving for your university. We've got some money in your RESPs, but nowhere near enough."

Shannon pocketed the envelope with a rather sharp "Fine then!" and then a softer "Thank you." She stood up to leave, gathering up a backpack half her weight. "Gotta go. When do I see you next?"

"How about a week from today?" I suggested. "I'll be in the area. I'm doing a Grim Reaper at Credit Valley Hospital."

Shannon grimaced. "Seriously? Maybe funny for your victim, not so funny for some of the other people there."

I shrugged. "I'm just the messenger. So how about it? Next week work for you?"

Shannon took her iPhone out of her back pocket and gave it a few swipes. "Oh, no," she said. "I'm totally booked. After morning classes, I'm meeting up with Jody. He has a doctor's appointment in the afternoon and I want to be there for moral support."

"Is he getting his operation soon then?" I asked hopefully.

"Nowhere near," Shannon pouted. "This is a therapist he has to see. To make sure he really wants to become a guy."

I shook my head in amazement. Unless you stripped Jody naked in public (which I don't think is allowed), the crowd he casually walked among daily had no idea this good-looking boy had female genitalia. Yet the poor kid had to jump through hoops to prove he was heart and soul a man.

"Well, it's the process he has to go through, I guess," I offered up weakly.

"Oh, and prom is coming up?" Shannon began. Inside, my heart skipped a beat and then sank. I'd totally forgotten about prom. My friend Lisa and I had kids in the same grade; we often spoke of the horrendous cost of proms and dreaded when our kids made it to Grade 12. Hair, nails, smashing dress, heels, limo, the ticket...

"Oh, that's right...," I managed to squeak out, trying to quell an approaching anxiety attack.

"I hope you don't mind, but I'm not going to go...," Shannon began. My eyes bugged open. "Don't worry! It's not because of your...situation. Here's the deal – the office called me and Jody in and told us Jody couldn't go to prom." My eyes somehow managed to widen even more. "If he goes, he can't wear a tux, he can't use the men's room, he can't slow dance with me..." Shannon's eyes teared up but she shook it off. "So who needs a high-school prom anyways? Cuz you know if he can't go, I'm not going."

My eyes teared up as well, sorry for Jody's ongoing battle with know-it-nothings, but also with gratitude that Shannon was saving me about a thousand bucks in prom foolishness. I gave her a hug, my arms encircling her backpack. People on either side of us munched on their Big Breakfast Specials or enjoyed their coffee-and-a-muffin deal. Nobody really took notice of us; nothing special about a mother and daughter getting together.

I apologized for not having enough room to drive her to school but she assured me she had plenty of time, and the exercise wouldn't hurt her. We agreed to keep in touch and to meet again soon, especially if a few cheques came in the mail.

Where to go now? With nothing to do until the next day, a cop singing telegram in Brampton, I grabbed a coffee to go and motored off to my pine tree. Once there, I killed time by trying to figure out how to play games on my cellphone. When you live in your car, time does not fly. It moves more like a sloth.

Twice I left for more coffee. It was chilly out and I was guzzling them fast so they wouldn't get cold. Close to nine p.m., I had nothing better to do so I made for my bed.

Around midnight my bladder urged me to awaken. Swearing, I turned on the interior light and crawled over the mound of costumes on my front seat. I opened the door and quickly threw on my coat. Hustling to my litter box, I wished I'd had a flash-light, even the little penlight attached to my keychain.

Heading for the pine branches, I saw a faint glow coming from the tunnel. I tried to hold my bladder but the need was too great. If that light was a train coming, all they'd get was a fleeting glimpse of my butt. It wasn't like they'd brake to a complete stop.

As I let forth my offering to the soil beneath me, I could neither hear a train or discern a change in the light. Rather, a shadow played off the tunnel wall, a flickering, shape-changing form. *Looks like a fire going*, I deduced. Maybe the 'artistes' are back at work? But I could hear no sound, so thought I could be wrong. Or maybe they'd already left? It didn't matter. There was no concern or fear; I just wanted to get back to my warm bed-in-a-box.

The next day was beautiful, a sure sign that spring would once again miraculously make its appearance. It seemed the Toronto area had been covered in snow since October. Taking out the police costume, I laid it across the front seat. There were many components, from the handcuffs to the walkie-talkie. I wanted to make sure I was fully prepared for my singing telegram this morning.

I had just finished my morning routine at a local Tim Horton's, disregarding the odd looks I got as I brushed my teeth, when my phone chirped. It was Barb, the agent at one of my many agencies.

"I hope you haven't left yet," Barb said. "The show's been cancelled."

"Oh, no!" I wailed. Usually I don't take cancellations so badly but for the next while, until I raised $100,000, every job counted. "Did they say why?"

"Yeah, the guy's not coming into work today," she informed me. "I don't blame him. It's his 65th birthday. Guess he didn't tell the staff his plans though."

"They should fire him," I groused.

"Well, now they want you to come in tomorrow," Barb offered. "He should be back at work then."

So now my job was tomorrow instead. With the day empty in front of me, I decided to save gas and stick close to 'home', which was no longer my old address but now my pine tree in the park. Industrial park, but still...it had a tree. I didn't want to spend the whole day there though, so I drove to the Meadowvale Town Centre, where there was a decent library. I knew Ben wouldn't visit there; we'd lived in the area fifteen years and he probably didn't even know there was a library in the mall.

Early in the day, the library had few patrons, mainly older folks. Some sat reading on couches, some sat reading in cubicles, some just sat. For awhile, I browsed magazines. I skimmed a how-to book on Suzuki car maintenance (my hub caps seemed to be making an odd noise) and then finally settled on a thick copy of *The New York Times*.

In the deepest corner of the library sat an alcove with a couple cubicles. These were rarely used, Shannon and I had discovered, when we used to come here for homework projects. Situated right behind the children's section, it didn't qualify for being the quietest place in the library. At this hour though, the area was kid-free, so I eased into a high-walled private seat.

I was almost at the end of the paper, enjoying this constructive use of my afternoon. I was up on today's New York Stock Exchange and I stopped reading the obituaries after the sixth murder. Hours later, a hand was shaking my shoulder. I opened up bleary eyes to see a lady with an armful of books.

"I'm afraid you'll have to go," she said, once she'd seen I had her in focus.

"Was my snoring that bad?" I queried seriously.

"Just under our allowance levels," she snickered, "but barely. I'm afraid we're closing now."

"Closing!" I sat straight up, and the librarian snickered some more. I cast my eyes to her.

"I suggest you use the washroom before you leave," she advised. "You can thank me later."

It was a good suggestion, as I was always looking for a washroom. As I waited my turn for the ladies' room to be free, I startled the woman coming out. I wondered if my hair was a mess, or if I'd drooled on my chin.

Looking into the mirror, and even though I had to read it backwards to understand it, I saw the words MAYOR PREDICTS DOOM GLOOM. I knew it was supposed to say 'mayor predicts doom AND gloom', but the word 'and' was lost in my eyelid crease. Hhhmm, wasn't that a headline I'd read somewhere? I correctly surmised that I'd fallen asleep across the newspaper and the print had etched itself across my forehead and cheek.

With it being nightfall already, I just jumped into the car and drove back to the industrial lot. I nestled into my usual spot. Damn, I should have grabbed something to eat. Instead, I munched on some leftover cold chicken nuggets, making sure not to get the police uniform next to me greasy.

Around midnight, I decided I should crawl into the back and get some sleep. My gig was first thing in the morning, at an import/export store. I only had my Toronto Police uniform and I was heading into Peel Police territory, but only once in about two hundred cop jobs have I ever been questioned on that. That one time was when I performed in Niagara Falls. The person who busted me had just turned 19, first year of university. No dummy there.

Sleep wasn't coming. I played Brickbreaker on my cellphone until the power ran out. I started doing mathematical equations in my head (how many jobs at $120 a pop would it take to get me home?) and that seemed to work. Soon I could feel myself drifting off into a light sleep.

Through the opening sequence to a dream, an unusual noise broke through. It sounded like a definite CLICK. I tried to discount it but then I heard it again, CLICK, immediately followed by my thought, "That sounds like my door, like somebody's trying to open my door."

Part of me wanted to sit up and see what was going on, but the rest of me, the majority vote, held me pinned down in utter fear. I waited a moment. I had left my window open a crack and suddenly, whispered voices hissed.

"Hey, I think it's an abandoned car," somebody whispered.

"Nah, I don't think so," the other whispered back. "There's a ton of stuff in it."

"You think there's anything good?" the first voice asked. Suddenly I heard two clicks, different clicks, the sound of lighters flicking. Huddling deep in my sleeping bag, I left just enough room for one eye to peek out. I could see two flames burning and two dark hooded heads trying to peer in.

"Hard to say," said the second guy. "We should get going though. What if the owner comes back?"

Again I heard a door click, this time on the passenger side. I wanted to do nothing more than leap into my driver's seat, start the engine and zoom out of there. As long as my doors were locked, I knew I could make a safe getaway.

As it was, I felt trapped. I still felt like making the move, but knew it would take a few minutes to get behind the wheel. What if those guys were mad rapists carrying sledgehammers? They could break my windows and have their way with me before I even got four costumes off my driver's seat.

"I'm gonna leave a tag," the first one said. I had no idea what that meant. Was he going to pee against my car? This time I heard a click like the top of a can being removed, followed by a shaking sound. I wondered if they were about to throw a Molotov cocktail at the car. The next noise was quite feeble though, a hissing sound.

I saw a lighter spark up at the passenger window, and a face press itself against it. I was ready to scream, I could feel it rising, and I couldn't stop it. The guy with the flame managed to nip it in the bud though, when he dropped his lighter and shrieked.

"Holy fucking shit, man! There's a cop uniform on the front seat!" he squealed, backing out of sight. "This is some fuckin' unmarked police car! Fucking run!"

I could hear the two of them take off. After about twenty minutes, when I was finally able to breathe at a normal rate, I finagled my way into the front seat. Starting up the car, I set my GPS for Brampton.

Arriving uber-early for my show – okay, it was the middle of the night – I parked in the visitors' section, right in front of a spotlight that illuminated the front entrance. I changed out of my clothes (not my pyjamas; I seemed to have dispensed with wearing them, though I did pack them) and put on my costume for the gig. There was no reason for putting it on with hours to spare pre-show, but I felt safer sitting there wearing a police uniform.

The next morning, I drove to the rear of the building, before anybody showed up, and had my pee. I could have driven to any coffee shop but once I was in the cop costume, I tried to keep a low profile. My greatest fear was that I'd get arrested for impersonating a police officer.

As I re-buckled my Sam Browne holster and remembered to zip up the fly on the heavy-duty pants, I relived my harrowing moments of the night before. Obviously I wouldn't be using the back-seat bedroom anymore. The front seat, as uncomfortable as it was, even when reclined, would also have to serve as my bed. I felt I had to be in a safer position to get out of Dodge, if needed.

Thinking of those hoodlums made me wonder if they'd done any damage to my baby. I stepped away from the driver's door, avoiding the puddle I'd just made. Everything looked fine. I strolled over to the back and saw nothing. Walking around to the passenger side, a snaky letter began to emerge.

"Oh, no!" I yelled, clenching my fists and stamping my foot. In a messy scrawl, in a black dripping paint, the word SEEK had been sprayed. "Now what the hell is that supposed to mean?" I asked aloud. I was so angered, I kicked at the rear tire of my car. Police brutality, I know, but this was just ridiculous.

"Seek? Seek what?" I asked the tranquil sky. "Is this some kind of message?" I wondered if some Christian graffiti artist was spreading the word. Well, what could I do? I wasn't about to fork over money to get my car repainted. I'd just have to live with it, until I made my $100,000 goal.

That sickly looking word would just have to be my new motto. SEEK. Seek Money. Seek My Freedom. Seek Happiness.

Chapter Six

This was one week I was happy to be living in my car. It was a week filled with misery, cheats, assholes and frustration.

Having endured a slow weekend work-wise, I was happy to get a Monday show. A Madonna for a guy working in a cargo warehouse out by the airport. I woke early, took care of business at a Burger King for a change (sneaking out when a crowd came in so I wouldn't have to buy any food), grabbed breakfast at Mickey D's and then spent ample time composing a terrific song. My make-up was spot-on and I hoped I wouldn't be mistaken for the real deal as I drove to the gig.

That's where the day pretty much went to shit. The airline's cargo hangar was next to impossible to find. I finally realized it was a dinky little hangar belonging to a sad-sack airplane company. Already fifteen minutes late, unable to reach my contact on my cellphone, I pulled up to the security gate.

"Hi, I'm here to do a singing telegram," I quickly told the guard, no Madonna at all in my delivery.

He merely looked at me, shut his window and picked up his phone. He hung up and then seriously stared at me.

I waited a moment and then loudly asked, "Well?" Nothing. "I'm late, can I get in?" I tried with more volume. He didn't move; only his eyes slid over my corset. I opened the car door to step out, one leg emerging. My fishnet stockings caused him to jerk.

I started to approach the closed window when I saw two security cars, yellow lights flashing, race up behind my Suzuki. I thought maybe my car is in their way; I should move! I turned to get back into the driver's seat when I heard two car doors slam.

"Stay right where you are!" one guy shouted.

I slowly turned around. "Who, me?" I asked in disbelief.

"What business do you have with FlyRight Airlines?" asked

the guard who's uniform jacket was four sizes too big on him.

I had nothing to hide. "I'm just here to do a singing telegram," I politely replied. "For a Michael McMann, in cargo."

"Ha! In cargo?" the second guard snorted. He was a good foot taller than his mate, and his belt was cinched in to show off his physique. "You have the proper papers to get into the hangar?"

"Well...I...I have a singing telegram," I explained. "My agent gets the call and just sends me to them. I didn't know I needed any special papers. They have a cheque waiting for me, you can call them, they know I'm coming!"

I don't always pick up cheques, but the odd time I do. Some clients just don't like to pay until the performance has been rendered. If the entertainer doesn't show, it saves them the hassle of getting a refund. Then most will mail the cheque, but a few prefer to just hand it over to the gorilla.

"I'm sorry, but those are the rules," the boy in a man's suit shrugged. "In this day and age, those are rules that can't be broken."

"And you want to go to cargo?" the other guard sneered. "Ha! I don't think so!"

"Oh, come on!" I threw open my arms. "Do I look like a terrorist to you? Do I look like I'm carrying weapons?"

Like synchronized swimmers, the guards' eyes swept the car from front to rear and then stopped at the same point. I turned to look at my car and saw various unusual pieces sticking up here and there. Wigs, pantyhose, balloons on a stick...but most prominent was the Grim Reaper's scythe.

"Seriously?" I laughed. "That's plastic and you know it."

The tall security guard took a deep breath and for a moment, he resembled a big-breasted rooster. "Look, we don't know what all kind of stuff you got in that car. So you better get the hell outta here now or you can wait for the airport police."

I left, but as soon as I reached a neutral zone, I pulled out my phone and called Dawson, the agent at AAA Absolute

Entertainment. I explained the situation and he was just as perplexed as I. "But I did get all dressed, I wrote the song, you'll still pay me a cancellation fee, right?"

Almost all the agents I dealt with were true business professionals. If a show got screwed up through no fault of my own, I would receive fifty per cent of my pay. Dawson, however, walked a fine line between shady and disreputable. His response? "Well did you pick up the cheque?"

"Dawson, I couldn't get past the security gate," I reminded him.

"Then I guess neither one of us gets paid then," was his comeback.

I drove to a Rabba convenience store, grabbed some overpriced junk food as well as their delicious cheap croissants, then motored off to Mississauga. In less than 24 hours, I'd be having lunch with my daughter. Till then, the world could stay away.

Tuesday started off with hope and promise. It ended with betrayal and spite.

Shannon and I met a the Loblaws grocery store across from her high school. They had a snack area on an upper level that overlooked all the shoppers. My daughter and I had been coming here often since she was a toddler, spending quality time in girl talk and people watching. For a change, by the end of lunch today, people were watching me.

We dug into our pieces of chicken and potato wedges. Shannon quipped, "This sure is a nice change from pizza."

Maybe I was stressed, maybe I didn't get a good night's sleep, but I went into a tirade. "Pizza! Shannon, I give you barely enough money to afford meat, how can you be ordering pizza?" I assumed they ordered; Ben wouldn't touch a store-bought one. "Don't tell me you're spending your hard-earned pay to buy your dad pizza!"

"I'm not buying him pizza, Mom, so chill," Shannon shushed

me. "And it's not just pizza. He's got new video games, a better stereo for his car...."

"What the fuck?!" I shrieked. The high-school boys at the next table snickered and gave me a thumb's up. Shannon looked at me disapprovingly. I leaned forward and whispered at the top of my voice. "Where'd he suddenly get this money then? He's supposed to be suffering the same as me! Or what, did he finally get a job?"

"I would have told you if he got a job," Shannon said. "It would be breaking news...history in the making."

Unfortunately, Shannon could offer no idea as to how Ben was able to still live a life of luxury. After that, lunch wasn't quite so memorable. Shannon gave me my mail (hooray! Four cheques totalling $1600!) as well as a few household bills. We parted on a sombre note, Shannon giving me a tight hug.

"Come home, Mom," she whispered. "Sleep in my room."

I squeezed my tears back into their ducts, then pulled away. Adjusting the collar of her jacket, I put on my current oft-used fake smile.

"Not yet, Shannon, but if it makes you feel better, I'm keeping that as one of my options." We parted ways.

She walked back to school and I, having nowhere to go until Friday, motored over to Erin Mills Town Centre. I took my pile of mail, went inside, grabbed a nice cup of coffee from a barista, and found myself on the bottom level of the mall.

In one section, around a large coffee table, sat three big overstuffed chairs and a long couch. The chairs were filled with senior citizens, all of them playing some form of lottery (Cash for Life cards, Nevada tickets), but the couch was empty. I set myself up to do some 'office work' and began opening my letters.

What was this? A lot of the bills were simply statements, as I allowed most companies to directly take their fee out of my checking account. But the heating bill was double the usual price! So was the Rogers phone bill and the water bill. All basically double what I usually paid.

I scanned the statements and saw the problem...none of the previous month's bills had been paid due to insufficient funds at the time. I wondered how that could be possible. Every 1st of the month, I made sure I had $4,000 in my household account. The bills usually ate up most of that, but it also left a couple hundred for whatever reason. Never had this account gone below the zero-dollar amount. Something was wrong, there had to be a mistake!

The Visa bill, which I'd casually tossed aside, gave out a silent whistle. I glanced at it, debated opening it but figured, what for? I rarely used Visa, maybe once every three months. I preferred my AirMiles MasterCard. It often awarded me ten bucks of free gas. Still, something told me the Visa bill could be a big clue. My palms suddenly sweaty, I ripped the envelope open and pulled out a...oh my Lord....a TWO-page bill.

EB Games. Dominoes Pizza. Pizza Hut. Game Play. 2 for 1 Pizza, 3-4-1- Pizza, the PlayStation Network, XBox, Pizza Pizza... Ben must have been desperate when he ordered Pizza Pizza, his least favourite, but the only ones who deliver after two a.m. Hundreds and hundreds of dollars in charges. I shoved all the bills into my purse and stewed for a moment.

I hadn't called Ben since I'd left but how dare he? How dare he ROB from me? Obviously I'd have to pay all this money back to Visa and Enbridge Gas and who knows how many other companies I'd stiffed. I pulled out my phone and was just about to dial Ben's number when a couple teens from the local Catholic high school showed up. They plopped down on the couch next to me, set their large Tim Horton's Ice Capps on the coffee table and then began to make out. Damned if I was going to give up my seat though. Instead of calling Ben, I scrolled through emails. Nothing but a reminder about my show on Friday, days away. I switched to playing Brickbreaker, but the cellphone game had its usual effect of lulling me to sleep.

Some sixth sense woke me up. I discovered I'd stretched my

legs onto the coffee table. After a momentary panic of *Where's my purse?! That couple must have stole my purse!* I found it had slid onto the floor. The coffee I'd been drinking, what little there was left of it, had been knocked over, a small pool of liquid congealing on the marble tabletop. But what woke me up was that I'd sensed someone watching me. I glanced up and the first thing I saw was a security guard staring at me from the upper level of the mall

As I grabbed for my purse and adjusted my clothes, I could see the guard making a bee-line for me. I immediately jumped up and even though it was on the opposite end of the mall from where I'd parked, I took the nearest exit.

I drove to the home branch of my bank. It wasn't far. I would sort this problem out face to face with a teller. I drove into the plaza lot and all I could see were fire trucks, ambulances and police cars. I parked at the far end, gathered my bills and walked over to the bank. Coincidentally, that happened to be where all the action was taking place.

"Excuse me," I said to a police officer guarding the entrance. "I've got banking business."

"'Fraid not," the officer said, not even making eye contact. "Bank's closed."

"Did somebody have a heart attack or something?" I asked, trying to look around him.

He moved to block my view and when he finally did make eye contact, it was pretty scary. "I said, bank's CLOSED."

I backed away from his intimidating manner. Walking back to my car, I decided to make a pit-stop at Price Chopper and use their handy-dandy washroom. En route, in the fruits and vegetables section, is where I heard the bank had been held up.

Certain they would re-open for business as usual in the morning, I camped out in the plaza parking lot for the night. It was a restless sleep, as I kept dreaming I had to be on the lookout for a bank robber.

Wednesday morning, I was the first customer in line when they opened at nine a.m. I didn't leave there until lunchtime. By then, I had cried buckets, I wreaked havoc on the name of my husband, I got a nosebleed, I pounded desks and curled up in a fetal position in the office's visitor chair. The first person to assist me, a nice Indian man, helped me for about an hour. He listened to my problems and then, bless his heart, realized I was heading for a nervous breakdown. He left the room, promising to be right back.

He never returned, but he did send a sweet lady, Jacinta Gonsalves, her name tag said... She had me start from the beginning. By the end of my tale of woe, I had a perfect stranger holding me, her hands patting my back consolingly. "Let it out, Mrs..." a quick glance at her computer screen, "...Magee. Just let it come. When you are able, we will sort this out."'

To make a short story long, my dearly beloved was sucking me dry. In my desire to remove myself from Ben, I seemed to forget the things in life we shared. Namely, a joint bank account as well as both our names on a Visa card. I didn't even think Ben still had his Visa card (I found it half a dozen times in the bowels of the couch) and though he signed papers at the bank when we first married, papers to do with all sorts of financial things, I didn't believe he knew he could withdraw from this account. Ben had his own account that I'd set up, $500 a month for whatever. That, plus the continuously empty wallet I always found myself with, gave him more than enough money for thirty days.

For three hours, I cancelled everything I could – the joint account, the Visa, the direct deposits. I had to sign triplicate forms to stop all the utility companies and Highway 407 ETR and Rogers Telecommunications, as well as the life insurance, pension and other investments, from taking any more money from my account. I had to set up a new household account in my name only. I used the $1600 of cheques to pay off the line of credit Ben was already into (having cancelled that as well) and then asked the big question.

"I have an account at another bank," I revealed. "It's still CIBC. Can you check that balance?" Ben didn't know I had a nest egg. From the first week of marriage, something told me I was married to a lunatic when it came to money. Within one month of wedded bliss, I secretly opened a bank account in just my name, to be used in case of emergency. My income had been so plentiful back then that Ben didn't notice. I happily kept contributing to that fund until times got tight.

Jacinta brought the account up onto her screen. "Oh, my, you have plenty of funds here! You should take a few thousand and beef up your RRSPs, and you should consider TFSAs, the tax-free savings account...you don't want all this money sitting here doing nothing!"

"Oh, it's busy, it's doing something," I informed her. "Just leave it where it is. But, I guess, take out what you need to cover all these insufficient-funds bills."

The nest egg was badly cracked when I left the bank. Ben's cost of living had depleted it by nearly half. Had he used the money for repairs to the house or perhaps on Shannon, I wouldn't have been as upset. It galled me to think that all those years of scrimping disappeared in a puff of pizza and video games.

As of this moment though, Ben no longer had any access to my funds. I paid off the Visa bill and then spoke to an agent to cancel it. I couldn't wait for Ben to order his favourite meal and have them decline it. But I had a hell of a lot of catching up to do to reach my goal of $100,000.

I felt grumpy and frazzled from my lack of a good sleep. I needed a strong coffee. Yesterday's brew at the Erin Mills Town Centre entered my mind. It was so strong, such pure coffee, that my taste buds tingled. Thinking of that Kenya Blend java then brought to mind the couch where I drank it, and how comfortable I'd made myself there. I sure could use a dose of comfort.

Twenty minutes later, I was in the same spot as yesterday. I brought in a canvas bag from The Bulk Barn, which held all my paperwork. I needed to go through my notes and see who owed me money. I had to get back on track.

I sat in the middle of the couch, with paperwork spread out on either side. Hardly anybody was behind in payments, except for Dawson at AAA Awesome Entertainment. That company owed me close to $3,000. After gathering all my data together, I gave Dawson a call.

"Awesome Entertainment," he growled into the phone. Nobody ever used the 'AAA' when they mentioned the company name. Those extra letters were strictly for the telephone book's yellow pages, so that it would be the first name you saw when you searched for entertainment.

And get this, AAA Awesome Entertainment was a name they'd only started using a couple years ago. Before that it was AAA Awesome Erotic Entertainment, specializing in strip-a-grams and stag-party entertainers. But one year, the phone company blundered and forgot to add the word 'Erotic'. So besides getting the ad for free the entire year, the unexpected bonus was that now people were calling for clowns, impersonators, magicians...anything to do with general entertainment. Dawson's business had quadrupled.

"Yeah, hi, Dawson, it's me, Maggie," I said. "Look, I don't want to get into the reasons why, but I really need that money you owe me."

"Oh, well, send me the figures you have and I'll take a look at it," he suggested. "If everything seems in order, then I can mail you a cheque."

"No, that's going to take too long," I sighed. "I have all the paperwork together. These are jobs that have been completed and you simply owe me for them. I don't want to get mad, I don't want to fight, I just want my pay."

"OK, but I need to see the dates and stuff," he persisted. "Do you have an idea how much it is, approximately?"

"Yeah, approximately $3,430," I replied.

"No, really," he said, thinking I was being funny.

"That's it!" I almost shouted. "I'm going to email you all the dates and jobs and then I'm going to drive to your house to get a cheque. Tomorrow."

I expected his usual excuses for it not being a good time, but he agreed. "OK, I guess I'll see you tomorrow. But it's got to be early," he warned me. "I'm leaving at ten to catch a flight. Going to Vegas for a few days."

Wow, Vegas? I wanted to get my cheque and have it cashed before his plane landed. I felt like my finances had just dodged another bullet. We made plans to meet at 8:30 in the morning, at his house in Etobicoke.

The next two hours were spent numbing my fingers as I sent a lengthy invoice to Absolute Entertainment. Had I been at home, maybe this would have gone quicker on my laptop computer. But all my forms of communication were reduced to my Blackberry phone. Twice I hit the wrong button and deleted my entire message. When I finally pressed SEND, I leaned my head back on the couch and immediately fell asleep.

My snoring woke me up. I was still on the couch but my paperwork was all over the floor. Sitting to my left was a tiny person, maybe you call them 'little people'? He was eating a pretzel. To my right, studying her receipt from Sears, was another 'little person'. Something told me they were a couple...what were the odds of having two height-challenged people sitting on each side of me? Had I been awake, I'd have offered to switch seats. I wondered if they'd rudely dumped my papers.

"Excuse me," I said as I bent to retrieve them. The tiny woman kindly helped me. As I stood up, I caught a whiff of a bad odour. Was it the man's parmesan pretzel?

Walking away, heading back to my car, the nasty smell stayed with me. I did one of those cliche moves, pretending to stretch but then sniffing my underarms. Yikes! I reeked of BO. I couldn't have an agent see me like this. Next time somebody wanted to book a beautiful French maid, Dawson would probably think of me and say, "Beautiful? Hell no, not the last time I saw her!"

I headed off to the Erin Mills Town Centre washroom to take a sponge bath.

Thursday was supposed to be better...I was to come into money. The night before, I decided to drive into Etobicoke to avoid the morning rush hour. As one a.m. rolled along and I still couldn't sleep, I thought it an even better idea to drive right to Dawson's house. I was sure he was asleep; he'd never know I was parked on his street.

What I wasn't prepared for was that there was no parking allowed on his street. Since there was space in the driveway next to Dawson's Land Rover, I pulled up alongside it and bedded down for the night. For sure I'd be on time for this 8:30 meeting.

At seven a.m., I was rousted by a shrieking teenage boy carrying a large guitar case. "Dad! Dad!" he was screaming. "Somebody's sleeping in our driveway! Call the cops"

I tried to wake up quickly and dampen the situation. I rolled down my window. "Hey, buddy! Calm down! I'm just here to see..."

"Dad! Quick, before she tries to get away!" the boy ran back to his front door. I realized I'd be seeing Dawson sooner than I'd planned, so I quickly grabbed my make-up bag. I barely had lipstick on when Dawson came to the front door.

"Where is this person?" I heard Dawson ask his son, and realized he couldn't see my car very well beside his Land Rover. I didn't want him to see the mess in my house, ha ha, so I jumped out of the car and up to the front walk.

"Dad, that's her!" Dawson's dramatic son pointed at me. "Probably a crazy lady! Let's get in the house!" At this point, a lady in a business suit and runner, walking two poodles, hurried past us. Neighbours on one side took their time getting into their

Saab, curious as to how this would play out.

"Maggie?" Dawson questioned. "You're awfully early!"

"Well, I wanted to beat rush hour, got here too soon, and thought I'd just grab a nap in your driveway until 8:30 came around." I basically didn't lie. I wanted to add that his son was a crybaby and deserved a kick in the pants. However, Dawson owed me over three grand and no way was I going to kibosh that cheque's delivery.

He had all the information at his disposal as we sat ensconced in his home office. Computers, filing cabinets, a calendar on the wall. I had my measly Blackberry. Yet Dawson would inquire as to the veracity of certain larger-paying shows and I'd have to search and scroll my messages until I'd find the corresponding booking. Then Dawson would miraculously find his own record of the gig. When 8:30 rolled around, we were ending our meeting. I was happy to leave with my $3,400; Dawson looked like he was going to have to cut his Vegas vacation short.

Where to go now? I had a couple gigs the next day, a Friday, the first in Mississauga and the second in downtown Toronto. A vision of a CIBC bank branch floated into my mind; it was back in Mississauga, at the Erin Mills Town Centre. That was my reasoning for driving back to the mall.

After depositing my cheque into my new account, my mind wandered to the lower-level seating arrangement, the couch and chairs. My 'home away from home', I laughed to myself. Well, I'd rather be comfortably sitting there than in my cramped car. I grabbed a pen and some paper to write tomorrow's songs, locked the car and headed for my sanctuary.

The chairs were full; so was my couch. Undeterred, I made a mother, cooing away to her nursing baby, slide over. Setting my Orange Julius hot dog and juice down, I went to work composing tunes for 50-year-old John and bride-to-be Deidre.

An hour later, two perfectly written ditties. A few weeks ago, they would have been even more impressive, typed with a cool font on crisp themed stationery. These days, I practiced my best printing skills as I handwrote the songs on stock white paper. Writing them left me in a state of fatigue. I looked at the math-studying Asian student to my right and then glanced at the chow mein-eating Indian to my left. The three chairs were occupied; one had a senior citizen fast asleep, another held a couple in the mating stage and their friend sat in the third chair. He was leaning forward, describing a hockey game to his uncaring pals. They acted like he wasn't there but the hockey player didn't seem to notice as he pulled his chair closer to the lovebirds.

The mall was busy as well. I was thinking I needed a coffee to perk me up, but would an empty seat be awaiting me on my return? Would I be reduced to sitting in a hard chair in the food court? A litany softly drummed through my head...should I stay or should I go? Should I stay or should I go? Should...

It was like counting sheep. I could feel myself drifting off and just went with the flow.

A couple hours later, I woke up to a voice saying, "Some people!" I wondered if she could mean me, though I didn't know why. As I fluttered my eyelids open, I became aware that I was no longer vertical. I was now totally horizontal; comfortably stretched out, taking up all the room as I slept on the couch.

In embarrassment, I quickly sat up. In less than ten seconds, both seats next to me became occupied. You must have looked like a bum, I thought. I wanted to move but felt disoriented from my deep sleep. Now I really needed a coffee and went back to that fancy coffee place.

I decided to return to my comfort zone, drink my coffee and then work out the rest of my busy weekend schedule. I was able to reclaim my seat on the couch, empty possibly because of the man who now occupied the corner seat. He had a shopping cart that didn't come from any of Erin Mill's stores. In it were empty pop cans. The man wore shapeless clothes and scuffed shoes. He was drinking a can of Pepsi but I could detect a strong odour of alcohol on him.

I took a sip of my coffee and frowned. Something tasted distasteful and I sensed I had been served the bottom of a long-brewing urn of coffee. It almost tasted burnt. Thing is, it cost me three dollars so I was going to have to drink it anyway.

I watched two security guards making their way through the mall. One was the guard from a couple days ago; I hoped he wouldn't recognize me as I tried to turtle my head into my shirt. They almost marched in unison towards my haven. I stole a look at the vagrant next to me and thought, "Uh oh, it's him they're after!"

"You might want to beat it," I whispered to the guy, giving him the red alert. He looked at the approaching mall cops and on his third try, managed to stand up. He was old and weary and not making a very quick getaway. I sat back to watch the drama unfold.

The guards didn't even spare the man a glance. They strode right in front of me, managing to squeeze in between the couch and the coffee table. "Hey, watch my coffee," I said as I tried to reach around them to grab it.

"Will you come with us, ma'am?" they asked politely.

I looked behind me, sure they were talking to somebody else. What possible reason would I have to go with them? Shoplifting? All I had on me were car keys, a pen and the change from a ten-dollar bill. Oh yeah, and a couple songs.

"Me?" I asked. "Whatever for?"

Seems I was being charged with loitering. Trying not to cause attention to myself, I explained I'd just got there, with a hot, not-so-fresh coffee to prove it. But one of the smarty-pants guards pulled out his iPhone and showed me a couple photos he'd snapped. He missed my snooze on one day, but had pix of the first nap and the last. Today's stupor showed me with an arm hanging off the couch, mouth open, people staring.

I'd never been in trouble with the law. Suddenly I had

committed a crime, and it sounded so lurid, so lower-class. I'd have felt the same way if I'd been wrongly accused of being a prostitute. That's how I felt; falsely accused. Maybe I'd look up the definition of loitering later, but I vowed to fight that charge.

So much for killing the day at the mall. I went back to my beloved seat in the Suzuki. At least I could recline it.

* * *

Friday morning, I was up with the newspaper delivery boys. I drove over to a McDonald's in the same plaza that I'd slept in and went inside to take care of business. I grabbed a coffee and a Sausage McMuffin. I probably ate four of those sandwiches a week, and they were really hit and miss. Somedays the sausage was hot and greasy, yum yum, the bun nicely toasted, the cheese still visible. Other days the bun was too soft and chewy, or the cold cheese was added at the last second or else microwaved into an orangey glaze or the sausage was dry as a hockey puck. Today they managed to prepare a sorry sandwich that encompassed all the bad points available. I ate about a third.

The good thing about living in my car was that I rarely had anywhere to be, or anything to do. No housework, no trips to the grocery store, no more visiting my friends. Just the pursuit of work. Thus, I was able to arrive super early at most of my shows. Hell, I'd often arrive two days early.

I've been to many places in my long career, logged many miles on my vehicles. I always claimed I could just as easily become a cab driver. Today was a different story. I found myself in a part of Mississauga that seemed like it was erected just yesterday. The building where I was going, a pharmaceutical company, was gigantic. The parking lot, rather, lots, had acres and acres of cars parked at eight a.m. in the mooring.

My show, a 'tacky bride', didn't start until ten a.m., likely their coffee break. That's how my shows usually booked when I went into an office – first coffee break, just before lunch, last coffee break, just before work lets out. I didn't want to park in the visitors lot just yet; getting ready in front of the building's windows could give away the shock value for when I arrived. I drove around, looking for a place to park, but it seemed like I just kept getting too far away.

Turning back towards the building, circling it, I came across a dumpster full of garbage. Next to it was a small open space. I don't know if it was an actual parking space but I knew I could make my little baby fit. Sometimes my 2004 Suzuki Swift amazed me. It would hold so much stuff, I swear it thought it was a cargo van. And at other times, when space was tight, my ride imagined itself to be a tiny circus clown car.

The tacky-bride costume was one that I'd debated leaving behind. It seemed I wouldn't get a show for six months and next thing you know, I was doing three in a week. This was the first one I'd gotten since I'd left my house. It was packed at the very bottom of all my possessions, and it took me some time to get to it.

I had taken out boxes and bags in order to get to the costume and just put it back willy-nilly for now. After this show, my next gig wasn't until 4:30 p.m., so I would have plenty of time to rearrange my car before that.

The yellowed wedding dress was totally wrinkled, the bouquet of flowers were bent and the 70s permed wig a disaster. This was all good when it came to the tacky bride. I enjoyed this costume; it usually got such belly laughs. The coffee-stained dress was beyond ugly and when I walked in, I liked to have the back of it all bunched up in my bloomers (as if I'd just taken a leak prior and my dress got stuck in my panties). My knee-high beige hose were visible and the garter rested around my ankle. My make-up and hair were overdone, my white gloves with the ripped seams were too tight, my plastic flowers still carried the Goodwill price-tag...so many components to get a laugh. My dress's zipper had broken, wouldn't do up past the waist, so I wore a zebra-print bra under it. A veil, attached to a large comb, fit over my head like a bubble.

I got into my get-up and then started the car to go find a visitors' parking space. As I cruised the lot, remembering to smear my teeth with lipstick, I saw that every space was full. That included the handicapped parking...not that I'd use it.

Twice more I circled the lot. Time was ticking, my show had to start in under ten minutes. "Screw this," I thought. "I was better off parked where I was." With that, I returned to my tight spot beside the jumbo garage cans. I could see I was on some yellow-painted diagonal lines but I'd only be here, hopefully, fifteen minutes or so.

Gathering my balloons, fake rose and song, I locked up my car. It was a chilly wind as I ran around the large building, looking for the entrance. My wedding dress billowed around me, my veil threatening to fly away. As I watched a couple also walking towards the building from the direction of the Excess Parking Lot about a half-mile away, I slowed down. Surely they knew where the entrance was.

The lady's scarf flew off and the two went running after it. I felt only a twinge of pity for her; more so I felt *Come on, come on, forget the scarf, get to the building already*. However, the guy, with a dramatic flair, managed to plant his big shoe on it. He stayed frozen, holding the scarf in place, until the woman retrieved it. They again began walking to the building and I resumed my steps, hoping to time our 'accidental' meeting at the entrance together.

Finally the conservative, unembellished entrance to this medical building appeared! No longer needing the couple's help, I surged ahead of them. The wind gave one more blast and my hands flew to cover the front of my dress. I didn't mind my back end being purposely exposed but not my front.

Somehow my balloons escaped. I tried to dash after them, the couple also trying. We spent maybe a minute doing this but then the lady's scarf flew off again. Her date, or maybe co-worker but he should be a date because he was going the distance here, once again ran after it. Just as it threatened to take to the skies, the guy jumped two feet in the air and brought it down.

He looked at his watch as he gave the scarf to the woman. He said something to her in a foreign language, which she was kind enough to relay to me. "We have to go now," she said in a precise-yet-artificial manner. "We have a meeting. We are so sorry about your balloons."

Not a word was mentioned about my get-up, which I thought considerate. And speaking of meetings, I was also supposed to be at one. I entered the building with them and reported to the security desk. The guard was busy on the phones, so I waited impatiently while he dealt with three different issues.

It was getting late; they probably had a secret room ready for the show, or a cake with candles lit, or fifty gals hiding behind a door somewhere. I wished I'd brought my cellphone with me so I could call the contact, let her know I was in the building. Yet I held my annoyance in check, just discreetly letting the guard know I was in a rush.

Let me tell you right now, when it came to security guards in office buildings or fancy condos...wherever I found one behind a desk...I had the utmost respect for these people. They have a phone and contact numbers at their fingertips, as well as access keys and codes for elevators. Since I can sometimes get confused with too many details (I'm always just trying to remember the telegram recipient's name!), they've often left their command posts to escort me to a party room or through maze-like corridors. Six times they've helped me find my car in their under-ground parking lots.

He finally had a moment to spare for me. "Sorry," he said as he hung up the phone. "It's really crazy here today. Got a big conference and the plane with the main speakers on it just got in.

Guess the wind held them up."

"I'm not here for that," I said. Obviously. I explained my mission and he checked a sheet. He was about to speak when the phone rang. He held up a hand while he answered it.

"Yeah, the speeches are delayed, but not by much," he informed someone. I heard him add, "A cab would be easier," before he turned his attention back to me. "OK, before the phone rings again, here's what you do. You take the elevator to the third floor, you turn right, you punch in 1234, and the door will open. Got that so far?"

I nodded. 3rd floor, turn right, 1234. "So far, easy enough," I said.

He nodded back. "The rest is easy too. You go through the door, turn right again, take the hallway to the end, where you make another right. Go to the end of that hallway and you'll see an office door. There's a sign on it, says Monica Schwinn. That's who you want to see."

"Yup, that's her!" I said, whirling to leave, rushing to the elevator, slapping the 'up' button. As the doors opened, I heard the guard call out to me.

"Ma'am, you might want to fix your dress in the back," he suggested. I just jumped into the open elevator and jabbed at the '3' button then start poking repeatedly at the 'Close Door' button. As soon as I arrived on the third floor, I turned right and there was a locked door in front of me. No problem, I thought, as I keyed in '1234'. The door clicked open and I entered.

Here is where the fun would begin, as people would notice me and trail me to my final destination. From there, the festivities would start, laughs would ensue, the victim would be sufficiently embarrassed and honoured, and I'd leave amid applause and kudos.

Today, not so much. As I opened the door upon the hallway, I saw an ocean of desks, cubicles, work stations...all filled with busy personnel. Some glanced up as I entered through the door, most just kept their noses buried in a computer screen. I put on a big smile but only one person nodded in response. A couple gave me a quizzical look, a couple looked at me in distaste. Hey, I know I'm not perfect, but I'm supposed to look tacky!

I approached my final right turn. I started singing out, "I'm looking for Monica! Monica Schwinn!" This would surely entice my longed-for Pied Piper line. Instead, a couple people just pointed me in the direction I was already headed. I finally reached the bride-to-be's closed door. With one last effort, I loudly called out, "Singing telegram for Monica Schwinn!" A girl, with her chair pulled up to another work-mate's desk, glanced up but quickly went back to the instructions she was receiving.

Knocking on the door, I was told to come in. I burst through the door, leaving it wide open for others to eventually come and see what the hullabaloo was about. "Monica Schwinn?" I trilled. "I've come to deliver a very important message from..."

"Close the door, please," Monica interrupted.

My performance stalled for just a brief second. "Oh...oh...well, it's not important in the way you have to shut a door for! This is a SINGING TELEGRAM! Monica, your big sister..."

She got up and moved around me, causing me to stop my over-the-top performance once again as she reached for the door. "That's great," she said with a smile. "Just let me shut this so we're not bothering the employees. Management kind of frowns on lost time." With the door closed and the blinds pulled, she went back to her seat. "Ok, you may resume," she said.

With an audience of one, the usual ten-, fifteen-minute show gets reduced to half its length. Audience participation is so key to a show's success. Don't get me wrong; I've done amazing shows when there's just one person. Top-hat-and-tails classy 'grams where the bereaved widow had the amazing frame of mind to call my agent and bless his soul for having such a touching performance delivered to her. Or the Marilyn Monroe telegram to the gent who turned 100. When he passed away a month later, a story was written about him in the paper. It said his last fond memory was of a visit from a blonde bombshell.

But those jobs, because of the small audience, still didn't last the usual time. With this in mind, I still tried to get some laughs. I kept portraying my backside, hoping Monica would notice I had my dress tucked into my panties. She kept her attention mainly on what she was hearing, as her eyes were drawn onto the computer screen and her fingers occasionally clicked a few words onto the keyboard.

Giving up on getting a laugh from the physical comedy, I reverted to the song I'd written. I was given a lot of information to work with and thought I'd managed to cram a bunch of telling points into the song. She simply nodded at the end of each line, almost like a silent command to keep going.

At the end of each singing telegram, if I'm not doing Marilyn, I still sing 'Happy Birthday' (or a version of it – Happy Anniversary, Happy Retirement, etc.) and manage to turn it into a comical dance with the recipient. At the end of it, with the victim usually managing to hold up my extended leg, I always freeze, enabling all cameras and iPhones to capture the moment forever.

Today, the show was about to get shorter. I was about to ask her to step away from the desk so I could sing her a second song, as well as include her in a dance. Usually, with a crowd watching, this request is always allowed. Something told me she would refuse...maybe she didn't want to get too up close with a perfect stranger. So I wrapped up the song, sent from her sister in Calgary.

"Thank you," she responded. "I'll give her a call later tonight. You know your way back to the elevator?" I assumed she was okaying that I could leave now, after what was no more than four minutes. I nodded my head and exited her office, closing the door behind me. My veil got caught as I tried to walk away.

Reeling myself back in, I opened the door quickly to pull the veil out. I whispered, "Sorry to bother you again," and making sure all of my tacky-bride apparel was out of her office, closed her door again. The walk back to the elevator was even more quiet than before, as now I wasn't calling out for my Monica. Now I was making a quick getaway.

I couldn't wait for the elevator to arrive fast enough. Worse than being stared at because you look ridiculous was not being stared at. That meant the general population figured this was my normal appearance. If I was doing a bag lady or a police officer, sometimes I took a simple pleasure in fooling Joe Public. But come on, today I was wearing a wedding dress!

As I got off on the ground floor, I blew by the guard, who was giving directions to three women in identical lab jackets, holding identical binders. Each also had a pull-along briefcase in tow. They didn't give me a second glance. As I exited the building, I was reminded of the weather.

My dress was so voluminous, it was blowing a hard sideways now with the wind's force. Every three feet I had to stop and disengage it from bushes and tree branches. Grateful I wasn't carrying much, I clutched my veil and car keys in one hand and used the other to wrench myself free of car mirrors and bumpers.

Finally finding myself at the back of the building, I looked towards the dumpsters, another big walk. From here I couldn't see my car; it was probably blocked by the red minivan next to it, but I was sure it was waiting for me.

My car was gone. Surely this was the place I'd parked it! But come to think of it, I didn't recall that red van there earlier. Maybe I was in the wrong place? Instead of retracing my steps, I went around the building the opposite way. "This is new," I thought, as I saw sights I hadn't seen earlier. Immediately around the corner was an employee's entrance/smoking area. A few hardy souls were still attempting to get their cigarettes lit when I blew around the corner. "Is there another dumpster around here?" I asked as an opener.

They just stared at me so I decided to elaborate. "I parked my car by a dumpster, and now I can't find it. Are there more dumpsters around here?" One guy pointed to the back, from the way I'd just come, so I shook my head. "No, that's the wrong dumpster. There's got to be another one." They all shrugged, so I moved along, only to observe more new details.

Didn't see all these picnic benches...didn't see the windows with fake birds painted on them...didn't see the parking lot marked for Executives Only. I turned the corner again and encountered a little parade. An airport taxi-bus was disengaging a group of people. Obviously three of these men were rock stars or famous scientists, as they walked forward imperiously, carrying nothing. Each man had two minions following, one carrying briefcases and the other working on iPads or Playbooks.

When the first man saw me, he slowed his pace and lowered his glasses. This caused a minor traffic jam, almost a pile-up, with the other eight people behind him. He spoke sharply to his personal secretary and the secretary instantly began to press and slide his iPad. With all of us frozen in place for a micro-minute, I saw the guy finally raise his electronic gizmo and snap a photo of me. The other lifted his Playbook and said, "Over here!" and I obeyed his command.

After I'd posed for a few shots, I backed up. "Sorry, I have to go!" and disappeared around the corner. I gathered my gown to myself and waited a moment, nodding solemnly to a Vice-President of Accounting driving into his marked spot in the lot. He pulled out a batch of paperwork and without paying me much notice, he quickly walked past. As I stepped away from my corner, I almost bumped into the same guy returning to his car. He merely snarled as he veered around me. He went into his car and retrieved a large lunch box. As I peeked around the corner to make sure the photo-snappers had gone, the Vice-President sped-walked past me again.

"Excuse me, I'm looking for a big dump..." I began as he

hurried past. I could see he wasn't willing to be of assistance.

I wound up back at the entrance and decided to simply try it again. Maybe I'd looked on the wrong side of the dumpster? Buffeted by the wind, simply letting my dress fly where it pleased, I click-clacked my way over the pavement back to the garbage container. That was another part of the tacky-bride's ensemble – white high-heeled shoes with the heels eroding so badly that the exposed nails made that telling sound.

I searched all four sides of the dumpster but could plainly see my Swift had disappeared. How could that be...unless it was stolen! But how, when I had the keys on me? Well, I was sure criminals had their ways. I hiked my dress up over my knees and ran back to my precious security guard.

This time I wasn't so patient when I found him with a customer. I barged into their conversation with, "I think my car has been stolen!" Apparently this was enough of a conversation-starter to grant me the floor. "I parked it at the back, since there was no room in visitors' parking..." I began.

"I had to park in the excess parking lot," the stranger at the desk said. I glanced at his fit form, his comfy loafers.

"It doesn't matter where I parked!" I shouted. "What matters is my car is gone!" I turned to the security guard, seeing his name for the first time on the pin clipped to his chest. "Vishran... Veeshran? Listen, it was parked right next to the dumpster..."

"Oh!" Vishran's eyes lit up. "Yes, I saw it happen! On my video monitors."

"Saw what happen?" I asked. "You saw the people who took it?"

"Yes, I saw them," he confirmed.

"I should call the cops," I stated.

"Maybe you should," he agreed.

"May I use your phone?" I asked, as he turned it towards me. "Did you happen to get a description of the guys who made off with my car?" I asked him. Maybe the camera's footage would help as well.

"Oh, yes, I did," he announced. "Peel Region Towing Services."

I stopped dialling and looked Vishran in the eye. The stranger next to me started giggling, and it wasn't at my outfit. "Are you telling me my car did NOT get stolen?" I asked the guard.

"Moo Moo," the stranger inexplicably called me, "You got towed!"

Vishran spoke up. "That was your car? I saw the garbage truck pull up but his crane could not reach the dumpster. Your car was blocking it. Then two minutes later, the tow truck pulled up and took you away."

Great. All this while I was doing a five-minute show. Suddenly a realization dawned on me and the tacky bride turned wacky. "OH MY GOD, oh fuck me!!!" I yelled, causing the stranger to stop laughing with a final bleat. "All my stuff is in my car! My LIFE is in that car!"

Without thinking, I ran behind the guard's desk, tripping over the front of my gown. The stranger caught me as I fell out of my heels. I left them on the lobby floor as I sidled next to Vishran.

"Give me the number to Peel Towing!" I commanded. As he looked it up, the phone began to ring. He looked at me apologetically and picked up the phone.

"Bio-Medicinal Industries, this is Front Desk Security, Vishran speaking, how may I help you?" He listened for a moment and then asked, "Where do you remember leaving your iPad?"

I made an 'oh, COME ON!' face, causing Vishran to frown. "OK, I will check with the cafeteria as well as the Conference Hall. I will get back to you as soon as I can." At this, I rolled my heavily blue-eye-shadowed eyes. The guard took down more information and made plans with the caller to keep in touch.

As soon as he hung up the phone, I whined, "Can we get back to MY problem now?"

Vishran held the phone away from me. "That may be unimportant to you, but to Dr. Shania Thishnamnam, that iPad is HER life. She does very intelligent work here. Who knows what formulas for curing cold sores she has on that iPad?" He pulled out his list of contacts. "I have to make some calls on her behalf."

FINE. Leave me standing here, shivering in the cool lobby, my back open to the elements with nothing but a veil to warm me. I waited a few minutes until Vishran got a call that made him smile. "I am so very glad, Doctor," he said. "Thank you for letting me know. I do not know if I would have checked the ladies' washroom." They shared a giggle and he hung up.

I pounced on that phone immediately. "I'll dial, just give me the number," I ordered.

Vishran began. "905..." and stopped when he could see another number lighting up. I tried to shield it with my ripped glove but Vishran moved my hand aside as he took the phone out of my other gloved hand. "Bio-Medicinal Industries, this is Vishran speaking..." I blocked my ears...did he really have to go through that spiel? "It's a Maserati, you say? And no handi-capped sticker? okay, you wait right there, sir, you'll have a space in no time. I'll call for a tow truck."

He hung up and reached again for his contact list. I could see five towing companies listed. "Just finish giving me Peel's number," I begged. "You can get them to tow it away."

Vishran looked hesitant. "My sister-in-law's brother works for Fast and Friendly Towing. I have an arrangement with him. I help him when it is possible for me to do so."

I gave him a pleading look. "Vishran, give him the next job, I won't tell on you, just please, PLEASE get Peel Towing here!"

Vishran reluctantly made the call. He was muttering. "It wouldn't hurt him to make a tow once in a while. Does he pay for his room? Doesn't even help with the chores..." Now in a surly mood, Vishran ordered me to wait on a chair in the reception area. It was low to the floor, and the cushions soft and welcoming. I sat with my dress all pouffed up around me.

About three minutes later, I sensed Vishran had left his post. I moved aside a few layers of taffeta and saw the guard standing outside. He was talking to a burly guy wearing a backwards-facing baseball cap. The big guy hooked up the Maserati as easily as if he were making a ham sandwich. I heaved myself out of the chair, squeezed my aching feet back into the not-so-funny-anymore stilettos, and ran outside.

"Hey! Hey!" I shouted to the tow truck driver. "I think you took my car!" I teetered on over as he gave me a startled look. Finally somebody who could appreciate a person in costume.

"Oh, shit," said the guy who had the name Burt stitched onto his overalls. "Was it last Saturday? Saturday nights are when I tow at the banquet halls. Wow, I bet this is a first! I never towed a bride and groom's car before!"

"Oh come on!" I barely held in my contempt. "This is Friday! You think a bride wears her dress all week?"

"Maybe...I hear they can cost a fortune," the burly Burt replied.

Vishran added to the conversation. "My cousin Prajash is marrying a white girl and they say her dress is costing as much as the rental of the hall."

Burt nodded. "I'm telling my daughter it's an elopement or nothing. She's been...."

"CAN WE DISCUSS MY CAR?!" I screeched. That shut them up. "It was towed from this location...well...in back of here, about thirty minutes ago. Did you take it?" I accused Burt.

"Thirty minutes ago?" Burt repeated. "Nope, not me. I've spent the whole morning towing student's cars out of the teacher's spots over at the Philip Pocock High School. Man, those kids can swear like an X-rated movie!"

I turned to Vishran, almost clutching him by the lapels before stopping myself. "You said Peel Towing took it!?"

Burt piped up. "Hey, Missy, or is it Mrs? Maybe it was one of the other guys? We got a bunch of trucks on the road."

"Can you find out?" I implored.

The tow-truck driver looked at the car he'd hoisted, all ready to go. "I could radio it in, but I'd kind of like to get a move on before this guy gets back. Owners of cars like these...they're usually not very pleasant."

I thought fast. Even if my car wasn't there, what was the use of waiting in this Mississauga wasteland? I decided to move along. "Can I ride with you? I'm sure I'll find it in your lot." I was already clopping my way to the tow truck.

Burt opened the passenger door, steadied me as I got in and then tucked my dress in with me. He hustled over to his door and with an easy move, swung his large frame behind the wheel. "Hang on," he said.

The speed bumps in the lot sent me flying to the roof of the truck and I buckled myself in. As soon as we were out of the lot, Burt picked up his radio. He called in his co-ordinates and his expected time of arrival at the lot. He asked if there were any more tows, or if he could take his lunch. I finally gave him a prod in his ribcage. With a glance at me, he asked about my car.

"Oh, by the way, did anybody else make a tow at Bio-Medicinal today? It was a...." he looked at me. "What kind of car was it?"

"A blue Suzuki Swift," I quickly answered. He radioed that information, then put down the radio and turned on its loudspeaker. He was making his entrance onto a highway.

"Safety first," Burt said.

A voice crackled through the airwaves. "License plate, Burt?" I relayed that pertinent bit of information. "Oh, yeah," the voice replied. "That car was towed about a half-hour ago. Should still be on the lot. I know Tom picked it up. You want me to check?"

Burt looked over at me. I nodded forcefully. *Yes, please check!* The urge to be reunited with Suzie grew strong. Surely she would be missing her driver by now!

Burt pressed a button. "We're almost there but you can tell Tom to radio me."

The exits rolled by. We were getting farther from my next gig. I watched the faces on other drivers when they saw a Maserati was being towed. Nothing but sympathy. Finally, as we exited off the highway and pulled onto a service road just south of it, the radio came to life.

"Burt! Tom here. You called about that Suzuki?" it asked.

"Yeah, you towed it?" Burt inquired. "It's in the yard?"

"Nah, I never brought it here," was Tom's reply.

"What? Why not?" I bugged out. Burt radioed that in.

"What?" he said. "Why not?"

"Ya shouldda seen it," Tom snorted derisively. "Full of junk, covered in graffiti...I think there was a dead fox on the dashboard..."

"That's a clown wig," I retorted. "And there's one piece of graffiti!"

Tom continued. "And they think they can just leave it by a dumpster and that the garbage guys are gonna haul it away like it's some couch?"

"Excuse me, can you tell Tom I'm sitting right here?" I asked Burt. "Just find out where it is now."

By this time, Burt had pulled into the gated lot. He keyed in a code that raised the barriers. As we slowly drove through, Burt picked up the radio again. "If the car is not in our lot, where did you take it?"

I could hear papers riffling. "Region of Peel Waste Management Metal Shredding Station," came the odd reply.

Burt and I just stared at one another. Again he spoke into the radio. "Tom, did you get my question? Where's the Suzuki?"

"Burt, did you get my answer?" Tom played cute. "At the Peel Metal Shredding Station."

"What does that mean?" I wailed. Visions of my car being shredded played like a bad movie scene before my eyes.

"What does that mean?" Burt radioed back.

"It means they're gonna put it in a big container, squish it 'til it's the size of a beer cooler, and then who knows? Who cares?"

"I care! It's my car! I live in it!" I cried out. Burt almost drove into the line of vehicles to his left. He turned to stare at me. The look he gave me was unreadable – was it disgust? Concern? Shock? I nodded. "It's true. And I need it back! How can I stop this?"

Burt snapped up the radio. "Tom, give me that address, and be quick about it!" Gone was the buddy-buddy talk. He whipped the Maserati into a space as I heard the address given. "Shit, that's halfway across the city, get me their phone number too," he ordered. Burt gave me a pad of paper and pencil, as he jumped out to unhook the car.

Tom came on, sounding a bit petulant. "Jeez, you don't have to sound so bossy."

I pressed the button attached to the radio. "Tom! Just do it!"

"Alright, alright, don't get your panties in a knot already, Burt," the other tow truck retorted. He came back with the number, but his comment about the panties oddly made me think about my own set of underwear...what was it about them? I knew I was wearing a pair, but what made them so special today? Oh yeah! I always had to remember to stuff my wedding gown into them, to get that initial big laugh. Then, as the tacky bride, I'd act embarrassed and pull them out.

I reached behind me and felt my butt. Sure enough, the dress was still bunched up in them. Burt had obviously noticed as well, but being the courtly Canadian that he was, decided to keep quiet. I had to give him credit for that. This time, with actual embarrassment, I pulled the dress out of the granny panties.

The door opened and Burt jumped back in. "Didja get the number?" was his first line. I nodded and presented him with the pad of paper. He reached for the glove box and tried to open it but there was too much dress in the way. I gathered as much of it towards myself as I could, and I heard the glove box open and shut as Burt retrieved his cellphone.

"Now this time, really hang on," he warned me.

The impound-lot gates had barely opened before Burt barrelled through. As he drove, he called the shredding lot. An automated voice came on, giving all sorts of instructions. "If you have paint cans, press 1. If you have a metal ladder, press 2. For wooden ladders, please call the Recycling Line at blahblah or consider visiting their website at blahblahblah. If you have patio furniture, press 3."

Sheesh! When would junky car come up? Press 226? Burt pressed 0. Through the loudspeaker on his phone, which he'd set on the dashboard, we heard a different voice come on. This one, though she sounded ethnic, was as automated as the first voice. "You've reached reception; the operator is currently unavailable. Please hold and somebody will be with you momentarily."

I groaned as Burt swung onto the highway at a speed much over the posted limit. "Momentarily!" I sputtered, grabbing onto a handle I found above my door. The radio crackled.

"Burt? You on your lunch yet? Got a tow if you want it, Royal Oak Retirement Centre. Right near that souvlaki place you like," the dispatcher said.

My tow-truck driver picked up the radio and stared into it. In a curt voice, he snapped, "I'm on lunch. Then maybe a bit of personal time. We'll work it out later." He shut the radio off and placed it between the seats. With ease, he whipped around an 18-wheeler and then glided around a school bus that had braked.

For a change, I was getting a point of view that came from NOT being a driver, seeing those mad tow trucks racing up behind you, blaring past you, trying to be the first on scene at the accident up ahead. The only difference this time was that it was a sole tow truck being King of the Road.

Burt was silent all the way. I fretted. As the shredding station came into sight, Burt mumbled something. "What was that?" I asked, as we waited for the gate security guard to approach us.

"I said...I said I'm sorry," he again muttered, more distinctly this time.

"What for? You didn't tow my car," I replied.

"I'm sorry that you have to live in your car," he clarified.

What was the use of explaining? Besides, the guard was almost at the door. "Me too," I simply said.

Burt got instructions on the fastest way to get to where my car could be found. He didn't bother with visitors' parking; he just flat-out drove to the front of the building. I guess he wasn't too afraid of being towed. He leapt out of the truck and rushed to my side. I was already halfway out, trying to disengage my dress from the stickshift.

Like my knight in shining armour, Burt extended his hand. I took it and stumbled out on my high heels. A gust of wind seemed to find its way right through the back of my open dress and I shivered violently. Burt noticed and before he shut the passenger door, he reached behind the seat and withdrew an oily plaid jacket. "I do apologize, it's all I've got," he looked forlorn. I let him drape it around my shoulders as he quipped, "But hey, everything goes with white! Now let's go find your car."

We raced up to a clerk who was just putting up her 'Closed' sign. "The other clerk will be able to help you when she's through," we were told.

We glanced at the other clerk, who was in a hot debate with a man holding a large tub of disposable name-tags. Clerk #2 was explaining that he had to separate the plastic from the metal. The irate man claimed she was being discriminating. Burt shook his head. "We don't have time for this," he told our clerk, who was already pulling up her purse from its hiding place. "Listen, believe me when I tell you this is urgent. You have a car here. I think it's about to become impacted. We need to stop it."

My eyes widened at Burt. An hour ago, he was just a cliché tow truck driver; now he was turning into a superhero. The clerk turned to a computer and brought up a screen with a bunch of numbers. The clerk looked at me, then at Burt. "Would you have the VIN number?" she asked him.

In turn, he looked at me. "I don't have anything except the keys to my car!" I cried, stepping back, holding out my keys to prove it. "Everything you might need of me, my driver's license, my proof of ownership, my...my expensive Estee Lauder lipstick! It's all in my car!"

The clerk twisted her mouth to one side. She said, "Well, when cars are about to get impacted, that's about the only information we take off of them."

"I know the license-plate number," I feebly offered.

"That won't help, even if it's still out there," she said as I cringed. "Let me try something else. I'm going to pull up the site where..." she clicked a few buttons... "I can pull up an aerial view..." as a screen full of cars appeared... "and maybe you can spot your vehicle." The clerk looked at the screen. "Whoa, busy day for those guys today. Lucky you, we have a hundred or so of these cars to impact."

"Lucky me?" I almost wanted to slap her.

"Lucky 'cuz maybe there's so many, they haven't had a chance to get to yours...yet," she corrected me. Our eyes studied the screen, Burt's head peering over mine.

"How can you tell what car is what?" I said. "They all seem to look alike. You know, my car can look like a Ford Focus, or a Yaris Toyota... Sometimes my car can look like an SUV if it wants..." I stopped my blathering and concentrated on the monitor. *Suzi, you impersonator of all cars, where are you?*

"I know what a Suzuki Swift looks like," Burt said. "This is kind of a long shot of the lot," he told the clerk. "Is there any way you can get a better look at what's down there?"

"I believe this button..." the clerk did a manoeuvre on her computer "...allows me to zoom..." as a battered old K-Car came into view "...and track as well," she finished as the shot moved next onto a motorcycle, almost bent into a 90-degree angle before it had even met Mr. Shredder. "Does your car have any distinguishing features?" she asked, as the cursor moved onto the next beaten-up mode of transportation – an ice-cream cart with no wheels.

"Yeah, for one thing, it's not a wreck," I exclaimed. "Move that cursor faster." The clerk breezed through all the vehicles, one trashy eyesore after another.

"On the other hand," she shrugged, "looks like we might have ate it already."

Her cursor slid past an image that showed a car at its pure length, proudly standing bumper to bumper between a burned-out Cadillac and a muscle car that resembled a squeeze box. "Wait!" I yelled. "That's it!"

"Wow," Burt mumbled over my shoulder. "Looks like a Dodge Neon."

The clerk scrolled just a bit more, showing my car was third in line to become compacted. "Oh my, you may be too late to stop it," the clerk declared.

"What?! But it's not even through yet! Stop them! Make a call, do something!" I begged, yelling through the hole in the glass partition.

"I'm going to try, I'm going to call them right now, and their supervisor will radio them up in the compactor," the clerk said, scurrying to make the call. "But those guys...it's so loud up there...they never hear the radio..."

SuperBurt sprang into action. "You stay here," he told me. "I'm gonna run out there, try to get their attention." With that, he took off out the door.

The clerk I was dealing with made her call to the supervisor, told him it was urgent, and the supervisor immediately radioed the compact guy. And that's where my hope ended. The guy wasn't answering. By this time, Clerk #2 became interested and had wandered over. She watched the drama being played out on the computer screen with me. We saw the tiny figure of Burt race to the foot of the compacting machine. He waved his arms, ran in circles, he performed jumping jacks...all as my car inched forward.

Suddenly, all the jolting on the screen seemed to stop as the compactor was shut off. A guy leaned out of the machine. We couldn't hear what was being said between Burt and him, but the guy reached back into his cabin and pulled out his radio. We could see him speaking into it and then waving at Burt. Burt turned around and we saw him walk away.

In a moment, my tow-truck driver walked back through the door. "Wow, that was close, but we saved your little car."

I ran up to him and gave him a big hug.

"Oh, is he your groom?" Clerk #2 asked.

"Don't I wish!" I said. He sure did about 900 percent more than old Ben would have ever done.

Soon the good feelings kind of dissipated. I thought that'd be it; I'd retrieve my car and get out of there. Mosey on to my next show with a few hours to spare to come down from this horrible experience. But no, first they had to remove all the cars that blocked my vehicle. I refused the kind offer of them using the gigantic claw machine to lift it above and over the mess of cars. Instead, the claw was used to clear a path for my car.

The shredding company used their own tow truck to move Suzi to the front of the building. I rushed out and hugged my car as best I could. I was about to unlock it when Clerk #2 came out of the building. "Hang on, you can't just drive off," she said. "There's papers to sign, and then you gotta get it towed to the Peel Region Towing Services lot."

"You mean...I can't just go?"

"Sorry, that's not how it works," she replied. "I know you've been through a rough time, but rules are rules. You still gotta pay for your tow, and the fine, and the storage...all the stuff that comes with being towed."

"Just go sign the papers," Burt told me. "I'll give you a tow back to the lot. We'll make it quick."

Burt hoisted up my baby with obvious care. He drove the speed limit back to the impound lot. With a delicate touch, my Suzuki was unloaded, the tires hitting the ground with a soft kiss.

Inside their messy compound sat a bunch of loud, complaining customers. Some were crying, some yelled into cellphones, some sat morosely. All held numbered tickets in their hands. I went to grab one but Burt said, "You don't need it. Follow me."

Leading me to a door marked Office Manager, he told me to wait outside. Fifteen minutes later, after I'd used the filthy tow-truck drivers' private washroom to freshen up, I was still waiting when Burt reappeared.

"OK, I'm going to show you what happened," he explained, displaying an invoice. "You still have to pay for the towing charge, that's on Tom's bill and I can't do anything about it...but I got them to remove the storage and I'm not charging you for the tow back from the shredders. You may still get a fine for parking illegally, but that will come in the mail."

"Oh, man, Burt, I don't know what to say," I began.

The dispatcher popped his head out of a door. "Burt, there you are! Still got that car waiting to be towed at the retirement home. Can you do it?"

"Yeah, sure, why not?" Burt replied. "I'll go be the bad guy as usual. Radio me the details. I'll be in my truck in two minutes." I was about to continue my thanks when Burt pointed me in the direction of a long line-up of people. "If I were you, I'd join that line. It moves at the rate of about two people an hour."

Burt gave me a clumsy salute and then an even clumsier hug. Maybe he instinctively didn't want to get too close to a woman who lived in her car. I again wanted to explain my situation but he turned and hustled off to his job.

By the time I finally reached my car, I knew it was going to be iffy if I would make it to my next gig in time. I had barely made contact with Suzi earlier, having just quickly opened the car door to retrieve my wallet. I still had no time to check if everything was okay with her as I raced downtown.

Doing the usual 'drive and get ready at the same time', I transformed myself from leftover tacky bride (oh, where did this plaid jacket come from?) and into a clown. The clown suit still lay where I'd draped it earlier, over the front seat. The orange wig was still on the dashboard. It was almost showtime as I debated where to park. Try one of my tricks to get free parking? Oh God, not today. I couldn't handle getting towed again. Instead, I drove into the parking lot attached to the stockbrokerage.

The clown act went fine, other than the victim's co-workers asking why his wife would send a clown. Why not a stripper? Why not a Marilyn Monroe? One of his buddies, a guy I thought I recognized from somewhere, mentioned he'd had a Madonna for his 30th birthday. I left the stockbroker's office and returned to my car.

Only to find it missing again. I almost became physically sick. I staggered to the garbage can I remembered seeing next to my stall – I saw the red lettering on the wall that said "Small Car Parking Only." A SmartCar was in residence instead of my Suzuki. Oh, no, no, no! My car is small! That's why I parked there. Unless it thought it was being a big car again...but that was only my imagination getting the better of me.

I'm going nuts, I figured. *But if my car has really been towed again, I think I will go off the deep end.* With despair, I looked along the garage and my eyes lit on the columns spraypainted '5B'.

Wait a minute...FIVE B??? 5??? No, no, no...even in my haste, when I parked, I saw a column that read '4B'. I recalled a fleeting thought, me saying, *4B. For Burt,* and blowing it a kiss as I ran for the gig.

On foot, I ran down to the next level and found the column

that read 4B. There was my Suzuki Swift, right where I had left it. From afar, I beeped it open, then started running towards it. It was corny and romantic, and if the car had run toward me as well, it would have been clichéd, as well as paranormal.

I reached my car and my hand caressed the door handle. I slowly pulled it open and slid behind the wheel. The seat was in the exact position I'd left it. The mirrors were still set at the perfect angle. And all of my stuff was there, from my fancy lipstick to my dirty laundry.

I was never so glad to be home.

Chapter Seven

What other country gets a snowstorm in May? Maybe the Antarctic, but by now, Canadians should have been planting their gardens. Trees had already sprouted buds, lakes and rivers had melted and my winter-wear was stuffed in the bottom of my trunk. Yet here we were, first week of May and snowflakes the size of dinner plates were dropping heavily from the sky. Five of those snowflakes landing on my windshield was enough to impair my vision.

I drove to my Bag Lady job in Minden, wondering if that town had even seen a bag lady before. Poor choice, but it wasn't my call. Thank goodness I'd driven two thirds of the way the night before, finding a truck stop off the 401 highway and bedding down there for the night. It was only another hour to my show, but with the bad weather it took three. I was pleased with myself for allowing plenty of time. I was almost there when the phone call came. Due to the forecasted blizzard, all the employees were being sent home. Even though I whined that I was ten minutes away, according to my GPS, my agent still cancelled the show.

I pulled into the nearest – you guessed it – Tim Horton's and grabbed some breakfast. I also washed up and brushed my teeth, seeing as how I no longer needed to work the Bag Lady look. The place was packed; the weather the hot topic. I debated my options and looked outside. Though it was snowing hard, I considered myself a good, careful driver. I decided to make some headway back to Toronto. Besides, there wasn't a seat to be had in the coffee shop.

I rushed to my car, determined to get a headstart on this impending storm. It was now a traffic jam of cars trying to get into the parking lot; I was the sole driver making an exit. I knew it was going to be a long drive so I had my usual XL two-cream, two-sugars coffee as well as a box of Timbits. I'm not a big donut fan but I bought them for a change of pace. I popped a Sour Cream Glazed into my mouth and glanced at the GPS.

In one moment I saw the GPS read 8 kilometres to the highway. That highway would take me to the big highway 401, which would pretty much take me home. In the next instant, the screen changed and simply read 'Lost Signal'.

"Oh, great," I muttered. But I wasn't about to start worrying. I was sure it would come on again. And at times it appeared it would, only to revert back to the annoying Lost Signal screen.

To make matters worse, every time I passed an open field, huge drifts of snow would blow off the barren areas. I would almost slow to walking speed, and remembered to put on my four-way flashers. Soon, probably with ten minutes of my leaving the coffee shop, the open fields weren't solely responsible for causing white-out conditions. The snow was coming down like mounds of cotton batten.

Out of the blue, Moneypenny, the name I'd given to the current British voice on my GPS, piped up. "In one kilometre, keep to the right on Highway 89." Then it went back to saying Lost Signal.

What were my options? I didn't want to pull over. There wasn't even room to pull over, other than in the ditch, and I was certain I'd get rear-ended by someone in a four-wheel SUV still driving like it was normal road conditions. Once I got onto the highway, which would certainly be plowed clear of snow, I would be able to better make an informed decision. A green highway sign almost passed by without my taking notice. "Whoa!" I said aloud. "Almost missed my exit!" At a turtle's pace, I turned a rather sharp right onto the road and began to speed up, ready to make my entrance onto the main highway.

In seconds, I was pumping my brakes. A freaking deer? On the on-ramp to a highway? The only reason I saw it was because it jumped right over the hood of my car. And then, maybe another ten seconds later, I almost made my entrance into a lake, having not seen I was coming into a major curve.

"What the hell!?" I yelled. "Did I miss the fucking highway?"

As if in response, Moneypenny chimed in. "In three kilometres, make a legal U-turn."

"Three kilometres!" I shouted in disbelief. "You're crazy!" Yes, I often spoke aloud to my GPS. This British babe, with her precise, clipped form of speaking, combined with that winning English accent, had been my best buddy for the last few weeks.

I figured I'd just pull into someone's driveway and turn the car around. However, I could see all the pathways leading into homes were covered with drifting snow. Chances were high to certain that I'd get stuck.

"Make a U-turn," Moneypenney commanded me. But where? Obviously this was the place to do it, but it appeared to be nothing but fields and snow. The GPS seemed to snort in contempt. "In two kilometres, make a legal U-turn."

I glanced to my left and in a quick instant, saw the outline of a big grey building, some kind of assembly plant. I debated stopping and trying to reverse back to that factory. I had just slowed down to ready myself for this move when a loud blaring horn almost gave me a heart attack.

A big semi-trailer passed me on the left side, close enough to actually move my outside mirror to the farthest position. I hadn't even seen him in my rearview mirror, and his multi-lit truck's momentary brightness disappeared once he was barely ten feet in front of me.

I quickly looked behind me to make sure no more trucks, hell anything, were coming my way. I could barely see out the back window. I had kept my rear wipers going but that had been my one ongoing complaint since I'd bought the vehicle. The rear wipers never seemed to quite meet the window all the way, only creating a small pane of clean glass. That pane was hidden behind bags of costumes.

Okay, better to keep going to the next legal U-turn, and figure it out from there. Taking it easy, I awaited Moneypenny's assistance, and I kept my eyes peeled, but I saw nothing but a sheet of snow. I realized I hadn't fixed my mirror and attempted to open my window. It was frozen shut but I kept pressing the button until there was a popping sound, and the window slid down. Immediately sideways flying snow blew into my car. I quickly popped my mirror back into place and shut the window.

The GPS came on, almost yelling at me. "In one kilometre, make a legal U-turn!"

"Sheesh, alright already, calm your britches," I told Moneypenny. And it was a good thing I was only going ten kilometres an hour, because the snow again broke for an instant and I saw a clearing to my right. A huge bank of snow had blown onto some kind of barricade, so I barely had room to squeeze my car into the remaining space. I almost hit a sign that sprung up as suddenly as that deer. I glanced up and saw it read 'Scenic Lookout'. I had no idea what there was to see...by this point I was so turned around, it could have been a farmer's two-headed cow. I didn't really have anyplace to go, but I didn't want to be where I was.

I gave it a moment's thought. Seemed the legal U-turns were coming closer together; ergo, I must be coming up to a town. Surely those factory people needed somewhere to get coffees in the morning. Again with the ergo, and being in Canada, there must be a Tim Horton's around. And even if there wasn't, I'd settle for a Country Style or Coffee Time. At this point, I'd have settled for a sexual deviate's offer of a cup of java at his place.

I took my GPS in hand and saw the reminder of Lost Signal. I cursed at the skies for blocking reception and held the GPS in a number of positions. Finally, stretching towards the far corner of the passenger seat, it came to life. Moneypenny immediately barked out, "Make a legal U-turn! Now! I'm tired of talking to you, you stupid idiot." Okay, she only said the first line, but I could hear the rest in her tone of voice.

I wasn't about to make that U-turn, legal or not. I had no desire to go back that way. I just wanted to get somewhere, pay for however many coffees it'd take to wait out the storm, and get back to Toronto. I punched in my query to the GPS – any coffee shops around?

And no surprise, Tim Horton's was the first and closest one to pop up. It was less than a kilometre away! I threw the GPS onto the seat, where it promptly lost its signal again. With caution, I slowly eased back onto the road. I kept up the slow pace when I realized I was headed down a steep hill. The snow plows had yet to make their appearance and I could tell the person who'd driven ahead of me had some pretty scary moments. Their tire tracks went straight, then wide squiggly tracks, then a set that actually looked completely sideways.

I rode my brakes going down that hill. I stayed right in the middle, just praying that nobody else was coming up or down. My eyes were raw from staring out the windshield, searching for my beloved Tim Horton's. And then, for a microsecond, I saw a big coffee cup up in the sky, with the Tim Horton's logo. It wasn't a mirage; it was the sign, high up on a post, for my destination. As suddenly as it'd appeared, it was again lost in the relentless snowstorm.

I finally felt the sense of being level once again, so I'd made it down the hill. I breathed a sigh of relief, only to be followed by a sharp gasp when Moneypenny screeched, "In 100 metres, turn right!" she rushed me.

"Whaa....?" I searched the skies for that Tim Horton's cup.

"TURN RIGHT!" Moneypenny screamed.

I turned right, just allowing myself to believe. Yup, I was on a little dirt road. Probably the dirt road to a quaint Tim Horton's restaurant. I slowed down completely, expecting to run into a hundred other cars escaping the storm. There was nothing but the snow-covered road. I inched forward, now unable to see anything in the storm.

"Hey!" I yelled at the GPS. "Wait a frickin' minute!" There should have been well-worn tracks if this road lead to a Tim Horton's. Snowstorm or not, somebody would have come along every minute for their Timmy's. "You sent me the wrong way!"

I stopped the car and just sat there. Now what? I realized the road I'd just travelled along was a tiny, unused one that was already becoming filled with huge growing mounds of snow. Backing up held no appeal to me.

I considered walking out, back to the main road, and finding that Tim Horton's on foot. Bundling up in my hoodie with a spring coat thrown over (mitts and scarf not handy, never mind snow boots), I shut the car off, grabbed my purse and cellphone and stepped out of the car.

The wind snapped the door shut, almost catching my fingers. I patted my Suzuki Swift and uttered a phoney chuckle. "You just stay here and wait 'til I get back, ya hear me, Suzi?"

I turned around and started walking down the road I'd recently driven. I tried to stay within the tire tracks I'd made, but the gathering snow had pretty much obliterated them. Head down, trying to find my trail, I walked head-on into a tree. That caused a pile of snow to jar loose from its limbs and almost turn me into a snowman. Backing up, shaking off the snow, I banged my tailbone into a huge metal container. In anger, I turned to push it over, which only helped to injure my shoulder muscles when it wouldn't budge. The can had a weird odour, and I saw a sign on it which read 'FISH GUTS ONLY'.

I stood stock still, afraid of causing my body any more damage. My cheek stung where I'd walked into the tree; I just knew I'd scratched it on a limb. I looked around and meekly wondered, "Where did the road go?"

I decided to walk ten steps in one direction and if I didn't stumble back onto the road, I'd turn around and walk the ten steps back to Fish Guts Can. But when I walked the ten steps, found no road and so retraced my steps back, it seemed Fish Guts had also gone for a walk. The can was nowhere to be seen.

Forget it, stay with the car, I smartly decided. Easier said than done. Now the question became, "Where did my car go?"

Back when my Suzuki was fairly new, and I'd lose it in a parking garage or shopping mall, the solution to this problem was blatantly simple. Press the panic button on the key chain and the horn would let me know where to find the car. The batteries kept blowing though. Last year, even with new batteries, the alarm stopped working altogether. When I tried to get it fixed, I was told something had corroded and it would cost a couple hundred to replace the key fob completely. I just decided to better remember where I'd parked.

So the key alarm was useless. And as close as Suzi and Moneypenny and I had become, calling out for them would be of no use. All I could do was stumble about, hoping to come across it. Part of me held out hope that if I didn't find the car, maybe I'd find the front door of Tim Horton's.

I could have let myself panic, but I was more concerned with keeping warm. I had the hoodie's drawstrings cinched as tight as possible, the hood pulled over my forehead and up to my eyes. I put my hands into the sleeves of my coat and tried to shield myself from the stinging icy snow. I wasn't terribly cold and knew I could last a couple more hours wandering around, looking for my light blue car.

Twice I came across Fish Guts Can. My legs were tired from lifting them through snow banks so, despite the rancid smell, I moved some snow away from the can so I could sit down and lean against it. My digging managed to turn up a dead seagull, its body half-eaten by scavengers before the snow drove them back into hibernation.

"Oh, ga-ross!!" I spat out as I recoiled backwards. Now I just wanted to be back in my car. I didn't care about Tim Horton's one bit; I'd be fine and dandy waiting out this blizzard in the comfort of my home. I just had no idea what direction to make my weary legs move.

I glanced at the can and figured that every time I left it, or came back to it, I always saw the neon letters. I moved to the opposite side of the can and decided to walk away from it. "Suzi!" I called out foolishly. It was only a ruse to keep myself from going back to Fish Guts Can and laying down next to the seagull. "Where are you?"

My words flew away with the big wind that whooshed through. I covered my eyes against the snow it brought, and just started to walk. I'd taken maybe a dozen steps when, just as the wind died down, I heard an odd sound. It wasn't a nature sound; it sounded man-made. A ping...ping...ping...

I stopped, like the mantracker who's caught wind of his quarry. *I know that sound...and it's not the sound of Tim Horton's cash registers...it's...Fucking right! It's the sound of my car!* The noise it makes if you don't shut off your headlights or close your door correctly.

I took three galloping steps towards the sound but then slid to a stop. Wait! I had to do this delicately! I listened for the pings but sure enough, all I could hear was silence. Before I even bothered to analyze anything, I just ran backwards three giant steps and froze.

Yes! There was that constant pinging sound again. This time I used a different approach, more ninja-style. I walked almost in slow-motion until I was certain I was headed in the right direction. The pings were noticeably louder and I ever so slowly inched towards the noise.

My car was about a foot in front of me before I actually saw it. The alert sound was being made because, when the door had slammed shut, the seatbelt (as it was wont to do) had slid out and got caught in the door. Normally I notice when this happens; it makes an awful sound. The poor seatbelt was pocked and misshapen from being slammed on so often. This time, what with the roaring wind, it obviously went unnoticed.

With cold fingers, I clicked the lock door open and jumped into the front seat. My shoes dragged in enough snow to build an igloo. I started up the car then moved my frozen fingers onto the control panel, flicking every switch I could find to maximum. I dispensed with defrost and went straight for total heat.

After fifteen minutes, I was warm all over except for my feet. I needed to get my wet socks off. But as soon as the shoes and socks came off, I placed my bare feet onto the floormats, where the snow was still melting. That put another chill over my entire body.

Knowing I had a few hours to kill, I tried to set the GPS again for that mystical Tim Horton's. However, now Moneypenny was just plain irritating. When it would speak, all she would say was "Make a U-turn." And then the screen would fizzle out and a now a new slogan was in order – 'Acquiring Signal'. It was like Moneypenny was saying, "I'm trying, Maggie, just give me time," when I knew that GPS was probably as lost as I was.

"It's been fun, Moneypenny, well, not really," I told the GPS in my hands. "But lately, you've changed. We have to break up. You're snippy, bossy and you have no patience. It's not me; it's you." And with that, I went to a male's voice. I tried the British guy. He sounded nice but I think he was into other guys. I wanted some company I could flirt with, so I went with the American male. He even sounded like he had an ever-so-slight Southern twang.

When I got myself into this predicament, I had about 3/4 of a tank of gas. After an hour of running the car, I began to worry about how long that gas would last. I turned off the car but it was only fifteen minutes before I began freezing. On with the car again. I'd heat up, almost so much that I was sweating, and then turn the car off again until I was chilled.

The car's clock read four p.m. and still the snow came down, even heavier than earlier. My gas gauge read half-full. A sixth sense told me it was probable I'd be there all night. Time to stop wasting fuel – I'd likely need it during the night – and time to think like a survivor.

First, since I was starving, a snack. That consisted of three Timbits and the rest of my cold coffee. Then I reached under seats and retrieved four water bottles, most half-drained. The only other food I could find was an old protein bar I was given when I sang to the company at their grand opening presentation. I had yet to see the bar on grocery shelves. An energy bar composed of prunes, apricots and dates held no appeal. I remembered I had breath mints in my Marilyn bag and chewing gum in my Madonna gear. The food groups were covered.

Next I had to find a way to stay warm for a long period of time. I had my sleeping bag, but I wanted to use that as a last resort. A bit of expert's advice came to me – for warmth, dress in layers. I didn't want to make too much of a mess so I put on the clown suit first. While I awaited the cold to come over me, I laid out my next few sets of layers.

Two hours later, I decided to run my car for a few minutes. By this point, the Grim Reaper's gown was bunched up over my clown suit. Over that I wore the cop's bullet proof vest that I'd miraculously picked up at a yard sale years ago. Over that was the doctor's smock, with the gorilla suit serving as the final furry layer. I was puffed up and could barely move. I was pretty warm...except for my toes, now wearing the gorilla feet (which were actually slippers but looked so real! Thank you, Walmart clearance sale!).

I wanted to run the floor heater for a bit, to toast my tootsies. I soon realized I had a new problem to worry about. I had to pee. Only place I would dare to go would be right outside my car door. I'd have used the Tim Horton's washroom, if only I could find the bloody place!

Blasting the heat to stay warm, I took off the many layers of clothes. I braced myself for the cold and opened the door. At least

I tried to open it. Maybe I'd locked it by accident? I checked and nope, it was unlocked. I tried again but the door wouldn't budge. It was frozen shut. I tried the other three doors of the car but the same refrain.

Well, who'd see if I just hung my butt out the window and took a leak? That proved to be impossible as well, since all four windows had also frozen solid. It appeared I wasn't going outside for a pee. "No big deal, no biggie," I reassured myself. "It's not the end of the world."

As much as I liked to think I had a home on wheels, my car never claimed to have a bathroom. The only concession I'd made was that my Suzuki was always equipped with a roll or two of toilet paper. Pissing outside had become the norm. Pissing inside my car? That was a whole different and disgusting story.

For thirty minutes, I huddled under my sleeping bag, ran the car, and tried to be the master of my bladder. I kept trying my cellphone, but there was still no service. Where had Moneypenny sent me? To the Arctic Circle? Finally I reached behind the passenger seat for my current bag of garbage. I reached into the large Swiss Chalet bag and pulled out an empty extra-large Tim Horton's cup.

"How ironic, yet fitting," I observed. Adding contortionist to the many characters I portrayed, I angled my body as best as I could to take this pressing pee. My head was pinned sideways against the roof, one arm balanced myself across the passenger seat headrest, one leg stretching to the floor, the other leg bent up on the reclined back of the driver's seat. With my left hand, I positioned the cup under myself, smack up against my genitals so I wouldn't miss.

Ahhh, it was a good plan. The only thing I didn't take into account was that I had to take a wicked whizz. I could tell by the weight of the cup that I was close to filling it. I tried to stop so that I could find another cup, but that was like trying to stop a tsunami. I wildly looked into the back seat, at the mound of discarded costumes not needed to keep me warm.

Without hesitation, I grabbed the cop hat and stuck it under my bottom, quickly exchanging it for the Tim Horton's cup. Just a little transfer got onto my seat. The cup was about a quarter-inch from spilling. I laid it gently on the dashboard, to be dealt with later. I almost filled the hat to the brim, and was grateful for its plastic lining.

Still acting like I worked for the Ringling Brothers, now I had to manoeuvre myself to avoid the hat of horror. I reached again into the Swiss Chalet bag and pulled out a styrofoam container. *This will work!* I emptied the debris from the container into the garbage bag, and poured the contents of the cop's hat into the box my chicken-wing special came in. I carefully snapped the lid shut and placed it next to the Tim Horton's cup. Since my entire car was a pigsty, the only clean area was my dashboard. That had now become a biohazard zone.

The gas was getting lower, so I blasted the heat as I put my clothes back on in the same order. Night was starting to fall and still the storm was blowing, icy pellets having completely frosted all my windows. I started wondering how carbon monoxide poisoning worked, and as soon as the gorilla costume was squeezed over everything else, I shut off the car.

God, I was hungry. I drank the third of my four half-filled water bottles, and ate the last two Timbits, then munched a couple breath mints. I managed to doze off for an hour but woke up cold, though I still had fresh breath. Instead of turning on the car, I wrapped myself up in the sleeping bag. I fell asleep for another hour, but hunger woke me this time. I knew I had that power bar, but I planned to eat that tomorrow if the storm hadn't let up. I scavenged around the car and found two sugar packets as well as a vinegar and a ketchup. I created an amusing recipe and called it supper.

I probably dozed off and woke up twenty times in the night, starting the car up about half the time. I'd try the doors, try the windows, but Mother Nature was still holding me captive in my Suzuki. I couldn't wait until morning arrived.

The only thing that told me it was morning was the clock in my car when I started it up again for heat. I didn't know if I believed it; was it six a.m. or six p.m.? The car had a surreal feel, like I was in a bubble in outer space. I could hear loud noises, which I assumed was the storm still raging. But the front, sides and back of my vehicle were all encased in a solid white snowdrift. My Suzuki Swift had become one with the earth.

Now I knew for certain that my tailpipe was probably blocked with snow, and the fear of dying by carbon monoxide poisoning increased. I spent the whole morning cocooned in my sleeping bag.

By lunchtime, I emerged and decided to admit defeat. I would eat that disgusting power bar. As I reached for the glove box where it'd lain for the past year, my peripheral vision caught sight of the Swiss Chalet bag. Hey...I had chicken wings a couple days ago...I grabbed the bag and looked inside. There was the wadded up tinfoil where I'd discarded the bones.

Oh glory be! I'd eat every scrap off those bones, maybe the bones themselves! And it turned out to be not much in the way of quantity, but it ranks as one of the best meals I've ever had. Tiny slivers of Suicide Hot chicken that still adhered to the bone, the cartilage at the end of the drumstick pieces, the very marrow itself. Lo and behold, there was the skin to the baked potato that came with the meal. Cold baked potato skin...don't knock it if you haven't tried it.

And though I only ate about 200 calories of food, the spiciness of it all came through loud and clear. I drank most of my remaining bottle of water. I turned the car's key onto auxiliary to listen to the news. All of it was about the weird weather; not one report about a missing singing-telegram performer.

It took a long, long time to pass that day. I had no urge to urinate and if I did, maybe I had the smallest of tinkles in my pants. I was parched, and so hungry I chewed two sticks of gum at once. As of yet, I wasn't going to succumb to tears. Surely this blizzard would end?

Around midnight, I chose to play a version of Russian roulette. I'd start the car a couple minutes, just enough to bring some feeling to my body. I was so frightened by thoughts of perishing due to the exhaust fumes having nowhere to go but into my car. By reflex, I again tried the window.

It took me by surprise, how fast it slid down. I cringed, preparing for the snow to descend on my head. It didn't move. I was still encased in my snow tomb. I closed the window and figured, if the window works, so will the door!

Yes, the door worked, but it would only open a millimetre. A ton of snow held me prisoner. Suddenly I desperately wanted to see what the world looked like outside. I positioned myself, opened the window again, and started punching out at the snow. The disturbance caused loaf-sized chunks of blocky snow to fall into my car. I changed my tactic and started to kick out at the snow with my gorilla feet.

Finally a hole appeared and I worked at it. Fresh air flew into the cabin of my car. That was appreciated, as the smell from the containers of pee were almost as lethal as the carbon monoxide I feared. I ran the car to warm up, knowing I could breathe the air. Since I was down to very little gas, I bundled up again and shut off the car. I filled up my lungs with the air coming through the snowbank hole, then closed my window, leaving it open a wee bit.

I figured the snow came directly from the sky onto my car, having met no dogs along the way. I rolled down the window once more, grabbed a hunk of snow and sucked on that until I fell asleep.

When I next opened my eyes, the sun had not yet risen, but there was a strange light in the sky. I heard nothing but silence, telling me the storm was over. I debated starting the car but actually, I wasn't all that cold. I opened the window and enlarged the opening through the snowdrift. With little effort, I created a hole big enough for me to sit on my open window and look outside.

The sky was filled with stars. The dark shapes on either side of my car told me they were trees and in front of my car, all I could see was a white plain, probably some farmer's field I'd almost driven into. After grabbing another hunk of snow to suck on from the car's roof, I wrapped myself back up in the sleeping bag and fell into a deep slumber.

I thought I woke up dead, sentenced to a life in hell. An intense heat enveloped me, far different from the coldness to which I'd become accustomed. At the same time as I struggled to free myself from the sleeping bag, I fumbled for the ignition switch. Surely I'd turned on the car, full heaters blaring, while I was sleeping. How stupid!

But once my sweaty head emerged from the sleeping bag's confines, I could see the car was still idle. As I rolled the bag off me, I did a double-take at the scenery. Where in the name of Jesus H. Christ was I? My windows had completely cleared; there wasn't a hint of snow to be seen. On either side of my car were the trees, as I somewhat recalled, but through the windshield, I saw nothing but water. I had parked in front of a great lake, possibly one of THE Great Lakes.

With a sense of incredulity, I leapt from my car and ran to the front of it. To my utter shock and awe, I saw my beloved home-on-wheels parked on the very edge of a dock. The front wheels were actually extending over the edge. With all my wandering about in the blizzard the first day, it's a miracle I didn't walk right off the dock. For some reason, I had had no desire to investigate what was in front of my car; I just knew Tim Horton's was behind me. For the love of God, that GPS almost got me killed!

I was so glad to be alive, my immediate reaction was to praise Christ for allowing me to stay out of the lake so that I could freeze in my car for two days. I actually raised my arms to the sky and plunged them back to my chest a time or two, sign language telling the Big Guy up there "I heart you!"

About to get down on my knees to thank him properly, I heard a man's voice shout out. "Hey, looky there by that blue car! What the fuck is that? Is that like a sasquatch?"

I swung my attention over to the man, and saw him tending to a boat in a little parking lot. Next to him stood a woman in a tank top and shorts. In a split second, my eye caught the fact that the road I'd driven to get here was clear. Maybe a little muddy, but no ruts of snow to get hung up on. Lots of puddles everywhere, especially the one I was standing in next to my car. Finally I realized the temperature had risen to...well, shorts and a tank top degrees...and in my gorilla suit, I was way too overdressed.

I needed to unburden myself of clothes, but as I ran back to the driver's door, I saw another car enter the lot, pulling a trailer with two jet skis. The eyes of the occupants widened.

"Take a picture, Laura, take a picture!" the male driver ordered.

The woman held up her cellphone and snapped. I shielded my face as I fumbled for my door handle. I almost lost the wig I had been wearing for warmth (the French-maid black pageboy number) in my haste. I was glad to hear the woman whine, "Shoot, I'm trying! Memory full!"

"Erase something! Anything!" the driver commanded, driving closer, narrowing my escape route.

I squeezed behind my steering wheel, fired up the car, took one calm moment to make sure I was in reverse, and then backed off the dock. I reversed into the parking lot then pointed myself forward, one thought prominent in my brain. "Timmy's, here I come! Screw you, gross power bar!" With the Tim Horton's destination in mind, I gunned that Suzuki Swift forward.

Suddenly I was drenched...and stinky. Damn if I didn't forget about those two containers of urine resting on my dashboard.

Chapter Eight

Feeling the usual urge to pee, I parked a few spaces south of the Coffee Time at Yonge and Lawrence. It wasn't my usual choice of coffee shops, but I had to go in a hurry. After doing my business, I shuffled up to the counter. The cashier had seen me come in and anyhow, they had cheap giant apple fritters. That would be my breakfast the next morning.

A commotion began at the front door and continued until a woman settled herself at a table. She carried all sorts of plastic bags overflowing with assorted goods. From an outdated Eaton's bag, she pulled out a tambourine and tipped it upside down. Nickels, quarters, loonies spilled out. With a sweet smile, she ambled behind me. I moved aside.

"Go ahead," I offered. "I'm in no hurry."

"If you insist," she replied. "And that's a considerate gesture in an inconsiderate world."

"No problem," I said.

As we waited for the waitress to finish her phone call, I studied the back of this woman. I noticed plastic bags were obviously a valuable commodity in her life. She even managed to find a way to wear them, from the Food Basics bags wrapped around her shoes to the Real Canadian Superstore bags forming some kind of diaper. A heavy-duty utility belt helped keep most of her lower garments from sliding off her body. I stole a look at the stuff stuck into the pouches of the belt. Where there should have been a measuring tape, there was a can of Skol chewing tobacco. Where there should have been a hammer, there was a half-eaten submarine sandwich. One pouch held hundreds of bobby pins while another one oddly held packages of flower seeds. I jerked my eyes away when I realized I was being spoken to.

"...good thing I'm a regular of this fine dining establishment, or I may register a complaint with the manager. Oh, wait, she is the manager!"

Homeless person or not, that was pretty funny. I laughed aloud and that seemed to grab the attention of Chatty Cathy. She ended her call and looked over at her customers.

"The usual, Daphne?" the cashier asked.

"Yes, if it's no bother," Daphne replied. I sniggered quietly behind her, letting her know I got the joke.

"One small tea, six sugars, six milk, coming up," the cashier said. "You know, Daphne, there's barely any room for the tea when I add all this stuff in."

"'Tis the way I've taken it since I was a wee child," the old lady said. "Memories of old are always gold."

My turn was next. I had wanted to pay for the bag-lady's tea, but felt a little embarrassed to do it. "Your order, ma'am?" I was asked.

"Uh...an apple fritter and...I'll have the same drink as Daphne there," I decided.

"You can't be serious?" was the cashier's take on my order.

"Why not?" I replied. "She got me curious."

"Bravo!" came Daphne's reply. "And if you're not in any hurry, perhaps you'd care to join me?"

What else did I have to do? Where else did I have to go? Nowhere until the day after tomorrow, when I had two gigs downtown. I pulled a chair away from another setting, since the empty chair at her table had her bags on it. Daphne moved the tambourine aside so we could set our drinks down. The ornate sides of the instrument me reach out for it.

"It's gorgeous," I said, as Daphne handed me the tambourine. "And it's got such fancy writing on it!"

"Calligraphic writing is meant to look that way," Daphne informed me. "It reads 'Croydon Davis'. He was a rather famous musician in these parts in the early 1900s. Back then, he made wonderful music...now the sound of coins falling into it is the music it makes. And what glorious music it is!" Again she gave a beatific smile.

"You know, you have such clear skin," I commented. And she did. It looked so white, with a shine to it, as if it had been sandblasted. It looked as if it had been scrubbed so much, she was onto her second layer of skin.

"I know," she replied. "How old do you think I am?"

I don't think she took my comment correctly. When did age come into our conversation? But I was brought up to be polite, and I went into performer-mode. No matter what their age, you always knock it down ten, twenty years. This woman was likely a senior citizen, but I guessed, "I dunno...I hope I'm not too high, but 42?"

"Nope!" Daphne giggled. "I'm 45! Now try your tea!"

I was stunned. She easily looked twenty years older. I picked up my tiny cup of tea and took a tentative sip. Daphne waited with bated breath. I made a bit of a face. "Wow, that's sweet!" I exclaimed. Six damn sugars sweet.

"I know, isn't it delicious?" Daphne giggled.

I took another wee taste. "You know, if you don't think of this as tea...it actually tastes like a dessert." I promised myself to drink it all in her presence and then never order such an atrocity again. "What's in all your bags?" I asked.

"Pretty much the most valuable possessions I own," she said without effect. "The stuff outside, if it gets stolen, it can be replaced. My newspapers, my cardboard, my tarp...even the shopping cart." I glanced outside and saw her buggy. It was parked right up against the window, so she could still keep an eye on it. I wasn't that careful with my car, and it had my whole life in it as well!

The next hour was spent with her showing me different objects from her many bags. From a Chapters Books bag, she displayed a tattered, worn notebook, with half-written stories and the signature of Margaret Atwood on it. From an Aren't We

Naughty? bag, she pulled out a stack of Polaroids, showing a guy I recognized as a former politician. In each one, he appeared with a different stripper, having the time of his life.

"I live for garbage nights," Daphne gushed. "You never know what you might find."

I waved the Polaroid sac. "You mean these were left out there, for all to see?"

"Oh, no! Sometimes you really have to get in there and search!" she said emphatically. "I get a feeling sometimes...and you know, I did go to university to study art. I do have a good eye. Tomorrow is garbage night in the Yonge/Lawrence village...and these people have a lot of money, they don't realize the value of what they're throwing out... You should come dumpster diving with me!"

Awkwardness set in as I tried to search for words. "Uh...wow...well...uh...wow...that sounds like it would be fun."

Daphne noticed I had not actually agreed to anything. "You probably don't want to be seen with me, is that it?" she asked, rather forlornly.

"Oh, don't be silly!" I said quickly. "I'm being seen with you right now, aren't I?"

"Two grown women enjoying a spot of tea," she replied. I looked into my cup. I'd been with her over an hour and had yet to finish my drink. The sugar had congealed at the bottom; I needed a spoon to finish it. "So let's meet again tomorrow, and I'll show you a night on the town you won't soon forget!"

That was a pretty enticing pitch, even if it did come from a bag lady. And besides, she wasn't bad company. I could use a night on the town and it would actually give my boring current existence a needed jolt. Still...

"I can't make you any promises, Daphne," I began, as her lower lip started quivering. "But look, look...if I can free up my evening, I'll be back tomorrow night."

"You promise?" she asked.

What had I just said about not making her any....? Oh, screw it. I nodded my head.

"I promise."

* * *

The following night, I went to meet up with Daphne as planned. I didn't think she'd show up. As for myself, I'd been half-hoping for a last-minute gig that would be a valid reason to bow out. But my momma didn't raise me to be impolite and I felt compelled to fulfil my obligation.

I was there promptly at seven p.m.. Daphne wasn't. I'd give her five minutes. Just as I was counting down the last few seconds, I heard a raucous banging outside. It was Daphne, parking her cart right up close to the window where I was sitting. That way she could keep an eye on it.

"Madeline, m'dear!" she called out as soon as she walked in. Daphne acted like she was right at home in that Coffee Time. "I knew you'd be here, sure as I know mankind will rise again." I couldn't make sense of that last statement, and I hoped I wasn't in for more of that malarkey tonight.

I shrugged. "This dumpster diving has me intrigued," I said. Truth be known, I'd have shown up if she suggested clam digging or taking belly-dance lessons. I just wanted to get out of my car and DO SOMETHING. The only thing I did, other than work and search for safe places to sleep, was go to coffee shops to kill the boredom. I read the *Toronto Sun* and the *Toronto Star* daily and if perchance somebody left a *National Post* behind, that would be a highlight of my day.

"You'll see why I've come to cherish Thursday nights," Daphne beamed. "We'll have a wee cup and then we're off to dig for buried treasure!"

I quickly held up my cup of coffee. "I'm good," I said.

She brought her small cup of tea to my table, which was a

two-seater arrangement. Daphne frowned. There were no extra chairs for her personal baggage. There were also no bigger tables available. "Tis only a momentary setback." She relaxed her pout. "Madeline, as a royal prince once declared, never pass up a bathroom. I suggest you use this one before we set out on our journey."

"I'm good," I said. Soon I was sure to progress to actual conversation.

"I insist," she urged. "After we leave our barista, we'll be reduced to begging restaurant hostesses to let us use their facilities...or the bushes in the playground."

I had not used playground bushes but there were more than a few times where I've been denied access to urinals. Shopping at Goodwill for an accessory to my French-maid costume, I got the urge to pee but was denied access to their washroom. Leaving the store without the white lace headpiece, I made it to my car and simply put Plan B into effect. Open the driver's door, open the rear door as well, give a good look around, peel down my pants and have at it. Though I still intensely disliked pissing in parking lots, after these few months, it was getting easier.

"Yeah, you're right," I gave in. As soon as I stood up, Daphne loaded my chair with a Metro bag. I saw it was filled to the brim with packages of fruit, all marked with a .99 cent sticker. Five blackened bananas, four withered apples, three gouged oranges. The total unappealing look of it all caused me to shudder.

"Quelle score already!" Daphne trilled. "Didn't want to leave it in my cart for any dogs to be poking at. So what happens is I took a shortcut on my way over and caught the gentlemen at Metro throwing out their garbage. I didn't even have to dig for this; they saw me and said I was welcome to anything I wanted. We're going to get hungry tonight and..." she pointed both arms toward the bag like a badly-dressed Vanna White, "Voila! I brought snacks!"

I just meekly nodded, keeping my mouth closed in case I

vomited into that Metro bag. I used the washroom out of courtesy to Daphne and then rejoined her. She was throwing back the last of her tea. I stood by the table as there was no room to sit, and noticed a bit of an odour around Daphne. Almost like she didn't need to use the washroom anymore.

She stood up. "Now I'll just be a moment. Sit down and please, keep an eye on my stuff." She pointed at her cart outside. "That's my life."

She cling-clanged her way into the washroom. I was going to sit down but call me rude, politically incorrect, elitist, hoity-toity, but the bag lady had just sat there and there was a possibility of bag-lady cooties. If not that, the bad smell still stuck to that chair.

For the next ten minutes, I stood moronically beside the table until Daphne re-appeared. She gathered her Metro bag of fruit as well as another thing which looked like an old-time newspaper delivery bag. Though it looked heavy as hell, I didn't offer to help.

Outside, she loaded the bags into her cart and moved it away from the wall. She pointed her already-bulging buggy north. *Oh, great,* I thought, *we're travelling with her shopping cart.* I hadn't anticipated that and it left me with an immediate rueful feeling; it would look like I was hanging out with a bag lady...maybe that I WAS a bag lady! Still, I just went with the flow.

"We'll walk up Yonge Street." Daphne plotted our course. "There are certain streets I like...we have to visit them. Others we can skip, or go back to them if we feel like it, but they usually don't yield much."

"Yield much like in what way?" I asked. I couldn't imagine we would be walking away with a slightly used couch set.

"Oh, there's so much thrown out that we could use!" she exclaimed. "Crumpets and croutons, dishes and diamonds!" Again my mind said just go with it.

We were approaching my parked car and I pretended I didn't know good ol' Suzi. Daphne startled me though when she gasped. "Oh, would you look at that car!" I glanced briefly, very non-interested. "Madeline, you can tell somebody lives in this car! I can see their clothes, I see their toothbrush, I see toilet paper..." Nodding furiously, still trying to act like I didn't care, Daphne went on, "...lots of take-out food...yeah, it's a woman, she lives in her car. But my, oh my," as she pointed to Marilyn's unpacked boa, "she does live in style, don't you agree?"

"C'mon, Daphne!" I picked at the material at her elbow and tried to pull her along. "Let's go! Crumpets and diamonds, remember?"

"Oh, yes, I'm dallying. Dillying and dallying," she pronounced, as she began to walk along again. "Keep an eye out for a small mattress. My friend Leroy has made a lovely home out of U-Haul boxes, but he needs a mattress. I always find mattresses, but this needs to be small."

Yay. Now I had an objective. Look for a used garbaged small mattress. I hoped I wasn't also expected to touch it.

* * *

I walked along beside Daphne...well, actually trying to stay a few feet behind. To passing pedestrians, it seemed apparent though that I was Daphne's associate. We were given a wide berth and sympathetic glances. How I wished I'd worn some kind of disguise. Here I had a car full of costumes and I was walking around looking fully like Maddy Magee.

Daphne was babbling from one subject to the next and since she didn't seem to need any replies from me, I mainly kept silent. One moment she was talking about buying a pencil for her sister's wedding anniversary gift, the next she was explaining how the tap water in Toronto is mainly shipped from Saskatchewan swamps. A small but clear thought bounced into my head – *She needs a pill.*

I just decided to, if not enjoy, at least tolerate the company I was keeping. The truth was, I missed my real girlfriends something fierce. The three pals I had that I could completely confide in. Melanie, who knew my every secret but this current one – the scandal of living in my car. Therese, my French-Canadian friend who could always lift my spirits. Priti, who loved to host parties, give away tickets to shows, knew the best places to vacation or shop or send your kid to camp.

On a lesser scale, but still missing them more than I thought possible, were the three moms I met at Shannon's school every Tuesday and Thursday. Only thirty minutes of fast walking around the school's track, but it was companionable. And the parents on Shannon's baseball team – they were a lively bunch and I knew they must be wondering where I was these days.

Daphne would have to be my comrade-in-arms. There was no guarantee we'd be BFFs for life but with her, I didn't have to explain my situation. We didn't have to discuss Ben or Shannon's awkward love life or the fact I was missing in action. I didn't have to avoid Melanie's intuitive questions or find a way to excuse myself from babysitting Therese's bratty kids on her Thursday-night dates with her husband. I wasn't looking for a new best friend; I just wanted some interaction with another adult.

"Would you looky-loo?" came a shrill, jarring me from my reverie. I looked over to where Daphne was pointing and saw nothing but a couple people putting out parts to a crib. They laid them out on the ground next to their garbage bins then turned to walk back into the house. Daphne and I stood there watching them; the man and I actually made eye contact.

After they walked into the house, I turned to Daphne. "OK, that was...uh...interesting? Shall we move on?"

"Wait for it...," she whispered, quivering with anticipation. "You know what they're going to throw out next..."

"The baby?" I joked, but Daphne completely didn't get it.

"The mattress!" she said gleefully.

"So we just stand around and wait 'til they throw it out?" I queried. "If they're even going to throw out a mattress..." We waited a couple minutes and then I said, "I say we move on. It feels like we're stalking the place."

Daphne's eyes widened. "Watch your language! We wait five more minutes and see if they decide to part with the crib mattress."

"And if they come out with it, do we just pounce on them?" I asked, again joking, again knowing Daphne wouldn't respond.

"Oh, no no no no no," my new friend declared. "No contact. Let them throw it away. It must obviously and absolutely be garbage before we can take it." The front door to the house opened and the man came out alone this time, carrying the objective of our search tonight. A mattress for the crib, looking somewhat stained and definitely due for the trash. Again he passed me, giving me an odd glance. I looked directly ahead and didn't say a word. He leaned the mattress up against a tree and almost bumped into Daphne, who had gotten into Ready Mode. As soon as he turned around to head back into his home, Daphne was grabbing for the mattress.

"Oh, the planets aligned today for this fortunate stroke of good luck," she said, hugging the mattress close to her. "And with more luck, Leroy will appreciate this gift so much, he will invite me into his new home and into his bed for a passionate night of reckless abandon."

I guess this was girl-talk with my new friend. The thought of two homeless people making out on a baby's mattress in a big U-Haul box, however, made me grimace. Daphne caught my look as she brought the mattress to her cart.

"People got needs, you know," she reprimanded me. "And Leroy is a prince living a pauper's existence. Inside his house, there's no dirt floor. Leroy put a TARP down!" Daphne announced this like he had laid the finest Italian marble in his home. "Now help me get this mattress in my cart."

Easier said than done. Even though the mattress was small, it stood three feet above the cart and almost looked like a thick sail. We had to move bags of assorted goods around to make the mattress fit. Everything seemed to have a sticky feel to it and I craved a hand washing. Even a shot of hand sanitizer.

"So we got lucky, huh?" I sad. "Guess we can call it quits then?"

"Oh, we've only started," Daphne replied ominously. "We still need to find, shall we say, the bread and butter of our search."

"You mean the diamonds and stuff?"

"No, more like the bread and butter," Daphne reconfirmed. "Food is always our main objective. Fruits and vegetables, buns and rolls, those can keep in my cart for days. But Thursdays...you'll grow to love Thursdays, I assure you...for that's the night we dine like kings."

Assuming that all of this dining meant from food that came from garbage cans did nothing to whet my appetite. "Oh, I'm not hungry," I said. "Not one bit."

Again Daphne blazed me with a harsh look. "Hungry or not, you eat on Thursday nights. Right now, we are going through the alley behind a row of fancy-pants restaurants. In two hours, we will make another pass. Prepare for oysters eclair, squid marinara, duck eggs on foie gras..."

"Geez, all stuff I had for lunch today," I joked, to nobody's laughter. "Well, we'll see, Daphne. This is all kind of new, you know..."

A muffled sound caused Daphne to tense like a hunting hound. "You hear that? That's soft garbage being thrown out! Come on!"

A man in a white busboy outfit was just going inside the back door of Le Brasserie Restaurant. Daphne, pushing the cart ahead of her as if they were all part of the same body, hightailed it to the garbage dumpster. Opening the lid, she reached in and pulled out a white bag. Steam was still rising from it. She quickly opened it.

She ripped off a popular phrase. "Now this is what I'm talking about!" I marvelled at how she could be so oddly eloquent one moment and so weirdly hip the next. Daphne carried the bag over to me and I took a peek inside. There was a pan-load of baked macaroni and cheese, surrounded by egg shells, potato peelings and the ends of zucchinis, eggplants and cabbages.

"Yeah, I see, the chef forgot about his mac and cheese," I felt compelled to say. "Look how bad the bottom is burnt. No wonder they threw it out."

"So what if the bottom is burnt?" Daphne retorted, pulling out a handful. "Oohh, it's still hot! The top is still good, see?" She took a bite. "Oh, it's delicious, you must try it! This is the best restaurant in town, I swear. They use only the finest of ingredients. Take a bite, taste the incredible cheese they've used!"

She talked a good game and I was sorely tempted because I was starting to feel quite hungry, but the residue from the egg shells worried me. Doesn't eating raw egg lead to something? "Oh, damn, it looks so good, but I have to pass. I'm...I'm lactose intolerant. Cheese can kill me."

Daphne softened. "Oh, not to fear. Next door is a classy Chinese-food place. We'll find you some nice noodles."

If that's your thing, then it was a good night for garbage picking. By the end of the alley, the cart was almost overflowing with food. "One more dumpster and then let's take some time to pig out," Daphne suggested. "You've watched me enough; now it's your turn to dive."

"I say we skip this one," I said. "You have enough to feed an army."

Daphne shook her head. "By this time tomorrow, half this food will be inedible. This is the best dumpster on the block. We're not skipping it. Open the lid."

At this point, I was completely ready to walk away. I really didn't owe this friendship much more and didn't think I would be seeing Daphne again. Yet I went through with her suggestion. I opened the lid to the dumpster and then recoiled at the stench.

Daphne rushed forward. "YES!" she declared triumphantly. "The aroma of wellbeing and good health. Now that's the smell you seek!"

"Are you serious?" I finally got mad. "That smells like something died in there...twice!" It was all I could do not to hurl violently; I could feel my stomach muscles contracting. I willed it down and hunched over, drawing deep breaths.

"Don't be so dramatic," Daphne chided me. She stepped closer and took a deep whiff. "Definitely bananas...always bananas here. Why do they buy so many when they throw so many out?" She inhaled again. "Something new...what is that? Smells exotic, like passionfruit, maybe pomegranate..."

"But what else?" I played the spoilsport. "Used Kleenex? Floor sweepings?"

Daphne gave me an innocent look. "You just wipe it off, dearie. Now let's see what else our grocer has left for us." She stepped back. "Go ahead, your turn."

What possessed me? I dragged a milk carton over and, holding my breath, I simply reached in and started pulling out bags. Before I ran out of air, I had a dozen garbage bags sitting on the ground. I leapt off the crate and took a deep hit of oxygen.

My fellow scavenger praised me. "Good job. Now let's see what there is, quickly, before an employee catches us."

I didn't like this air of danger; no way would I have participated had I known we could get in trouble. I ripped open the bags and was disgusted at what presented itself. Besides the almost-rotted fruits and vegetables, there were an old pair of runners, a broken mirror, unrecycled newspapers, sanitary pads, even a mousetrap complete with a dead varmint. I backed away in horror.

Daphne, on the other hand, was a complete professional. With quick hands, she sorted through the bags. Beside her, she made a growing pile of food – wizened apples, flexible carrots, potatoes with Medusa-like tendrils growing from them. She glanced up. "You can see what bags I've gone through already. Tie them up and throw them back in the dumpster."

Obviously she was the boss. I did a very slipshod job of tying the bags up and returning them to the reeking bin. With the last bag shipped off, I turned and saw Daphne putting her disgusting treasure into a BabiesRUs shopping bag. She was beaming.

"We did well tonight, my Miss Maddy!" she said. "Of course we'll share it, even-steven."

I was about to put up an argument when voices were heard coming from the back door of the grocery. One guy was laughing while another guy was yelling to open the door, this fucker was heavy. Daphne's happy smile had suddenly turned upside down.

"Don't run, we'll look guilty," she whispered. "Just walk away normally, like we're just strolling the alley."

Off we went, just as the back door opened. Daphne pushing her cart like the bag lady she was, me doing a fast walk, trying to look like I belonged in this back alley. The men didn't speak to us and I didn't turn to look at what the "fucker" was that was so heavy.

As we got onto the street, Daphne commanded me to turn right. "There's a school half a block way. Their entrance is hidden from the street. We can eat on the steps."

Oh goody. After this scare, now I get to look forward to e-coli. With a full realization that I wanted to bring this evening to an end, I still found myself tagging along. We made our way to the Stephen Leacock School and settled on the cool steps of its entrance. Daphne started digging through the food we'd picked up from the restaurant dumpsters.

"This is from the French place!" she murmured. "Look! Fancy pork medallions, covered in some kind of Hollandaise sauce!" She tasted one. "Hhmm, I don't think I'd order this if I was paying for it." She dug out another piece of meat. "Oh, my, steak! Cooked medium-rare, just the way I like it, and just a few—"

I interrupted her. "Daphne, no! There's a bite taken from it!"

"—bites taken from it," Daphne finished her sentence. She pushed the bag over to me. "Dig in."

Lying never came so easily. "Wish I could, but that's meat. I'm strictly vegetarian." She reached over and grabbed the Chinese-food offerings. I shook my head. "Don't know what's in there...can't take a chance."

Daphne looked over the assortment of food we'd gathered; enough to feed an entire homeless shelter. "Looks like you're stuck with the food from the grocery. That should please you – it's all fruit and vegetables."

"I don't even think I'm that hungry," I said, just as my stomach let forth a mighty gurgle and growl. "Well, maybe a little. I'll find something." Remembering the debris that came with the windfall of food, I tried to make a sensible choice. I didn't want to eat the skin on anything that came in contact with actual garbage. I finally settled on a brown-spotted banana. Even as I peeled it, I noticed white spots of who-knows-what clinging to the skin.

I may as well have been slurping baby food; the banana was that soft. It did assuage the hunger in my belly though. Something else would have made me feel better but though the Shanghai noodles smelled delicious, the melted spatula adhering to it was an appetite inhibitor.

Daphne re-bagged the food she didn't eat and placed it into her overstocked shopping cart. She patted the mattress. "All in all, a successful night," she pronounced. I took that as a sign this cursed evening was over until she continued, "Though we have miles and miles to go."

I jerked, as if she'd actually hit me. "Oh, no! Not me!" I replied. "I don't have miles and miles left in me..."

"It's just a saying," she stopped me. "Let's take a walk down this street, see if we can find some interesting junk."

This was a little better. At least we weren't inserting our bodies into giant garbage bins. Now we were just out sightseeing, looking at what people had put out for trash. Daphne, sated from her meal, desultorily lifted lids and poked around a bit through the contents.

From one can she extracted a ratty old stuffed animal. "Your name will be Boo Boo!" she exclaimed. She gave it a hug and then squeezed it into her cart. In one recycling box she pulled out a *Hello Canada* magazine, with a picture of Ben Mulroney on the cover. She gave that a hug as well. "Just you wait, Ben," she whispered. "Your time will come."

At the end of the street, we came upon a beautiful house, more splendid than the rest. A lone garbage can rested at the end of the circular drive, under the last streetlight on the block. In the can, on top of a small bag of trash, rested an old vintage suitcase. I would have loved to take that case, if only my car had space for it. Maybe I could make room?

I rushed forward, finally excited by a find. I wasn't prepared to be rudely pushed aside by Daphne. "I go first!" she said quite frostily. "How dare you!"

"Whoa, chill out, Daphne," I retorted. "I just want to see the suitcase."

She blocked me from the garbage can. "Then I will extend my apologies. If you like the suitcase, then it's yours." As if she owned it in the first place! "I'll take whatever is inside...if it's of any value to me, that is."

She stepped aside and I pulled the case out of the trash can. Immediately I could see the latches were broken. Daphne opened up the case and again my nasal senses were assaulted. This time is was an ancient musty smell. I stepped away from the case.

"You certainly don't have a nose for this, do you?" Daphne asked. "To me, this is another special aroma...from a long-ago era..." She pulled out a few dated Valentines. "Look at these –

cherished mementoes of love...." Next came a well-worn pair of ballet flats, followed by some dated piano songbooks. "Artistic people...," Daphne mused. For a moment she studied a bundle of photographs, then looked up at me. "I have a passion for culture, you know, and I think I recognize some of these people. My memory fails me at the moment, but I think they were stage stars."

In the next instant, my newfound friend went from quirky to downright freaky. She reached into the bottom of the suitcase and pulled out the last item. It appeared to be a stage script, with the cover darkened by many scribbled signatures. In one breath, she's gushing, "Ohh, directed by Alan Lund...," and in the next, her eyes are bugging out as she sees something written on the cover.

I reached for the script, intrigued by her reaction. "What is it, Daphne? Let me see!"

I was denied. Daphne strong-armed me out of the way and then shoved the script into her shirt. She sprang to her shopping cart and started walking away in a hurry, as if she'd stolen something.

I ran behind her. "Come on, Daphne, you've got to show me what you found!"

"Go away!" she shouted. "Take the suitcase. This is mine!"

"Whatever it is, you can have it," I said. "I don't want it. I just want to know what you found."

"You want to take it from me!" she screeched.

"No, I don't!" I said, as a porch light came on at a nearby house. "Quiet, you're making a scene."

"Then go away!"

"Fine!" I said. "I'm going!" However, the only way back was the same direction Daphne was headed. I followed along about ten paces behind her. She kept glancing back at me.

"I don't trust you!" she decided. "Cross the street!"

"What's your problem?" I had to ask. "Why are you acting

this way?"

She patted her chest. "This could be my ticket," she said. "The golden ticket. MY golden ticket, and you're not getting any of it. Now cross the street!"

"You can stop telling me what to do anytime," I suggested. I'd decided I really had enough of her. Who needed friends like this? I so badly wanted my real girlfriends back in my life. I'd even OFFER to babysit Therese's rotten kids.

"CROSS THE STREET!" Daphne suddenly started shrieking. "CROSS THE STREET! CROSS THE STREET!"

Jesus Christ, she suddenly scared me so much, I didn't just cross the street. I began to run away from Daphne. I ran back through the alley, my peripheral vision catching sight of one garbage bag I'd tossed over the dumpster by mistake. A raccoon was already into the mess. I ran until I reached the Coffee Time shop, where my car was parked.

First, real food was in order. I walked in, ordered a large roast-beef sandwich, and used their washroom facilities. Cleansing my hands of the night's escapades used up a ton of soap. How I yearned for a bath, but the coffee-shop's sink was the next best thing.

It felt so good to be 'home'. Even though I didn't live in a house, I didn't live on the streets like Daphne. I shuddered when I thought of the surreal evening I had just spent. For one moment, I thought it would be such a good tale to share with the girls. Ahhh, but it wouldn't happen. And I knew this would be the first and last time I would engage in social contact until I got my life sorted out.

Speaking of Daphne, whom should I see in my rearview mirror? The cacophony of her cart was what drew my attention. I couldn't make out her face; the mattress obscured it. I watched her approach.

Don't ask me why, but I guess what I did next was catty. She deserved it though, for turning feral on me. Just as she passed by my car, I honked my horn. Daphne jumped, and then looked in my window. I gave her a wave as I pulled out of my parking spot.

Daphne had admired whoever the lady was who lived in this car. Well, that lady was me, and I felt such pride as I drove by her stupefied look. Even my Suzuki purred like I've rarely known her to do, acting as if she were a Rolls Royce.

Eat your heart out, Daphne, 'cuz this is the high life.

Chapter Nine

Living in fear of being busted by the cops was taking its toll. Every time I tried to sleep, and felt a car's headlights wash over my vehicle, I prepared to be rousted. And I wasn't just worried about a vagrancy charge; I also fretted when I was driving. Though I was a careful and obeyed all the rules and regulations of the road, I was sure I'd be pulled over for obstructed vision. There was so much stuff in my car, most of my windows were basically useless.

One evening, I drove through a Tim Horton's in Oshawa, having just finished doing a French maid to a boy who was turning 18 at midnight. When I performed for him, I felt like a pervert. Legally he was still a child. I was twice his age and it just felt gross. I hoped I was the only one who felt that way. The acne-ridden pudgy kid seemed naturally thrilled when I sat on his lap and turned a beet-red when I laid a kiss near the top of his unblemished ear. His parents, who had sent the gift, looked on with pride.

"Large French Vanilla," I said to the drive-thru's speakers. I had no idea why I'd ordered that. Maybe I was still in my French-maid mode. I was getting a little coffee-d out anyhow.

"Wow, you have a lot of stuff," the girl at the take-out window observed. "Are you moving?"

"Nah, it's just my work stuff," I replied. I took my cappuccino and left. I was about to hit the highway back to Toronto when I stifled a big yawn.

There was a Holiday Inn just to the left of me. This time I let loose with a giant roar of a yawn as I turned into the hotel's lot. I had nowhere to be until tomorrow afternoon, and nobody to miss me. Who cared where I stayed? I found my usual out-of-the way spot, where no prying eyes would stare down at me as I slept, and bedded down for the night.

A sharp series of hard raps at my driver's side window caused me to jump a mile high. As I instinctively reached for the keys to start the car and run, I glanced at the window. Standing there was an officer of the law.

I rolled down the window a few inches. "Yes?" I meekly asked.

"You're sleeping in your car," he duly noted. "You're parked at a hotel. Why aren't you sleeping in the hotel?"

"Oh, I'm not staying there!" I gave a half-hearted laugh.

"Then why are you parked overnight in their lot?" he continued his line of questioning.

And okay, I'll confess right now and hope the statute of limitations has passed, but I lied to the cop. Dramatically lied. I looked at my watch and played dumb and told fibs like they were raining from the sky.

"Oh my God! Is it really three o'clock?" I batted my eyes. "I'm supposed to meet a friend...I'm helping her move...she...she was waiting on keys...we were meeting up here...I must have fallen asleep...I wonder where she is?"

I hoped he wouldn't ask me her name. I was plumb out of falsehoods. If they took me to court on this, I wouldn't be able to stick to my story. Already I was forgetting half of it.

The cop looked over at his cruiser, where I could see another officer through its open door. He was obviously running my plates through the system. That grated on me; as I said, perfect driving record, no criminal activity, I was a certifiable saint.

The policeman in the cruiser answered a call on the radio, then called to the cop standing by my car. "She's okay," he said. "Let's roll, domestic disturbance."

"Alright, listen," the cop by my car slammed his palm on the rooftop, "you might want to get moving. Or get a room. Just don't be sleeping here." He joined his mate in the squad car and, with sirens quiet but lights flashing, they shot out of the lot.

I left as well. I didn't care for my stay at the Holiday Inn.

* * *

The very next night, I was feeling pretty pleased with myself as I drove away from my last show. It was a top-hat-and-tails telegram to a very appreciative crowd at a 50th-anniversary party. The husband was a real ladies' man, which only helped make the show more entertaining as I rolled with his one-liners.

"I wouldn't mind a shag with you one night," he quipped as he drew me into a tight one-armed squeeze.

"Gee, I don't know, you handsome devil," I returned. "Let me ask your wife of fifty years how she feels about that."

I asked the wife if I may give her husband a kiss on the cheek and she agreed. I gave him a little peck and then pointed behind the wife, saying, "Oh, that lady wants to take a picture." There was no lady but as always, the missus turned her head to look. That's when I grabbed the hubby and started planting a load of kisses on his cheek. His face was tattooed with red lipstick. That got such a good laugh, I had the seniors at this party pissing their pants.

The two shows before that went just as smoothly; that is, once I found the nurse's costume. I was sure I'd packed it, but I recalled see-sawing on whether I should. I rarely got calls for it...but it wasn't a bulky costume... After parking in a Home Depot lot, I unloaded my trunk. Tucked right beside my spare tire was a black garbage bag. I didn't recall seeing it since...forever, it seemed. Obviously it had managed to wedge itself under the mat and into the bowels of my car trunk.

Inside the bag, the top level revealed some magazines I'd probably intended on reading. My *Good Housekeeping*, my *Chatelaine*, my *Taste of Home*...all filled with recipes I'd planned on clipping out. Under that level was a bag of jewellery, hair pins and a fancy dress. That had been added last-minute and I have no idea what I was thinking when I'd tossed it in. Did I plan on socializing while I lived in my car? To the point where I'd need an elegant blue velvet dress with matching shawl? My current wardrobe stayed the course between fishnet stockings, halter dress, white gloves...to sweats and a t-shirt. When I wasn't performing, my everyday wear still managed to resemble my Bag Lady costume.

To my relief, the next item to appear was the Once Upon A Time bag in which I kept the nurse's costume, complete with giant thermometer, stethoscope, clipboard, official-looking name tag... The show would go on! I saw one more bag under that, The Shoe Company, and dug into it. Whoa, my nun outfit! It was another small costume; the crosses, little bible, simple robe and straw belt packed easily. Just the nun's headpiece needed some future work.

The nurse's gig led to a gorilla-gram. I didn't have to drive far until I found the address, but drove completely around the block once. There were no cars anywhere except in their own driveways. My house had a single car in its drive. I became the sole vehicle parked on the street as I tentatively made my way to the front door.

Gorilla mask on, I went into performance mode the moment the door opened. There was a moment of laughter and whoops of surprise, but then I had to stop my act for a couple minutes while the mom dealt with a freaking-out baby. Since she was also taking a video, she asked me to hang on for one quick second. She disappeared and I gave a sly look at the three-year-old and five-year-old kids watching me. Sometimes I forget I'm wearing a mask; I don't know what kind of look it appeared the gorilla was sending.

"So you're 30, huh?" I asked the birthday man conversationally. He nodded as the three-year-old hid behind his leg. "Three kids, huh?" I continued. Just the gorilla and the dad, shooting the breeze. "Must be a lot of work," I went on.

"What was that?" he asked. I forgot I had to ENUNCIATE, speak loudly and clearly, when I was wearing that oxygen-sucking mask. And why was I wasting breath anyhow? With that mask on, I had JUST ten minutes before my brain screamed for oxygen.

The wife scurried back. I went back into my gorilla posture, let out one grunt, and she said, "Wait, wait, I have to turn this thing back on." She fumbled with the video camera and then said, "Action!"

I went into my act but cut it about four minutes short. I could see, through the gorilla's forehead actually, that the kids cringed whenever I got a little too vocal. Taking a step in either direction caused the three-year-old to cower. I was wondering how I would go into the 'Happy Birthday' dance with the little guy attached to his dad's leg. Suddenly the lad began to whimper.

"The monkey man is scaring me," he said, clear in his speech.

"It's not a real monkey," his mother blew the scam. "It's just a person wearing a costume."

"No, it's not!" the boy began to sound like he was going to start crying. "He scared Tanner and now I'm scared."

The mother turned to me. "Why don't you take off your head?" she suggested.

Inside the costume, I grunted. If I was a child, that suggestion alone would have given me the chills. The dad said to me, "You don't have to, it's not necessary," and to the little boy, "Noah! Suck it up! Be a man!"

The three-year-old tried to be tough for a moment, but big snorts were emitting from his nose. The mom again asked, "Please? Take off your head? I don't want Noah going on all night about this after you leave."

So I knelt down on the carpet and removed my head. Noah instantly calmed down. "You're a monkey girl!" was his first comment. I held out my mask to him and even let him hold it. He was stroking the fur as I tried to fix my own hair. I hadn't expected to be seen in public. I was glad I still had pretty-girl make-up on from the nurse's gig.

Before I even saw it happen, I heard a juvenile grunt and turned to look at Noah. He had my gorilla mask on his head. It looked pretty funny and we all laughed, but mine was a little forced. Within seconds of me putting on that gorilla mask, I'd begin to sweat. I didn't want to envision the grossness that kid felt when the inside of the mask touched his own face. No need for the parents to know, I figured, as I took the mask back.

Having spent enough time there to warrant a decent telegram show, I went to my third gig of the night. I was pleased with having three in Toronto. Some days I'd have three shows but I'd total 500 kilometres on my car. Today I racked up about thirty k's.

As mentioned, a third show that went swell. Never mind all shows being in close proximity, I didn't have to do much with my make-up, other than keep the pretty-girl face going. No beauty marks to apply, no red nose, no gap in my teeth. Before I got into my driver's seat, I took off the tails and the top hat, the cummerbund and the tie, and tossed them into the costume bag. I'd change out of the rest later when I got to my spot of the night. Not knowing where that was to be yet, I got into the car and drove away from the scene of the show.

Driving along the Queensway, my phone began to ring and I could see it was Shannon calling. I swung down a side street as I connected. "Hang on, Shannon, I'm driving," I said swiftly. "I'm pulling over, just give me a second."

There was a huge box store with a big parking lot, a Costco. At this hour, it was closed so I simply parked my car at a strange angle, disregarding the painted lines. I resumed my conversation. "OK, I'm back," I said, "and somethings's got to be up. You never call me on a Saturday night. What is it?"

"I don't think it's anything important," she assuaged me right off the start. "It's just...I did something...it's probably illegal...and it's really eating at me."

"Illegal!" I gasped. "That's important!"

"PROBABLY illegal, is what I said," Shannon cleared it up.

"What is it? You shoplifted?"

"No, that's definitely illegal," Shannon said. The only thing that could get on my nerves what when she talked to me like she was the adult and I was the kid. "This is like...you could say I tampered with mail that wasn't mine."

"Whose?" I asked loudly. I was thinking it was the guy three houses down. In the last year before I'd left, he had FedEx and UPS at his door daily. We were naturally curious. "The guy with the boat in his driveway?"

"Dad's," she stated.

Oh, big deal. "Relax, Shannon, you're not going to jail," I laughed. "I don't think it counts when it's family-related."

"That's not all of it," Shannon intoned. "It's kind of a strange piece of mail..."

"Don't tell me!" I cut her off. "It's porno!"

"No..."

"It's drugs!" I took another guess.

"No, it—"

"IT'S A CREDIT CARD!" I shrieked. "Please don't tell me he managed..."

"Mom!" Shannon stopped my oncoming rant. "Let me explain! You know how you told me to take care of your mail, right? So I see a letter, I figure it's one of those regular statements you get, from KidsCanLearn. It's always addressed to both you guys, but I know it goes into your tax file."

"OK, so get to the part about Dad's mail," I urged. KidsCanLearn was the RESP account where I monthly contributed a hundred bucks. All in the name of Shannon's education.

"I am," she replied. "So I take the letter, but then I notice it's only addressed to Dad."

"That's weird," I stated, as my heart began to pound faster. "So you opened it."

"Yeah, I confess. I opened it, and there's this letter with a form attached to it. It says that if he wants to pull out funds ahead of my scheduled start at university, he had to fill out the form and send it back." She hesitated a moment. "Do you know what that could be about?"

Oh, did I ever! That bastard lowlife scumbucket, denied access to his wife's thousands, was now going after money earmarked for his kid's university. Money I'd saved up over SEVENTEEN years! Ben was actually stealing from his own child!

"Listen," I began to speak, before realizing I sounded too harsh. I wanted to spill the facts – *Your Dad is so low in ethics, you'd better sleep with your purse, Shannon. Lock up the gold earrings your Grandma gave you as well as that 1967 coin collection you won with that Canada Day speech.* But I just didn't want to bend Shannon's ear with any more bad talk directed at her father. Lord knows she had enough to do with me gone – clean the house, do the laundry, buy the groceries, take care of our property, mind the big baby. Oh, and I think she also had a life of her own to lead.

I tried again, barely containing my anger. "Listen, sweetie, there's probably been some kind of mistake. I'm going to call KidsCan Learn first thing Monday and sort it out. But in the meantime, do not give your Dad that letter, understand?"

"Ok, got it, I just thought you should know," Shannon said miserably. I think she realized the truth.

We said our goodbyes right after that. I couldn't wait to get off the phone; I wanted to have a little wig-out. I used every curse invented, even making up new ones. Near the end, the words I was spouting didn't even make sense.

"That asshole wipe cocksucker, that fuckin' piece of tit licker, that dog...crap...fried rice-face...force-fed...con man!" came at the close of my twenty-minute meltdown. My voice was hoarse from yelling. I hate to admit to crying as well, but you may as well add

I did that too.

I laid back in my seat and wearily tried to see if there was any other way Ben could rob me blind. Ever since he'd managed to sabotage my finances a while back, with the line of credit and joint bank-account withdrawals, as well as maxing out the Visa, I became quite diligent about where my money went. I put stop-payments on anything with Ben's name attached. I made sure that his foolish expenditures wouldn't come back to haunt me. He was on his own, he had to be a big boy and make his own way. You'd think he would look for a job already.

But no, he went looking for some possible way to eke more money out of me. I'd completely forgotten about Shannon's university fund. Maybe I didn't even think of it as MY money, or OUR money; it belonged to Shannon. Ben must have tried every-thing before he came up with this brilliant plan. Those statements went immediately into my tax files, so he had to do some pretty intense searching. If only he'd search as hard through the help-wanted ads.

As I looked in my rearview mirror, I saw a long face staring back at me, eye make-up completely smeared down my cheeks. Any chipper feelings I'd had from the good day's work had been completely washed away in one fell swoop. Thanks, Ben.

A set of lights appeared in the mirror. In the parking lot's bright overhead lights, I could see it was a cop car. The desire to start up my vehicle and innocently drive away was strong, but I knew that would only make me appear guilty. I sat there and waited for them. *Please, please, just drive by, look me over, drive on.* I was still partly dressed in my top-hat-and-tails clothes; I felt confident that lent me some class.

The car made a wide circle around me, somewhat menacing. The driver pulled his car right up beside mine, so close neither one of us could open our door if we wanted to. He parked in such a way that we could talk to one another face to face.

"Can I ask what you're doing here in the middle of the night?"

the officer said.

"Of course you can ask, you're the police," I replied, somewhat crisply. That's not what I meant to say at all. Where did this attitude come from?

He just gave me a steady look. "You're alone in a parking lot. It's late at night."

The tears just burst through. The officer's partner, who'd been sitting silently by, filling out a report book, merely turned his head to look at me. I wanted to lie again, but not like before, where I couldn't keep track of my story. "I...I had a fight with my husband... Sorry, I just packed a bunch of stuff cuz...I'm leaving him...I didn't know where to go...I just parked here for now. I'm trying to figure it out..."

"Maybe you need a shelter," the officer in the passenger seat said, not even bothering to look up from his reports.

"Maybe I need a hitman," I retorted. Again, where did that come from? I never even spanked Shannon. I'm a total pacifist.

The cop who sat less than a foot away gave me a stern look. "You don't want to be talking like that, especially to a police officer."

Once again my lip started quivering. "Oh, I don't even know what I'm saying! I'm sorry, I'm sorry, do you have the address of a shelter?" I pretended to absorb their directions and thanked them for their help.

They took off, having done their civic duty. Instead of a shelter, I drove across the street to a used car lot. Squeezing Suzi between a BMW and a Lexus, I assured her she wasn't for sale and we both called it a (crummy) night.

* * *

Frimette from Top Choice Entertainment called. I was quick to answer. Frimette didn't call often but when she did, the jobs were top notch. She'd done many things to win my appreciation. For example, I'd tell her it would cost $175 for me to travel to Bowmanville. She'd say, "OK, I'm putting you down for $250."

"Hey, Madeline!" she greeted me. "You still doing a top hat and tails?"

"You bet. I'm looking at it right now," I said. The costume lay on top of the pile in the back seat.

She went into the job offer. To her, it was just another call that had come her agency's way and she was simply filling the position. To me, it was the job of a lifetime! As this particular point in my life, this gig would help to alleviate a couple of my current problems. Mainly, it would add money to my bank account and it would get rid of my B.O.

The bird baths were a lark at first, but my body was crying out for a full immersion in water. I wanted to feel bath water flow over my armpits and my genitals. I yearned to be fully clean. I could barely stand the smell of myself anymore.

"Here's what I have to offer," Frimette began. "I hope you can do it. For starters, it's in Windsor."

"I don't mind," I cheerfully replied. "I've gone to Windsor before." Long drive, little over three hours one way, but I'd spent that much time looking for a good place to bed down for the night.

"And it's a full day of singing telegrams," she went on. "They want you to arrive Monday, to make sure you are there for Tuesday's shows. On Tuesday, you go to Windsor Airport arrivals area. Throughout the day, there's a total of seven planes landing with groups of people attending a conference. You're to sing them a welcoming song. They don't want any more than five minutes."

"So arrive Monday and..." I prodded.

"It's all worked out," Frimette said. "You arrive Monday and check in at the hotel attached to the Windsor Casino...hey, maybe you can do a little gambling!" I laughed, although it was a phoney hardee-har. AS IF. I was reduced to picking up coins I found at drive-thru windows. "Check in is at four p.m.," Frimette continued. "You'll have to get up early Tuesday, first plane lands at 8:15, last plane is scheduled to land at 7. You go back to the hotel for the second night; it's too far to drive home afterwards. Check out is at 11."

"I love it!" was all I could say.

"You sure? You're going to be away from home for three days, you know," she warned. Little did she know.

Further jubilation ensued when I got the email with the details. Never mind the hotel, I was being paid $2,000! The cherry on top was that I was also given $100 a day for meals...$300 on food alone! Considering how I was using coupons to get two-for-one meals, this was a bonanza worthy of a T-bone steak, twice a day.

I did a show on Sunday afternoon, in Waterloo, a clown show. Seemed the client was trying to win back his girlfriend. The song I had to write was sickeningly sweet, but I had no comedic notes to work with. It was all about her deep blue eyes, her funny ways, her patience with him.

I went in all happy and bubbly and left with the same painted-on smile, but feeling miserable for my client. I had barely pressed the doorbell of the fancy house when it swung open with force. A young woman, maybe 23 or 24, glared at me. Despite her anger, I was transfixed by her eyes. They were a startling shade of sky blue, the beauty further enhanced by the kohl and the lush lashes surrounding them.

But polite and patient? Not so much. She opened with, "Did Carlos send you?"

I wasn't going to say; that came at the end of the song. "Charmaine!" I said. "The great and gorgeous Char...!"

"Cut it," she ordered. "If you're sent from Carlos, you can leave right now."

"Can I just sing you a song first?" I asked.

"Is it from Carlos?" she demanded an answer. I didn't say

anything so she began to close the front door.

I stuck my big clown shoe into the doorframe before it closed completely. "Look, it'll only take a couple minutes!" I said. "The guy went to a lot of trouble to send this. Can't you just hear his message? I won't even sing you the song." The message was saccharine as well, and he'd asked if I'd get down on bended knee to beg forgiveness as I read it. No problem! Never a problem; that's why I got the bulk of the work. I went the distance.

"Look, I'm not interested," she said, as I withdrew my foot to get down on my knee. "But you can pass on this message to him...bugger off!" And the door was slammed in my face.

I didn't mind. I did my job as best I could. I made the trek to Waterloo, I wrote the song, I delivered it. Having thought that, I left the song in the mailbox next to the door. Job well done! The client needn't know the outcome and I knew I would get paid. If Charmaine wanted to further speak to Carlos, she could tell him herself how it played out.

Where to next? Since I was already a third of the way to Windsor for my upcoming gig, I continued in that direction. I arrived about 24 hours before I could check into my hotel. Not knowing the city, I followed some signs that led me to the Windsor Casino and parked in its lot.

A big sigh escaped me. How long since I'd been living in my car? When had I last done anything remotely sociable or fun or exciting? I mean, I met people all the time. Geez, with my job, I met a thousand new people a year. But when did I last just do something to relieve boredom or take a break? And here I sat in my car, buried amongst Taco Bell wrappers and Harvey's containers and coffee cups from Starbucks to Timothy's, not a hundred yards from the Windsor Casino. I watched the people pour into the entrance, all looking expectant and eager.

Casinos were nothing new to me, and held little appeal. When Ben and I were newly married, we'd go out on dates to the casino now and then, and blow a couple hundred bucks. I'd play the slot machines, Ben would go to the gaming tables. I'd only see him once or twice in the next few hours, when he would borrow another fifty off me. Casinos lost their appeal soon after.

This afternoon, I felt the lure of the bright lights, the clanging bells and shouts of jubilant winners. I wanted to be near my fellow man. I wanted to drink free coffee. The idea of sitting in a car smelling of fried food, inhaling the equally foul odour of my unwashed skin, didn't thrill me. I looked at myself in the rearview mirror and saw my greasy-haired, pallid expression. No matter how hard I scrubbed with the make-up wipes, that white clown make-up was almost impossible to remove.

"Hey, Maddy May," I said to myself, "we're going out on the town!" I threw on mascara and red lipstick and fiddled with my lank hair. Finally I pulled it into a severe bun, hoping the oily look appeared intended. I pulled my wallet out of my purse and extracted a five-dollar bill.

I lasted a couple hours at the slot machines, but only because I hit upon a way to make the time stretch. Finding the penny machines, I sat between an old wheezing gentleman playing $2.40 every press of the button and another man, stooped and rail-thin, betting 80 cents. I slid my five into the machine and started to wager a penny per spin.

Even though the skinny man, dressed in clothes that enhanced his frame, was winning a tidy sum, he kept stopping his slot play to sniff the air. After a few minutes, he leaned back in his chair and inhaled loudly through his nose, his gaze directed at the gentleman to the left of me. I was right next to that big bettor, and he smelled like Old Spice cologne. I liked sitting next to him.

Finally Jack Spratt shoved back his seat and miffed, "I can't take it anymore! Be nice to come to the casino and not have to smell crotch rot!" He stood up and the man hooked up to the oxygen tank stared at him in disbelief. Jack gave the old gent an evil glare as he stalked off. I immediately took his vacated seat.

For the rest of the time, as best I could, I kept my distance from my fellow gamblers. I accepted two free cups of coffee from an attendant who was offering them. I played a variety of machines, avoiding any that weren't penny slots. But you know, one cent doesn't get you far. Had I played more, I could see where I may have won a bigger payout a few times. But the deal was – I was just out to have fun, not try to make enough to buy off Ben.

Down to my last 17 cents, I finally hit a jackpot! But because I didn't bet large, the maximum it could pay out was 50 cents. I took the win and cashed out. I didn't mind leaving with a bit of cash. Ever since I'd walked in, the thought of losing my $5 had been eating at me. I grabbed one more free cup of coffee and made my way back to the car.

Later that night, I took a walk and ate supper in a restaurant that looked starved for business. Since I wasn't yet using my per-diem food money, I order the cheapest thing I could find on the menu; a fried-egg sandwich and water. When I got back to my car, I could see it was safe and sound. Perhaps it would be okay to park here for the whole night?

I woke up early the next morning. Through the night, I heard the cars on either side of me start up and leave, only to be replaced a minute later by other cars. This happened more than once. Nobody hassled me. Grabbing my sealed plastic bag of toothpaste, soap, deodorant and the like, I re-entered the casino.

Security seemed to give me an odd look as I walked through. Feeling uneasy, I made a quick job of cleaning up and changing my hairstyle. I exited with a bounce in my step, hoping to be mistaken for a different person.

With hours to kill before check-in, I GPSed the Windsor Airport and made a trial run. I was always the professional in the past, but these days I had the time to be a perfectionist when it came to my job. Having the route down pat, I decided to check out a shopping mall. I'd not been out shopping in ages; maybe I'd find some cool stores.

Once inside the megamall, I walked around, burning with a desire to just spend some mad money. There was a chaise lounge, something I've always wanted and at a price I would jump at, if only I had the room. A shop full of discount party dresses, but a shopper with nowhere to go. I tried on clothes anyhow, just to see myself in full-length mirrors. Yup, as I suspected, I was putting on weight.

As always, a kitchen gadgets store drew me in. I checked out the new Rachel Ray cookware collection. Tested out a toaster oven. Marvelled at the wok demonstration. My hands were softly caressing an electric milk frothing tool when my eyes teared up unexplainably.

"Can I help you, miss?" asked a sales clerk.

I lifted up the frother, holding the cord in the other hand. "Does this come with a cord you can plug into your lighter?"

She frowned. "I'm sorry, it doesn't." She didn't even bother to check.

Since it seemed shopping was only rubbing salt in my wounds, I allowed myself to buy a pair of knee-high pantyhose for the shows the next day. I wanted something on me to smell clean and fresh.

I left the mall and returned to the hotel parking lot, which also served the casino. Still too early to check in, I sat in my car for awhile and played Brickbreaker. Prayed it would not incur roaming charges on my phone. After an hour, I left the car and went into the hotel.

"Is it possible to get an early check-in?" I asked. I gave her my name and she ran me through the computer.

"I'm sorry, that room is still not ready," she said. "Perhaps you'd like to try again in an hour or so? In the meantime, why don't you try your luck at the casino?"

"Hhmm, maybe," I said. Instead, I tried the handicapped stall in the ladies' washroom.

Going back to my car, I stewed for awhile. It was tormenting me, being this close to a real bed! An actual bath! I decided to make use of my time and write the songs for the following day. Same song over and over, just had to change the name of the country. "Hello People from America! (And Nigeria, China, Albania, Venezuela, Czechoslovakia and Japan. Japan had to ruin the run, but it became 'Japan-ah'!) Welcome to our country Canada! Greetings from President Keith Maha! He'll be meeting with every one of ya!" And so on. Didn't need to even leave a copy with anybody, so I just chicken-scratched it on the back of an old Beaver Gas receipt.

Exactly one hour later, I reappeared at the hotel lobby desk, this time with a little luggage bag. "Is my room ready yet?" I asked.

She retook my information and then gave me a smile. "I'm sorry, it's still not ready. Perhaps you'd like to wait in the casino?"

"Perhaps not," I said a touch loudly, then had to justify my rude behaviour. "It's been a long drive. I'd like to clean up first before I...uh, hit the slots." I took my little bag and sauntered my way over to a group of chairs. I had just chosen my seat when I heard my name called out.

It was the hotel clerk. Had I left something at the counter? We made eye contact and she said, "Your room is ready!"

Well, that was quick. I guess they wanted me to hit the slots sooner than later. I went back up to the counter. "Great!" I smiled. I couldn't wait; I hoped this fancy place supplied bubble bath.

"Just need a bit of info," she said. "I see the charges are all being looked after by Maha Industries, so that's good." I nodded. It was very good. "So I'll just need your address and your car's plate number and you're on your way."

I could see her holding a room key in her hand. I was like Pavlov's dog. Give the information, earn the reward. "2004 Suzuki Swift, 854 RKW," I droned.

Suddenly something struck me as wrong. Did she ask for my address, or the make and model of my car? The more I thought about it, I'm sure I didn't hear the phrase 'make and model' come out of her mouth. However, she typed away. "What city is that?" she asked.

"Mississauga, Ontario," I continued, adding the postal code.

"And what did you say your license plate was again?" she asked. I repeated it and waited for her to ask more questions, but then I saw her hit the 'enter' key. "Here's your room key," she said. "Enjoy your stay in Windsor!"

The room was pretty decent but the main thing was – it had a BED and a BATH. Before the door had even closed behind me, I had the tub running. I took a two-hour bath and used up all the allotted soap and shampoo. Afterwards, I debated on where I wanted to charge my per-diem food money. I'd seen a couple restaurants attached to the casino, but none held the same attraction for me as the bed I was sitting on. I ordered room service instead.

There was no way I was going to blow this gig. Already I was including Maha Industries in my thank-you speech, if I was ever given an award for anything. I set my Blackberry phone alarm, as well as the hotel room's alarm clock, and then called the front desk to ask for a wake-up call. All three alarms sounded at the same time the next morning.

That bed was so wonderful, my sleep so exquisite, I just didn't want to move. Reluctantly, I'd hit snooze on my cellphone, hit it every five minutes until I remembered the bed and I would be reunited again later. I jumped off of cloud nine, got into my top-hat-and-tails get-up and boogied over to the airport.

Rush hour was heavier than I'd thought you would find in Windsor. I'd anticipated some morning congestion but this was similar to Toronto! The cleansing bath from the night before was going to waste as I knew I'd be late for the first planeload of people, the good folk of Albania. I parked the car in the airport lot and ran, in my black high-heeled pumps, to the arrival section.

Hordes of people were streaming by. Many stopped to look at the woman wearing a tuxedo and top hat, but didn't linger; my anxious vibe was palpable. I heard a whoop and saw a group of men wave at a lone man in a limousine driver's costume. He held a sign that read MAHA. I ran to him and got there just before the surge of Albanians reached him.

"Is this the group for the Maha conference?" I asked the guy. He nodded so I stood right beside him as I went into my song. It lasted only about three minutes and I know they asked for short, but it felt too short. I was glad when each man took my hand and shook it, thanking me for the song. That added another minute or so to my act.

The guy with the sign herded the six men. "Come with me," he ordered them. "We have a limo waiting outside."

I ran into that guy six more times that day. It was a repeat of the first show. I didn't even bother talking to him; just hovered around until his sign-wielding ways got the attention it cried out for. As soon as Japan or the Chinese guys saw the MAHA cardboard sign and headed over to the guy holding it, I was on them like white on rice.

After my last song, to the Nigerians, I bowed low. Ooops, wrong crowd, as I sensed nobody bowing in return. As I stood up, I saw a man as black as my tuxedo jacket, holding up an open palm. I did likewise, assuming that was the Nigerian custom. He reached forward, slapped my palm and said, "High five!"

I nodded farewell to the Maha employee and made my way to my car. My plans for the evening could be the name of a store – Bed, Bath and Beyond. As I passed the attendant at the hotel lobby desk, I decided to push my luck with this job.

"Do you think I could arrange for a late check-out?" I asked

She checked her computer. "Check-out is at 11, but we can move it to 12. Is that okay?" The look on my face caused her to add, "I can make it one p.m., but that's the latest." I couldn't ask for more. My heels ached as I made my way to the elevators. Two young boys, likely brothers (since the younger one was howling he'd tell Mom), almost bowled me over as they ran out of an elevator just opening. As I whirled to miss them, I saw they wore nothing but sopping-wet swim trunks. I stepped into the waiting elevator car, hit the button for the fifth floor, then backed up a pace. A second later I was on my ass, having slipped on the puddles of water left by the boys.

Up in my room, I discarded the wet top-hat-and-tails costume and got naked. I ran my bath and lay down in its warmth. I couldn't stretch out completely but it was still more comfortable than my car. Two hours later I woke up in freezing-cold bath water.

Pulling the plug, I rushed out of the bathroom, as dripping wet as those two young boys. I jumped into my crisply made bed and huddled under the covers for warmth. As soon as I felt better, I remembered – I could watch T.V.! Oh, how I flipped those channels! I never realized how much I'd taken my T.V. at home for granted. A rush of homesickness for my 40-inch plasma television surged through me.

I spent a pile of Maha cash on my dinner, making sure I knew when the kitchen closed, as I planned on ordering dessert later. As I ate my coconut shrimp with wild rice and a side of poutine with a Greek salad, I thought, *This is the life!* I wished the mysterious Mr. Maha could use me on a daily basis.

After I was more than pleasantly sated, I ran another bath. This time I only soaked for an hour, as I wanted to catch the dessert menu. I also wanted to get some alone time with the bed. It was going to be the last night we spent together and I wanted it to be special. Ordering enough for three people, I wrapped two of them up. The brownie cake and the assorted cookie selection would go into my luggage, good for a snack on the ride home. I ate the ice-cream sundae.

I watched a little more T.V. after that, maybe half an hour, but it was just foreplay for the coming event. Around midnight, I shut the curtains as tight as possible. I made sure the room's alarm clock was OFF and that my Blackberry alarm was set for noon. I put a DO NOT DISTURB sign on the door. I got under the covers and hit the power button on the T.V. remote. The room went pitch black.

I stretched my body out completely and still had room to spare. I spread my arms and legs to either side of me and nothing hung off the edge of the bed. The pillows were soft and plump, unlike my flat pillow that smelled of dirty hair and bad breath. The sleep I had that night was beyond spectacular. I was so grateful for a rest where I wasn't still half-alert, listening for trouble. Or where my arm would get pins and needles because I had nowhere to put it but under my head. One night that the seatbelt connector couldn't anguish me. That sleep goes down in history as one of the highlights of my life.

My trusty loud Blackberry alarm woke me up at noon the next day. I didn't actually think I'd sleep that long and even then, I hit the snooze button six times. I finally dismissed it when there was a knock at the door. "Housekeeping," I heard a voice call out.

"I have this room 'til one p.m.," I called back. "I'll be gone at one!"

I could hear the cart move away. Now I was up, but a little dismayed that I'd stayed in bed this long. I had wanted one more bath before I had to leave. Now there would be no time. I felt really bummed by this as I gathered my clothes and toiletries together. Picking up my still-damp pants from the elevator slip, I recalled the boys...and their swim trunks...and the image of a swimming pool came into my mind.

Forming some kind of vague plan, I grabbed my stuff. I had to act fast, before one p.m. rolled around. Opening my door quietly, I checked the hallway for the cleaning staff. I could see the cart, but no cleaner. Shutting the door quietly behind me, leaving the DO NOT DISTURB sign on the knob, I quietly took big tip-toe steps to the elevator. In the parking lot, I threw my stuff onto the front seat. *No time to dally, pack it better later!*

Opening up the hatchback, I threw a few bags onto the ground. I needed to get to a suitcase I rarely used. It had clothes in it that I just hadn't gotten around to wearing, like my long denim skirt (too uncomfortable to sleep in), my shoes with the double buckles (I now preferred ones easy to kick off or slip on), my pyjamas. I found a bathing suit.

I didn't see any need to talk to the hotel lobby clerk. There were signs everywhere telling me I could Express Check Out. I didn't incur any more charges than I was allowed and I imagined they'd figure out I'd left when they saw my room. With seconds to spare, I used my plastic key card to enter the swimming area.

For the next four hours, I bathed...I mean swam in the pool of the Windsor Hotel. The water was a bit cool, and maybe too much chlorine was in it, but that only helped to make me feel cleaner. Every now and then I'd get out, lay on a lounge chair, and cover myself up with towels. Hardly anybody was in the pool all afternoon; I felt like I owned the place.

Around five p.m., I saw a new pool attendant come in and take the PH levels of the pool. I swam over. "You probably know there's too much chlorine in here," I mentioned. He looked at me like I was some kind of nosy know-it-all, packed up his kit and walked out.

A couple minutes later, I was feeling chilly enough to come out but I could see the towel rack was empty. The pool attendant came back and sat at a desk, doing his best not to stare at the bevy of beauties who had just dropped their LuLu Lemons to reveal skimpy bikinis. "Excuse me!" I called to him, then again when it appeared lust had impaired his hearing. "Excuse me! You're out of towels. Can you get some?"

He stood up but instead of going to the spare towel room, he walked over to me. "You staying at this hotel?" he asked. I nodded. "What's your room number?"

I don't know why he asked – maybe he had to record it? But

the earlier pool guy didn't even look at me, never mind ask that question. "Room 516," I replied. He left and I did a few laps until I saw him return. Sans towels.

"Hey, I just called to verify your room," he said seriously. "There's nobody registered in Room 516."

BUSTED! Even though the attendant was nothing more than 20 years old, with a pathetic attempt at a moustache and an already-receding hairline, I felt he could make trouble. I just wanted to get out of there without making a scene. I scrambled out of the pool and ran to the lounger where my clothes were resting.

"I didn't say 516," I brazenly lied. "I said 416!" I hoped this would require another trip to check out this room number. In his absence, I'd be long gone. "Oh my God! Is it really 5:30?" I shrilled, looking at the clock. "I should have been gone by now!" I cried as I threw my shirt on over my wet bathing suit. "This pool was just so relaxing. I don't know where the time went!" I didn't allow him a word in edgewise as I struggled with my pants over my wet legs. "I've got to get ready for dinner!" I spouted as I squeezed my shoes onto my dripping feet. "It was nice to meet you," I told the slack-jawed pool attendant. Thank goodness one of the bikini babes had a wardrobe malfunction. The guy, enjoying this job perk, didn't speak to me again.

Balling up my socks, bra and panties, grabbing my jacket, I made a hasty retreat to my car. I didn't know where I was going next; I only knew I wanted to get away from the Windsor Hotel.

I hoped the magnificent Mr. Maha wouldn't catch wind of this.

* * *

That night, I found myself in Mississauga. I'd made the drive from Windsor, smelling nothing but the odour of chlorine that stuck to my skin. It didn't bother me; that aroma brought back fond memories of my stay at hotel. The cookie assortment that I pulled out of my overnight bag staved off my intense hunger.

I didn't see any point in driving further. My gas gauge read empty and I also needed fuel for the belly. The first exit off the highway and into the city presented everything I needed. Gas station. Restaurants. A health-food store, though I had no intention of going there.

After gassing up, I drove throughout a giant plaza. One side had about fifteen rather high-end restaurants where you had to sit down to eat. I drove to the opposite end of the mall and found twice as many fast-food restaurants. Though the variety was large, nothing seemed to appeal to me. Any future meals would pale in comparison to my coconut shrimp and poutine combo from the Windsor Hotel room service.

With a resigned sigh, I pulled out my coupon holder. It held no 50-cents off a tub of yogurt type of coupons. Rather, they were deals for fast-food restaurants. I checked to see if I had one for any of the joints in this plaza. Sure enough, I had a 'buy one burrito, get one free' offer from Taco del Mar. I wasn't a big fan of Mexican food and had never tried this particular restaurant, but I was getting value for my money, so that would be my supper.

A busy restaurant is a good sign, and Taco del Mar was half-full, with pleasant and efficient staff. Back in my car, I unwrapped my first burrito and too big a bite. The smell of it was deliciously fragrant; the taste of it made me want to gag. I suspected it held refried beans, a childhood food I'd despised. Put it this way – I will never try a burrito again.

As cheap as I'd become, I could not force myself to eat that meal. Pulling out the coupons again, I found a Champs Chicken deal. I drove to that corner of the mall and bought a three-pack piece of chicken and fries at a discounted price. I left with a bit of a spring in my step. Champs Chicken would be ordered monthly when I lived at home. It was a special treat; week-old chicken still tasted great.

Tonight, something was wrong in a big way. I don't know if it was time for Champs to change their fryer oil or if somebody was trying to poison me. The fries were cold and bland, but that wasn't my complaint. It was the chicken. I took a bite out of each; one tasted like fries, the other tasted like it was cooked twice and the third was weird, almost tasted like fish.

I shoved it all back into the takeout box and threw it onto the dashboard next to the two uneaten burritos. The few fries I'd choked down weren't enough and now I wasn't going to bother being picky. I looked a couple doors down from the chicken shop and saw a Subway Sandwiches. I ordered a single sandwich, nothing but vegetables, and lots of them. I carefully watched her prepare my heaping meal, making sure I got my money's worth.

Unwrapping the sub, it was all I could do to hold it together. I took a big bite, barely able to get my mouth around all the cucumbers, lettuce, onions, etc. By the time I'd finished, and even though half the sandwich's contents lay on my lap, I was quite stuffed. "Good choice of restaurant," I congratulated myself.

A walk would be in order about now, I thought. *Still got to keep in shape.* A fleeting thought of my workout buddies at Lady Fitness crossed my mind; they must have been wondering where I was...or how fat I was getting without their support. As we tread-milled, we'd talk about inner-thigh fat. As we rode stationary bikes, we spoke of upper-arm flab. I had no desire to go back and let them know I had more concerning me than my thickening waistline.

The need for sleep was stronger than the need for exercise. It had been a long drive, it was a filling meal, and I was worn out. Besides that, my heels still ached from the shoes I'd worn all day yesterday. Decision made, I crimped up the Subway wrapper and threw that onto the dash as well.

The urge to drive, to find a spot for the night, just wasn't in me. I usually didn't spend the night in an open mall; I didn't like being the conspicuous only car in the lot. And if there happened to be a pedestrian taking a shortcut through the mall lot, they always had to walk right by my car.

Tonight I was willing to shake off my misgivings. To satisfy my conscience, I drove to the back of a Walmart store. There was just enough room between two large garbage bins, almost the exact height of my car, for me to drive into. I squeezed in and willed my car to become one with the garbage cans.

I had my usual secretive pee between my open driver's door and open rear door. How I hated to do that – take a furtive pee while keeping an eye out for any vehicles or worse, people silently walking by. Yet, it had to be done, over and over and over and...

Back in the driver's seat, I reclined as best as I could. Something in back was blocking the chair but I was too lazy to fix it. Tomorrow I would clean out my car and reorganize everything. Maybe even get an oil change.

As I nestled into my pillow, another whiff of chlorine enveloped me, bringing a wistful smile to my face. I fell asleep, only to dream of the Windsor Hotel's bathtub.

A soft tapping at my window startled me. Though I didn't rise, my eyes flew open. "It's only the seagulls," I said. Earlier I'd seen a couple flocks of the birds in the lot by the fast-food outlets. They were eating any leftovers found on the road. "Nothing to be afraid of..." My head left my lovely smelling (now like chlorine!) pillow and I slowly sat up and looked out my windshield. Over the mound of leftover food on my dash, I saw nothing but the hood of my car.

I swivelled my head to the left and saw a policeman looking down at me. I unrolled my window. With one hand, I moved my hair out of my eyes and again, aahhhh, a whiff of chlorine. You know how they say smells can trigger memories? That malingering odour of chlorine only brought back comforting thoughts of the Windsor Hotel. "Yes, sir?" I asked.

A flashlight shone in my face and I instinctively shielded my eyes. When I looked again, a second officer had joined the first guy. Officer B was female, barely. Taller, broader, heavier than her counterpart, she shone her own flashlight over the stuff in my back seat.

"Did you want me to move?" I asked.

"Well, you can't park here," Officer A said. I could hear Officer B at the rear of my car, speaking into a radio. My license-plate number was mentioned.

"OK, I can leave," I acquiesced. I looked into my rearview mirror. "You'll just have to move your police car."

"In due time," he said as his light played over my blanket and pillow. Once again the beam was aimed into my eyes. I averted the light for a brief moment and then realized he may be checking to see if I was impaired. I looked back into the light, blinking hard. "Would you step out of the car, please?" the officer ordered.

I unlocked the door and opened it. There was very little room so the officer stepped back so I could exit. Once the door opens, the interior light comes on. Clearly illuminated was the puddle of pee I was about to step into. Giving the policeman an apologetic look (words need not be said; we both knew where he'd just been standing), I stretched my leg over the parking-lot stain and got out of my car.

The lady officer was now on the other side of my vehicle, still talking on her radio. "Light blue, Suzuki Swift," I heard. "So it's all a match then. Thanks. Say hi to Doris for me." She walked to the police car, threw the radio on the seat and turned back to us. "Car checks out clean," she reported.

Both turned to me. I leaned against the car, giving Suzi a pat. *We're going to get through this, gal.* The guy began to interrogate me. "Let's start with your name," he said.

"Madeline Magee," I replied. The officer looked at his partner and she nodded. Yup, that was the owner of the car on record.

"Your address?" he continued.

Remembering the Windsor Hotel check-in, the last time I had

to state my address, I smirked and said, "2004 Suzuki Swift."

Neither cop cracked a smile. They were all business. I wiped the smirk off my face and looked at them levelly. I wasn't going to lie; Mississauga was monitored by the Peel Police Department and they had a rep as being the best in the country.

"Okay, obviously that's my car," I said. "My real address is on Montevideo Road, but...I don't live there right now. Hopefully I will be there again but for now..." and I looked them straight on, "I'm living in my car."

The feeling that washed over me was cleansing. Go ahead and book me, but the truth was on the table. I wasn't on the street, but I didn't live anywhere anymore. My car was my rolling address.

The woman played her light over the mess on the dashboard. "Looks like she's been going through the garbage, looking for food," she said. I wanted to deny it, give myself a little dignity, but she took me by surprise when she shone the light back on me. "You okay, honey?" she asked, not sounding as brutish as she appeared. I just nodded. "You need a couple bucks for food?"

"No...no, I'm okay," I stammered. "This is just a temporary situation."

The male officer walked back to the passenger door. "You take care of this, Frida," he suggested. "Be quick, it's quiet, we can take our coffee break." He got into the squad car and waited for his driver.

Frida looked into my car. "You been sleeping in here long?" she asked softly.

"Few months," I admitted.

"I can give you some addresses, if you like," Frida said, taking out her pad and a pen. "There's a place on Matheson...doesn't look like a shelter so it's kind of hard to find but...."

"That's okay, Officer," I stopped her. "I've...uh...already checked out all those places. To be honest, this is the way I want to do it."

"You sure now?" I nodded. Officer Frida shrugged. "Well, we're done here then." She snapped off her light and headed back to the police car. She began to lower herself into the driver's seat but then stepped out again. "Look, if you want, you can spend the rest of the night here," she offered. A wry grin spread across her face. "It's a pretty good spot. We almost didn't see you there."

"I'll do that," I replied. "Thanks...for everything."

She got back into the car and they drove off. Giving me a goodbye wave, I sketched one back at her and made sure they were totally gone before I took another leak. I got back into my own driver's seat and got ready for bed again. My confession to the cops had lifted a burden off my shoulders. The emotional weight of this secret had left me a mental wreck, but I no longer felt like I was the scum of the earth.

So I lived in my car. Big deal.

Chapter Ten

After months of living in my car, I came to the realization I had a love/hate relationship going on with two different establishments – Tim Horton's and McDonald's. I loved them because whenever I had to use the washroom, whether to pee or brush my teeth or wash my body, there was no second glance if I left without buying something. And they were open 24/7, and there was a McDonald's or Tim Horton's every 40 feet, it seemed.

The hate part came in because I was so sick and tired of their food. I'd completely gone throughout the menu, tried every muffin, donut and sandwich going, and just felt annoyed when I found myself hungry at three a.m. I'd pull up to the drive-thru and just stare at the order board, while "Can I take your order?" would be repeated a time or three.

And then I had a total love and a total hate for something else. The love? My Clorox Wipes. One day, I walked into a Canadian Tire store, looking for Windex to wash my inside windows. I saw Clorox Wipes on sale and bought a large package. The whole inside of my car needed a clean and those things were just amazing. I used maybe 35 of them, but my entire car was scrubbed until it looked new. That night, trying to sleep was difficult as I was nauseous from leftover fumes but since then, I used at least one Clorox Wipe a day.

The total hate probably overwhelmed all else. It affected something very important to me, and that was what little sleep I could get, between worrying about being busted or towed away. And that thing was my seatbelt. Actually, just the hard plastic part where you plug the strap into. It did not lie flat in any way. No matter how many layers of padding I put on top of it, I could always feel it in my sleep. I'd be comfortable, sleeping flat out, and then I'd try to turn onto my side, and that seatbelt connector would press itself hard into my ribs or my knee. I absolutely loathed that thing with every ounce of spit I could muster.

Even though I was on a roll professionally, I felt at an all-time emotional low. Lately I had to keep rationalizing to myself the reason why I was living in my car. Why couldn't I spend $100 to get a hotel room, just for one night? To sleep one solid eight-hour shift without swearing at that seatbelt contraption?

The better part of me explained the reasons why – it would be a waste of money, it would set me back, it wasn't part of the game plan. As it was, I was clipping two-for-one coupons out of newspapers. That sure was fun – trying to quietly rip out the coupons as I sat in the library, hoping nobody was watching or listening. Or wanted to read that particular page.

To be fair to Suzi, the $100 I'd blow on a room could probably be better spent on my current accommodations. My car needed an oil change badly and I got honked at hard three times that day while making a left turn, leading me to believe I had a wonky turning signal. The windshield had a small crack in it which was recent, and I prayed it wouldn't get any bigger. 'SEEK' was still painted on the side, though hidden under dirt. Most of all, she needed a car wash. Maybe I could splurge on that for her.

May and June were great for business. Tons of weddings, anniversaries, graduations... My schedule was packed, my top hat and tails at the ready. Though I was getting older, my reputation was still gold, and I got the lion's share of the singing-telegram work. Maybe the French maids were slowing down, but if they wanted comedy and a dynamite show, I was your performer. If you want a so-so act from a beautiful young thing, I was never that girl.

So even though I was doing well, I wasn't doing well. My joie de vivre was MIA. Today was Monday. I'd just come off a splendid round of shows and I knew my agents would be in for a few happy emails about my performances. If only the customer saw what went on between shows.

I was booked solid all weekend, and no two shows were the

same character. Friday night I started as a clown at a high-school prom. Worried that the poor kid (whose grandparents had sent it) would be embarrassed, I went in big and paid more attention to his classmates than I did to him. I was a hit, allowing them to lift me high in the air for a group photo.

After that I had to rush to do a gorilla-gram. I didn't bother removing the clown make-up; who would be able to tell? And of course, having made it to the gig with a minute to spare, they kept me waiting. Apparently the guest of honour had yet to arrive at his party. Thirty minutes later, I was just about to leave my car again and tell the customer sorry, I had to go to another show (knowing I'd still get paid 50% from the agent who'd booked this one), when I saw a car take a wide swing onto the street. Twenty cars lined the street and the little red SmartCar almost sideswiped the entire row on the driver's side. I hid low in my seat as he turned into his empty driveway and parked at an odd angle.

A man slowly emerged from the tiny vehicle. He quietly shut the door and then tended to his appearance, running his hands through his hair, pulling up his pants. He took a couple wobbly steps forward and then stopped. Once more he fixed himself; again with the hair, this time tucking his shirt into his pants, though he completely missed in the back. He walked on, carefully considering his steps as he approached the front door.

The bannister lining the steps came in quite useful as he pulled himself up. Ever so slowly, he turned the doorknob, trying to make a silent entry. I would give them five minutes and then make my appearance. I knew he'd still be greeting his guests but they had kept me waiting...the client would understand.

Even from outside, I could hear three distinct sounds come next. First, the expected loud "Surprise!!!" Secondly came an astonished collective gasp. Third was just a melange of groans and shrieks. I couldn't wait to see what all this amounted to when I appeared at the party.

Throwing my mask back on as soon as I left my car, so nobody would see the gorilla was really a clown, I monkey-walked over to the front door, which had been left wide open. With my limited vision, I could see women bustling about. I went straight into my routine as I walked in, only to be stopped in my tracks.

"Don't come in!" a lady, wearing all white with a strange spotty design, yelled at me. I had already made my entrance but immediately froze. "Oh, well, now you've done it, you're standing right in it." I had no idea what she meant, couldn't see a thing, but to appease her, I moved a couple steps over to a door that was shut. Maybe they could hide me in there?

"Oh, God! You're only making it worse! You're in more of it now," the lady griped. "Can't you see where you're going?"

"Not really," I said. "Where's the birthday boy?"

"The asshole's in the washroom," the lady answered. "Spence!" she said, not very lovingly. "Get out here!"

Spencer came out of the washroom and even through the mask, I could see sheepishness when I saw it. And then – one of the job perks; their shock when they see the gorilla. He took a wide step away from the door and positioned himself across from me. A teenager showed up with a mop and pail but was told to wait five minutes.

I took that as my cue and gave a short-but-to-the-point telegram. Funny, in the information I was given to write the song, nothing was mentioned about his love of drink. It seemed the wife knew best when, after five minutes, it appeared old Spence needed to get back into the washroom.

Once I got back into my car and into my seat, I pulled off the gorilla mask. As I reached for the passenger seat floor, in search of wipes to take off my smeared clown make-up, it didn't take long for the most wretched smell to greet me.

"What the fuck?" I said aloud as I scrambled to open my car door again. Now I didn't give a shit what anybody saw; I just wanted fresh air. I looked down at my gorilla feet and they looked fine. So did my costume. I undressed right out in the open and I could still smell the distinct odour of vomit. Once the suit was off, I looked at the feet again. Sure enough, the bottoms were covered in Spencer's last meal.

I had time to kill before my next show, downtown in a nightclub. I quickly drove to a gas station with the gorilla feet wrapped in a Longo's food bag (best day-old sushi I've ever had). With my head low and my shoulders hunched, I made a bee-line for the washroom, only to discover I needed to get a key from the clerk first.

Once back in the washroom, I immediately took off the clown make-up. When I did my show, freshly made up, I was as cute as a clown doll. Now I was a contender for the sequel to the Stephen King move *IT*. One scary clown dude. Then I went back to work on the putrid gorilla feet. I would have preferred to have just thrown them out but these were one of a kind. I went back to Walmart once to get a spare pair; they never restocked them after that one time.

I did the best I could but I knew they needed a laundromat. Thankfully I didn't have any immediate gorilla shows coming up. I attempted to dry the slippers but at this point I'd been in the PetroCanada can for almost thirty minutes; somebody was banging on the door.

"Sorry, didn't hear you over the dryer," I apologized as I exited. A woman with a crying baby and a crotch-holding three-year-old were waiting. "Here's the key."

I drove right across the street, to an Esso gas station. Most of them carry Tim Horton outlets, some more higher-end than the others. I was delighted to see this was one of them. I ordered a coffee from their little shop within a gas station and sat down at one of their three tiny tables to eat my meal. Something different, still on the cheap, but I'd never had a sun-dried-tomato bagel before. Now I have, and probably won't again in the future. A medium coffee as well. Lately I've been trying to downsize, as I've grown tired of drinking cold coffee. In the past, I'd nuke my coffee a couple times in the morning to heat it up again. With the lack of a microwave oven, changes had to be made.

I decided to do my make-up in the Esso station. That was a luxury I rarely granted myself, but if there was one thing about my Suzuki I could bitch about, it was the lack of interior light it emitted. I just needed more when it came to getting ready to do a professional show-biz job. Not just emerge from my car with overly red cheeks and unmatching eyebrows. In five minutes in the Esso establishment's ladies' room, I transformed into an attractive nurse.

Jobs downtown are a curse, have I mentioned that? And if Friday-night rush hour is bad, there is still nothing worse than a weekend night in the Entertainment District. People walk in the streets, they cross against traffic lights, fights break out of nowhere. Parking is non-existent and tow trucks circle the cash cow like vultures.

After cruising the area, I could see no street parking available. The four parking lots in the immediate vicinity all had LOTS FULL signs posted. I briefly tried to make Suzi fit into a spot and even though there was only an inch from my back bumper to the other car's, the front end of my vehicle still extended beyond the 'Don't Park Past This Sign' warning. I almost decided to give it another try when the beaming smile of a passing tow-truck driver made me reconsider.

Even though I'd gotten to my show location early, the usual parking crisis was about to make me late. I decided it was time to put my usually foolproof plan into action. I drove to the commercial building where the Canoe Nightclub was located. Instead of trying to get into their full lot, I turned into the aisle marked 'Delivery Vehicles Only'. Was I making a delivery? I definitely was, though my delivery tended to take a little longer than FedEx.

Tonight worked even better than usual. Arriving to an empty dock, I parked my car as if I'd done this a thousand times. A security guard appeared and I explained why I was there. The guy was young; I was older and wiser and seemed to know what I was doing. I said I'd be "about ten minutes" and if he could point me in the right direction?

The nightclub was packed and the noise level was high. I greeted the hostess, who was expecting me. She led me through a throng of dancing bodies to a table just off the dance floor. I yelled, "Do you know which one's the birthday boy?"

She yelled something back but I couldn't make it out. She saw my confused look and simply pointed to the table, which held two men and two women. Both men looked 40. I figured the odds weren't too bad I would figure out who Scott was on the first try.

Of course I picked the wrong guy. I'd played a third of my act before I could hear one of the ladies telling me, "The other guy is Scott!" The bloody place was so noisy that I ended up shouting the song into Scott's ear. The rest of the table, by necessity, missed out on the 'show'. I dispensed with the rest of my act – pretending to administer to the 40-year-old's heart. I would have to pantomime it, and miming was not my forte. I cut the act short by half. As long as Scott knew he'd received some sort of oddball gift from 'The Struthers Family', my job was pretty much done there.

On Saturday, I didn't have a show until later in the afternoon. That usually meant I could sleep in, but when you're sleeping in your car, pretty much anything could wake you up much earlier than planned. The night before I parked at the end of a road leading into an underdeveloped park. Quiet, dark, out of the way...and I was tired and in no mood to search for primo cover.

The next morning I awoke to excited voices. I raised my seat and saw a bunch of guys in uniforms. Everybody was carrying big bags and shovels. I craned my neck around and saw my

Suzuki was the leader of a long row of cars. Rubbing my eyes, I tried to focus on the people surrounding me. It slowly dawned that they were boy scouts with their leaders. A massive tree-planting session was about to take place.

Carefully making a three-point turn, avoiding the hundred boy scouts looking into my overloaded car, I drove back up the road and turned onto a busy street. I found the closest place of business that was open (McDonalds), found their washroom, and began my day.

First on my schedule was a tacky bride at a bridal shower. Usually I don't much care for performing 'woman-to-woman'; I had so much schtick when it came to men. But I had fun with this character and her zany mismatched costume. Even if I did a bad show, my appearance was so striking, it was enough to get a huge belly laugh. Listen, if you have the crowd laughing, you have them in the palm of your hand.

Next up was the singing nun. Coincidentally, this show was in the same banquet hall, but in another room. I ran back to my car, threw the many assorted pieces of the tacky bride back into its garment bag, and wiped off the make-up as thoroughly as possible. Not a trace could be seen on the nun's face. I put on the costume, assumed a holier-than-thou look, and walked back to the hall.

The bride-to-be, whom I'd just performed for, was outside having a cigarette with a matronly woman dressed in black from head to toe. The white cigarette the older gal was holding seemed completely wrong with her outfit, but she was sucking on it like she'd smoked since birth. A little too late, I tried to avert my face without seeming obvious. The young woman did a classic double-take when she saw me. I may have fooled her, had I not been carrying the same two balloons on a stick that I'd brought to her event. I didn't even say hello, just went through the doors to Salon B.

A complete change of character, but still a dynamic show. I

was so pious at the opening that when I got into my act and made the nun a bit sexier, the shock loosened everybody up. Same 'bit' as when I do Marilyn... "My heart's pounding so hard, can you hear it?" and I pull their head to my chest. Laughs when I do it as Marilyn, gasps of astonishment when the nun does it.

From this show, I had to travel quite a distance to be a Grim Reaper, one of my least favourite characters. The garment was made of a thin nylon and was actually an inexpensive Halloween costume I'd gotten online. When I opened the packaging, I was astounded to see how well-made it was, and quite scary-looking. It was a problematic outfit though; my vision was blurred from the dark netting covering my face and the garment was too long. If I didn't belt it just so, I would be tripping all over the place.

The drive out of town was quite unpleasant. The lingering stench of vomit filled the car. I was sure I'd given the gorilla slippers a thorough washing but obviously it wasn't good enough. The smell seemed to fill my nostrils, even with the windows open.

I had an address in Ancaster, a town about an hour from Toronto. Assuming it was a house, I was surprised when my GPS informed me that I was at my destination. A bingo palace? Oh well, as long as Henrietta was in there... I went into my Grim Reaper persona, tall, brooding, ominous, and entered the bingo hall.

I heard, "O 66, 0 66, clickety-click," as I walked in. The brightness of the place aided my vision and I could see a wave of people turn to stare at me. Before I could say anything, a large shape lumbered toward me.

"Hi, I'm the manager, I know why you're here but you're going to have to wait...we have a game in progress," he quietly whispered. "Just until somebody calls Bingo."

Not wanting to attract more attention, I stood stock still as the players continued their game. People kept staring at me and behind my netted face, I stared back. Oh crap, about 75% of the crowd were senior citizens. I'm sure they loved seeing the Grim Reaper come around. My pose seemed menacing, silent but deadly.

Finally, "Under the B, number 5, B 5, stayin' alive..."

Followed by a "Bingo! I got Bingo!"

The attendant dutifully checked to see that the excited 90-year-old actually did have a Bingo. He turned to the bingo caller and nodded his head. In the dull monotonous voice, the caller told the folks, "Ladies and gentleman, chicken dinner, we have a winner."

The manager of the bingo hall appeared on stage and whispered to the caller, before scampering off towards me again. The bingo caller, in the same drone, spoke into the microphone. "Folks, we're going to take a short pause while we have a spot of entertainment."

At this point, about half the hall emptied out and I saw cigarette packages clutched in everybody's hands. Some even had the unlit cigarette already in their mouths, their lighters in hand, ready to flick as soon as they cleared the no-smoking area.

The manager pointed out Henrietta, who was seated at the same table as the gleeful bingo winner. When she saw me up close, the happy old biddy clammed up, her eyes blinking rapidly.

"Don't worry, bingo winner," I calmed her. "Today really is your lucky day. I'm not here for you." With that I wheeled around and pointed my plastic scythe at Henrietta. "It's YOU, Henrietta, that I've come to see!" Henrietta (though I was told she was called Henny since birth, so why did they give me her formal name that nothing rhymed with? 'Henny' would have been a cinch, anything ending with an 'ee' sound) was just entering her senior years. Her sister had sent the telegram as a joke that now that Henny was 65, she was at death's door. Only a family member could get away with that joke. Henny knew a prank when she saw one and completely went with the scenario. She was quite the ham and basically made the show a hit.

Back at my car, I stood in the parking lot and peeled off the costume. I opened the trunk to get my French maid out; may as well get into it before I started the long drive to Pickering. I love my job but hated all the driving. Back in the 'old days', after a long day of shows, I couldn't wait to get home, get out of the damn car (sorry, Suzi!) and just be glad I was off the highways. Now, after a similar long day of shows and driving, I was forced by circumstances to remain in my car.

I sat on the driver's seat to put on my fishnet pantyhose and gagged at that awful vomit smell again. This couldn't continue! It was affecting my quality of life! I threw the fishnet stockings aside and went back to the trunk. Pulling out the bag that contained the still-damp slippers, I gave it a tentative sniff. The bag didn't smell at all, so I opened it up and took out one slipper, again cautiously smelling the underside. There was definitely a lingering bad aroma, but it wasn't ground zero of the REALLY bad smell.

I went back to the front of the car, leaned in and inhaled. Now, for some reason, I couldn't smell it that much, so I sat down on the seat in the same way I'd been doing moments earlier. Maybe the odour was stronger again, but by now I was simply confused. Deciding to just carry on, I again started to put on my fishnets. As I raised my food towards me, the smell came in loud and clear.

Oh, dear God, my feet stink of vomit! I shuddered to think that whatever had seeped through the slippers and onto my feet had been there all night and day. I was sure I would lose a foot from some disgusting infection I was bound to get. Once more, my inner spirit wavered... *Had you been in your home last night, you'd have had your usual nightly bath!* I'd developed a habit of dropping into various hotels, acting as if I had every right to be there, and using their lobby washrooms to seriously wash up. McDonald's and Tim's had too much traffic, even at midnight. Gas stations rarely had toilet paper, never mind the thick hand towels offered by The Delta Inn.

There would be time to worry about this after my French maid show. I had to get going before I'd be late, so I sprayed my feet with perfume and finished dressing. I drove to Pickering in record time, windows rolled down as far as possible before clothes and boxes could fly out.

The French maid was thankfully outdoors. I was a gift from the wife. Other than the fact that my spike heels keep slipping through the cracks in the deck, the show went spectacular. FiFi the French maid pulled out all stops, anything to make them forgive my stinky feet. The happy couple walked me to my car after the show. I turned down their awkward request for a threesome for later that night by saying I was happily married. Joke's on them.

My last show of the night was at the Old Links Golf Club in Bolton. Another long journey. Now that I knew my feet were in mortal danger of a fungal outbreak, the rest of my body began reacting in sympathy symptoms. I started to get a headache, (though I hadn't eaten in quite a few hours, food had lost its appeal. How I longed to even boil an egg or toast my own toast the way I liked it toasted), I got stomach cramps, my back ached. Something had to give.

En route, I came up with a plan and prayed it would work. For my sanity, it had to work. As I entered the long winding road to the golf course, I pulled off to the side. Using my trusty Blackberry (who needs ya anyhow, laptop?), I googled the Old Links Golf Course and came up with their phone number. I pressed the button for 'call' and was connected to reception.

"Hi, I'm going to be coming by there soon," I began. "I'm doing a singing telegram..."

"Yes, " she interrupted, "we know about it. Are you lost, honey?"

"Oh, no! Actually I'm here already," I replied.

"Aren't you early?" the receptionist asked, a worried tone in her voice. "They just served the main course."

"I'm calling to ask you for a favour, if it's possible," I was as polite as could be. "You see, the lights in my car don't work that great and...I want to look good for my show. I was wondering...do you think I could get ready inside the golf club somewhere? I just need a public washroom, if that's okay?"

"Awww, sweetums, you come on in," the receptionist said. "You're the entertainer, you're the big star, of course you want to look nice! Listen, nobody uses the member's lounge at this time of night. You're welcome to it."

"Oh, I can't thank you enough!" I gushed. "I'll be there in two minutes!"

I quickly parked my car and grabbed my top-hat-and-tails costume. In my haste, with my feet afire, I swear, I almost forgot three of the four things I always made sure to take to my gigs – rose, balloons, song and car keys. Grabbing them, I locked up and ran to the rustic-looking Old Links Golf Course door.

The receptionist, a woman about forty years younger than I'd imagined, stood up to greet me. Her smile instantly faded when she saw my get-up. "You're a French maid? I thought Mr. Wilson booked a...."

I lifted up my garment bag. "This is my costume for the show." I pointed to the skimpy French maid I was wearing. "This was my last show."

She almost swayed in relief. "Thank Betsy! The couple celebrating their anniversary tonight – extremely religious! Just make sure you keep it clean."

That was good information. In the info I was given to write a song, no mention was made of their devoutness. I'd have to do away with the sexual innuendoes, the double-entendres, the full-on flirting. There went half the show. And if she wanted clean, my perfumed feet didn't make the cut.

I was shown to the member's lounge and had the washrooms

pointed out to me. Assuring the receptionist, LizBeth (really, no space?) that I'd be seeing her in thirty minutes, I closed the door on her. Dropping all my stuff immediately onto a couch, I shot into the washroom.

Ooowee! Luxury! There were three giant sinks, with enough space between them that I could sit up there and stick my feet into the basin. And even better, separate faucets so that I could control the water temperature! I'd become almost obsessive in my hatred for those sensor-controlled one-temperature single taps found in every public washroom these days. The coup de grace were the thick towels to dry your hands (or feet) and the lilac-smelling soap. With the water turned as hot as I could stand it, I scrubbed them until they were beet red and starting to swell. Finally I stood up and with some dexterity, I lifted each foot up to my nose and sniffed.

Aahhh, back to normal! Even better, I could say. And while sniffing my left foot, I happened to take in the rest of the washroom. Three lovely toilet areas to go with the three sinks. And tucked farther back, a small sauna, which held no interest for me. What made me scurry over was the sight of...be still, my heart...showers! And even though I'm a bath person, I've been known to take the occasional shower. Usually a power shower, in and out in under five minutes. Could I do that now...?

Glancing at my watch, I saw I had less than fifteen minutes to get ready. My make-up was fine; the French-maid look could work for the top hat and tails, though the eyeliner was a bit thick. Not enough time for a badly needed shower. Oh well, at least my feet were clean.

Going up the stairs, I went back to reception. LizBeth perked up. "Oh, what a difference a change of clothes can make! You look much more presentable!"

I didn't know whether that was a compliment or a diss, but I let it pass. "I want to thank you for letting me use that room," I said. "I'm going to have to run back down there after, to get my stuff."

"You have another show after this?" she asked. I didn't, but I nodded anyhow. "If you want to use that room again, go ahead. I know you said you had bad lighting in your car."

"Seriously?" I asked. Now she nodded her head. "Wow, you're the best," I told her. She was my angel in disguise, and I'm sorry I was rude about her name. She had no idea of what I planned on doing in that members' lounge. Refreshing my make-up was not one of them.

The top-hat-and-tails telegram went superb. I had been worried about losing a good portion of my show but somehow I still managed to give them fifteen minutes' worth. It was a different show than usual, for some reason. I was affectionate with the elderly couple, I went to the trouble of meeting their children and grandkids, and I shared words of wisdom on the sanctity of marriage. I was not just smiling, I was ebullient. Maybe because I had the best-smelling feet in the room. Or maybe because I was about to put my devious plan into action.

After a final photograph with the grateful couple, sent from their niece in California, I wished them many more years of wedded bliss and walked out of their lives. I passed the lovely LizBeth on my way to the members' lounge.

"Sounds like they had fun," she commented.

"It's my job," I replied. "I'm going to change now...don't panic if you don't see me for twenty minutes or so."

"Take your time," she offered, as her computer made an odd sound. "Oh, no, not again!" LizBeth pouted as she jabbed at a key. I simply slipped away, turned a corner and literally ran in my high heels to the stairs. By the time I'd gotten to the bottom, half my clothes were already off. I ran into the lounge and directly to the glistening, clean shower stalls.

I stayed in that heavenly shower for a long, long time. I knew I should get going but I just couldn't seem to get out. After thoroughly cleaning my body and washing my hair twice, I just let the water cascade over me. I figured they'd have to remove me by force. Suddenly, after what was maybe forty minutes? the water began to get cooler. That's happened to me before in my house...but was I using up the entire golf club's supply of hot water? I got out immediately.

Standing there naked, dripping wet, I couldn't see any large towels. Was I supposed to bring my own? I picked up my costume jacket with the long tails and used it to dry myself off. Going back into the washroom area, I upgraded to the little hand towels.

Definitely time to split. However, I didn't want to get dressed again in my costumes. I picked up the French-maid dress and put it on, sans bra or panties. Squeezing my damp feet into the heels, I packed everything else away into the garment bag. It was time to make a stealthy getaway now, especially since I was wearing a micro-mini dress with no underwear on.

I quietly went up the stairs, then tip-toed to the wall shielding me from the reception desk. I slowly peeked around it and saw LizBeth on the phone. It seemed apparent she had called somebody about her malfunctioning computer, as she was listening and then pressing the odd key.

With haste, I made a fast bee-line to the exit. Once I had the door open, I turned around and called out to the receptionist, "Thank you, LizBeth!" She glanced up, gave me a perfect receptionist happy smile, and waved goodbye. I'm glad she didn't notice I hadn't one spec of make-up on my face...and that my hair was awfully damp.

Back at my car, I exchanged the French-maid dress for the most comfy old sweat pants and baggy t-shirt I'd packed. I enjoyed a big yawn. It had been a busy day of work, and the steaming shower had left me feeling drowsy. All I wanted to do was get some sleep before I had to do it all over again tomorrow.

I was in Bolton. The danger of getting in trouble with cops or management were slim. I didn't drive far that night, looking for a place to sleep. About fifty metres, to be precise. The far corner of the Old Links Golf course, a nice place to golf, shower and sleep.

* * *

Sunday dawned early to the sounds of the course-maintenance workers mowing the grass. That always meant one thing – time to get out of there. Today I had three shows, the first one at 11 a.m. downtown. I took my sweet time getting there, travelling the back roads instead of the highway, turning a 45-minute drive into double the time.

Today I had to show up at a brunch as a Bag Lady. That was usually a favourite character of mine; clothing-wise, anything worked as long as you looked down and out. A lot of laughs came from the costume, a lot from my character's quirks – scratching at her head lice, phlegm-filled coughing before I sang the song, the begging for a penny, nickel, quarter, dime.

As well, the location for this show could not be more perfect. Where else do you find the homeless? Usually downtown! I would park my vehicle and then walk to my gig, getting in character before I arrived. Downtown, I wouldn't get a second look from bystanders; the homeless are a common sight. Often when I'm booked to do a show in some quaint villages that have never even heard of the phrase 'bag lady', I have to say, "Hey, don't be alarmed, I'm really a singing telegram." And they kind of acknowledge that they get it, but I know they don't because they still look alarmed.

Today felt different though. Walking the block and a half to the Fred's Not Here restaurant, I had somewhat of an epiphany. With one stroke of bad luck, like my car getting into a wreck, and I too could become a bag lady. For God's sake, I hadn't even changed out of my t-shirt and sweats, nor bothered to put on underwear. I was even wearing my battered old slippers, which I'd brought with me and slipped on when I was running into restaurants to pee. Was I subconsciously preparing myself for a future life of living on the street?

I started to get anxious, maybe I was going to cry, when I glanced into the window of a closed sushi place. I could see the reflection of my painted face and relaxed. I saw someone that didn't look like me at all; she looked like Hagatha the Bag Lady. In that brief instant, I snapped back to normal. *Don't be silly*, I chided myself. *Besides, no bag lady smells as clean as I do.*

Entering Fred's Not Here, I went into my tried-and-true routine. I scrounged a bun off a platter, I pretended to sneak a slice of bacon off someone's plate. As soon as the crowd seemed to turn against me, demanding management evict me, I suddenly noticed my 'victim' and acted like he was an old boyfriend.

Today, Seamus, the new 40-year old, was taken off-guard. He denied it and seemed to fear any contact with me. It wasn't until I told him I wrote a song about him and proceeded to sing it that he then realized it was a set-up. The entire audience gave me a standing ovation.

However, I still looked like a bag lady as I left the restaurant. Just for kicks, I dragged my ass getting back to my car until I saw a couple well-dressed women stop to crack open their Starbucks coffee containers. They were close to my vehicle and I made sure they saw me get into it. Their dumbfounded expressions, one with her cup frozen halfway to her lips, made me love the character all the more. It was a role I could play until retirement!

I had almost the whole day to kill before my next show, a Madonna. This one was up in Barrie, over an hour north of Toronto. With nothing better to do, I drove up there immediately. Being at a party seven hours early always ensured I got a good parking place.

Dark clouds were rolling in as I made the drive. After stopping for gas, washroom, snacks, the usual, I GPSed the party's address. My current GPS pal, the American Dude, told me to continue up Highway 400. Once at the address, I donned a baseball cap and sunglasses, even though the sky was seriously overcast. I just didn't want the people at the event to later recognize me as the woman loitering in her car on their street all day.

I wrote the song for Zak, which didn't take long. The telegram was being sent from his girlfriend and apparently, she didn't know much about him. He liked video games, he liked burgers, he liked rap music, his girlfriend's name was Bronte.

Hours to go until my show. I could take a walk, but with my luck the rain would start. I could go to a mall and drink more coffee and look around, but I just didn't want to lose my parking spot. As soon as this gig was done, I had to race back to Toronto for my final show of the evening. I wished I had a house to clean.

That thought naturally led me to look at the mess in my car. Maybe I could spend time cleaning it? I had removed the bulk of my belongings and had just started doing a fine job of repacking it all in when fat raindrops began to fall. As fast as possible, I put the rest of my stuff in but it wasn't as neat as I was aiming for. Rain doesn't scare me, but being conspicuous in sunglasses is what hustled me back into my car.

The sky turned black. Even though the rain came down steadily, it was still warm. A refreshing breeze wafted through the car. The water droplets that came in through my open windows felt like a spray of mist from a waterfall, just delightful! I tilted my seat back, tucked the pillow under my head and picked up a cooking magazine I'd been reading intermittently. Fictional reading, you could say. Studying a difficult recipe for brined turkey, I drifted off to sleep.

Hours later, I awoke to a huge crash of thunder. I was drenched from the rain and had a chill. As I rolled up the window, a burst of lightning lit up the street. Though it was only about 5 o'clock, the darkness made it appear later. I saw a woman walk out of the house where I would be performing. She was carrying a bunch of helium-filled balloons, all saying '25!' on them. She placed them on the lawn and scurried back inside. Within seconds, the heavy rain was pushing the balloons to the ground.

I turned on my interior light and decided to write the song for my last show. Looking at the Blackberry attachment that contained Braxton's information, I groaned aloud. Another one of those instances where the person sending the telegram just couldn't tell you enough about the birthday boy. His many accomplishments. Every school, course and class he'd taken since junior kindergarten. The many names of his friends (and spouses!), all the jobs he'd held since his first paper route. Didn't these people understand they were hiring me to write a little song, not his autobiography!

With that done, I blew up the balloons for the next two shows and then considered my make-up. Time was of the essence; I had to rush from my Madonna gig to Marilyn. Except for their famous beauty marks, the make-up was identical. As long as I remembered to switch beauty marks, I'd be okay. I took extra care with my make-up because I wanted it to look fresh for the next couple hours and because my final gig was going to a well-known wealthy man. He'd have discerning guests who knew a quality act when they saw one.

I was ready to go into my show at eight p.m. There were quite a few cars on the street but only a couple were by the party house. I made my entrance and I could see Zak wasn't that impressed. He turned to his girlfriend and said, "You sent this?"

She nodded, all pleased with her inventiveness. With the $250 she spent on this telegram, she could have gotten him an iPod or rims for his Ford Fiesta. Instead, she thought this gift would be more appreciated. "You said you liked Madonna," she gloated.

"I said I liked Gwen Stefani," Zak reminded her.

"I remember you said you liked Madonna," Bronte said, urging him to like me.

"I said I liked that one song of Madonna's," Zak clarified. "The

Virgin one. That's it."

"I don't remember anything about Gwen Stefani," Bronte pouted.

"Oh, come on, I love Gwen Stefani!" Zak retorted. "You should know that by now."

"Well, sorrrr-ree!" Bronte retorted.

It was time to interrupt this lover's quarrel. "I'm still here!" I broke in. "And I do have a new song to sing! I call it 'A Song for Zak' and it goes like this...." I went straight into the singing telegram. What with the fake flirtation and the appreciation of the six Madonna fans at the party, the act went over well enough that Zak gave his girlfriend a kiss on the cheek at the end.

"Thanks, Bron," he said. "But next year, Gwen Stefani, okay?"

Like that couldn't wait until I was out of earshot? *Well, good luck, Zak, finding a Gwen Stefani lookalike. I'm in the business, and there is none.*

Through a torrential downpour, with intermittent flashes of lightning, I headed back to Toronto. As soon as I got into the city and off the highway, back in the land of traffic signals, I began changing my costume every time I had to wait out a red light. Before I'd driven 10Ks, Madonna transformed into Marilyn. The beauty mark above the lip now appeared on my cheek. Best of all, it appeared I would get to this show on time.

The lack of parking is what astounded me. I guess Braxton was quite the popular man with the upper echelon of society. Porsches, Bentleys and BMWs lined the road as far as I could see. I drove around the block and couldn't find a spot. Often I will block the driveway at my show's location if I can't find a place to park; I know nobody will leave while I'm doing my act. This time, not even that option was available. The foot of the drive was taken by the caterer's truck.

Even the spaces by fire hydrants were taken, not that I'd allow myself that dangerous luxury. I finally parked about half a kilometre away when someone vacated a spot. To make matters worse, the rain was coming down in buckets. How I despised it when people ordered up expensive entertainment and expected them to show up looking mint, when they couldn't supply parking. Don't blame me when the gorilla's sopping-wet feet leave marks all over your hardwood floor. You didn't supply parking, the ape had to walk through puddles to get to your soiree – put the blame on your damn self.

An umbrella would sure come in handily and I knew I'd packed one, but I didn't have the time to dig through my car to find it. Grabbing the balloons, rose and my song, I reached for my issue of *Bon Vivant* magazine. It was nice and big and only cost a quarter at the library's used-book sale. So I splurged one day, but it helped to shield most of the rain from my wig. In my high heels, I did a fast walk to the mansion where I'd be performing.

I got more pissed off the closer I got. Ringing the doorbell, I waited for somebody to answer. The music coming from the lower level of the house was deafening. I rang the bell three more times then brazenly tried the door. The knob turned easily in my hand so I walked in.

The inordinate style of the foyer was remarkable but what was most appealing was the tiny washroom tucked right beside the front door. Nobody saw me come in, nobody saw me duck into the little cubicle. The entire washroom was encased in mirrored tiles.

The sight staring back at me made me want to run back to my car. I was a trashy, has-been, slutty version of Marilyn Monroe. For obvious starters, my white dress had become rather sheer; my nipples were clearly visible. Even though *Bon Vivant* did its best, my wig held a thousand droplets of water. The boa's red feathers clung to me, the dye rubbing off on my dress, gloves and shoulders. Worst of all was my beauty mark. Instead of that perfect round dot, now there was a long black line running down my face.

Fire me, ask me to leave, but I definitely planned to be late for my performance. There was no possible way I would even allow myself to be seen like this. I took a towel and rubbed hard at my wet dress, trying to dry it enough so that all eyes would not be on my boobs. I took off the wig and gave it a hundred good shakes before placing it back on my head. I fixed my make-up as best as I could, without having my make-up bag with me.

Picking up the rose (looked like it lost a few petals), the telegram song (about to tear apart from its sodden state) and balloons (still glistening wet), I made my exit from the washroom. A woman in black pants and white shirt was just passing by, a silver platter of appetizers cradled in her arms. I asked her for Elinor, my contact, and was told to wait, she would get her.

Five minutes later (all good, I was getting drier), Elinor showed up and asked if I could give her ten minutes so she could get everybody together in one room. I guess my being twenty minutes late (though she didn't even seem to notice) gave her the right. Fifteen minutes later, she showed up again. I'm glad I didn't have anywhere else to skedaddle to – all this waiting around would have put a wrench in my schedule. Often people will do this – assume that their party is the only thing you have to do, and they can keep you waiting all night if they wished. "Oh, sorry, can you wait until the bride and groom have had their first dance?" Me: "Oh, do you know how long that will take?" Them: "I don't know, they haven't finished eating, they're still on their salads."

I was led down the stairs and by rote, went into the same routine I've done for twenty years. Maybe the crowd was liquored up, maybe it was a boring party with too-loud music, but the guests were loving me. After a multitude of photos taken with the male guests, and one with Braxton's mother, I bid adieu and walked up the steps. Elinor followed me to the door.

Now, I'm not greedy and I don't always expect to get a tip. I know I'm already paid quite well for my services. However, when you're doing a show for one of the richest men in Toronto, a gift sent from the wife, you can't help but hope for a few bucks. I'm sure the caterers were getting a tip. So I lingered by the front door.

"That was fun!" I laughed. "Good crowd! Very appreciative." Subliminal hints.

"They loved it," she agreed. "Thanks for coming in this rain. Did you have an umbrella?"

"Oh, yeah!" I remembered. I opened the door to the little bathroom and reached into the sink, where my Bon Vivant magazine still rested. "Well, thanks for the job," I said.

She opened the front door. "Drive safe now," she said in a kind voice. I could see that Dame Elinor, in her Dior dress and Tiffany jewels, was not about to bequeath any extra of that wealth onto me.

As I turned to leave, a voice boomed out. "Elinor!" She froze and I could see the top of Braxton's head peering from the stairwell. He strode up. I didn't know whether to leave or see if I was part of this. "Did you give her a tip?" he asked his wife.

"N...no," she stammered. "I...I was going to mail it to her agent..."

"Like hell you were," he spat out. The lovey-dovey couple I'd seen downstairs were nowhere to be found on this floor. Braxton suddenly appeared tyrannical. He reached into his pocket, pulled out a gleaming money clip choking with bills, and peeled off a hundred. He held it out to me. "Take this."

"No, it's not necessary," I said, with my hand already on the money. "But thank you, you're very generous!" Tyrant or not, I liked his style.

"I enjoyed your show very much," he said. Leaning forward, guaranteeing that I never work for Elinor again, he gave me a soft kiss on the cheek. "Sorry my wife is so cheap."

On that note, I left. I clutched that hundred-dollar bill tighter than the magazine shielding me from the rain. I got back to my car and made sure to put the money into my glove box. I drove off, with the usual predicament ahead of me – where do I sleep tonight?

About five minutes later, stopped at a red light, a honking noise caught my attention. A woman in black clothing covering every inch of her body except for her eyes, driving a fancy SUV, rolled down her window. Me, in my body-exposing white dress, rolled down mine.

"Your dress is hanging out of your car door!" she shouted.

I looked down, followed the line of my dress, and saw I'd shut the door on most of the skirt part. I groaned then said, "Thank you!" to the lady. I made an immediate right-hand turn into a Sunoco station.

I pulled into a spot quite a distance away from the entrance to the gas station. Hopefully nobody would bug me and I could sleep the night away here. I opened the door to see if any damage had been done to my costume. The whiteness of the dress that had remained in the car was a stark contrast to the mud-splattered wet black mess that hung outside.

Great. I'd just done my laundry four days ago – about a month's worth. Obviously I'd need to visit the laundromat again. Taking it off, I stuffed it into a Thai One On plastic bag, which I then wedged onto the seatbelt thingy (always trying to pad the damn thing). I changed into my regular clothes and then felt queasy. I don't know if I was hungry but the Tim Horton's down the street held zero appeal. After a brief visit to the gas station's washroom to wash away Marilyn, I bought some peanuts and celebrated the end of a lucrative weekend.

* * *

The next morning, I understood why I'd been having a sore back, stomach cramps and a headache. Sorry to have put the blame on you, my vomit-covered feet, but my period had arrived. In the past, I knew to the hour when I could expect my 28-day visitor. Since moving into my car, my period ceased to be regular. Now it was every 40 days or so.

Maybe my menstruation started during the night, in my sleep. It had gone on long enough, without protection, to soak through my sweat pants and onto my seat. It looked like a chicken had been killed in my car. So now I had a Marilyn dress to clean as well as my car seat.

As mentioned, I was in a precipitous state. Here I was, making tons of cash, but all I could do was gripe. Things weren't panning out the way I'd planned. Though I claimed otherwise to my daughter Shannon, I wasn't enjoying my stay in my Suzuki Swift. It was nowhere near as fun and exciting as I thought it would be. It was outright boring and monotonous and scary and unpleasant.

Here I had a $100 burning a hole in my glove compartment, begging to be spent on a hotel room. But no, that lovely tip would go to the Suds N' Bubbles laundromat, and the Lucky Coin Wash. As well as tampons and Midol.

Maybe I was PMSing, but lately I REALLY hated living in my car. And did I mention how much I detested that goddam seatbelt doohickey?

Chapter Eleven

The rut that I'd been spiralling into had to be put on pause. Life got in the way of my burgeoning antipathy. Once again, Shannon unknowingly pulled me out of my funk just by being a daughter who needed her mom.

She called me first thing Monday morning, as I sat outside my car. I was parked in Syntex Park and was seated on a picnic bench under the shade of a tree. It wasn't even eight a.m. and the temperature must have been close to 100 degrees. I'd just swiped a spider off my leg, the second once since I'd been sitting here, when the phone rang.

"Eww! Yuk! Get off me! Hello!" I said, answering the phone.

"Mom, you okay?" Shannon quickly asked.

"Yeah, there was a big spider on me," I gasped. "You know how I feel about spiders." I looked under the picnic table and could see more critters awaiting their turn to frighten me. I booked it out of there. *Go to hell, nature.* I went back into my sweltering car. "So what's up?"

"I don't know where to start, it's such a busy week," she began. She was always on the go, so I didn't see how anything could be different. "First of all, graduation is Thursday, you know."

She said that as if I did know. I wanted to slap myself for being so wrapped up in my own world that I kept forgetting about my only child and her life. Then, with a further jolt, I knew I'd probably taken a show for the upcoming Thursday. And yes, I did have a gig, a couple actually, but they would both be done by noon. I made sure to scratch out the rest of the day as I continued the conversation.

"Yeah, Thursday," I replied. "It's in my book."

"Will you be there?" she quietly asked.

"Will I be there?" I repeated. "It's your graduation! I'm your mother! Of course I'll be there!" And the truth is, even if I had a singing telegram for the Prime Minister of Canada, I would have blown him off for this momentous, though probably boring, event.

"Great!" Shannon sounded more enthused. "It starts at four p.m., and I've got you a seat next to Jody's parents. But I need your help tomorrow, if you're available?"

Back to my schedule. I had two shows, both in the early part of the day again. "I'm busy 'til lunchtime. When do you need me? And what for?"

"I've been looking at cars, you know," she said. "Mine is leaking oil all the time and it's gonna cost too much to fix it. I've been saving up for a down payment but I need you to co-sign on a loan for me."

"You've got a car picked out already?"

"Not quite. I've narrowed my choices down to two but I want your opinion," she explained.

"You didn't take your dad to look at them?"

"No, I took Jody," she replied. "I talked to the sales guy, I told him what I had for a down payment, and he said it all looked good." She hesitated, then continued. "I didn't take Dad cuz...I guess I just didn't want him to know how much money I'd saved up."

Could I ever relate.

* * *

My days (and nights, since this heat wave began) had been spent finding air-conditioned places to while away the non-working, non-sleeping hours. However, whether in a mall or a coffee shop, I had become so terrified of getting another loitering ticket that I barely sat for the allotted twenty minutes before I went searching for another cool location.

Driving with the air conditioning on in my car was not an

option. That ate up my gas consumption at an alarming rate. Driving with windows wide open was also not an option. The only pair of pantyhose I had left with no runs flew out my back window; a newly written telegram blew off my dash in the front. In more ways than one, I felt like I was living in Hell. And there was no fire escape.

I decided to make the upcoming graduation the focal point of my existence. I hoped to present myself that day as a respectable mother of an accomplished student. I wanted to look nice and I wanted to arrive in style. I looked over the interior of my car. Where was the passenger seat? Nothing but costume pieces mixed with take-out food containers. Maybe Shannon would need a ride and this time, I meant to be of some assistance.

From where I sat, I could look across the expanse of the park. It ended at a busy street, and I could see the large yellow sign of a business. It read 'Mini-Storage'. I didn't stop to think; I just started up the car and drove on over. It couldn't hurt to ask a few questions.

Mini-Storage had tiny spaces to rent, from just one day to however long you wanted. I told the clerk I needed it for more than a day, less than a week. Choosing a space about the size of a clothes closet, and as long as I cold vacate by noon on Friday, I was given a special deal on the locker.

"You unload your stuff and lock it up," she informed me. "Ya got a lock, don't ya?" I shook my head. "Well, you can buy your own or buy one from us. Up to you."

I bought one from them, which cost almost as much as the locker rental. A large moving van passed by the window. "He must have a lot of stuff," I commented. "What did he do, rent a hundred mini-lockers?"

"We got more lockers in the back," she informed me. "And the whole second floor level is full of storage rooms. Just the main level has the small lockers." She went on to explain the rules of renting storage space. One rule was that the main gates closed at

11 p.m.; if you had to get into your locker, plan on being there by 11. But you didn't have to leave at that time, she explained. You could leave whenever you wanted.

I asked to see one of these storage rooms. A soft idea was forming...at the cost of $150 a month, I could possibly sleep in one of these rooms! The storage desk clerk grabbed a battery-operated fan and led the way. Within moments, I kiboshed that idea. There was no air-conditioning in this massive warehouse of storage units; the air was still and dusty and I could barely draw a breath. I gave up on the idea of stretching out fully for one night.

Back in the lot, I drove my car closer to the door that led to my storage locker. I wanted to get some stuff in it immediately. However, what should have been a quick run in and out turned into a whole day's process. The cramped and disgusting interior of my car underwent a makeover. I completely filled a garbage can that had been totally empty earlier.

That night, after a cold supper of my leftover Sausage McMuffin and the remains of the Wok This Way lunch combo, I motored over to Syntex Park again. From the confines of my car, I watched a baseball game being played out under the lights. The temperature actually dropped to the mid-80s, and I finally felt comfortable in my skin. With the crowd cheering and the sounds of balls being hit, I fell into a deep sleep.

When I awoke, I was the only car left in the parking lot. The baseball lights had been shut down and the place had an abandoned feel to it. My windows were wide open and what caused me to open my eyes and immediately turn the car on was...I thought I heard a giggle. I didn't care if it was a mutant grasshopper and I didn't even bother to look. My instincts told me, from past history, to just gun it out of there.

I got back onto Derry Road and glanced at my car's clock. 10:57 p.m. I was less than a kilometre from my storage locker. I decided to check out their rules and raced to Mini-Storage. At

10:59 p.m., I was sliding my entry card into the slot. The gate magically opened and I shot through.

Once inside the huge lot, I drove around a bit until I found a parking space that suited Suzi. For the next couple hours, I sat in my car, waiting for some security guard to order me out of there. Nothing happened though. It was like I owned the place and could do whatever I wanted. I could even visit my locker, but the thought of wandering around at night deterred me. Instead, I drifted off to sleep.

The next morning, rather than the usual rude awakening I was accustomed to, I was gently roused by a quiet U-Haul unpacking a load of what appeared to be bags of salt. They were so considerate, the two men not speaking as they quickly unloaded their truck. Sure, it was barely six a.m., opening hour, but I had to get up anyways. I had two songs to write and two people to be – Madonna and Marilyn.

* * *

On Tuesday, Shannon met me at the Mazda dealership right at three p.m. We looked at different vehicles but she was drawn to two in particular. Both were compact cars and I wasn't pleased at all.

"What's your problem, Mom?" Shannon asked. "What's not to like about them? They're both cheap, both good on gas..."

"It's hard to say," I began, "but look at the seat in this one...," I reached into the red Mazda. "It doesn't recline all the way." I pointed to the silver car. "And that one has no trunk space to speak of..."

Shannon gave me an odd look and then said, "Let's go get a coffee from their machine."

Free coffee? Free! I trotted off to the beverage machine. Away from the salesman, Shannon came to the point. "You don't like the cars I picked because they wouldn't work out well if I had to

LIVE IN THEM. That's it, isn't it, Mom?"

"Don't be silly," I said, in my defence.

"I just need to get to school and to my jobs and to visit Jody," she said, adding cream and sugar to my cup. "I want a small car. I don't want to pay a lot. And I love the red car."

"But the seat...a total recline is vitally important!" I stressed.

"Mom! That's the last thing I'm worried about in a car!"

I gave in. "Well, it actually is pretty gorgeous. And it looks like a total sports car." Suddenly an alarming thought jumped into my mind and I ran back to the red Mazda. Sitting in the front seat, I pulled the seatbelt across me and watched where it made its connection. Jealousy momentarily washed over me. Shannon would be getting herself a car with a seatbelt connector deeply recessed beneath the seat. You could barely notice it, it was so unobtrusive.

Stepping out, I said, "Go get the salesman. Let's make a deal."

We made them an offer, they came back with their offer, we made a final counter-offer, and were asked to wait while the manager considered it. We were told it could take up to fifteen minutes so Shannon and I both went back onto the showroom floor. I checked out the luxury vehicles and salivated at their roomy interiors. I sat in one, flipped the visor and saw a mirror complete with a row of lights. I turned on the interior lighting and not just the roof dome lit up, but a strip of lights around the door as well. This baby was HOT!

The salesman came back into view, all smiles and holding a thumb up. He waved us back into his office. I was enjoying myself, sitting in the deep plush leather seat, my hands stroking the supple steering wheel. Shannon strongly gestured for me to get out and then followed the salesman. I still didn't feel like getting out until, through the plate glass window of the showroom, I saw my grimy Suzuki sitting out there amidst the gleaming new vehicles.

Ashamed, I beat a hasty retreat out of the stunning Mazda.

She may have been one beautiful babe but somehow, I almost felt like I was cheating on Suzi. *Don't worry, Su, you're still my one and only!*

Besides, you were paid off two years ago.

* * *

"Is someone sending you a message, Mom?" Shannon asked, pointing at my car.

I followed her finger to the passenger side of my car, a view I rarely see. Written into the dirt were the words 'Pig Pen' and 'Wash Me' and 'Kill Me Now'. The spray-painted word SEEK could barely be seen under all the dust.

I blanched. I spent the previous day completely cleaning out the interior of my car. I'd circled it twenty times and did not see those words, though I thought a dozen times about getting a car wash soon. This morning, I did a Madonna show at eight a.m. One of those 'grams where Mom thinks it's funny to have the performer wake up the victim, get his birthday off to a roaring start. Meanwhile, we both know he has morning breath and has to take a leak and wishes he looked more presentable.

I had parked in a wealthy residential area; surely nothing would have happened in those 15 minutes. My Marilyn was to a glass blower who lived in a farmhouse in Fergus. Not another soul but him and his two daughters. Basically, I was with my car the whole time. I saw no one! When...where...could this have been done?

Then that giggle came back to me. Some hooligans, probably teenage pranksters, had written this while I slept in the baseball park. I'm positive they saw me snoring there and still decided to be mischievous. I commend them though for not using a paint can to convey their message, as well as not murdering me.

"It'll be clean for your graduation," I managed to squeak out.

"You should see Jody in his brother's tux!" Shannon

exclaimed. "Talk about handsome!"

Blanching became my new tic. "Oh, shit, I totally forgot about that!" Shannon gave me a questioning look. "Your dress? You're gonna need a dress for grad!"

"Oh, don't worry about that," she dismissed it.

"No, you need a dress," I decided. "I didn't get you one for prom so I should get you a new one for graduation. Do you have time to go shopping now?"

"I don't need a new dress," Shannon stated. "You only wear it once and most of the time, you're wearing your grad gown over it. Waste of money."

Money. I was so tired of everything boiling down to money. For once I just wanted to throw caution to the wind and open up my purse strings. "I don't care. You deserve a new dress. Let's go shopping."

"Sorry, Mom, I can't. I'm almost late for work as it is," Shannon said, looking at her watch. "But I do appreciate the offer. Have no fear, I'll be okay. I'm borrowing a dress and I'll return it just as soon as grad is over."

For a second high-school event requiring copious amounts of spending, Shannon denied me. I drove to the Esso station located down the road from Mini-Storage. They had a car wash and I ordered the deluxe treatment. I almost didn't recognize the new-and-improved Suzuki.

I knew where I was sleeping tonight, and every night until my five-day locker rental contract was over. In the safe and sound sanctum of the Mini-Storage compound, it was almost like living in a gated community!

* * *

Before heading 'home', I killed time at the gigantic Walmart up the road. I didn't actually need anything; I just wanted to get out of the heat. I entered hot, sticky and sweaty and immediately headed over to the frozen foods aisle. Maybe I spent an hour or two checking out the T.V. dinners and various ice-cream products. In my flip-flops, tank top and sweat pants I'd cut down to shorts, I knew I couldn't be suspected of shoplifting. My car keys were clipped to my bra strap and I carried nothing else. I guess I wouldn't be suspected of purchasing anything either.

When Walmart announced they were closing at 10 p.m., I left feeling nice and chilled, like a good bottle of wine. Gee, I couldn't remember the last time I even had a sip of alcohol? It's not like I'm a lush but I do like the occasional drink now and then. But now, if I were to have a drink in the privacy of my home, I ran the chance of an open liquor charge.

As soon as I reached my car in the parking lot, I was back to feeling overly warm. I splurged and ran my air conditioning on the three-minute drive back to my storage locker. Arriving an hour before they completely locked their gate, I saw the place was a swarm of activity.

At first I parked in a corner lot, got out and went to my trunk. I had a case of water back there; not a usual purchase but these days, I was drinking two, three bottles an hour. I felt a rare moment of complete bliss, just marvelling at how easily I got to the water. No moving cartons or costumes out of the way – the case of water simply sat there, visible and accessible.

Half my stuff was in the storage locker. Why not all of it? At least until my contract was over. I knew I'd already decided to sleep here the next few days; now I was making this my home base.

Getting back into my car, I drove to the area of my locker and backed into a space. I had to re-arrange my storage bin to fit whatever was left in my car, but I managed to wedge everything in and force the door shut. Something slipped but I slammed the steel door quickly so it wouldn't completely fall out. A piece of whatever it was – something plastic looking – peeked through the seams of the locked vault. I'd deal with it later.

Glancing at my watch, I saw it was past 11 p.m. and now too late to make a run for the Esso station. I liked to do a good wash-up at night, if only to keep the flies off me. Never mind the luxury of using an actual commode, but I've discussed that ad nauseum. A door banged at the end of the hallway where my storage closet was located. I didn't know I had company.

A man emerged from a room, not even glancing at me as he zipped up his fly and fastened his belt. My eyes widened – oh my God, what was going on in that room?

Curiousity led me to quietly walk closer to that room. It was quiet at that end of the storage warehouse. I could see the door was ajar. Moving like a ninja, I got down low and peeked around the opening.

The shock that greeted me could not be contained. I whooped with glee and jumped high in the air. Then I did it again when I saw I could touch the ceiling of the hallway. A freaking, honest-to-goodness live washroom! Of course there was no bath or shower but the toilet and sink told me I'd be living large the next three days.

I skipped back down the hallway, past my locker and out the door. I stopped for a moment, caught by surprise at how shiny and clean my Suzuki Swift looked. A lone spotlight shone over the storage area, catching Suzi in all her glory, as if she were in a showroom at a car store. Empty of the bins and garbage, she looked good enough to purchase all over again.

I reached onto the floor of my passenger seat, the only spot designated for important stuff. I grabbed my toiletries bag and sped back to that wonderful room at the end of the hallway. Taking the longest sponge bath yet, I must have spent a good thirty minutes in there. Nobody pounded on the door, I had paper, and there was a mirror large enough that I could see my entire face at one time.

Tomorrow was a free day. I planned on spending it on myself, maybe getting a haircut, shopping for a graduation gift for

Shannon...oh, the list was endless. Mainly I just wanted to be seen driving around in a clean car.

* * *

Parked in the same place as the previous night, I was again woken up the same two gents in the salt (?) truck. They were as quiet as before but I still kept half-awake when I slept. By accident, when the driver jumped back into the truck, he hit the horn. A short beep emitted but his fellow worker came up to him and quietly gave him a whack in the head. The driver seemed to accept it as he started up the vehicle. Without a word, they drove off.

The elation of my washroom find had worn off. I must have had a bad sleep as all my bones ached. I reached for a bottle of water and noticed I had trouble swallowing, my throat was so sore. Oh no! Don't tell me I was getting sick! I finally had a social event to attend, one where I wasn't being paid, and there was no describing how much I wanted to go.

I blamed it on Walmart's frozen-food section. Perhaps I did stay too long in the store; my teeth had been chattering and I had to cover my breasts so my rock-hard erect nipples wouldn't embarrass me. And then to walk out of Walmart into 90-degree heat....

Today I had a big ME day planned and I had to get on with it. After using the storage facility's washroom, as well as half a roll of their toilet paper to blow my nose, I drove over to the Esso gas station. Fuelling up on gas and coffee, I spied the vacuums in the corner of the lot. That would be the final touch on beautifying Suzi.

Vacuuming took up all my energy. Even finding $1.33 in loose change did nothing to excite me. And as soon as I got the car started, the 'Check Engine' light came on. How was that for gratitude? I knew it had to be the oil; I kept saying I'd get it done.

What was the use of cleaning Suzi if she couldn't run? So I went to one of those quick-lube places and got an oil change. That took care of the Check Engine light.

I got to sit in the waiting room of the lube place, but all I did was fill it up with germs as I coughed and sneezed. My 30-minute oil change took 20 as they hustled me out of there. All I wanted to do was sleep, as I felt a headache coming on. I made a pit-stop at Rabba Foods, bought some oranges and dragged my ass back to the storage facility.

My cellphone rang and I swam through layers of sleep to answer it. Too late, missed call. Actually there were a couple missed calls from Shannon, as well as a couple from the dealership where we bought her new car. I looked at my watch and then tapped it. Surely I'd broken it because there was no way I'd slept all day in this sweatbox.

I resorted to my cellphone and saw my watch was accurate. I called Shannon back. "Hey, sorry, I missed your calls," I immediately said. "I'm not feeling great today...I just woke up from a huge nap."

"Oh, no! Can I bring you something?" she asked.

I thought of my medicine cabinet chock-a-block full of aspirin and cold and flu remedies. Back then I'd spend $20 on cough syrup; now I was relying on $2 worth of oranges to do the trick. "It's okay, I'm managing," I lied. "And I'll be at your grad tomorrow." I prayed. "So why'd you call?"

"The car place phoned me!" she said excitedly. "My car is ready!"

"Y...yay," I tried to sound gleeful but my throat croaked.

"I can pick it up tomorrow as long as you sign some kind of release form," she explained. "I so so SO wanted to drive it to grad!" There went my plans of transporting her, but I didn't really mind. I had been somewhat worried that I'd have to go to my old house to get her. Part of me knew that Ben would probably drive her anyways; now he wouldn't get to have the honour either. I'd just have to worry about seeing him at the graduation ceremony.

"OK, I guess I can do that," I said. "Oh_.but I have two shows tomorrow! Can I do it tonight?"

"As long as you get there before they close," she warned. "Jody is going to drive me over first thing in the morning and then I have to get ready for grad. Big day for me!"

I couldn't spoil this. Heaven knows, lately I wasn't doing much for my kid. This was important for her and I had to make every effort to make it happen. First I had to look presentable, which meant digging into the storage closet for respectable clothes.

Opening the door was difficult and the plastic thing sticking out turned out to be the tip of the Grim Reaper scythe. Now the end bent at an awkward angle, resembling some kind of giant dental pick. Getting to the suitcase with my regular clothing made me work up a hell of a sweat, as well as a voracious thirst.

Back at my car, I devoured two oranges and squeezed every ounce of liquid from two bottles of water. I went back into the storage warehouse and into the washroom with my bag of toiletries and my wrinkled summer dress. Looking in the mirror, I saw a lank mess of blonde hair. Even the pinned-back, tight-bun look couldn't hide the fact that it shone like frying oil.

My toiletries bag held hotel-sized bottles of shampoo and conditioner. I looked at the tiny sink, barely big enough to fit two hands. Glancing into the garbage can, I saw, amongst other debris, a large-sized Tim Horton's cup. I laughed, then had a coughing fit, as I thought how often Tim Horton's figured into my life.

Rinsing the cup out, I put one of the recycling rules into effect by re-using it. I thoroughly wet my hair, stood there sudsing it and then, holding my head above the sink, I rinsed it as thoroughly as I could. I used the same cup to try to take somewhat of a shower. I was making a terrible mess all over the floor and hoped nobody would be needing the washroom soon.

Feeling somewhat more refreshed, I went back to my car. There was a breeze passing between the windows that felt so soothing, I decided to just sit there a bit with my eyes closed. A brief respite from the non-stop heat.

My stomach grumbled and I thought, *How can that be? I just ate two oranges!* I opened my eyes and the first thing I noticed was that the sun was setting. I almost hit myself in the face as I brought my watch up. *Oh God, oh Jesus, what's wrong with me??? I mean, yeah, I know I'm getting sick but do I have to keep falling asleep?*

I was still in my dress, more wrinkly than before, and dispensed with make-up as I slammed the car into drive and sped out of my parking place. The gate to the exit had barely cleared Suzi's roof as I shot out of Mini-Storage. My foggy brain tried to remember the best route to get to the Mazda dealership as I popped a breath mint. There, now I'm presentable.

Mazda closed at 9 p.m. and I probably had six minutes to spare as I parked right in front of the doors, on the diagonal lines. I ran in, already grateful to find the front doors still unlocked. "Hi! I'm sorry I'm late! I have to sign some paper?" I yelled out to the general showroom, to nobody in particular.

Our salesman from Monday came out of his office. "Oh, hi!" he said. "I've been trying to call you."

"Yeah, sorry, but Shannon called me," I replied. "Her car is ready? I just have to sign some paper?"

"Come on in," he said. "It'll only take a minute."

He had the forms waiting on his desk. "I'm glad you made it," he smiled. "Shannon said she's coming in first thing tomorrow morning to pick it up."

I smiled back. "She wants to show it off, I guess. She says she wants to drive it to grad..." My face contorted. "GRAD! Oh no! No, no, no...." Because the salesman looked confused by my sudden emotional change, I felt I had to explain. "I was supposed to get her a present today! I have no time tomorrow..."

The sales guy looked around his office. "I wish I could help...I mean, we have Mazda baseball caps and t-shirts..."

"OK, here's what I'm going to do," I looked the salesman in the eye. "I want to give you a cheque that covers the first month of her payments. Is that okay?" Shannon would never accept money from me; in this manner, it was already a done deal.

"Perfectly fine," the salesman nodded his head. "Or you can pay it with a credit card. It's faster that way."

I hesitated. Using credit cards had become a thing of the past but I just wanted this one thing to go right. "Let's do that," I said, fishing it out of my wallet. Then I realized I should actually have something tangible to give Shannon. "You sell Mazda key chains?"

* * *

Graduation day! You'd think I was the one graduating. I wish I could say I was elated because I was proud of my daughter but the truth was – I was going out socially! Chances were high I'd run into acquaintances – parents of Shannon's fellow students, the ladies I'd walked with, teachers. I longed for the Maddy Magee of old, who could hold a conversation, be witty and charming. Now I just felt like the dumpy troll who lived under a bridge.

On a more positive note, I was feeling better! My nose was still running and I was not quite in form vocally but this singing-telegram performer was ready to go to work. First up was a nurse and as I got ready in the parking lot at Yorkdale Mall, I wrote the song for the manager of Black's Cameras.

The show went pretty good. I had to stop a couple times, have a couple good coughs, ensuring I left as many germs as you could find at a real hospital. The next show was for a retiring elementary-school principal and I was a clown for that. I thoroughly approved of their choice.

In the parking lot of the school, after all my make-up was on, I knew I'd better blow my nose. That mussed up my look a bit, but I had to rush in. I felt that gig went amazing; teachers laughing and following me as I led the way to the gymnasium where they were holding a fake assembly. It was actually a party and I was glad I was on time. I saw the principal looking at a speaker, who appeared to be talking jabberwocky nonsense when I made my appearance. With apparent relief, the speaker dramatically yelled "Surprise!" into the microphone.

Yup, felt pretty good about that show...until I got back into my car and looked at my face. As mentioned, the red nose had been smeared when I blew my nose, but what sickened me was that I should have checked the interior of my snout before I left my car. Or not have blown my nose at all. I could only hope they found the clown's boogers funny.

I raced back into town, back to my storage 'residence'. Time to get ready! I knew exactly what I would wear – that dress I'd packed away long ago, with the jewellery and the pumps. They hadn't even been taken out of the bag since I'd left. I pulled it out of the storage locker and headed over to my private washroom to try it on.

FUCK ME. The dress didn't fit! I knew it! I had been gaining weight! Where the zipper would glide up easily before, now I tugged and pulled to get it up. Having finally zipped it shut, I could barely breathe. Plus I had more impressive back cleavage that I had in the front.

I pulled the zipper down halfway. Oxygen returned to my lungs and the dress felt much better. I remembered the shawl and found a way to drape it, hiding the fact that my zipper was glaringly open and my bra was showing. Shades of tacky bride flitted through my head and I shook off the feeling that I was turning into my characters for real.

Hair and make-up were carefully dealt with. I didn't pack my curling iron or hair dryer, but I fluffed, back-combed, sprayed and pinned my rat's nest into a rather fetching version of bed-hair. I exited the storage facility, half expecting my parents to show up with their camera. Again I had to remind myself it wasn't my party, but who cared? Maddy Magee was going out on the town! Well, as far as my kid's high-school gymnasium, but check out the hot mama!

* * *

I drove to the school early, wanting a chance to speak to my daughter before the ceremonies began. By habit, I drove to the far corner of the parking lot. Once there, I remembered I should no longer feel ashamed of my ride; Suzi sparkled like a gem! I drove back to park closer to the school's entrance and had turned off my car when a couple teens walked by. One male pointed out the passenger side of my car and they both sniggered. It took me a second but I remembered I had been vandalized by that graffiti 'artist' and had yet to remove the word SEEK from my car. I returned to my original parking space. A monstrous weeping willow hid the offensive side of my car from onlookers.

I decided to join the burgeoning crowd as it was becoming impossible to spot Shannon. I did notice Jody drive in with both his parents sitting in the back and his younger brother in the front seat. My stomach churned at the thought I'd be seeing Shannon's other parent soon.

Jody parked their car and his family went inside. I saw Jody wave to a blonde beauty and then scurry over. I squinted my eyes as I watched him give her an overly friendly hug. Who was he being so touchy-feely with? Then my eyes popped when I saw it was my daughter.

I also ran over to her. "Shannon!" I yelled out, as she began to enter the building with her boyfriend. "Shannon, wait! It's me, your mother!"

Shannon turned and then squealed with the sound of pure

joy. Did she actually think I would miss her graduation? She ran over to me and we hugged and danced around as if we hadn't seen each other three days earlier.

I held her at arms' length. "Oh my God, I love your dress!" It was of sky-blue colour, with a rhinestone encrusted, form-fitting bodice and a skirt made of iridescent tassels. "I think I've seen it before, like maybe in a magazine or something."

"Maybe you saw it in a trunk in our garage?" she asked. "That's where I found it."

"You mean that's mine?" I asked. She nodded. "I was never that small," I declared.

"Yes, you were. It's the first costume I ever remember you wearing," she reminisced. "Your Baby Spice character?"

Baby Spice, a member of the Spice Girls, had been an integral part of my income when Shannon was just a toddler. I did telegrams for six-year-old girls, I did a sexier version of her for the 60-year-old men. For two years, she was a hot ticket. Then the girl band broke up and the work stopped soon after.

"I barely remember it," I said, admiring the bejewelled shoulder straps. "Did you get it altered? It fits you like a glove!"

"Nope," she shrugged. "Just pulled it out of the trunk and gave it a delicate wash in the machine."

"Oh, here, before I forget!" I said, passing her a small gift box. Inside was the Mazda keychain, along with the 'Paid in Full' statement for her first month's car payment. I looked around and then spoke in a ladylike voice. "I imagine your father is already inside?"

With a look of regret, she said, "No, he's not coming. But you're sitting with Jody's folks. You'll have company."

"Shannon, I can't understand Jody's parents. I've known them how many years? It's agony trying to talk to them." Then I got to the point. "And you're telling me your father is not coming to your graduation?"

"He figures you two will start up a fight," she acknowledged.

I snorted in disbelief. "But he did tell me to pass on a message," Shannon added. "'Get me my money.'"

"Oh, piss on him!" I almost shouted. "So there's nobody representing the Magee side of the family then?"

She uncharacteristically hemmed and hawed until, "Well...I thought I should invite somebody..."

At that moment, Shannon's best fried MiMi came running up. She grabbed my daughter's arm and shouted, "Let's go! Everybody's taking photos in the library!"

Shannon looked around. "Where's Jody?"

"I saw him go in already," MiMi kept tugging at Shannon. "Let's go! They're asking where you are. And I didn't spend two hundred bucks on my hair and make-up to miss photos!"

Shannon gave me an apologetic look. "I'll see you after the ceremonies, okay, Mom?"

We reached out for one more impulsive hug. I whispered into her ear. "You look so beautiful, Shannon! How much did you spend!?"

She stepped back, gave the skirt a sexy little swish and in a convincing British accent, said "Most of it was spent on the dress." She blew me a kiss as she ran off. I 'caught it' and pretended to put it in my purse. It's still there.

* * *

The Garcias spotted me first. I could hear a strange word being shouted. "Olamadee! Olamadee!" It was urgent enough to make me search out the caller of that word. I spotted Ernesto, Jody's father, wildly waving, and then realized he was yelling, "Hello, Maddy!" but in Spanish. I dreaded the next two hours plus. The only thing that might save the evening was seeing who the other recipient of Shannon's two-guests-allowed invite was.

I waded over some knees to get to my seat. Ernesto, in jackhammer style, shook my hand for thirty seconds. My wrist was left feeling sore. I was glad Carlotta's handshake was more of the 'just touch the fingertips' variety. I looked at them and wondered how to start a conversation we could all carry.

I fanned myself. "Hot in here," I tried. Ernesto nodded but Carlotta looked confused.

"Es tu habitol du fille Shannon?" Carlotta asked.

The only word I could understand wasn't even a word; it was a name. I frowned and said, "Por favor, come again?"

"Mi cassia es Shannon cassia," Ernesto tried to help. My limited knowledge of Spanish translated that to mean 'his house is Shannon's house'. In a split second, I guessed that Shannon had been spending a lot of time at her boyfriend's house. They probably knew the whole story from Jody. What could I say but "Gracias"?

A voice rang out loud and clear, causing me to cringe. "Well, well, here you are! The Queen of Sheba!" I glanced up and saw my mother-in-law Phyllis coming down the stairs. Of all people Shannon could invite, why her grandmother!? It was true that Phyliss and Shannon had a different dynamic that Phyllis and I had going. They got along, they enjoyed shopping together, Shannon was a bridesmaid at two of her weddings...

I made introductions, not caring how English I sounded. "Ernesto, Carolotta, this is Shannon's grandmother, Phyllis Colarucci..."

Phyliss interrupted me. "Soon to be Mrs. Jagarsumthum." I paused the intros. Not because Phyllis getting divorced and often remarrying weeks later was any surprise, just that she was going out of her comfort level with the future groom's nationality. She jeered back at me. "Maybe if you would keep in touch with your own husband sometimes..."

As we waited for the ceremonies to begin, I controlled an urge to start a public fight with Phyllis. Every remark she made to me had a double meaning, or was flat out a stab to the heart. "Maddy worked so much when Shannon was born, I had to step in and be the mother," she told the Garcias.

Horrified, I said, "It wasn't like that at all!"

Ernesto looked solemn. "Hablo uno bebe?"

OK, I know he said 'baby', but what else? Suddenly Phyliss leaned in and started yapping in Spanish to Ernesto and Carlotta. "Hey," I broke in. "Where did you learn Spanish?"

She gave me a disdainful look. "When I was married to Alonzo," she said. "June of '02 to June of '04."

I shook my head. "I can't keep up." I stood and said, plain and clear for all English people to understand. "You know what? Let's change seats. Phyllis, you can talk to the Garcia's and I'll..." I smiled sweetly, "I'll not talk to anyone."

We exchanged seats. The Garcias seemed thrilled to be speaking their mother tongue. I sat next to an Asian couple. The mother had a walkie talkie and she was radioing Chinese directions to a couple of their children seated in other areas of the gymnasium. The father was fidgeting with a hi-tech video camera.

All in all, it wasn't that bad a ceremony. The Asian parents, with their info-gathering operation going ahead with military precision, were quite entertaining. The object of their mission was the eldest son, who garnered about a third of all the awards being handed out that night.

My pride and joy won an award, as I knew she would. When her name was called and Shannon confidently strode up to the podium, I wanted to whoop and holler. Thankfully I reined myself in. Phyllis, on the other hand, yelled out, "That's my girl!" A bunch of people turned to look at the big mouth.

It wasn't me. I was the respectable lady sitting down the aisle from her.

* * *

In the throng of people filling the hallways after the ceremony, I searched for my daughter. Phyllis and the Garcias followed behind me. I spotted Shannon and Jody near the exit.

Carlotta grabbed her son and sobbed. She was so proud; every day of high school had been a trial for that family, yet Jody stuck through it. Even Ernesto, whom Jody claimed couldn't get a handle on the whole transgender business, seemed on the verge of tears as he shook his child's hand.

The touching-yet-awkward moment was broken when Phyllis screeched, "Wait 'til you see what I got you, Shannon!" She thrust an envelope into her hands. "Open it now!"

With a bemused smile, she slit the envelope open and pulled out a card. Only I, who knew her best, could tell her gratitude was a bit forced. "Oh, wow!" she said. "A season's pass to Wild Water Kingdom!" I knew, with her work schedule and her usual summer studies, that she'd have little time to go swimming. Plus the pass was good for only one person.

Phyllis nodded smugly. "I remember how much you loved that place when I had to look after you all those summers. It's from your father and I."

"I'll put it to good use," Shannon promised.

"Well, I have to go," Phyllis said. "Jag is taking me to an Indian buffet tonight." She made classy barf actions and then turned to face the Garcias. In her broken-yet-workable Spanish, she bid a fond adieu to Jody's parents.

I didn't want to leave Shannon's side. It seemed I barely got to see her. I said hello to a few parents I recognized and wished their kids well in their futures. A boy walked by that Shannon used to tutor. I stopped him and asked if he'd take a couple photos of my daughter and I. All I had was my cellphone but that was perfect for my needs. A new screensaver to replace the old photo of my house.

The kids mentioned there was an after-grad party they were going to attend. The Garcias and I walked out together, after I gave Shannon one final hug. "So, keep in touch, okay?"

"I'll call you tomorrow," she replied.

Slowly, feeling a little bummed out, I walked back to my car. I was about to start it up when I realized I had nowhere to rush to. I could drive to the storage lot and sit there in my finery looking pretty, or I could do that where people might actually see me. I felt a little like crying; it all seemed so anticlimactic.

Most of the parents had left the parking lot. The noise level suddenly swelled as perhaps fifty students exited at the same time. The party had already started. I could hear graduates yelling, "Can somebody give me a lift to the party?" and "Who's buying the beer?" and "Who's old enough to get liquor?"

Shannon and Jody broke away from the crowd and walked over to her new Mazda. The car started up and was about to exit the parking lot when I saw it do an impressive reverse, all the way to where I was parked. Shannon, obviously enjoying her air conditioning, rolled down her window.

"Mom, what are you still doing here?" she asked.

"I dunno," I mumbled. "I'm all dressed up...and nowhere to go."

Ever so polite, Shannon said, "I'd invite you to the grad party but it's all going to be kids our age. You might feel out of place."

I burst out laughing. "No, I don't want to go. You two go ahead, I'm okay. Just gonna sit here and do nothing but be so proud of you, Shannon." Again with the foolish tears threatening to spill.

Shannon said nothing, just gave me a fierce look. She rolled up her window, turned to Jody and they spoke. She started to drive off. What did I do? I was about to open my door and run after her when I saw she was merely angling her car to form a V-shape with mine. The Mazda was shut off and the couple emerged from the car.

I became alarmed. "No, no, no! You guys aren't staying here on my account. I said I'm fine! Go to your party!"

Shannon went to her trunk and pulled out a couple chairs.

"It's a Bring-Your-Own-Chair party," she explained. "Guess they didn't have enough chairs for the 500 kids expected to show up."

"Yeah, they won't miss us if we're a bit late," Jody added. "Besides, we don't see enough of you."

Shannon opened the camp chairs and apologized to Jody. "Sorry, hon, only two, you'll have to stand." Jody leaned against the new Mazda and Shannon gave out a wolf-whistle. "Jody, if you could see how sexy you look in your tux, standing there against my new car..."

He moved away, toward the open trunk of the car. "Control yourself, woman," he cautioned. "Parental unit in the vicinity." He came back with a bottle of wine, a corkscrew and two re-usable Starbucks coffee cups. "Why don't you two ladies enjoy a drink?" he suggested.

Shannon reached for the cups. "Why, a splendid idea, my kind sir!"

"Wait," I party-pooped, "aren't you driving, Shannon?"

"Just until I started celebrating," she said, raising her glass. "Jody is staying sober. It'll be his first chance to drive my car, when he takes us home tonight."

It took Jody a while to get the cork out of the wine bottle, but that was only because he was 18 years old and had little practice. I could have jumped in and opened it in a couple seconds, but I didn't want to spoil the moment. I could also have reminded them they were both underage still, not legally allowed to drink, but I left my motherhood medal behind as soon as that cork popped out of the bottle.

Shannon and I clicked our Starbucks cups together and then did the same to Jody's can of Dr. Pepper. Even though our chairs sat on asphalt, the general feeling was one of camping, enjoying a drink and camaraderie in the early evening hours. The wine, with a $10.95 price tag, seemed to be of the highest quality.

Jody looked over my ride. "What year is your car?" he asked.

"2004 Suzuki Swift," I said, then giggled. "Mississauga,

Ontario." Okay, the large cup of wine was already getting to me.

"It still looks pretty good," he noted.

"That's cuz I got her washed and oiled and vacuumed," I stated. "Only thing I'm worried about...ever since I got the oil change, for some reason, it seems like she wants to stall."

"Maybe they hit the idle?" he suggested. I stared at him dumbly. "Do you want me to take a look?"

"You know about cars?" I asked incredulously.

Shannon piped up. "He got top marks in auto shop," she said proudly. I could sense she was doubly proud of his achievement, since he wasn't actually a card-carrying member of the male race yet.

Again he walked back to the trunk of the Mazda as he took off his tuxedo jacket and rolled up his sleeves. "I got Shannon a tool kit for her car for graduation," he said, pulling it out. He looked over at his girlfriend. "Who knew it would come in so handy so soon, hey, babe?"

"I got Jody a year-long membership to Premier Fitness," she said. "Oh! And thank you for the key chain!"

"You're welcome," I replied, then waited for more. Nothing. "Did you see the paper that was also in the box?"

"I didn't really look at it," she admitted. "It's the receipt in case I want to return it, right? But I'm keeping it."

Bless your heart, my only offspring. She thinks I got her a simple keychain for her graduation gift, and she's happy as a lark. I explained the essence of the paper and how pitiful a gift it was.

Shannon was ever so grateful though. Then she giggled and said, "I don't want to sound mean, but if you want to talk about pitiful gifts..."

We burst into loud laughter as we both stated, "Wild Water Kingdom??"

Shannon ran to her car and returned with the season's pass. She handed it over to me. "You know I'm not going to use it. But maybe, seeing as how it's so hot...maybe you want it?"

The thought of lying in a wading pool like a beached whale held far more appeal than sitting in a sweltering car. Thank you, Phyllis!

I was pleasantly shocked when Jody got my car running smoothly. He put the tools away and came back to pick up the empty wine bottle. Shannon simply raised her glass at him. Jody returned to the trunk and brought out a second bottle of wine. As he lifted the corkscrew, I tried to stop him.

"No, you guys, that's for your party," I said.

"Mrs. Magee, if we take this to the party, a hundred kids will want some," Jody replied. "I'd rather see two beautiful women enjoying it." This time he opened the wine with ease.

"You did that much better this time," I commented.

"I hope so!" Jody retorted. "I'm going to bartenders' school; this is probably the first thing they want you to master." He held the bottle out to Shannon.

"I have to pee first," Shannon said.

"Actually, I do too," Jody admitted.

"Let's all pee in the great outdoors!" I shouted. Like it was a wild and crazy idea when in reality, it had become so humdrum.

Jody walked into the branches of the willow tree and even though I was starting to get pie-eyed, I swear he did it standing up. God bless technology. Shannon and I took opposite corners of my car. We didn't want to mess up the Mazda's tires.

Back in the chairs, I mentioned the university Shannon was attending in September. "So did you two manage to find schools in the same city like you planned?"

Jody came to stand between our camp seats and placed a hand on Shannon's shoulder. "Well, things change fast, you know," he began. "In September, my darling Shannon and I must go our separate ways."

I over-reacted, came close to turning into one of those crying drunks. Reaching over, I wrapped my arms around Jody's leg.

"Noooo!" I cried. "You two can't break up! You're both so good for each other! What happened?"

"Whoa, chill, Mrs. Magee," Jody said, stepping out of my embrace. "We're not breaking up. We're still good."

"Jody changed schools," Shannon explained. "He's staying in Toronto; there's a good bartending course at Ryerson College."

"But why not Waterloo?" I asked. "I was so happy you two would be together. It can be scary, being a new student at a big school..."

"I'll manage," Shannon said. I had no misgivings about that. She'd probably be president of something by her second semester. "And we'll still be seeing each other at least every two weeks."

"Basically," Jody butted in, "my doctors and my therapist are in Toronto. If I go to school in Waterloo, I can't make any of my weekday appointments. If I stay here, I can probably have my surgery by the time I'm 21."

"Oh, boy," I foolishly said. "I can't wait."

"I know the feeling," Jody replied.

The second bottle of wine was being drained quickly, mostly by me. I chided Shannon on not keeping up. "I still have to make shumwhat of a reshpectacle entrance at the party," she slurred. I knew she was nowhere near as drunk as I. "You, on the other hand, are going nowhere tonight. When we leave the party, we're going to do a drive-by and we better find your car right here, under this tree."

That meant no storage locker, but I didn't care. I was ready for beddy-bye right now, warmed by the setting sun, the wine, the love of my kid. She tucked me into my car seat, put my keys in the cup holder and pecked me on the cheek. "Sleep tight, call you tomorrow," she said.

I watched my Baby Spice sashay to the passenger side of the Mazda as Jody gladly hopped into the driver's seat. He rubbed his hands together before he started up Shannon's new car. I thought he'd do something to show off but he drove out of the school lot like he was driving the Pope-Mobile.

I recall waving goodbye before I pretty much passed out. The next morning I awoke with a wicked hangover. I was thirsty as hell and even though it was only about six in the morning, I could tell it was going to be another scorching June day. I spotted my keys in the cup holder and put them into the ignition.

It was Friday. I had to get all my stuff out of storage by noon. After that, nothing to do but sweat in my car all day. It was then I noticed a rose lying across my windshield.

Clarity rushed at me. Shannon had returned to check on me! Warm memories of the previous night flitted through my mind, and the belly laugh we had shared over Phyllis's ridiculous idea of a graduation gift.

I glanced into the second cup holder. The Wild Water Kingdom's season pass rested there. Opening my wallet, I carefully placed it where I'd be sure to find it.

Today, and every hot day I could manage, I'd be trading Suzi's car seat for a water slide. Hope was on the horizon.

Chapter Twelve

Just my luck to have a Marilyn telegram in Mississauga, my old stomping grounds. Let me tell you, Marilyn was not looking so fresh these days. I simply needed sleep...even four uninterrupted hours would be a godsend.

Instead, I lathered on the concealer, made sure to add the beauty mark and took extra time aligning my false eyelashes. If I could afford it, I'd invest in those fake mink eyelashes and have them lay it on thick. But they were costly and had to be redone every couple months. Sure, my Marilyn would look stunning, but for the Bag Lady?

The Bank of Montreal crowd loved me. I don't think the Indian manager even knew who Marilyn Monroe was; the Iraqi, Iranian and Pakistan staff also seemed confused by my identity. No matter. I flirted with Hardeep, referred to myself 'accidentally' as Marilyn Mohammed (Hardeep's last name), and gave that bank a show they won't forget.

As an aside, I recalled performing at the bank five years before. The person who had booked me today, the white bread assistant manager who assumed EVERYBODY must know who Marilyn Monroe is, hadn't worked there then; she had seen my act at her cousin's wedding. I simply told her I had performed here before; I didn't give her the details. Last time had been as a gorilla. However, upon entering and making my usual grunts and swinging my arms about, I was immediately set upon by a security guard. He informed me that masked people were not allowed in the bank. So in front of the birthday teller victim, I had to remove my mask and show my face to the cameras attached to the walls. Then, the illusion having been totally ruined, I put the mask back on and went on with the show.

Today I was rewarded with a ten-dollar tip. Not enough for lashes, but I decided lunch would be courtesy of the Bank of

Montreal. Next door to the mall where the bank was located was one of my favourite greasy spoons, the John Anderson restaurant. I was going to drive over and enjoy a nice artery-clogging meal inside a restaurant, and not in front of my steering wheel.

After a quick change in the car, adding a bra but noticing with dismay that I had worn polka-dot panties (and Marilyn's white white dress warranted strictly white white panties), some sweat pants and a t-shirt, I ambled up to the counter and surveyed the menu. So much to choose from, all so affordable! And that ten-buck tip enabled me to order one of my most desirable meals in the world – a steak sandwich combo. Large steak-cut fries, a chilly Diet Coke and a huge sandwich.

My deal with myself was not to be a pig. If I could make a meal stretch into two servings, I was saving money. I knew I couldn't eat this sandwich in one sitting anyhow, but I didn't care for cold fries. So I gobbled those up quickly and then savoured half of the fried-onion laden sandwich. The other half was wrapped up in foil and placed back into the Styrofoam container. The two sips of Coke weren't worth saving, so I chucked that into the trash.

Since I was in the city where I'd once resided, I decided to sneak a drive-by of that beautiful home I'd once lived. I planned on driving by quickly, horrified I might be caught in the act. Once I got within view of the old homestead though, I almost braked to a complete stop. What had happened to my house??!!

The grass was at least knee-high in the front yard. The screen door seemed to be stuck open. The garbage cans were still on the street, three days after trash-day pickup. My peaceful front-porch swing was laden with beer cases and the whole building had a dejected feel of neglect. I curbed my desire to race in and start cleaning up. Instead, I drove up the street and pulled out my cellphone.

"Shannon!" I shrieked. "What the hell is going on with the house?"

Her voice came back to me in its usual calm manner. "Whaddaya mean? I was just there an hour ago."

"Well, for one thing...the yard!" I sputtered.

"You mean the grass? Dad said he'd cut it," Shannon replied.

"When? Next year?" I retorted. "And why can't you get Jody to cut it?"

There was a moment of silence. Then, "I wasn't going to say anything, but Jody and Dad aren't really getting along."

I sucked in my breath. Shannon and Jody had a tough time of it as it was. In their world, they were as near normal as could be (without 'going all the way'). In everybody else's eyes, they were 2016's version of *The Odd Couple*. When I was at home, Shannon had me to talk to about the bullying and snide remarks, or the progress being made. While I was away, I'd hoped Ben would continue the parental support. *Please, let it be over something minor...like Ben caught Jody playing his video game (thus perhaps destroying his 'rank'?).* "Was there an incident or was Dad just being his usual self?" I asked.

"Little of both." Shannon sighed. "Actually, it happened when Jody came over to mow the lawn. It was hot and he was wearing shorts, which you know he rarely does. Dad started teasing him about how hairy his legs are."

"Big deal. He's a guy. Guys have hairy legs," I stated.

"And Dad's legs are even hairier," Shannon declared. "But Jody's hair is so black, it really shows. Dad just wouldn't stop talking about it."

"And that was it?" I asked.

"And he's been making other weird comments and stuff," Shannon confessed. "A couple days after that, when Jody was leaving the house, I gave him a kiss goodbye, just a little peck. Dad saw and made these actions like he was going to throw up."

"Well, that was rude! But maybe it was just because it was you kissing," I suggested.

"Maybe...I don't know. But ever since then, Jody said he

doesn't feel comfortable around Dad," she lamented. "So I've been spending even more time away from home."

I moved on to another topic. "And what's with all the beer bottles on the front porch? That looks real classy."

"Oh yeah, that and the front door," Shannon snorted. "Don't think Dad has turned into a drunk, it's not like that. But I guess he had a little party on the weekend."

A stun gun would have had less effect on me. Shannon knew it and waited for me to speak. "Your...father...had a party?" I managed to get out. "In all our years of marriage, we maybe went out socially five times. I even attended the Magee family get-togethers without Mr. Magee. And you're saying he actually threw a party?"

"Oh, I don't think he planned to have a party!" she said in his defence. "But he went out to the bar and came home with a bunch of people on Saturday night. They got pretty rowdy...somebody broke the screen door...Mr. Gonzoli from across the street came over to complain about four in the morning..."

"Oh my God, you're gonna have the cops there! Were you home for this party?" I asked her. Somebody needed to chaperone.

"Yes, Mother, but I had to leave at 5:30. I have to be at Cora's by six to help open." She reminded me of her weekend job at Cora's Restaurant. Almost every waking hour was devoted to her many part-time jobs, all going to pay for her university education. Momma was too busy trying to pay for her freedom.

"So, were they all gone when you left?" I asked.

"Most of them were...the loud obnoxious ones anyway. There were maybe six people sitting around when I left," she said. I could tell something was being left out.

"People? What kind of people?"

"Just people. Not like bikers or the Klu Klux Klan, if that's what you're worried about."

"I'm not worried," I said. I don't know what I was. "But were there...uh...boy people as well as girl people?"

"Yeah, there were men and women at this party, if that's what you're getting at," she replied. "But when I got back later in the afternoon, they were all gone. Dad slept for a solid day after that."

"Well," I choked out. "I'm gonna let you go."

"Mom, wait!" she delayed me. "We have to meet up! You have important school papers to sign. Super important, they have to be signed in the next couple days! Don't forget, in four weeks I start school. In four years, I start my career!"

I took a deep breath to stop the roiling rage I felt brewing inside me. "I'll be in the area tomorrow. Do you have time for lunch?"

I could feel her brighten over the phone line, daughterly love being sent my way. "It's a date! Say 11:45, Gabriel's?" She chose my favourite restaurant as well as my preferred beat-the-lunchtime-rush meeting time.

I tried to send the same loving vibes back her way. "Great," I snapped out. "See you then." I pressed END and threw my phone onto the seat.

DAMN YOU, Ben! Now you've moved on to a social life? Fine, I guess it was to be expected. And you're having women over? Maybe you're sleeping with one, maybe not. For a certainty, he wasn't sleeping with me and never would again, so I guess moving on was his prerogative. Act social, have people over, be normal.

But what was my normal? Could I date? Get all gussied up in a Shell gas station, have to meet my date at a pre-arranged location so he couldn't see my car and afterwards? Could he come to my place? Uh...no. Any scenario just played out awkwardly.

Suddenly the idea of living in my car seemed ludicrous. Before, I justified it in so many ways. It was for the best...it was a temporary situation...it wasn't so bad...I was making it work...I was adapting...an answer would present itself soon... But now? It just all seemed so pathetic.

One of those big crying jags seemed to be in order. Either that or a big shopping spree. And seeing as how I was still $70,000 short of my goal, the tears would have to do. But not on my old street, with kids skateboarding by and dogs being walked and neighbours chitchatting across their immaculate lawns.

I knew I had a clown singing-telegram the next day, in the airport area. This was a fairly important gig – to the people booking the show and to my ethics. It had been booked a month before by a sick little girl's grandparents. The kid was flying to Houston, Texas to see a brain specialist. I was to meet them at the airport and do my foolish act; anything to make her forget, even for an instant, the scary surgery awaiting her.

So I headed in that direction. It was only twenty minutes away and I didn't have a lot of gas in Suzi Suzuki. But as I drove around, looking for a place to 'Park n' Cry', I berated my bad memory. In the last few years, all the airport hotels started to charge for parking in their lots. Unless I was staying there, which was a joke unto itself.

I found myself cruising down Silver Dart Drive and recalled taking Shannon there as a toddler. We would grab a coffee for me and a donut and juice for her, and park our car on Silver Dart Drive. From there we would watch the planes fly into the airport, so close you felt you could almost throw a baseball at it.

There were a few cars pulled to the side, probably doing the same thing I'd done years ago. I saw an SUV with 'Baby on Board' stickers and one car with a stroller folded into the front seat. I decided to pull over as well, a few cars back so nobody would stare at the overladen vehicle. I was sure the sounds of incoming planes would help drown out my sorrowful cries.

For the next two hours, I howled louder than a Boeing 707. At first I wept in anger at Ben, but then realized I wasn't mad at him. He was simply moving on with his life. So then I cried at my situation. I wasn't able to do anything but subsist moment to moment. I was in limbo...in a holding pattern...just living in my 2004 Suzuki Swift. Life wasn't fair and I felt like a total loser.

Of course, after a big cry, a big sleep was in order. Reduced to those hiccups that remind you of the pain yet feel so satisfying, I rearranged my car as best as I could so I could grab a nap. Perhaps I should cry more often, because I slept soundly for hours. The only reason I woke up was because of that stupid seatbelt. For the 9,340th time, I tried to squeeze it down and make for a level sleeping area, but it was of no use.

I sat up, buckled myself in and was about to start the car when a thought hit me. Where was I going? Until I showed signs of having to use a washroom, I may as well sit there and watch the planes come in.

Twilight was just settling in and hunger pangs filtered through to my brain. I realized it had been about eight hours since I last ate, which was that very tasty steak sandwich. And speaking of that, I still had half of it left on my passenger seat! It may be cold, but it was so fine at lunch that it was bound to still be delicious.

The truth was, the sandwich was dry and the cold fried onions had a slight addition of congealed fat to them. As I scraped off the onions, I watched the last remaining vehicle pull away from the roadside. They pulled a U-turn and of course had to stare at the lone occupant of the overstuffed car. I took a sip of my water to wash down the bite I had just taken.

The driver of the van stopped and rolled down his window. "You okay?" he called out. "I notice you been parked here awhile."

"I'm...I'm fine," I croaked out. My throat felt raspy from trying to swallow that last bite. I returned the water bottle to my lips and drained it.

"K, just thought I'd ask," the kindly man said. "You have a good night then."

I waved goodbye and rolled my window up. I looked at my

sandwich and debated finishing it. However, the GAME PLAN had to be adhered to! Save money every which way you can! That meant the remainder of the steak sandwich must be my next meal.

I didn't plan on it being my last meal.

With an air of resignation, I took a big bite. *Don't have to savour it, Maggie, it's just fuel for your body at this point.* I chewed, and chewed, maybe 200 times I chewed, before I finally forced myself to swallow it. I could feel the mushed-up meat and bun lurch down my throat, but it only made it to the halfway point before it chugged to a stop.

Oh, oh, I thought, as my throat started to try swallowing a few times by reflex. Nothing happened. On the contrary, it seemed to only help make it more stuck. I quickly reached for a bottle of water; I always had a bunch of waters in my car. But oh yeah, the car was such a mess, every time I wanted a fresh bottle, I'd have to move costumes or bags to find one. Of course none was handy.

OH, OH, I thought again. Funny how I could come up with nothing more interesting to say. Maybe a prayer to God, or a swear word.

Coughing it up didn't work. I swirled my head around quickly, hoping another plane-watcher had shown up. The entire length of Silver Dart Drive was empty. I briefly considered driving for help but at this point, my vision was blurred by bright white shooting stars. These weren't in the sky, they were right in front of my eyes.

For a moment, my being seemed to split into two. There was the physical being, who was being wracked by a choking fit. Poor pitiful Maggie, almost banging her head on the steering wheel as she tried to dislodge the meat that had set up camp in her throat.

Then there was the soul part, who was probably already packing its bags. *I'm a goner*, was the first thought to cross my mind. In a flash, I saw my coffin, and knew that Shannon had spared no expense. I wanted to thank her for that, because I knew

I'd be able to stretch out completely, no gas pedals or floor mats to stunt my sleep. Resting in peace never sounded so apt.

And though it's cliché, cliché is often the truth. The truth was that odd snippets seemed to microburst through what remained of my vision. I saw myself again with Shannon, on this very street, her eyes wide with the sight of the ferocious planes descending. The same look on her face going through a car wash. The time she slid into home base, winning the game. The loitering ticket cut in, followed by my mom's face looking sad. I didn't want her to look sad; she'd always been so proud of me!

I saw the last dog I owned. My house the first day I saw it. Shannon getting the award at her graduation. Her beau, Jody, caulking my tub. For some reason, Bruce Willis. My bank account statement, showing $31,233. My two best friends made a quick appearance, first laughing and then turning a disapproving look on me. Don't judge me, I wanted to say, but too late now.

Then Ben's image flew by, reversed and stayed frozen on the screen of my mind. And that's when I prayed to God. "Oh, God, don't let me die with his face being the last thing I see!"

All of this seemed to take a few minutes, but it was more likely seconds. And as Ben's usual unsatisfied look presented itself, I seemed to hear the one good piece of advice he always gave out. "Never panic." He could elaborate on various scenarios and go on and on about this topic, but it boiled down to one thing. When in trouble, panic will only get you into more trouble.

With that, body and soul reconnected. Taking a quick breath (impossible) to calm down, I surveyed my situation – pretty close to dead at this point. I almost decided to say, "Screw it, go back to panic mode." Instead, I threw open the car door and jumped outside.

The plane that was coming in for a landing roared its arrival. I'm quite positive the little heads I saw in the windows could see the weird sight below. A shabbily dressed woman, jumping up and down, ramming her hand down her throat....

"Give up," a voice whispered. "Accept it. We all gotta go sometime..." And besides, I was getting so tired of trying to take a breath and just hearing that awful squawk of a sound emit from my eroding voice box.

Then, as if she were standing right next to me, I heard Shannon's voice. "Mom, I NEED you to sign those university papers for me. It's important!"

OK, Shannon, for you, one last effort. The ol' college try, ha ha!

Another look around for anybody, but I was alone. *THINK!!! What to do with choking victims?? Uh...uh...you HEIMLICH MANEUVER them!* But how to do it alone? I feebly tried punching myself in the stomach but, already weak, my jabs had no effect.

I hung onto the open car door, ready to call it a day, my glazed eyes staring dumbly into the lit interior. *Fuck you, loitering ticket,* was my last thought. But I wanted to change it so I tried *Fuck you, Ben.* That didn't feel right though; I didn't want to leave this earth with hard feelings between us. The last of my vision rested on that hated seatbelt connector. Yes, a worthy last thought. *Fuck you, seatbelt connector, or whatever your name is!*

That connector seemed to defy me. The light from the little roof bulb seemed to shine directly on it. The connector stood up strong, tall and erect. Even in the throes of my death, that seatbelt contraption tormented me.

But wait...was it tormenting me or was it offering salvation? The word 'Heimlich' seemed to teletype itself in twinkly bluebirds when I blinked my eyes. Without even thinking about it, I reached down for the lever that lowers the front seat. The seatbelt connector became even more prominent.

I knew I had about six seconds left before my brain shut down. I closed my eyes, thought, *This is for you, Shannon,* and then, with the little breath I had left, I opened my eyes and whispered to the seatbelt connector, "You owe me."

With that, I threw myself down onto my nemesis.

* * *

You could tell the seatbelt connector and I had become quite intimate by this time. With deadly aim, I rocketed, free-fell you could say, right onto that connector and boy, did we connect. That thing spiked right into my solar plexus. The left side of my brain felt the intense pain (did it hit my spinal cord as well?) while the right side of my brain allowed me to absorb the end result. The meat, as well as spots of mashed-up bread and droplets of blood, shot out of my mouth, hit my still-unpacked Marilyn Monroe dress, ricocheted off that and came to rest in the rear cup holder.

There was no drama after this. I simply rolled onto my seat and gulped in a few breaths of life-enhancing Toronto smog. After a moment, I reached onto the passenger seat floor, picked up the container of Clorox Wipes and scrubbed the mess away as best as I could. Using the last wipe, I picked up the regurgitated steak and threw it out the window.

There was one thought in my mind. Marilyn needed cleaning. *That blood needs to come out immediately. She's my main source of income. I need a washing machine and I need it now.* And the one I had in mind washed whites just like the ads said it would. That machine was located in my house. MY house!

My mind briefly dwelled on the images I'd received. I had a momentary guilt trip when I realized, had I died, that poor little girl waiting for the clown at the airport would only have had another blow dealt her way. Then, just like a movie, I saw a flashback where I had to press rewind.

The bank statement. Little over $31,000. Not even close to the $100,000 that I'd been working towards for the past six months. And those six months? Felt more like six years that I'd been living in my car. I loved my little Suzuki but at this point, give me a toilet to scrub. Give me meals to cook, a daughter to coddle, a lawn to mow.

I started the car and for the hell of it, picked up the GPS. "OK, Miss USA," I told my current best friend. "Here's one you haven't tried, from the golden oldies list. It's called 'Home'." I smiled at the thought of seeing my daughter. Maybe I wouldn't be sleeping in my bed but the couch seemed a purely wonderful alternative. With a widening grin, I patted the dashboard of my car.

"I got money in the bank, my pet," I lovingly told my constant sidekick for the past half-year. "Enough to take care of that soul-sucking loitering ticket and plenty left over to get out of my marriage. I love you, sweet Suzi, but fuck this shit. I'm getting a lawyer."

At Roundfire we publish great stories. We lean towards the spiritual and thought-provoking. But whether it's literary or popular, a gentle tale or a pulsating thriller, the connecting theme in all Roundfire fiction titles is that once you pick them up you won't want to put them down.

By Lillian Hellman

Plays

THE CHILDREN'S HOUR (*1934*)

DAYS TO COME (*1936*)

THE LITTLE FOXES (*1939*)

WATCH ON THE RHINE (*1941*)

THE SEARCHING WIND (*1944*)

ANOTHER PART OF THE FOREST (*1947*)

MONTSERRAT (*An adaptation, 1950*)

THE AUTUMN GARDEN (*1951*)

THE LARK (*An adaptation, 1956*)

CANDIDE (*An operetta, 1957*)

TOYS IN THE ATTIC (*1960*)

MY MOTHER, MY FATHER AND ME (*An adaptation, 1963*)

THE COLLECTED PLAYS (*1972*)

Memoirs

AN UNFINISHED WOMAN (*1969*)

PENTIMENTO (*1973*)

Editor of

THE SELECTED LETTERS OF ANTON CHEKHOV (*1955*)

THE BIG KNOCKOVER: STORIES AND SHORT NOVELS
BY DASHIELL HAMMETT (*1966*)

PENTIMENTO

PENTIMENTO

A Book of Portraits

Lillian Hellman

A PLUME BOOK
NEW AMERICAN LIBRARY
TIMES MIRROR
NEW YORK AND SCARBOROUGH, ONTARIO

Portions of this book originally appeared in *The Atlantic, Esquire* and the *New York Review of Books*.

Library of Congress Catalog Card Number: 73-7747

This is an authorized reprint of a hardcover edition published by Little, Brown & Company, Inc. The hardcover edition was published simultaneously in Canada by Little, Brown & Company (Canada) Limited. First appeared in paperback as a Signet edition.

Ⓟ PLUME TRADEMARK REG. U.S. PAT. OFF. AND FOREIGN COUNTRIES
REGISTERED TRADEMARK—MARCA REGISTRADA
HECHO EN MANCHESTER, PA., U.S.A.

SIGNET, SIGNET CLASSICS, MENTOR, PLUME and MERIDIAN BOOKS are published *in the United States* by
The New American Library, Inc.,
1301 Avenue of the Americas, New York, New York 10019,
in Canada by The New American Library of Canada Limited,
81 Mack Avenue, Scarborough, 704, Ontario.

First Plume Printing, October, 1975

1 2 3 4 5 6 7 8 9

PRINTED IN THE UNITED STATES OF AMERICA

For Peter Feibleman

Contents

PENTIMENTO

OLD paint on canvas, as it ages, sometimes becomes transparent. When that happens it is possible, in some pictures, to see the original lines: a tree will show through a woman's dress, a child makes way for a dog, a large boat is no longer on an open sea. That is called pentimento because the painter "repented," changed his mind. Perhaps it would be as well to say that the old conception, replaced by a later choice, is a way of seeing and then seeing again.

That is all I mean about the people in this book. The paint has aged now and I wanted to see what was there for me once, what is there for me now.

BETHE

THE letter said, says now, in Gothic script, "Bethe will be sailing between November 3rd and November 6th, the Captain of the ship cannot be certain. Be assured, dear Bernard, that we have full trust in intentions you have been kind enough to give to us. Her mother has put aside the pain in knowledge that nothing is here with us for her but a poor life. We have two letters from the Bowmans, Ernest and Carl Senior, assuring us that the arrangement will not be 'forced upon, etc.' and we know that yourself will make the final approval only if the young people should wish joinment. Bethe is well favored, as the sister you remember, some say even more. How strange the name New Orleans sounds to us, in the Southern States of America. As if our daughter is to travel to the lands of the Indies, we think it no less far. But nightly we

7

say prayer that we will live to cross the sea, all our families to meet again."

The letter is blurred and the pages are torn in the folds, but the name Bowman appears several times and it is still possible to make out a sentence in which the writer tells of having sold something to make the voyage possible.

Bethe for a short time lived in the modest house on Prytania Street, sleeping on a cot in the dining room, rising at five o'clock to carry it to the back porch, to be the first to heat the water, to make the coffee, to roll and bake the German breakfast rolls that nobody liked. Then, to save the carfare, she walked the long distance to the end of Canal Street, where she carried shoe box stacks back and forth all day for the German merchant who ran a mean store for sailors off the wharves.

Two or three months after she arrived — there had been, through those months, a few short visits to whichever lesser Bowman was not too busy or too bored — she was taken to one of the great Bowman houses and there, finally, was introduced to Styrie Bowman, the husband planned for her in the long-distance arrangement. Many years later, when people had given Styrie up for dead, I was told that a journalist wrote a book about the period. Bethe entered the book for a reason she did not know on the day she met Styrie. I do not know the book or the journalist's name, but there is a cutting from the book pasted in a family album. "This same Bethe Bruno Koshland married Styrie Bowman, who was cousin to the powerful New Orleans cotton merchants. Styrie came and went so often and so far that it is impossible to trace his years between the time he was twenty and forty. He was described by many as having powerful force with women and yet all reports say that he was about five feet six, one side of his face an earth brown, and of almost fiend-like distortion. But like many ugly men he had success with women. The last traces of him occur in the home of Mrs. Finch of Denver, who supported him in style."

I do not know who Mrs. Finch was. In fact, I never knew much about Styrie, except the bare accounts, told to me so many years later, of the marriage that was arranged between him and Bethe. The Bowmans had been looking for someone who could clean up Styrie, keep him out of the hands of gamblers — there were too many forged checks that bore their names — and nothing better could be found than sensible, handsome, hardworking Bethe, who was also a third cousin and therefore to be trusted.

Two thousand dollars was raised by the Bowmans, a decent sum in those days for young people to begin a life, and a job was found for Styrie in a Bowman warehouse in Monroe, Louisiana. I never heard anybody say what Bethe felt about Styrie or the marriage, but certainly Styrie's feelings were clear, because six months after the marriage he disappeared, and Bethe returned to New Orleans. I remember breakfast talk about all that, and somewhere in those years I knew that Bethe was acting as governess — or whatever word the Bowmans had learned from their fellow Northern industrialists to call those who cared for their children — to one of the less important — less important meant less money — Bowman families.

I know all that I have written here, or I know it the way I remember it, which, of course, may not be the whole truth, because my grandfather was the Bernard of the letter sent from Germany and it was with his family that Bethe slept in the dining room and rose early to make the coffee. I am, therefore, a distant cousin to the Bowmans, but the only time they have ever acknowledged me was once, in a London hotel, when the Queen Mother Bowman complained to the manager that I played a phonograph in the apartment above her head.

Bethe arrived in New Orleans long before I was born, long before my father was married, but my grandfather and my father were great letter writers, competitive in what was then called a "beautiful hand." My father had little style — perhaps because he was so busy with the formation of the alphabet into shaded curls — but my grandfather, who had a few undergraduate years at Heidelberg, made charming, original observations in his letters and in the children's copybooks he used to make bookkeeping-household entries on one side of the page, and comments and memories and family jokes on the facing page. What isn't blurred, or isn't in code, is good to read: his memories of the Civil War — he became a quartermaster general of the Confederate Army in Florida, a job that pleased him because of its safety — oddly phrased comments on New Orleans, his children, his friends, his self-mocking comic attempts to become as rich as his cousins, the Bowmans. Many of these copybooks and letters — he evidently made a copy of every letter he wrote — were lost before I was born, but a surprising number of them remained by the time I first saw them, when I was sixteen, and I remember my pleasure in them, particularly the ingenious mathematical puzzles that he invented for himself and his friends.

That year, the year I was sixteen, Jenny, my father's sister, sold the boardinghouse she had owned for so many years and she and her sister Hannah moved to a small half-house that could not accommodate the massive furniture, the old family portraits, the music and the books of their long dead father, much of which had come so many years before from Germany. For a few days I made myself useful to my aunts, but then the debris of other lives, the broken stickpins and cameos and ostrich feathers and carefully wrapped pieces of exquisite embroidery, pleased me so much that I was allowed to carry them to the back porch and sit with them for days on end. This puzzled my aunts, who like all sensitive older people were convinced that youth had no interest in what it sprang from and so were careful not to bore the young with their own fancies or regrets. (I am now at the

same age myself and the interest of students in my
past has bewildered me and taken me too long to
understand.)

My father's family, more than most, I think, did not
speak of the past, although, if pressed, they had loving and funny stories of their mother and father. But
I never knew, for example, until that time of their
moving from one house to another that they had lost
a brother in a yellow fever epidemic twenty years before I was born. I think the three of them, my father
and my two aunts, had a true distaste for unhappi-
ness, and that was one of the reasons I found them so
attractive. In any case, it was on that porch, that six-
teenth year of my life, that I discovered my grandfather's letters and notebooks and asked if I could
have them for my own. Jenny and Hannah seemed
pleased about that and for weeks after interrupted
each other with amused, affectionate stories of my
grandfather's "culture," his "eccentricities." When I
returned to my mother and father in New York, I carried with me a valise with the letters and notebooks.

I suppose all women living together take on what
we think of as male and female roles, but my aunts
had made a rather puzzling mix-about. Jenny, who
was the prettier, the softer in face and manner, had
assumed a confidence she didn't have, and had taken
on, demanded, I think, the practical, less pleasant
duties. Hannah, who had once upon a time been more
intelligent than Jenny, had somewhere given over, and
although she held the official job, a very good one in

those days of underpaid ladies, of secretary to the president of a large corporation, it was Jenny who called the tunes for their life together. I don't think this change-about of roles ever fooled my father, or that he paid much attention to it, but then he had grown up with them and knew about whatever it was that happened to their lives.

And so it was Jenny who wrote before my visit of the following year, asking me to bring back the letters and the notebooks of my grandfather. That seemed to me odd, but I put it down to some kind of legality that grown people fussed with, and carried them back. Perhaps I told them, perhaps I didn't, I don't remember, that during the year I had them, I had copied out some of them for what I called my "writer's book," a collection of mishmash, the youthful beginnings of a girl who hoped to write, who knew that observation was necessary, but who didn't know what observation was. All I really remember was the return of the valise and my conviction that it would come back to me when my aunts died.

Jenny died twenty years later. Hannah, lonely, bewildered, uncomplaining, lived on for another seven years, and one of the pleasant memories of my life is a visit that Dashiell Hammett made with me to see her. She was waiting for me at the New Orleans airport. She had never met Hammett and I had not told her he was coming with me. I was nervous because I knew she had never, could never approve a relationship outside marriage. As I came toward her, old now,

13

the powerful body sagging, the strong face finally come into its own, outside the judgments of youth, the open, great smile faded as she realized that the tall figure behind me was Hammett and that she would finally have to face what she had heard about for many years.

The first day was a strain, but since Hammett was not a man to acknowledge such strains, the week's visit turned into a series of fine, gay dinners that worried Hannah at first by their extravagance, but came to please her when she realized that Hammett didn't even understand her protests. More important, all my father's family liked jokes, good or bad, and when Hammett, on the second day, told Hannah that all he had ever wanted in the world was a docile woman but, instead, had come out with me, the cost of the dinner at Galatoire's ceased to worry her, and she said that she, too, liked docile women in theory, but never liked them when she met them, and didn't he think they were often ninnies with oatmeal in the head. He said yes, he thought just that, but ninnies were easier women to be unfaithful to. She laughed at that and told me on our walk the next day that she thought Hammett was an intelligent man.

A year later I had a telephone call from a doctor I didn't know to say that Hannah was in the hospital. I went to New Orleans immediately to find a quiet, frightened old woman who had never been really sick in her life, and certainly never in a hospital. At the end of the week she seemed better and I made arrangements to go home, sure that she would recover.

(I have gone through my life sure that the people I love will recover, and if, in three cases, I have been wrong, at least I did them no harm and maybe curtained from them the front face of death.) I had, during that week, gone several times to her house to bring underwear or other things that Hannah needed in the hospital and I had seen the valise I had brought back so many years before. It was tied with the same cord I had put on it then, with the same red mark I had scratched on its side. It was standing in a closet next to a portrait of my grandfather and some old photographs, and I remembered that I had seen Jenny put it just there the day that I returned it.

But Hannah did not recover. She died a few days after I left New Orleans and I went back to give away the sad, proud, ugly things of her house. (She had left a will, giving me everything she had, more savings than I could have guessed from the deprived life she and Jenny had led.) Daisy, a Negro woman, who had come once a week for many years to clean the house for my aunts, brought her son and nephew, and as they hauled away the furniture to sell or keep or give away, we spoke about my aunts and what they would have liked me to keep for them. I decided to take a chocolate pot that had once belonged to my mother, my grandfather's portrait, family photographs, all the broken pieces of antique jewelry that had been piled in a tin box, a box of letters I had never seen before and, of course, the valise. But the valise was not to be found.

But I had seen it ten or twelve days before and

Daisy said she had seen it after that. A few hours later we found Hannah's door keys hidden in a flowerpot on the porch. Daisy said that was a habit of my aunts and it meant that somebody had been given the keys and told where to leave them when they were finished. Finished with what, Daisy asked me, but we both knew immediately that Hannah had given instructions to somebody to remove the valise. What friend, most of them too old or infirm to do such an errand? And why? Perhaps, I told myself, the last act of a private life. Or was it suspicion of me, a different breed, a writer, and therefore a stranger? But I had already seen the contents of the valise many years before and so that made no sense. On the plane going back to New York, thinking about it as the only alien, unfriendly act of Hannah's life, I remembered I had never read all that was there and when asked to return the valise I had told my aunts that and protested its return on that ground.

I don't know when in the next few years I came to believe that Bethe and Styrie and Mr. Arneggio had to do with the disappearance of the valise. When I thought about that, forcing myself into sleepless nights, knowing my memory is always best when I am tired, I pictured again old newspaper clippings and at least one long letter from Bethe in a German I couldn't read.

I am all out of order here — as most memories are — and even when I read my own childhood diaries, the notes about Bethe make no pattern, or they make a pattern in terms of years and seasons. But I cannot separate now what I heard described from what I saw or heard for myself.

I first remember Bethe, a tall, handsome woman in her late thirties, come to call on my aunts, always on a Sunday afternoon, carrying a large box of bad candy. Yes, her health was good, her small job was good, no, her coat was not too thin for the sharp damp of New Orleans winters, she had seen a good movie last Sunday and had a good Italian meal in a good Italian place for little money. I suppose it was the constant use of the word good, without a smile, that caused my mother, who was not to be predicted, to say to Bethe on one of the visits, "What a bitter life," and then leave the room with her hand over her eyes.

Bethe never stayed long on those occasional visits and would leave immediately when she was asked to eat supper with us, shaking everybody's hand and mumbling words that I often couldn't understand. Her accent was not German, but some strange, invented mixture as if she had taught herself English without ever hearing anybody speak it.

My aunts felt guilty about her, remembering their father's commitment, but my father would grow bored with their guilt and say that Bethe was a good-looking clod — he once said that she looked like him — and that he didn't believe Styrie's desertion had caused her anything more than a guttural sound in the throat. Jenny didn't like such talk, answering always that women were injured by the loss of husbands, no mat-

ter what stinkers, which is why she had never wanted
one, and Mr. Crespie, one of my aunt's boarders, a
former great lover of the town, would say that he had
never thought much of Styrie, God knows, but that
any man could be forgiven for leaving a German donkey like Bethe. I liked that kind of talk: I was coming
to the age when I wanted to know what attracted men
and what didn't; I would have liked to ask Bethe why
men thought she was an unattractive clod, a donkey,
when I thought her so handsome.

We were in New York when Bethe disappeared
from her job with the Bowmans, because I remember
Jenny telephoned my father to report it, and to ask
him what she should do. He said that if everybody
was lucky maybe Bethe had found a job in a nice
whorehouse, and I heard Jenny's cackling laugh at the
other end of the phone. But we were in New Orleans
when Styrie reappeared, came to inquire for Bethe at
my aunt's boardinghouse — I was miserable that I
had been out at the time — and two days later was
found beaten up somewhere along Bayou Sara. The
good side of his face, I was told by Carl Bowman,
Junior, older than I by a few years, wasn't good anymore, and the word Mafia came into Carl's talk, but
I had never heard it before and it therefore meant
nothing to me. I know Styrie stayed around New Orleans for a few months after that because Mr. Crespie
said he saw him with some people in fancy clothes at
a bar on Lake Pontchartrain. And then, suddenly, he
was in the hospital.

Something must have worried the Bowmans — they were well known for shrugging off people who did not succeed — because Styrie had a private room and a night watchman was moved from one of the family warehouses to stand guard outside the room. But on the second night the room was shot up by two men in doctors' coats. When it was all over, Styrie was found clinging to a fire escape with his right hand because his left hand was lying on the ground.

I was allowed to stay home that day from school, and toward night I heard that the Bowmans had found Bethe in "a strange neighborhood," but that she had refused to visit her husband, using more sounds than words, finally writing in German that a visit from her might bring him further harm.

Perhaps nobody understood or perhaps the Bowmans were so sure of Styrie's imminent death that they felt anything was worth a respectable farewell. The two elderly Bowman uncles who escorted Bethe to the hospital told my father that Bethe seemed to "change" as she stepped into Styrie's room, because she "demanded" to be left alone with him. They said she came out mumbling in her "low-class syllables," shook hands with them, and disappeared before the two old fellows could find out where she was to be found for the funeral.

But there wasn't to be any funeral because that night the fevered, amputated Styrie disappeared from the hospital — the night watchman from the Bowman warehouse had a doped glass of Coca-Cola in his hand

19

when they brought him around — and appears only once again, ten or twelve years later, in a letter from Mrs. Finch of Denver, reporting his death to Ernest, president of all the Bowmans, and asking for a memento or a photograph to remember him by. I know that caused a good deal of laughter in our house but Carl Bowman, Junior, my friend, said it caused anger in his.

It was a few years after Styrie's disappearance from the hospital — I was about thirteen, I think — that I was sent to Enrico's in the Wop section near Esplanade to buy oyster loaves for my aunts and me because on Sunday nights no dinner was served in the boardinghouse. I always looked forward to these suppers with my aunts, doors closed, jokes flying, Jenny singing after supper in a pleasant voice, regretting the opera that didn't come to town anymore, imitating her old music teachers.

I had chosen to go early for my walk on that pleasant spring night and have a good look at all the foreigners of the section around Enrico's. It was a conviction of my girlhood that only foreigners were interesting, had the only secrets, the only answers. A movie theatre — even now I can see the poster of Theda Bara, although I have no memory of the picture — was breaking between shows as I paused to examine Miss Bara's face, deciding to come back the next day for the movie. Then I saw Bethe. I started to call her name, never finished the sound, because she was with two men, a large, heavy man, and a young boy of about fifteen. When I did call her name, they were crossing the street and could not have heard me. I began to run toward them, but three oyster loaves, or the running time, or some warning, slowed me down and I came to follow so far behind that when they were a block ahead of me I lost them as they disappeared into a corner store. I took a streetcar home.

I don't know why I didn't tell my aunts that I had seen Bethe, but the next day I decided to skip school. I did this so often that my teachers, puzzled, in any case, by a girl who was shuttled between a school in New York for half the year and a New Orleans school for the other half, had ceased to care whether I showed up. I went immediately to the corner store. I walked around it for a long time until I saw two children go in. I followed them, having stopped to examine the window, full of sausages and cheese, canned goods and cheap candy boxes, and came into an empty store that had only two sausages hanging from the ceiling and one sparse shelf of canned stuff. And the children were not in the store. I waited for a long time and then tried a few soft hellos. When nobody came, I went out the door, rang a bell on the outside, and went back in to face the young boy I had seen in front of the movie.

I said, "I'd like a can of sardines, please."

When there was no answer, I said, "I like Italian sardines best. My father doesn't, he only likes the French ones. How much are they, please?"

The boy said, without accent, "We don't speak English here."

I said, knowing that many people in New Orleans liked only to speak the patois, *"Excusez-moi. Les sardines. Combien pour la boîte de sardines?"*

The boy said, "We have no cans of sardines."

"Yes, you have, I see them. Do you know my cousin Bethe?"

There was a sudden sound behind the door, and voices. The boy said, "Go, please, go out."

"That's not a nice way to talk. I wanted only to say hello to my cousin Bethe —— " and stopped because I heard a man's voice; and then Bethe appeared in the door, turned to look at somebody I couldn't see, put up her hand, and shook her head at the young boy.

I said, "Good morning, Bethe, I'm —— "

She said, very loudly, "How you find me here, *Liebchen?*"

"I saw you at the movies yesterday and I just wanted to say hello."

"Your family send you to this place?"

"No, no. I didn't tell them I saw you. I'm skipping school today, and I'd catch hell if they knew. What's the matter, Bethe, have I done wrong, are you mad with me?"

She smiled, shook her head, and turned to whoever was behind the door. She said something in a language I didn't know about and was answered. She listened carefully to the man's voice and said to me,

22

"No longer am I German. No longer the Bowmans. Now I am woman and woman does not need help."

She was smiling and I realized I'd never seen her smile before, never before heard her use so many words. But, more important to me, something was happening that I didn't understand. Years later I knew I had felt jealous that moment of that day, and whenever I have been jealous something goes wrong with my face. I guess it was going wrong then, because she said, "Do not sadden, *Liebchen*," and took my hand. She called out something cheerful to the man behind the door and we went for a walk.

We walked a long way, down toward the river, into streets and alleys I had never seen before. I don't remember her asking questions, but I told her about the books I was reading, Dickens and Balzac, about my beloved friend Julia in New York, and a joke about my mother's Uncle Jake and his money, and how bad it was to live without my old nurse Sophronia. As we waited for the streetcar that would take me home, I said, "Please, Bethe. I will never tell my family. I promise. I didn't come to see you for any reason at all except just coming."

But the words fell away and I knew that wasn't the truth. I was on my religious truth kick, having sworn on the steps of St. Louis Cathedral, and then in front of Temple Beth Israel, that I would never again in all my life tell a lie under threat of guillotine or torture. (God help all children as they move into a time of life they do not understand and must struggle

through with precepts they have picked from the garbage cans of older people, clinging with the passion of
the lost to odds and ends that will mess them up for all
time, or hating the trash so much they will waste their
future on the hatred.) And so sitting on that bench
with Bethe waiting for a streetcar, I went into an incoherent out-loud communication with myself, a habit
people complain about to this day, trying to tell her
what was the truth in what I had just said and what
wasn't. When I grew tired, she sighed and said that
she had not had much schooling in Germany, found
it hard to speak and understand English, but was doing better in Italian. I said I would give her English
lessons if she would teach me German or Italian and
Bethe said she would inquire if that would be allowed.

I have no memory of when we saw each other again
because the next meeting is merged with the others
that followed, that year and the three or four years
before she disappeared once more. I think in those
years I saw her eight or nine times, but nothing now
is clear to me except a few sharp pictures and sounds:
I know that I told her about the Druids and that I gave
her my copy of *Bleak House* and that she returned it,
shaking her head; she brought me a photograph of her
father and mother, and I know that only because I
still have it; once we went to the movies and a man behind us touched her shoulder and she pressed his
hand; I brought along my English grammar and tried,
one day in Audubon Park, to explain the pluperfect

as she stared at me, solemn, struggling, and I touched the beautiful, heavy auburn hair to console her and to apologize. I know that led to sad, sympathetic talk about my hair, blonde and shameless straight in a time when it was fashionable to have curls. And one Sunday, when I went to the corner store, she rolled my hair in wet toilet paper rolls and put a scarf around my head, saying that would do it, and after we had gone to sit in a Catholic church where the priest near the poor box seemed to know her, and we had not spoken for a long time, she unwrapped my curlers, and as the hair came from the curlers as loose and dank as always, she kissed me. It was not a good thing to do. I disliked Bethe for thinking I was "unattractive," a word of my generation that meant you wouldn't ever marry. My friend Julia, in our New York school group of four strangely assorted girls, was too rich to think about marriage and I envied her. I was impractical: I wanted to marry a poet. One of us did marry a young poet but he killed himself a few months after the marriage over the body of his male lover.

On another Sunday morning I went to the store to tell Bethe that we would be leaving for New York in a few days. The young boy who always answered the bell said Bethe was in church and so I went looking for her. She was sitting with a tall, bald-headed man so dark of skin I thought he was a Negro. Something kept me from them and I turned to leave. But Bethe saw me. She said something to the man, he answered, rose, and quickly moved ahead of her. She took my hand and we stood outside in the sun, waiting, I think, for the man to disappear.

She was trying to say something. Whenever she was ready to talk, she moved her lips as if rehearsing the words, and now I saw that what she was going to say she didn't want to say.

"Do not again come to church here, *Liebchen.*"

"I'm sorry."

"You are not Catholic. Some do not like it so, your coming."

"But you are not Catholic, either."

"I am. I become. I believe now God, Father, Holy Ghost."

I was accustomed to my mother's religiosity, a woman seeking and believing that salvation lay in the God of any church. My mother, therefore, had no church, calling in at many; but now, with Bethe, I recognized the assertive tone of the uncommitted because I had so long heard the tone of the committed.

In those days I said whatever came into my head, in any manner that my head formed the idea and the words. (It is, indeed, strange to write of your own past. "In those days" I have written, and will leave here, but I am not at all sure that those days have been changed by time. All my life I believed in the changes I could, and sometimes did, make in a nature I so often didn't like, but now it seems to me that time made alterations and mutations rather than true reforms; and so I am left with so much of the past that I have no right to think it very different from the present.)

I said to Bethe before I began to cry, "You lie because a man tells you to."

She stared at me, walked ahead of me, motioned to me to follow. We went back to the corner store and she disappeared into the back room and reappeared immediately to ask me if I would like to have a good Italian lunch in a good Italian restaurant.

I could now, I did a few years ago, walk to that restaurant; I could make a map of the tables and the faces that were there that Sunday, so long ago. Freud said that people could not remember smells, they could only be reminded of them, but I still believe I remember the odor of boiling salt water, the close smell of old wine stains. I had never been in such a place. Somewhere I knew I was on the edge of acquisition, a state of nervousness which often caused me to move my hands and wrists as if I were entering into a fit.

Bethe asked me what I wanted to eat, I shook my head, she ordered in Italian from a thin old lady who seemed to know her. We had a heavy sauce poured over something I could not identify and did not like. (The food in our house was good: at one end of the serving table there was always the New Orleans cooking of my father's childhood and, at the other, the Negro backwoods stuff of my mother's Alabama black-earth land. Food in other places seemed inferior.) This Italian food was a mess.

I don't know how long it took me to search each face in the restaurant with the eagerness the young have for strangers in strange places, nor how long it took me to recognize the man who had been in church with Bethe. He was sitting alone at a table, staring at a wall, as if to keep his face from us. I asked Bethe for a glass of water and found her staring at the man, her lips compressed as if to hold the mouth from doing something else, her shoulders rigid against the chair. The man turned from the wall, the eyes dropped to the table, and then the head went up suddenly and stared at Bethe until the lips took on the look of her lips and the shoulders went back against the chair with the same sharp intake of muscles. Before any gesture was made, I knew I was seeing what I had never seen before and, since like most only children, all that I saw related to me, I felt a sharp pain as if I were alone in the world and always would be. As she raised her hand to her mouth and then turned the palm toward him, I pushed the heavy paste stuff in front of me so far across the table that it turned and was on the tablecloth. She did not see what I had done because she was waiting for him as he rose from his chair. She went to meet him. When they reached each other, his hand went down her arm and she closed her eyes. As I ran out of the restaurant, I saw her go back to our table.

Hannah wrote to us in New York a few weeks later saying that Bethe had telephoned twice to ask for me, and wasn't that odd? My father wanted to know why

I thought Bethe had asked for *me*, but I had learned to smile at such questions and my father had learned that what had been childish bucking was, if pushed, turning into sharp, unpleasant stubbornness. We had had an uncomfortable winter; I was getting bad marks in school when, all my life, I had been given good ones; I was locking the door of my room and sometimes refusing to come out for meals; I was disappearing at odd hours, and questions about that were not answered. I had run away from home for a day and a night and was, as spring came, refusing to go back to the girls' camp where I had spent so many summers. And late one night I had tried to climb up ten fire escapes into my room to avoid my parents' questions on why I had cuts on my face. I didn't climb more than three fire escapes before the apartment house was in an uproar.

I did send Bethe a Christmas card, but I didn't see her on our next winter visit to New Orleans. It was to be the last regular visit we ever made. It was finally obvious to my parents that I couldn't be dragged back and forth from a bad school in New Orleans to a good school in New York: I was getting too old for such adjustments. I had, on that last visit, gone immediately to the corner store, but I did not ring the bell, telling myself I would come the next day. But I did not go back again.

I have very little memory of that winter in New Orleans or the summer in Biloxi, Mississippi. I know that I watched every movement that Carl Bowman, Junior, made as he dove off the pier, or pitched in the baseball game, or walked down our block, and one night I was wracked with gagging, the emotion was so great, as he put his arm around me. I must have thought about Bethe, because in my "writer's book" for that period I practiced a code based on her name, but now, looking at the book, I can't understand the code.

The last week of our visit — we had returned to New Orleans from Biloxi — we were sitting around Jenny's dining room table, her boarders having gone their after-dinner way, in the family hour that I always liked. My father was reading the paper, and when he made a sound in his throat I saw Jenny nudge Hannah. Hannah nodded, Jenny put down her sewing, Hannah closed her book, and they watched my father.

He said, "Well the boys are shooting it up again. Have you seen her?"

Jenny said, "No."

"Who?" asked my mother.

"Stay away from her," my father said to Jenny, "do you hear me?"

"Stay away from whom?" said my mother. "What are you talking about?"

My father turned his chair toward Hannah. "Stay away from her, I tell you. These boys are nothing to fool around with."

My mother's voice, soft, rose now to high. "It's always been like this."

Hannah, who liked my mother, whispered, "Now, Julia, he will tell you — "

But I was trying hard to listen to my father and Jenny, knowing from long experience that they would have the interesting things to say, the opinions by which the other two would abide. Jenny had said something I missed, was saying now, "Not for two years, maybe more, although one day I saw her in a car, a *car*, an automobile, I mean, and I hurried over — "

"Don't do that again," said my father. "Don't hurry over. If she comes here, say you're sorry, or whatever you can say that will curb your curiosity."

"Mind your business," Jenny laughed.

"I don't care who she sleeps with," said my father, "nor how many. I care that this one is a danger and you're not to go near her with any excuses to me later on."

"It is my belief," said Jenny, "that Hannah and I earn our own living — "

"Oh, shut up that stuff," said my father, "and be serious. These boys are killers."

"Killers," said my mother. "It's always been like this. You never answer me, I'm never told the secrets."

"O.K.," said my father, "you have relatives who are killers."

"Whatever you think of them," said my mother, "my family are *not* killers and even you have never said that in all the years."

"Oh, Julia," said Hannah, "you always let him tease you. You always do."

"What a sucker," said Jenny.

"Don't interfere between man and wife," my father said. "What is it you want to know, Julia?"

"My relatives are not killers and you ought not to say so in front of our child."

My father turned to me. "Your mother's family are not killers of white people. Remember that and be proud. They never do more than beat up niggers who can't pay fifty percent interest on the cotton crop and that's how they got rich."

"The child has no respect now," said my mother, "for my family."

"I didn't say *your* family were killers. I said you were now *related* to killers."

"Oh, God," said Jenny to my mother, "he means us, *our* cousin, Bethe."

"In a proper marriage," said my father, "the blood of one house merges with the blood of the other, or have I misunderstood the marriage vows?"

"You've misunderstood them when you wanted to," said Jenny, and Hannah rose nervously and puttered about. Then my father said something to Jenny in German and I couldn't understand much of it, although I could have managed more if my mother hadn't kept on saying, "Please translate for me," and "That isn't nice. You know I can't understand," and, "Very well, ignore me," until my father said to her, "Bethe's common-law husband, if that's the word," and Jenny said, *"Schweigen vor dem Kind,"* and everybody was silent.

I said, "I will go to bed now so you won't have to

Schweigen vor dem Kind and I've known what that's meant since I was three years old."

"You're smart," Jenny said, "but if you were smarter you wouldn't have told us that."

An hour later, when all the lights were out, I came down to the dining room and found the newspaper. There was a long story about the beating up of some men with Italian names because they were running bootleg liquor, and the headline included the name Arneggio and said he and his brother were being sought by the police in a suspected gang warfare.

At breakfast the next morning I said to my father, "Arneggio is the man in the corner store. You ought to help Bethe."

My father waited a long time, twice put up his hand to silence Jenny. "What corner store? What are you talking about?"

I had made a mistake and I was angry with myself. "I don't know. But you ought to help Bethe. She loves him."

"Come out on the porch," said my father.

"I'm late for church."

"*Church?* What church?"

"To understand is to forgive," I said, "and love she does, and so does he, and to her aid you must go."

"My God," said Jenny, "help us."

"It's *you* who have taught our child to go to any church and talk that way," my father said to my mother as he took me by the arm. "Come outside and let's have a talk."

"You will bully me," I yelled to my father, who never had, "or you will trick me. And both are immoral and I will not say one more word to a Philistine."

I was at my high-class moral theory stage, from which I have never completely emerged, and I had even had time to learn that it often worked.

"Immoral," I shouted as I ran from the room.

"That's not nice, baby," said my mother, looking in another direction.

"Immoral," I shouted, and sulked under the fig tree, refusing lunch, until late in the day when I asked permission to visit Grace Alberts, the daughter of my father's best friend, crippled at birth from the syphilis of her father. When Jenny said that was very strange because I had often said I didn't like cripples, my mother told Jenny that perhaps I was growing more charitable and she thought the visit to poor Grace was a good idea.

I knew where I was going — the house dictionary having failed me — so I stopped by Christy Houghton's on my way. Christy was the daughter of divorced parents, necked openly with the boys, and was two years older than I. I wanted to ask her what a common-law wife was. She explained it was a fancy name for just a plain old whore in this wide, wide world. The third time she said whore I twisted her arm and held it firm as I forced her to repeat after me, "Does love need a minister, a rabbi, a priest? Is divine love between man and woman based on permission of a decadent society?" and would not now believe those words except I liked them so much that they are written three times in my "writer's book."

When I left Christy Houghton she screamed after me that everybody knew about Bethe Bowman from the newspapers and I came from a family of gangster-whores. (One of the few clear memories I have of the opening night of *The Children's Hour,* almost fifteen years later, is Christy Houghton kissing me and saying, "I married a New Yorker. You're drunk, aren't you?")

But that day I went down to the corner store. It was boarded up and nobody answered the bell. I paced around the block and tried again, worried that I had lost Bethe forever. I took a page from my notebook, wrote a message, and slipped it under the door. As I walked back to the streetcar, a man behind me called, "Hey, young lady," and I began to run. He caught me easily after a block and made sure by a very firm hold on my arm that I couldn't move.

"What's your name?"

I was too frightened to answer. After a minute he took my small purse and went through it to find almost nothing except cigarette butts and my "writer's book."

"What are you doing at Arneggio's place?"

"Nothing."

"Nothing? You don't know the people?"

"I'm on my way home."

"I'll come along with you."

35

I said, "Please," didn't like myself for it, and heard the fear turn into anger. "Please take your hand off my arm. I don't like to be held down."

He laughed and with that laugh caused a lifelong, often out-of-control hatred of cops, in all circumstances, in all countries. Then the grip lessened and he said, "Nobody's out to hurt you. What's this mean?"

He held out the paper I had put under the door. I had written, "Stendhal said love made people brave, dear Bethe."

"Stendhal was a writer," I started, "who — "

"What do you know about the dame?"

"The *dame?* The *dame?*"

"Look, kid, what were you doing there?"

"Nothing. I told you. I just rang the bell — "

"What's your name and where do you live? Hurry up."

"I am on my way to church — "

I moved away from him. He let me go, or so I thought, until I got off the streetcar on St. Charles Avenue and saw him behind me. He smiled and waved at me and I turned around and got on the Jackson crosstown car. I had a soda in Kramer's Drug Store, felt better for it, and walked home.

Jenny and Hannah were waiting for me on the porch. Jenny motioned me back to the chicken coops, away from the house. She said, "The police were here. Fortunately, we all went to school with Emile. Why don't you mind your God-damned business?"

"No sense getting angry," Hannah said, "no sense."

"Why not? Why not get angry? Miss Busybody here — "

"Tell us," said Hannah.

"Does Papa know the police were here?"

"No. Not yet. But he gets to Memphis tonight."

"Then telephone him," I said, "and don't threaten me. I wasn't doing anything. I was looking for Bethe."

"Bethe? What for?"

Somewhere I knew why, but I didn't want to talk about it, and when they knew I wasn't going to answer, Jenny sailed back to the house and Hannah followed her. When I came in the door the phone was ringing, and as Jenny answered it she put up her hand to stop me from climbing the stairs. When she finished listening she said, "Very well," hung up, went across the room, and whispered to Hannah. I had never seen her face twitch before and was not to see it happen again until a day, many years later, when she first saw my father after he had been confined for senile dementia. It is not good to see people who have been pretending strength all their lives lose it even for a minute.

Hannah said, softly, "Well, don't let's make a fuss. Let's just go."

Jenny said to me, "Go wash your face. Put on a hat. Tell your mother we're taking a cake to Old Lady Simmons. And hurry."

When I came downstairs a taxi was waiting in front of the door. I had never seen my aunts take a taxi before. I think I knew where we were going, because when we drove up in front of police headquarters I wasn't surprised, although I must have taken such a sharp breath that Hannah took my hand.

Jenny, as always, went through the door first, and up to a man at the desk. "I'm Jenny Hellman. Tell Mr. Emile we're here."

"He's pretty busy," said the man, "pretty busy. Is that the girl?"

"Don't speak in that tone," said Jenny. "What is it you want with this child?"

"Is she a child?" said the man, and I thought of the Infant Phenomenon and laughed out of nervousness.

"Sit down, ladies," and the man rang a bell. Hannah gave me her handkerchief as we sat waiting on the bench and I said to her, "I love you."

"Oh, certainly, love is just what we need," said Jenny. "Give Hannah back that handkerchief. It was our mother's."

A man came out of an office, motioned us toward the door.

This time it was Hannah who said, "We'd like to see Mr. Emile. We went to school with him and he's been to our house all his life."

"He told me," said the man. "He isn't here. He's very busy." He turned to me. "How well did you know Al Arneggio?"

I was so surprised that I didn't answer until he repeated the question.

38

"I didn't know him. I never saw him — I saw him in a restaurant once."

"Who do you think we are," Jenny said, "knowing people like that?"

"I think you're nice ladies whose cousin lives with a man like that, that's what I think," said the man.

"*Schweigen vor dem Kind,*" Hannah said. "I mean that isn't a nice way to talk in front of a young, very young girl."

The man said to me, "What were you doing at that place? At the store? Don't you know it isn't a store?"

"It's a kind of funny store. But it's got some things in it and — "

"How many times have you been there?"

I was growing very frightened, perhaps more of the look on Jenny's face than of the man or the place.

"I don't know how many. I only went to see Bethe."

"Why did you go today? Did you have a message?"

"A message? No, sir. Bethe never wanted my parents or my aunts to know."

"To know what?"

"Where she lived, I guess."

"Or the gangster she lived with?" he said to my aunts.

"We've known," said Hannah. "A man in my office told me. I hope her poor papa is dead long since. In Mannheim, Germany, I mean, he must be."

The man said, "I want to know why the girl went there today."

"I do, too," said Jenny, "although she meant no harm, she never does mean any harm, she is just too nosy and moves about — "

He stood in front of me now. "Why did you go there today?"

I had already come near a truth I couldn't name, so close to it, so convinced that something was being pushed up from the bottom of me, that I began to tremble with an anxiety I had never felt before. It had nothing to do with my fear of the policeman or of my family.

"Answer me, young lady. Why did you go there today?"

My voice was high and came, I thought, from somebody else.

"I don't know. I read about Mr. Arneggio last night. Love, I think, but I'm not sure."

A long time later somebody, I don't remember who, repeated the word love, and I heard Jenny's voice and the man's voice, but I was so busy gripping my knees that I couldn't, didn't, want to look up, or to hear, and didn't care what they said. Somewhere, during that time, I found out that pieces of Arneggio had been discovered a few hours before in the backyard of the store, and I heard the man say to my aunts, "O.K. I'll tell Mr. Emile. But if you should hear anything about Bethe Bowman it is your duty, the Mafia and all, dangerous, and keep the kid away from there."

Hannah it was who poked me to my feet and said to the man, "Thank you. You are most courteous."

I don't think we spoke on the streetcar going home but I don't know because I think of it now as the closest I have ever come to a conscious semiconsciousness, as if I were coming through an anesthetic, not back into a world of reality, but into a new body and time, moving toward something, running back at the moment I could have reached it. I am sure my aunts believed that I was frightened of police consequences or my father's anger. I was glad they thought that and nothing more. Later that night Jenny said that since Emile had not phoned she saw no sense in ever telling my father or mother if I would promise to stay away from Bethe.

The next day and for days after that there were discussions of the murder of Arneggio. Bethe's name was mentioned in every press story but she was never called Bowman. In the boardinghouse so many questions were asked, opinions exchanged, that Jenny grew very sharp and took to defending Bethe, perhaps out of family pride, perhaps from the tangles of her own nature, so sure, so dismissive of "the ninnies of this world," and so sympathetic to them.

From the time I was fourteen until I was twenty-five, I had no news of Bethe, although I often thought of her. I thought of her as I got dressed for my wedding, deliberately putting aside the pretty dress that was intended and choosing an old ugly gray chiffon. As it went over my head, I heard myself say her name, and I saw again the man, Arneggio, in the restaurant. Then I don't believe I ever thought of her again through a pleasant marriage that was not to last, until the first afternoon I slept with Dashiell Hammett.

As I moved toward the bed I said, "I'd like to tell you about my cousin, a woman called Bethe."

Hammett said, "You can tell me if you have to, but I can't say I would have chosen this time."

Later that same year I went to New York from Hollywood to tell my parents about my divorce, and then, on my way back to California, I went to New Orleans to tell my aunts. It was an unpleasant errand: my parents and my aunts liked my husband, knew that I liked him, and had every right to be puzzled and disturbed about me.

I suppose, in an effort not to talk about the present time, my aunts and I talked a good deal about past times, and it was on that visit, as I opened a closet door to get a bath towel, that I saw once again the canvas valise that had been given me and then taken back. As my aunts moved about the kitchen I stood staring at it, wondering about me and them. I wrapped a towel around me and went to stand in the kitchen door.

I said, "Is the letter still there from Bethe? The one that says she now has good Italian friend and that maybe if they marry you will come again to see her?"

Hannah turned her back to me. Jenny said, "What does all that old stuff mean now?"

"It means that long before the day at the police station you knew about Bethe and Arneggio. But you didn't tell me you knew."

"That's right," said Jenny. "Why don't you put on a bathrobe?"

But I wanted to have a fight, or to pay them back, because that night I said, "I know that you will not approve of my living with a man I am not married to, but that's the way it's going to be."

"How do you know that," said Jenny, "how do you know the difference between fear and approve?"

"Because you deserted, sorry, you gave Bethe up, when she loved a way you didn't like. When she was in trouble, neither of you, or Papa, went to help her."

An hour later, reading on my bed, I heard through the walls of the small shoddy house an argument between my aunts. There was nothing remarkable about that — Jenny's temper was as bad as my father's and mine — but something was different, and as I opened my door I realized that it was Hannah who was angry. Neither I nor anybody else, I think, had ever heard Hannah angry, and so I walked into the dining room to find out about it.

Jenny said to me, "Your generation, camp and college and all those fine places, goes about naked all the time?"

"Yes," I said, "all the time. And we sleep with everybody and drink and dope all night and don't have your fine feelings. Maybe that's the reason we don't always spit on people because they live with low-down Wops and get in trouble. Each generation has its standards."

Jenny laughed, but Hannah rose, turned over her chair and said, "Sit down."

Jenny said to her, "We don't have to prove ourselves."

"Why don't you go out in the garden?" Hannah asked Jenny, and as I whistled in surprise at the tone, she turned into her bedroom. I could see she was unlocking a box. Something large had happened between them. I went to get dressed and stalled to give them time.

When I came out, Jenny said to Hannah, "O.K. Go ahead."

Hannah handed me an open savings bank deposit book and said, "Look at the date on that page."

The date was ten years before, in the first days of September. There was a thousand-dollar withdrawal from a total of thirty-three hundred.

I said I didn't understand. Jenny said, "Hannah doesn't want you to think mean of her ever because she loves you more than sense. I, myself, don't give much of a damn what you think. But so be it. That thousand dollars was withdrawn about a week after the police station visit and was used to get Bethe out of trouble. Your father didn't know, nobody knew, and you're to shut up about it."

"You are fine ladies," I said after a while, "the best."

Jenny was angry. "Sure, sure, now put all that sweet-time patter in the shit can."

"My!" said Hannah.

Jenny said, "Bethe paid it back. A long time ago, after she sold the jewelry and other stuff he gave her

44

and when the police finally left her alone, so don't start any stuff about you giving us the money because we are poor virgin ladies."

"I haven't got any money," I said, "but maybe someday."

"Then someday send us a steak."

"I will," I said. (The morning after *The Children's Hour* opened, four years later, I gave a porter on the Southern Pacific ten dollars to carry a package of twelve steaks to my aunts and got back a telegram saying, "Do we have to eat the porter as well?")

The next morning Hannah, who usually left for work at seven-thirty, was still in the dining room at eight-thirty, and as I ate the wonderful breakfast that brought back my childhood — tripe, biscuits, cold crabs, crawfish, bitter coffee — she said that she was entitled to a day's holiday when I came to visit. An hour later, Jenny appeared and said, "Come along, it's a long trolley ride."

I think I guessed where we were going, but I know so little about directions, and the city was so changed and grown, that I didn't bother to ask what direction we traveled in. When we reached the end of the trolley line, we began a long, long walk through flat, ugly, treeless land. Occasionally we would pass a small house, and once an old man came from a dilapidated outhouse to look at us. My aunts were tall, heavy women who never walked more than a few blocks, and now I heard Jenny's heavy breathing and became nervous when I saw Hannah take her hand. Near the end of the road, sitting alone on the plain, was a mean cottage, square against the sun. The half-finished porch had four tilted steps and a broken chair as if to show that somebody had once intended to use it but had grown weary of the effort. Bethe was standing on the steps, her body slanted with their angle, and I stopped at the handsome sight of her. She came down the steps to support Jenny with one arm, Hannah with the other. I followed them into the house.

I don't think many words were spoken that afternoon, and certainly I said none of them. We drank a bitter, black iced tea, we stayed about an hour, we made the long trek home with sighs from Jenny as Hannah hummed something or other off key. That night I telephoned Dash to say I would stay in New Orleans a few days longer, would return to Los Angeles on the weekend.

The next morning I went back to Bethe's, losing my way on the turn of the dirt road, then finding it again. As I came toward her house, I turned and ran from it, around another dirt path and then off into another, coming suddenly into a green place, swampy, with heavy stump trees and large elephant ears. I heard things jump in the swamp and I remember thinking I must be sick without feeling sick, feverish without fever. I don't know how long I ran, but a path brought me in sight of a roof and as I ran toward it, thinking that I must leave the sun and ask for water, I saw Bethe hanging clothes from a line that stretched from a pole to an outhouse. She was naked and I stopped to admire the proportions of the figure: the large hips, the great breasts, the tumbled auburn hair that came from the beautiful side of my father's family and, so I thought that day, had been lost in America. She must have heard the sound of the wet, ugly soil beneath me, because she turned, put her hands over her breasts, then moved them down to cover her vagina, then took them away to move the hair from her face.

I said, "It was you who did it. I would not have found it without you. Now what good is it, tell me that?"

She took a towel from the line, came toward me, and wiped my face. Then she took my hand, we went into the house, she pushed me gently into a chair. After a while she came back into the room, covered now by a cheap sack of a dress, carrying coffee. I must have fallen asleep in the chair because I came awake saying something, losing it, then trying to remember what I had wanted to say. I took a sip of the coffee, finished the cup and, for the first time in my grown life, I vomited. Then I must have gone back to sleep because when I looked down the floor was clean and Bethe was in the kitchen. I went to stand near her as she dropped heavy-looking dough balls into a boiling broth.

She asked me, half in German, half in English, how I was feeling. I tried to say I had never felt sick and, trying too hard, said, "I wasn't sick. Just the opposite. It was that day in the restaurant, you and Arneg-

47

gio — " and never finished, because as I spoke the man's name she put her hand over my mouth. When she took it away she said, "Now I go in bed maybe seven or eight P.M., in the night. He is plumber and like dinner when come home soon at four-thirty in afternoon. Come for visit again."

I waited for a dumpling to be finished, ate it, didn't like it, shook hands with Bethe, and walked down the road. Not far from the larger dirt road that would join the road of the streetcar back to New Orleans, I passed a very thin middle-aged man, carrying a lunch pail. Maybe he wasn't the plumber, but I think he was.

I was never to find out. Two years later my aunts wrote that Bethe died of pneumonia and they had only known about it because they had a note from a T. R. Carter. They said things like poor Bethe and they wished they had been able to help her, but they were getting old and the streetcar ride was hard for them, although they had always sent a present at Christmas and what they thought was her birthday. My aunts said they had written to Germany, had no reply, didn't know if any of Bethe's family were still alive, but maybe the next time I went to Germany I would try to find out and bring the news.

I never went back to Germany because now it was the time of Hitler, and I don't even remember talking again about Bethe with my aunts, although one drunken night I did try to tell Hammett about Bethe, and got angry when he said he didn't understand what

I meant when I kept repeating that Bethe had had a lot to do with him and me. I got so angry that I left the apartment, drove to Montauk on a snowy day, and came back two days later with the grippe.

WILLY

HE was married to my ridiculous great-aunt. But I was sixteen or seventeen by the time I knew she was ridiculous, having before then thought her most elegant. Her jewelry, the dresses from Mr. Worth in Paris, her hand-sewn underwear with the Alençon lace, her Dubonnet with a few drops of spirits of ammonia, were all fine stuff to me. But most of all, I was impressed with her silences and the fineness of her bones.

My first memory of Aunt Lily — I was named for her; born Pansy, she had changed it early because, she told me, "Pansy was a tacky old darky name" — is of watching one of the many fine lavallières swing between the small bumps of her breasts. How, I asked myself in those early years of worship, did my mother's family ever turn out anything so "French,"

53

so *raffinée?* It was true that her family were all thin people, and all good-looking, but Lily was a wispy, romantic specimen unlike her brothers and sisters, who were high-spirited and laughed too much over their own vigor and fancy money deals.

That is what I thought about Aunt Lily until I made the turn and the turn was as sharp as only the young can make when they realize their values have been shoddy. It was only then that I understood about the Dubonnet and recognized that the lavallières were too elaborate for the ugly dryness of the breasts, and thought the silences coma-like and stupid. But that, at least, was not the truth.

Lily was so much younger than her brothers and sisters, one of whom was my grandmother, that I don't think she was more than ten years older than my mother. It was whispered that her mother had given birth to her at sixty, and in my bewitched period that made her Biblical and in my turn-against period made her malformed.

I do not know her age or mine when I first met her, because she and her husband, Willy, their son and daughter, had been living in Mobile, and had only then, at the time of my meeting them, moved back to New Orleans. I think I was about nine or ten and I know they lived in a large house on St. Charles Avenue filled with things I thought beautiful and foreign, only to realize, in my turn-against period, that they were ornate copies of French and Italian miseries, cluttering all the tables and running along the staircase walls and newel posts on up to the attic quarters of Caroline Ducky.

Whenever we visited Aunt Lily I was sent off to Caroline Ducky with a gift of chocolate-covered cherries or a jar of pickles, because Caroline Ducky was part of my mother's childhood. Anyway, I liked her. She was an old, very black lady who had been born into slavery in my mother's family and, to my angry eyes, didn't seem to want to leave it. She occupied only part of the large attic and did what was called "the fine sewing," which meant that she embroidered initials on handkerchiefs and towels and Uncle Willy's shirts and was the only servant in the house allowed to put an iron to Aunt Lily's clothes. Caroline Ducky never came downstairs: her meals were brought to her by her daughter, Flo Ducky. Whatever I learned about that house, in the end, came mostly from Caroline Ducky, who trusted me, I think, because my nurse Sophronia was her niece and Sophronia had vouched for me at an early age. But then her own daughter, Flo Ducky, was retarded and was only allowed to deal with the heavy kitchen pans. There were many other servants in that house, ten, perhaps, but I remember only Caroline Ducky and a wheat-colored chauffeur called Peters. Peters was a fine figure in gray uniform, very unlike my grandmother's chauffeur, who was a mean-spirited slob of a German mechanic without any uniform. My grandmother and the other sister, Hattie, would often discuss Peters in a way that was clear to me only many years later, but even my innocent mother would often stop talking when Peters came into the room with Aunt Lily's Dubonnet or to suggest a cooling drive to Lake Pontchartrain.

Aunt Lily's daughter died so early after they returned to New Orleans that I do not even remember what she looked like. It was said officially that she died of consumption, supposedly caused by her insistence on sleeping on the lawn, but when anybody in my mother's family died there was always the rumor of syphilis. In any case, after her daughter's death, Aunt Lily never again appeared in a "color" — all her clothes, for the rest of her life, were white, black, gray and purple and, I believed in the early days, another testament to her world of sensibility and the heart.

The son was called Honey and to this day I do not know any other name for him. (He died about fifteen years ago in a loony bin in Mobile and there's nobody left to ask his real name.) Honey looked like his mother, thin-boned, yellowish, and always sat at dinner between Lily and his father, Uncle Willy, to "interpret" for them.

I suppose I first remember Willy at the dinner table, perhaps a year after they had moved to New Orleans, although because he was a legend I had heard about him all my life. For years I thought he was a legend only to my family, but as I grew up I realized that he was a famous character to the rest of the city, to the state, and in certain foreign parts. Depending, of course, on their own lives and natures, people admired him, envied him, or were frightened of him: in my mother's family his position in a giant corporation, his demotions, his reinstatements, his borrowings, his gamblings, were, as Jake, my grandmother's brother, said, "a sign of a nation more interested in charm than in stability, the road to the end." By which my grandmother's brother meant that Willy had gone beyond their middle-class gains made by cheating Negroes on cotton crops. But, in fairness to her family, I was later to discover that Willy had from time to time borrowed a large part of Lily's fortune, made money with it, lost it, returned it, borrowed it again, paid interest on it, and finally, by the time I met him, been refused it altogether.

I do not think that is the only reason Aunt Lily and her husband no longer spoke to one another, but that's what Honey's "interpretations" seemed to be about. Uncle Willy, his pug, good-looking, jolly face, drawn by nature to contrast with my aunt's sour delicacy, would say to Honey such things as, "Ask your mother if I may borrow the car, deprive her of Peters for a few hours, to go to the station. I will be away for two weeks, at the Boston office." Honey would repeat the message word for word to his mother on the other side of him and, always after a long silence, Aunt Lily would shrug and say, "Tell your father he does not need to ask for his car. *His* money bought it. I would have been happier with something more modest."

There were many "interpretations" about trips or

cars, but the day of that particular one, Willy looked down at his plate for a long time and then, looking up, laughed at my mother's face. "Julia, Julia," he said. "You are the charming flower under the feet of the family bulls." Then, puzzling to a child, his laughter changed to anger and he rose, threw his napkin in Honey's face and said, "Tell your mother to buy herself another more modest car. Tell her to buy it with a little piece of the high interest she charged me for the loan she made." We stayed for a longer time than usual that day, although Lily didn't speak again, but on the way home my mother stopped in the nearest church, an old habit when she was disturbed, any church of any belief, and I waited outside, impatient, more than that, the way I always was.

Aunt Jenny, my father's sister, who ran a boarding-house, would take me each Saturday to the French market for the weekly food supplies. It was our custom to have lunch in the Quarter at Tujague's, and my watered wine and her unwatered wine always made for a nice time. And so the next day after Willy had told my mother she was a charming flower, I said to Jenny, "Everybody likes Mama, don't they?"

"Almost," she said, "but not you. You're jealous of your mama and you ought to get over that before it's too late."

"Mama nags," I said. "Papa understands."

"*Ach.* You and your papa. Yes, she does nag. But she doesn't know it and is a nice lady. I said you must know your mother before it is too late."

She was right. By the time I knew how much I loved my mother and understood that her eccentricities were nothing more than that and could no more be controlled than the blinking of an eye in a high wind, it was, indeed, too late. But I didn't like lectures even from Jenny.

"Uncle Willy likes Mama," I said. "I think that's hard for Aunt Lily."

Jenny stared at me. "Hard for *Lily?* Hard for your Aunt Lily?"

"You don't like her because she's thin," I said to Jenny, who was six feet tall, and heavy, and had long been telling me that my rib bones showed. "I think she's the most interesting, the only interesting, part of our family."

"Thank you," said Jenny. "Your *mother's* family. Not mine."

"I didn't mean you or Hannah," I said, "really, I . . ."

"Don't worry," Jenny said as she rose, "about me, worry about yourself and why you like very thin people who have money."

I asked her what she meant, and she said that someday she would tell me if I didn't find out for myself. (I did find out, and when I told her she laughed and said I was thirty years old, but better late than never.)

It was that year, the year of my mother being a flower, and now, in my memory, the year before my sharp turn, that I saw most of Aunt Lily. I went to the house two or three times a week and whatever she was doing, and she was never doing much, she would put aside to give me hot chocolate, sending Honey to another room as if she and I were ready to exchange the pains of women. I usually went in the late afternoons, after school, but sometimes I was invited to Saturday lunch. The visits were hung in a limbo of fog over water, but I put that down to the way people who had greater culture and sensibility than the rest of us lived their special lives. I don't know what I meant by culture: in Aunt Lily's house there were no books other than a set of Prescott, and once when Jenny and I went to our second-balcony seats for a concert of Verdi's *Requiem* Aunt Lily sent for us to join her in her box. After a while, Jenny said to me, "Would you ask your Cultivated Majesty Aunt please not to hum the Wedding March? It doesn't go well with the 'Libera me' and there are other reasons she should forget it." But I put that down to Jenny's customary sharpness and went on with my interest in Aunt Lily.

Ever since her daughter's death Aunt Lily made soft sounds from time to time and talked even less than before, although unconnected phrases like "lost life," "the hopes of youth," "inevitable waste," would come at intervals. I was never sure whether she was talking of her daughter or of herself, but I did know that, for a woman who had never before used her hands, she now often touched my hair, patted my arm, or held Honey firmly by the hand.

And I thought it was the need to deny the death of her child that made possible the scene I once saw when I arrived for a visit while Lily was out shopping. The car came into the driveway to the side door and from the window I saw Peters reach in for Lily's hand. As she stepped from the car, she twisted and slipped. Peters caught her and carried her to the door. On the way there, her head moved down to kiss his hair.

I did not know how to cross the room away from the window, how to face what I had seen, so I ran up to the third floor to call upon Caroline Ducky. Past the second landing I heard Honey's voice behind me. He said, "He does it to her."

"Does what?"

"You're older than me," he said, and ran up ahead of me. He was larger, taller than I, and his face was now sweaty and vacant.

I said, "What's the matter?"

"Ssh and I'll show it to you."

I went by him and was caught by the arm. "Want to see it?"

"See what?"

"My thingy."

I hadn't seen a thingy since I was four years old and maybe my no came too slow, because my shoulders were held with his one hand, my dress lifted with the other, and I felt something knocking against my stomach.

"Open up," he shouted into his future. "Open up."

I sneezed so hard that he fell back against the stair-

61

case wall. I was subject to sneezing fits and now I stood in the full force of one violent rack after another. When the sneezing was over, Honey had disappeared and Caroline Ducky was standing a few steps above me. I don't know how long she had been there but I followed her to the attic, was told to press my upper lip and given a Coca-Cola spiced heavily with spirits of ammonia, an old and perhaps dangerous New Orleans remedy for anything you didn't understand.

Caroline Ducky looked up from her sewing. "You be careful of that Honey." (She was to be right: at twenty he raped a girl at a picnic, at twenty-two or -three he was sued by a Latvian girl for assault, and his later years in the Mobile loony bin were in some way connected with an attack on a woman who was fishing in the Dog River.)

Caroline Ducky said, "I knew what he was going to be the day it took him three days to get himself out."

"Out of what?"

"Out of the stomach of his mother."

"What did you know?"

"I knew what I knew."

I laughed with an old irritation. Such answers were, perhaps still are, a Southern Negro form of put-down to the questions of white people.

"His mama didn't want him, his papa didn't want him, and a child nobody wants got nothing ahead but seeping sand."

"Then what did they have him for? They don't like each other."

"She trapped him," said Caroline Ducky. "Mr. Willy, he was drunk."

"Things can't start from birth, that early," I said from the liberalism I was learning.

"That ain't early, the day you push out, that's late."

"What did you mean Aunt Lily trapped him? How can a man be trapped?"

"You too young for the question, I too old for the answer." She was pleased with herself and laughed.

"Then what did you start it for? You all do that. It's rotten mean."

Grown people were always on the edge of telling you something valuable and then withdrawing it, a form of bully-teasing. (Little of what they withdrew had any value, but the pain of learning that can be unpleasant.) And I was a particular victim of this empty mystery game because, early and late, an attempt was made to hide from me the contempt of my mother's family for my father's lack of success, and thus there was a kind of patronizing pity for me and my future. I think I sensed that mystery when I was very young and to protect what little I had to protect I constructed the damaging combination that was not to leave me until I myself made money: I rebelled against my mother's family, and thus all people who were rich, but I was frightened and impressed by them; and the more frightened and impressed I grew the more aimless became my anger, which sometimes expressed itself in talk about the rights of Negroes and on two Sundays took the form of deliberately breaking plates at my grandmother's table. By fourteen my heart was with the poor except on the days when it was with those who ground them under. I remember that period as a hell of self-dislike, but I do not now mean to make fun of it: not too many years later, although old shriveled leaves remain on the stump to this day, I understood that I lived under an economic system of increasing impurity and injustice for which I, and all those like me, pay with ridiculous wounds to the spirit.

"What's rotten mean," asked Caroline Ducky, "you snip-talking girl?"

"Rotten mean, all of you."

"I like your Uncle Willy," she said, "but he ain't no man of God."

She closed her eyes and crossed herself and that meant my visit was finished. She was the only Baptist I ever knew who crossed herself and I doubt if she knew that she used the Greek cross. I left the house and went far out of my way to back-of-town, the Negro section, to put a dime in the poor box of the Baptist Church. I did this whenever I had an extra dime and years before, when my nurse Sophronia had proudly told my father about it, he said to me, "Why don't you give it to the Synagogue? Maybe we never told you that's where you belong." I said I couldn't do that because there was no synagogue for Negroes and my father said that was perfectly true, he'd never thought about that before.

For years I told myself that it was from that day, the day Caroline Ducky said he was no man of God,

that I knew about Uncle Willy, but now I am not sure
— diaries carry dates and pieces of conversation, but
no record of family gossip — when I knew that he had
been a poor boy in Mobile, Alabama, working young
on the docks, then as a freight boss for a giant company doing business in Central America, and had married Lily when he was twenty-four and she was thirty.
It was said that he had married her for money and
respectability, but after six or seven years he couldn't
have needed either because by that time he was vice-
president of the company, living with the first fast
cars, a hundred-foot yacht, the St. Charles Avenue
great house, an apartment at the old Waldorf in New
York, a hunting place on Jekyll Island, an open and
generous hand with everybody, including, I think, my
father in his bad years.

Sometimes in those years, years of transition for
me, the dinner table of the St. Charles Avenue house
included other guests — the "interpretations" of
Honey between his mother and father still went on
but were circumspect when these people were present
— fine-looking, heavy men, with blood in their faces
and sound to their voices, and then I heard talk of
what they did and how they did it. I don't know when
I understood it, or if anybody explained it to me, but
there were high tales of adventure, with words like
"good natives," "troublemakers," and the National
City Bank, ships and shipments that had been sabo-
taged, teaching lessons to peons, and long, highly rel-
ished stories of a man called Christmas, a soldier of

fortune who worked for my uncle's company as a mercenary and had a great deal to do with keeping the peons quiet. At one dinner the talk was of "outbreaks," arranged by "native troublemakers" — two men who worked for my uncle's company had been murdered — and the need for firm action, revenge. The firm action was taken by Mr. Christmas, who strung up twenty-two men of a Guatemalan village, cut out their tongues, and burned down the village, driving the others into the jungle. Uncle Willy did not join in the pleasure of that tale, but he said nothing to stop it, nor to interfere with a plan to send a boatload of guns to Christmas to "insure the future."

The terrors and exploitations of this company were to become a world scandal, the first use of the U.S. Marines as private mercenaries to protect American capital. But even in my uncle's time, the scandal was of such proportions that the guns and the killings tapered off enough to convince me that the company had grown "liberal" as it established schools, decent houses and hospitals for the natives. When, in 1969, I told that to a graduate student from Costa Rica, he laughed and said he thought I should come and see for myself.

In any case, my reaction to those dinner tales at Aunt Lily's was an unpleasant mixture: my distaste for what I heard did not stop my laughter, when they laughed, at the shrewdness and heroics of "our boys" as they triumphed over the natives. I believed in Willy's personal affection and generosity toward the poor people he exploited. But the values of grown people had long pounded at my head, torn me apart with their contradictions.

But I could not now, in truth, get straight the tangled mess of that conflict which went so many years past my childhood: I know only that there were changes and that one day I felt that Aunt Lily was silly and that I had been a fool for ever thinking anything else. But I went on being sympathetic and admiring of Uncle Willy, interested in the days of his youth when he had ridden mules through Central and South American jungles, speaking always with an almost brotherly admiration of the natives from whom he "bought" the land. I am sure that his adventures made him interesting, the money he earned from them was different to me than money earned from a bank or a store, that his fall from high position seemed to me a protest, which it wasn't. And I had other feelings for him, although I didn't know about them for years after the time of which I speak.

But I already thought Aunt Lily foolish stuff the day of the outbreak. We had arrived in New Orleans only a few hours before she telephoned to ask my mother to come immediately. My mother said she was tired from the long journey, but that evidently didn't suit Aunt Lily because my mother told Jenny she guessed she'd have to go immediately, something bad must have happened. Jenny sniffed and said the something bad that had happened was probably the lateness of the Paris mails that failed to bring Aunt Lily's

newest necklace. My mother said it was her duty to go
and I said I would go along with her. Since I didn't
often volunteer to go anywhere with my mother, she
was pleased, and we set off at my mother's slow pace.
Lily was pacing around her upstairs sitting room, her
eyes blank and unfocused, and, annoyed with seeing
me, she said immediately that it was too bad my hair
was so straight and muddy-blonde, now that I was
fourteen. But she sent for my hot chocolate and her
watered Dubonnet, and my mother nervously chatted
about our New York relatives until I went to a corner
with a copy of *Snappy Stories*.

I guess Lily forgot about me because she said to
my mother, "You've heard about Willy."

My mother said no, she hadn't heard about Willy,
what was the matter, and Aunt Lily said, "I don't believe you. Jenny Hellman must have told you."

I don't think anybody in her life had ever before
told my mother they didn't believe her, and I was
amazed at the firmness with which she said that Jenny
had told her nothing, Jenny didn't move in large circles, worked too hard, and she, my mother, always
tried not to lie before God.

"God," said Aunt Lily. *"God?* He hasn't kept everybody else in town from lying at me. Me and Honey
and my brothers and sisters who warned me early
against Willy. It isn't the first time, but now it's in the
open, now that he says he's paid me back when, of
course, he still owes me sixty thousand," and she began to cry.

I saw my mother's face, the pity, the getting ready, and knew that she was going to walk into, be a part of, one of those messes the innocent so often walk into, make worse, and are victimized by. I left the room.

I met Peters in the hall. When he spoke to me, I realized he had never spoken to me before. "Miss Lily with your mama? Miss Lily upsetting herself?"

"I guess so," and started up the stairs toward Caroline Ducky.

"Miss Caroline Ducky don't feel good," he said. "I wouldn't bother her today." I went past him.

When Caroline Ducky answered my knock and we had kissed, I said, "Sorry you don't feel good. Your rheumatism?"

"One thing, five things. They mix around when you getting old. Sit you down and tell me what you reading."

This was an old habit between us. She liked stories and I would sum up for her a book I had read, making the plot more simple, cutting down the number of people, and always, as the story went on, she forgot it came from a book, thought it came from life, and would approve or disapprove. But I didn't want to fool around that day.

"What's Aunt Lily so upset about? She made Mama come right away. Something about Uncle Willy and the whole town knowing."

Caroline Ducky said, "The whole town don't know and don't care. Has to do with that Cajun girl, up Bayou Teche."

I was half crazy with pleasure, as I always was with this kind of stuff, but I had ruined it so many times before by going fast with questions that now I shut up. Caroline Ducky, after a while, handed me her embroidery hoop to work on and went to stand by her small window, leaning out to look at the street. In the last few years she had done this a good deal and I figured it had to do with age and never going into the street except for a funeral, and never liking a city where she had been made to live.

She said, over her shoulder, "I'm making a plan to die in high grass. All this Frenchy stuff in this town. Last night, I ask for greens and pot likker. That shit nigger at the stove send me up gumbo, Frenchy stuff. Tell your ma to cook me up some greens and bring 'em here. Your ma used to be a beauty on a wild horse. A wild Alabama horse."

I suppose there was something wrong with my face because she said, "Your ma's changed. City no good for country folk, your ma and me."

"What's that mean?"

"Your ma's a beauty inside out."

I didn't know why she was talking about my mother and I didn't want to talk about her that day, but I think Caroline Ducky meant that my mother was a country girl and the only comfortable period of her life had been with the Alabama Negroes of her childhood. New Orleans and New York, a worldly husband, a difficult child, unloving sisters and a mother of formidable coldness had made deep marks on my mother by the time I was old enough to understand her eccentric nature.

I said, "Uncle Willy going to marry a Cajun girl?"

"What? *What?* There ain't a white child born to woman ain't crazy," said Caroline Ducky. "Niggers sit around wasting time talk about white folk being pig-shit mean. Not me. All I ever say, they crazy. Lock up all white folk, give 'em to eat, but lock 'em up. Then all the trouble be over. What you talking about, *marry* Cajun girl?"

"All I meant was it must be kind of hard for Aunt Lily. Uncle Willy's being in love. I guess nobody wants to share their husband. My father isn't faithful to my mother."

"How you know that?"

"I found out years ago at a circus when . . ."

"Shut up," said Caroline Ducky, "this house pushing me to my grave."

There were sudden sounds from downstairs, as if somebody was calling. I opened Caroline Ducky's door but nobody seemed to be calling me, so I closed it again and went back to the embroidery hoop hoping to please Caroline Ducky into more talk, but the sounds downstairs grew louder and Caroline Ducky was too busy listening to pay any attention to anything I might ask.

She laughed. "Well, well. Time now for Miss Lily's morphine shot."

This was the richest hour I had ever spent and I was willing to try anything.

"Look, Caroline Ducky, I'll take you back to Demopolis. I'll get the money from Papa or I can sell my squirrel coat and books. I'll take you back, I swear."

"Shut the shit," said Caroline Ducky, good and mad. "Take me home! What I going to do when I get there? Nobody there for me except the rest of your shit catfish family. Home. What home I got?"

The door opened and Uncle Willy came in. "What's going on?" he said to Caroline Ducky.

"She's calling in the securities," said Caroline Ducky, in a new kind of English, almost without an accent. "Taking 'em from the bank."

"Christ," said Uncle Willy. "When?"

"Today's Sunday, tomorrow's Monday."

"God in Heaven," said Uncle Willy. "What a bastard she is, without telling me. That gives me sixteen hours to borrow three hundred thousand dollars. Maybe Peters just told you that to scare me."

Caroline Ducky smiled. "You too smart for what you're saying."

I had never heard anything so wonderful in my life and, although I didn't know what they were talking about, I knew I would, it was just around the corner. I suppose I was straining with the movements of body and face that have worried so many people in the years after that, because Uncle Willy realized I was in the room.

He smiled at me. "Hello, Lillian. Would you lend me three hundred thousand dollars for a month?"

I said, "You bet. If I had it, I'd . . ."

He bowed. "Thank you. Then maybe somebody else will. If they do, I'll take you fishing."

Several years before, Willy had taken my father and me and one of the big-faced men called Hatchey on his large boat and we had had a fine two days fishing in the Gulf. My pleasure in the boat had pleased Willy and there had always been talk of another trip after that. Now he left the room, patting my head as he passed me, and Caroline Ducky fell asleep by the window. I went downstairs. I heard my mother say to somebody that things would be better now that the doctor had arrived.

Walking back to my Aunt Jenny's boardinghouse, I said, "So she is having her morphine. Gets it often, I guess."

My mother stared at me. "What makes you think anything like that?"

"Caroline Ducky. Plenty makes me think plenty. Like what about all that money she's making Uncle Willy pay back because of his Cajun girl?"

"My goodness," my mother whispered. "Please don't speak that way. Please."

And I knew I had gold if I could get the coins together. But it was no use because my mother was moving her lips in prayer and that meant she had left the world for a while.

For the next few days I tried games on Jenny, hinting at the morphine, deliberately mispronouncing it, giving her pieces of the conversation between Uncle Willy and Caroline Ducky, saying that I had read in books that men often had outside women like the Cajun girl and what did she think, but I got nowhere. Jenny said we should mind our own business because rich people like my ma's family often got into muddles not meant for the rest of us.

It was a difficult time for me. I wandered about the house at night and Mrs. Caronne, Aunt Jenny's oldest boarder, complained; I wrote two poems about the pleasures of autumn love; I skipped school and spent the days sitting in front of St. Louis Cathedral and one night I wandered back-of-town and got chased home by a cop. I was, of course, at an age of half understanding the people of my world, but I was sure, as are most young people, that there were simple answers and the world, or my own limitations, were depriving me of a mathematical solution. I began, for the first time in my life, to sulk and remain silent, no longer having any faith in what I would say if I did talk, and no faith in what I would hear from anybody else. The notebooks of those days are filled with question marks: the large, funny, sad questions of the very young.

The troubles of Aunt Lily were not spoken about and my mother, as far as I know, did not return to the house. But I did, every few days, circling it, standing down the street, seeing nothing, not even Honey. But after two weeks that was unbearable and so I decided to take some pickles to Caroline Ducky. As I turned in the back entrance, Uncle Willy came out the side entrance to load his car with fishing rods and a shotgun. He looked fine and easy in old tweed clothes and good boots.

When he saw me he said, "I'm going fishing and maybe a bird or two."

"Oh," I said, "I wish I were going. I do. I do."

"I'd like to have you," he said.

It's been too many years for me to remember how long we drove on the river road, but it was a long way and I was happier — exalted was the word I used when I thought about it afterward — than I had ever been before. It was as if I had changed my life and was proud of myself for the courage of the change. The wilder the country grew, the more we bumped along on the oyster shell roads, the wilder grew my fantasies: I was a rebel leader going to Africa to arouse my defeated tribe; I was a nun on my way to a leper colony; and when a copperhead crossed the road I was one of those crazy lady dancers who wound snakes around their bodies and seduced all men. Willy and I did not speak for a very long time, not one sentence, and then he said, "Oh, Lord, what about your mama, a toothbrush, all that stuff?"

There are many ways of falling in love and one seldom is more interesting or valid than another unless, of course, one of them lasts so long that it becomes something else, like your arm or leg about which you neither judge nor protest. I was not ever to fall in love very often, but certainly this was the first time and I would like to think that I learned from it. But the mixture of ecstasy as it clashed with criticism of myself and the man was to be repeated all my life, and the only thing that made the feeling for Uncle Willy different was the pain of that first recognition: not of love, but of the struggles caused by love; the blindness of a young girl trying to make simple sexual desire into something more complex, more poetic, more unreachable.

Somewhere, after that silent time, we stopped at a small store where Uncle Willy seemed to know the old lady who was sitting on the porch. He telephoned my mother from a back room and came out to say that all was O.K. He bought me a toothbrush and a comb, a pair of boots, heavy socks, a heavy woolen shirt, and twenty-four handkerchiefs. Maybe it was the extravagance of twenty-four that made me cry.

The bayou country has changed now, and if I hadn't seen it again a few months ago I would have forgotten what it looked like, which is the measure of the strangeness of that day because I remember best what things look like and forget what it has been like to be with them. But even now I could walk the route that Willy took that day so long ago as we left the car and began to move north, sometimes on a rough path, more often through undergrowth of strange and tangled roots. Swamp oak, cypress, sent out roots above ground and small plants and fern pushed against the wild high dark green leaves of a plant I had never seen before. There was constant movement along the ground and I was sweating with fear of snakes. Once

Uncle Willy, ahead of me, called out and waved me away. I saw that the swamp had come in suddenly and that he was deep in the mush, pulling himself up and out by throwing his arms around a black gum tree. He was telling me to move to my left but I didn't understand what he meant until I sank into the mud, my feet, my ankles going in as if underground giants were pulling at them. I liked it, it was soft and comfortable, and I leaned down to watch the things moving around me: crawfish, flat small things the shape of salamanders, then the brownness of something the size of my hand with a tail twice as long. I don't know how long I stood there, but I know Willy had called to me several times before I saw him. Above me now he had tied a branch to his pants belt and was throwing it a foot from me. It could not have been easy for him to pull me out as he stood on uncertain ground with my dead weight at the other end. I watched the power of the shoulders and the arms with the sleepy admiration of a woman in love. I think he was puzzled by my slowness, my lack of excitement or fear, because he kept asking me if something had happened and said he had been a fool to try a shortcut to the house.

I don't know where I thought we were going, or if I thought about it at all, but the house was the meanest I had ever seen and, over the next two days, more crowded with people. There was a room with three beds, and two others of Spanish moss on the floor, a kitchen of ells and wandering corners, dirty with

77

coal smoke, filled with half-broken chairs and odd
forgotten things against the walls. Willy was as gay
as my father had always said he was, embracing people who came and went, throwing a small child in the
air, and cooing at a baby who lay in an old box. He
was at home here, this man who was accustomed to the
most immaculate of houses, the imitated eighteenth-
century elegance of Aunt Lily's house. The dirt and
mess pleased him and so did the people. I could not
sort them out, the old from the young, the relations of
the men to the women, what child belonged to whom,
but they were all noisy with pleasure at Willy's arrival, and bowls of hot water were brought from the
stove and an old woman and a young woman cleaned
his boots and washed his feet. A young girl of about
my age took my shoes to dry on the stove and gave me
a bowl and a dirty rag to wash with. I must have
drawn back from the rag — obsessive cleanliness
now seems to me less embarrassing than it seemed
that day, New Orleans being a dirty city when I was
young, with open sewers and epidemics — because
Willy said something in Cajun French and the rag
was taken out of my hand.

It was a good night, the best I had ever had up to
then. The dinner was wonderful: jambalaya, raccoon
stew, and wild duck with bitter pickles, all hot with
red pepper that made the barrel-wine necessary after
each bite. The talk was loud and everybody spoke
together except when Willy spoke, but we were deep
in Cajun country and my school French needed ad-

justment to the omitted sounds and dropped syllables. My pleasure in food and wine was, of course,
my pleasure in Willy as he chased wine with whiskey,
wolfed the food, and boomed and laughed and was
amused, and pleased with me. I remember that a
very tall man came into the room, a man in city
clothes, and that my uncle left with him to sit on the
porch, and everybody else disappeared. But after
that I don't remember much because I was drunk
and woke up in the bedroom that smelled of other
people and saw two women on beds and one on the
floor. I have never known whether I heard that night
or the next night three quarrelsome voices outside the
house, and my uncle's voice saying, "If it goes wrong,
and the last one did, I'll get the blame. Nobody else.
And that will be curtains." A man kept saying, "You
got no choice." I had heard that voice before but I
was too sleepy to think about it. Certainly by the time
Willy shook me awake at dawn he was in a fine
humor, laughing down in my face, saying I must
never tell my mother he had got me drunk and to get
ready now for the ducks.

I have been duck shooting many times since that
early morning, but I have never liked it again because
it never again had to do with the pleasure of crouching
near Willy in the duck blind. I was then, was always
to be, a bad shot and once Willy was angry with me
because I ruined the flight overhead, but later he did
so well and the dogs made such fine recoveries that we
came back with fourteen ducks by nine o'clock. The

house was empty and Willy made us giant sandwiches
of many meats and peppers and said we were going to
the store. We walked around to where we had left the
car and drove down the bayou road to a settlement
of twenty or thirty houses and a store that seemed to
have everything — barrels of coffee, boots, bolts of
cloth, guns, sausages, cheeses and ropes of red peppers, fur hats, oars, fish traps and dried fish.

I was standing on the porch when I heard Willy say
to somebody inside, "Wait a minute, please. I'm on
the phone. Certainly you can see that." Then a young
man passed me carrying to our car a case of liquor,
three or four giant bolts of cloth, a box of ladies'
shoes with fancy buckles, a carton of coffee beans
and a sewing machine. Inside, Willy said, "Hatchey,
Hatchey? Ask them to hold off. No, it's not too late.
Send a cable to the boat." (I don't know if I knew
then the name Hatchey belonged to the man I had met
on Willy's boat, and who had been outside on the
porch the night before, or if I recognized it a long
time later when my father told my mother about the
troubles.) Then Willy came out and got in the car.
The owner of the store called out about a check for
last month's stuff and now all this, but Willy waved
him away and said his office would send it. The owner
said that would be fine, he just hoped Mr. Willy
understood he needed the money, and the car drove
off without me. A few minutes later it made a circle
in the road and came back to the store. Willy opened

the door for me and said, "Forgive me, kid. It's not a good day."

When we reached the house, Willy got out of the car and strode off. I didn't see him again until supper and then, as people thanked him for the gifts, he was bad-tempered and drank a lot. There had been plans for treeing raccoons that night, but Willy wouldn't go and wouldn't let me go. He and I sat on the porch for a long time while he drank whiskey and one of the old ladies brought pitchers of water for him. I think he had forgotten I was there because suddenly he began to whistle, a short call, then a long call. A young woman came down a side path as if she had been waiting there. She sat on the porch steps, at his feet. The second time he touched her hair I made a sound I had never heard myself make before, but neither of them noticed. A long time later, he threw an empty whiskey bottle into space, got up from his chair, toppled it as the girl rose to help him. She moved in back of him, put both arms under his, and they moved down the road. I followed them, not caring that I could almost certainly be heard as the oyster shell path crunched under me. They didn't go very far. There was another house, hidden by the trees, and then I knew I had seen the girl several times before; a big, handsome, heavy girl with fine dark hair.

I went back to the porch and sat there all night in a state that I could not describe with any truth because

I believe that what I felt that night was what I was
to feel about myself and other people years later:
the humiliation of vanity, the irrational feeling of
rejection from a man who, of course, paid me no
mind, and had no reason to do so. It is possible to feel
many conflicts and not know they are conflicts when
you are young: I was at one minute less than nothing
and, at another, powerful enough to revenge myself
with the murder of Willy. My head and body seemed
not to belong together, unable to carry the burden of
me. Then, as later, I revenged myself on myself:
when the sun came up I left the porch, no longer fearing the swamps. On the way down the road I, who
many years later was to get sick at the sight of one in
a zoo, stumbled on a snake and didn't care. A few
hours after that, a truck gave me a ride into New
Orleans. I had been walking in the wrong direction. I
did not see Willy again for five years, and if he worried about my disappearance that night, I was never to
hear about it.

One July day, three or four years later, on a beach,
my father said to my mother, "What's the verdict on
Willy?" He was asking what my mother's family was
saying.

She said, "I'm sorry for him."

"Yes," said my father, "I am sure you are, but
that's not what I'm asking."

"What can they do," she said, as she always did
when my father attacked her family. "It isn't their
fault that he lost everything."

"Have they forbidden you to see him?"

"Now, now," said my mother.

"So they have forbidden you."

"I'll see him as my conscience dictates," said my mother, "forbid or not, but I don't want fights."

I was old enough, grown by now, to say, "What happened?"

My father said, "He sent down a shipload of guns with Hatchey Moore intended for Christmas to use. They stopped the ship. There was a scandal."

"Guns to put down the natives?"

"Yes."

"You forgive that?" I asked.

"It's always been a disgrace," said my father who, to the end of his life, was a kind of left liberal who had admiration for the capitalist victors. "But it wasn't all Willy himself. He was just acting for the company. He happened to get caught. So they fired him. That old shooting-up stuff isn't liked by the new boys. Too raw. So Willy took the rap."

"And you feel sorry for him?"

"Yes, I do," said my father, "he's stone dead broke. He was good to me."

I said, "He's a murderer."

"Oh, my! Oh, my!" said my mother. "We're all weak vessels."

During those years, because I had started to go to college, we went less often to New Orleans, three or four times, perhaps, for a month. On each visit, my mother went to see Aunt Lily, but I never again went

in the front door of the house. I would go to the
kitchen entrance to call on Caroline Ducky, the last
time a few months before she died. She looked fine,
that hot June day, more vigorous than ever. We spoke
of Uncle Willy. She took for granted that I knew what
everybody else knew: he had been thrown out of "the
big company," had started his own fruit import company and was, according to New Orleans gossip, having a hard time. Somehow, somewhere, my aunt's
money was again involved, but that made no sense to
me because I couldn't see why she gave it or why he
once again took it from her. But then I was a young
eighteen and so little of what older people did made
any sense to me that I had stopped worrying about it,
finding it easier and more rewarding to understand
people in books.

On one of the visits to Caroline Ducky, she said,
"You ever see your Uncle Willy?"

"No."

"Me neither, much. He come around this house
maybe once a month, pick up something, sleep in his
office."

"Or with the Cajun girl."

"What Cajun girl? The part nigger Cajun girl?"

"I don't know," I said. "It doesn't make any difference to me if she's part nigger."

"Well," said Caroline Ducky's loud voice, "it
makes a difference to me, you little white Yankee
know-nothing."

I had already come half distance up the slippery

mountain dangers of liberalism. "I think maybe it's the only solution in the end. Whites and blacks . . ."

Caroline Ducky's large sewing basket went by my head. The old lady had remarkable strength, because when she saw the basket had missed me she rose and pulled me from the chair. "Get you down and pick up the mess you made."

As I was crawling around for needles and spools, fitting thimbles back into the pretty old box, she said, "That a nice box. Your mama gave it to me. I leave it to you when I go to die."

"I don't want it. I don't like people to throw things at me."

"You got a hard road to go," she said. "Part what you born from is good, part a mess of shit. Like your Aunt Lily. She made the shit and now she sit in it and poke around."

I was old enough to know what passed for wisdom among ladies: "I guess she's not had an easy time, Aunt Lily. Uncle Willy wanting her money, and his girls and all. That's what many people say."

"Many people is full a shit." With the years Caroline Ducky said shit more often than anybody I ever met except the head carpenter at the old Lyceum Theatre in Rochester, New York.

"Willy's got his side," said the old lady. "Where and why you think the morphine come here?"

I was so excited that I dropped the thread I was rewinding and tried not to shout. "The morphine the doctor gives Aunt Lily for her headaches?"

"He don't give her no morphine 'cause she don't have no headaches. Getting bad now, she won't last long." And Caroline Ducky giggled. (She was wrong. Aunt Lily lived another twenty-three years.) I guess Caroline Ducky was savoring Aunt Lily's death because she kept giggling for a while. Then she said, "That Peters ain't all nigger. His grandpa had a Wop store on Rampart Street. Wops know about stuff like that."

"Stuff like what?"

"Morphine," she screamed. "You wearing me out. And Wops make good fancy men. Peters been with your Aunt Lily long time now, but Mona Simpson down the road had him before that."

Over thirty years later, when *Toys in the Attic* had been produced and published, I had a letter from Honey. I guess he was out of the Mobile loony bin, at least for a while, because the letter had a San Diego postmark. He wanted to know if I ever came San Diego way, were my aunts still living and did I ever visit New Orleans; he himself never went there anymore although he still owned the St. Charles Avenue house, and, by the way, had I meant Mrs. Prine in my play to be his mother and her fancy man to be Peters? If I had, he didn't mind a bit, he'd just like to know. I had not realized until Honey's letter that the seeds of Mrs. Prine had, indeed, flown from Aunt Lily's famous gardenias to another kind of garden, but I thought it wise to deny even that to anybody as nutty as Honey. I showed my denial to Hammett, who

talked me out of mailing it, saying that the less I had
to do with Honey the better.

And that was because years before the letter, and
years after that last time I ever saw Caroline Ducky,
Aunt Lily and Honey, on her yearly New York buying sprees for jewelry and clothes and furniture, came
twice to visit us on the farm in Pleasantville. I don't
know why I invited them, some old hangover of curiosity, I guess, wanting to fill in missing parts of myself.

The first visit was O.K., although Honey seemed
even more odd than I remembered and there was some
mention of his nervous troubles. After they left, the
cook reported that she had seen him kick our largest
poodle and put a half-eaten piece of chocolate cake in
his pocket.

A few years later Aunt Lily and Honey drove out
with my father on a Sunday morning. Honey and I
went swimming and I showed him the stables, where
he teased a bad-tempered pony who kicked him. At
lunch the conversation was disjointed. My aunt, as
usual, ate almost nothing, but Honey went four times
to the buffet table.

My father said, "You have a good capacity, Honey.
The fish is pretty good, but how can you eat that other
junk?"

"That other junk," I said, "is sauerbraten. I cooked
it for the first time, to please you. It's German and I
thought you'd like it."

"It can't be German," said my father, "it's Jewish.

87

I don't know where you learned to make bad Jewish food."

When Dash laughed I was about to say something about loyalty, but was interrupted by Aunt Lily, who said to Honey, "Go vomit, dear."

Honey said, "I don't want to."

Aunt Lily sighed. Then she turned to my father. "You still see my husband, so called?"

"I'd like to see Willy, but I don't get home much anymore, and Willy doesn't come to New York."

"Oh, yes, he does," said Aunt Lily, "he comes all the time. He just doesn't want to see you anymore. He has no loyalty to anybody."

My father's face was angry. "He doesn't come North and you know it, because he doesn't have any money. None."

"That's right," said Honey through a mouthful of something. "Mama took it all. It's for me, she says, but she gives a lot to Peters."

Aunt Lily seemed to be dozing, so Honey said it again. When he got no answer he said it the third time and added, "That's because of fucking."

My father laughed. "Remember, Honey, my daughter is in the room." Then he said to Dash, "Some nuts." And he got up from the table to get himself a piece of sauerbraten.

Dash said to me, "Your father who hates the stuff has now eaten four pieces of it."

"You have to try everything to know you don't like it," said my father.

Aunt Lily turned to Honey. "I don't like your talk. Shut your face."

My father said to Aunt Lily, "Never punish a child for telling the truth. Haven't I lived by that, Lillian?"

"And by much else," I said.

My father turned to Dash. "Lillian's got the disposition of her mother's family. My family were good-natured. Look what's happening to Honey."

Honey had gone out into the hallway and was standing on his head. Aunt Lily said, "It's his way of adjusting his stomach. The doctor told me Willy has syphilis."

"Oh, Christ," my father said to me, "any time your mother's family get stuck with anything, crazy children, bad stocks and bonds, other people gave them syphilis."

I said to Aunt Lily, "I don't believe you. Uncle Willy is a fine man. I admire him very much."

Dash said, "Watch it, you're not going to like what you're saying."

Soon after lunch, Aunt Lily said she wanted "a lie-down," was there a room to rest in. I took her upstairs, Dash went to his room, my father and I sat reading, and once in a while I watched from the window to see that Honey was doing nothing more than dozing on the lawn. Toward four o'clock their car arrived and I went to tell Aunt Lily. There was no answer to my knocks, but when I opened the door Aunt Lily was not asleep: she was sitting in a chair, staring out the window at the top of a tree. I spoke to her several times, moved in front of her, leaned over her. There was no sign of recognition, no answer. I went to get Honey. He was sitting in the car. Before I spoke he said, "She gets like that."

"What's the matter with her?"

"Peters takes care of it, not me. I'll send him back tomorrow."

"Where are you going?"

"To New York. I got a date."

I said to the chauffeur, "Wait here, please. This gentleman can't pay for the car without his mother," and went off to find Hammett. He put down his book and went with me to the room where Aunt Lily was sitting. He pulled a chair up next to her.

"You're a very handsome man," she said. "Handsome people have an easier time in this vale of tears."

"Your car is waiting," he said.

"I hope you are good to my niece. Are you good to . . ." and faltered over my name.

"Better than she deserves," said Dash. "Please get up. I will help you to the car."

"In our South," she said, "it is a mark of woman's trust when she allows the use of her first name. Call me Lily."

"No," he said, "one is enough," and reaching down for her arms he brought her to her feet. But he had not correctly gauged her humor, because she pulled sharply away from him, moved to the bureau, and held tight to its sides.

I think she saw me for the first time. She said, "What are you doing here? You like Willy. You're no good."

"We'll talk about that another day," Dash said and moved quickly to take away the alligator pocketbook that had been her reason for the move to the bureau.

"Give me my bag immediately," she said, "there's a great deal of jewelry in that bag."

Dash laughed. "More than jewelry. Come along."

I followed them down the stairs and stood on the porch as Dash moved her down the driveway to the car. Once she stumbled and, as he caught her, she threw off his arm and moved away with the overdignified motions of a drunk. As Dash shut the door of the car, I heard Honey laugh and he waved to me as they drove past the porch.

"Well," said Dash, "that will be enough of them, I hope."

"What was that about her pocketbook?"

"She wanted a fix. I don't know what kind and don't want to. A bad pair. Why don't you leave them alone?"

"What did you mean when I said Uncle Willy was a fine man and you said I wasn't going to like what I was saying?"

"You told me that even as a child you hated what his company was doing, the murders, and what it meant to you."

"I never told you Willy did the murders. He's a

good man. He just went where life took him, I guess."

"Oh, sure. Now let's leave that talk for another day or forever."

"Why should we leave it? You always say that when . . ."

"Because I want to leave it," he said, "maybe in the hope you'll find out for yourself."

I thought about that for a few days, sulked with it, then left it and forgot about it.

A year later Dash and I moved to Hollywood for four or five months, each of us to write a movie. Soon after we got there, we had one of our many partings: Hammett was drinking heavily, dangerously. I was sick of him and myself and so one weekend I took off to see my aunts in New Orleans. I would not have liked to live with them for very long, but for a few days I always liked their modest, disciplined life in the shabby little house that was all they could afford since each had stopped working. It was nice, after the plush of Hollywood, to sleep on a cot in the ugly living room, crowded with stuff that poor people can't bring themselves to throw away, nice to talk about what we would have for the good dinner to which one of many old ladies would be invited to show off my aunts' quiet pride in me. Nicest of all was to take a small piece of all the Hollywood money and buy them new winter coats and dresses at Maison Blanche, to be delivered after I left for fear that they'd make me return them if I were there, and then to go along to Solari's, the fine grocers, and load a taxi with delicacies they liked and would never buy, hear Jenny protest over the calves'-foot jelly she liked so much and watch Hannah's lovely, greedy eyes deny the words she made over the cans of giant Belgian asparagus.

The taxi driver and I were piling in the Solari cartons when I saw Willy staring at me from across the street. He was much older: the large body hung now with loose flesh, the hair was tumbled, the heavy face lined and colored sick. I crossed the street and kissed him. He put an arm around me and pressed my head to his shoulder.

He said very softly, "So you turned into a writer? Come and have lunch with me."

He paid the taxi driver to take the stuff to my aunts' house and we walked a few blocks to Decatur Street and turned into an old building facing the river that had a large sign saying, "Guacosta Fruit Import Company." As we went up the steps he said, "This is my company, I am rich again. Do you need anything money can buy?"

Directly opposite the stair landing was an enormous room entirely filled by a dining room table. Along the table, at intervals of ten or twelve chairs, were printed signs, "French," "Mexican," "German," "Creole," "Plain steaks, chops," and seated at the table, sometimes in groups of four or five, occasionally alone, were perhaps twenty men who looked like, and maybe were, the men I had seen at Willy's house on the Sundays so many years before.

Willy put his arm around me, "What kind of food,

kid? There's a different good chef for each kind."
When I chose Creole, he whispered to the two men
who were sitting in that section and they rose and
moved down the table. We must have had a lot of
wine because our lunch lasted long after everybody
left and I didn't get back to my aunts until six that
evening, and then I was so rocky that I had a hard
time convincing them not to send for a doctor and
during the night, through the thin walls, I heard them
talking, and twice Hannah came to turn on the light
and look down at me.

I was in the shower the next morning when there
was a knock on the bathroom door and Willy said,
"Come along. We're going to the country."

Going down the steps, I saw my aunts in the garden.
I called out and Hannah waved, but Jenny turned her
back, and Hannah dropped her hand.

Toward midday we went through the town of Hammond and Willy said, "In a few minutes." The long
driveway, lined with moss oak, ended at a galleried
plantation house. "We're home," he said. It was a
beautiful, half empty house of oval rooms and delicate colors. Beyond the great lawns were strawberry
fields and, in the distance, ten or twelve horses moved
slowly in a field.

I said, "I like my farm in Pleasantville. But there's
nothing like the look of Southern land, or there's no
way for me to get over thinking so. It's home for me
still."

"I'll give you this place," he said. "I'd like you to
have it."

Late in the afternoon, after a long walk in the strawberry acres, I said my aunts would be hurt if I didn't
have dinner with them. We had an argument about
that, and then we started back to New Orleans. Willy's
driving was erratic and I realized that he had had a
great deal to drink during the day. When we took a
swerve I saw that he had been dozing at the wheel.
He stopped the car, said he thought I should drive,
and he slept all the way to the outskirts of New Orleans.

I hadn't expected the voice, nor the soberness with
which he said, "Pull over for a minute."

We stopped in the flat land that was beginning then
to be as ugly as it is now.

"When are you going to Los Angeles?"

"Tomorrow morning."

"Do you have to?"

"No. I don't have to do anything," believing, as I
had done all my life that was true, or believing it for
the minute I said it.

"I've been faking. I'm broke, more than I've ever
been. Stone broke. That lovely house will have to go
this week, I guess, and I haven't got the stuff to pay a
month's rent on the office. I owe everybody from here
to Memphis to Costa Rica."

"I have some money now," I said.

"Don't do that," he said sharply, "don't say it
again." He got out of the car, walked around it and
came to my window. His face was gay and he was
grinning now. "I am going to Central America on
Friday. I'll move the way I first went as a boy, on

mules. I'm the best banana buyer in the world. I'll get all the credit I want when I get there, San José, Cartago. Three or four months. I can't tell you how I want to go the way I did when I was young. It's rough country and wonderful. Come with me. You'll see with me what you could never see without me. A mule hurts, at first, but if I were your age . . ." He touched my hand. "Anyway it's time you and I finished what we have already started. Come on."

That night, at dinner, I told my aunts I would not be leaving them until Friday. Hannah was pleased but Jenny said nothing. The next morning when I went into the dining room, Jenny pointed to a large florist box and watched me unwrap a dozen orchid sprays. She said Willy had phoned and left the name of a man who made fine riding boots, he had ordered me two pairs and I was to go down immediately, fit them, and come to his office for lunch. I was uneasy at the expression on Jenny's face and went to get dressed. When I came back she was sitting in the hall opposite my door, Hannah standing next to her. She raised her hand and Hannah disappeared.

"You're going riding on a horse?"

"Yes," I said.

"As I remember your riding, you don't need made-to-order boots."

"I'm going to Central America for a few months."

Jenny had rheumatism and always moved with difficulty. Now she got out of the chair, holding to a table. When I moved to help her she pulled her arm away from me.

"In that case," she said, "you can't stay here. You have been our child, maybe more, but you can't stay here."

I said, "Jenny! Jenny!" But she pushed passed me and slammed the door of the kitchen.

I lay on the bed for a long time but after a while I packed my bags and went to find a taxicab. It was raining a little and they were scarce that day and by the time I reached St. Charles Avenue there was a sudden, frightening curtain of rain, so common in New Orleans. I went into a restaurant and had a drink.

I phoned the Beverly Hills house from the restaurant. I said to Hammett, "I'm in New Orleans. I'm not coming back to Hollywood for a while and I didn't want you to worry."

"How are you?" he said.

"O.K. and you?"

"I'm O.K. I miss you."

"I miss you, too. Is there a lady in my bedroom?"

He laughed. "I don't think so, but they come and go. Except you. You just go."

"I had good reason," I said.

"Yes," he said, "you did."

"Anyway," I said, "I'll be back in a few months. Take care of yourself and I'll call you when I come back. Maybe then we won't have to talk about reasons and can just have a nice dinner."

"No," he said, "I don't think so. I'm not crazy about women who sleep with murderers."

"I haven't slept with him. And he's never killed anybody."

"No," he said, "he just hired people to do it for him. I was in that racket for a lot of years and I don't like it." He sighed. "Do what you want. Have a nice time but don't call me."

I flew to Los Angeles that night. I didn't telephone Dash but somebody must have told him I was there because after about ten days he called me, said he was on the wagon, and we had a nice dinner together. I never saw Willy again and never had an answer to the letter I had mailed from New Orleans.

On my birthday that year my aunts sent a hand-knitted sweater and the usual box of pralines with a note saying all the usual affectionate things and adding, as a postscript, that Willy had gone into bankruptcy and barely avoided jail for reasons they couldn't figure out. And not many months after that I had a telephone call from a man I knew who worked on a New Orleans newspaper. He said that Willy, driving up the road to Hammond and the strawberry plantation, with two men, had had an automobile accident that killed everybody in the car, and did I want to comment for the obit.

Years later, Caroline Ducky's grandchild, who had worked for Willy as a cleaning woman, said it hadn't been any mystery, that accident, because he had started out dead drunk from a one-room, cockroach apartment he had rented on Bourbon Street.

JULIA

I HAVE here changed most of the names. I don't know that it matters anymore, but I believe the heavy girl on the train still lives in Cologne and I am not sure that even now the Germans like their premature anti-Nazis. More important, Julia's mother is still living and so, perhaps, is Julia's daughter. Almost certainly, the daughter's father lives in San Francisco.

In 1937, after I had written *The Children's Hour* and *Days to Come*, I had an invitation to attend a theatre festival in Moscow. Whenever in the past I wrote about that journey, I omitted the story of my trip through Berlin because I did not feel able to write about Julia.

Dorothy Parker and her husband, Alan Campbell, were going to Europe that same August, and so we crossed together on the old *Normandie,* a pleasant trip even though Campbell, and his pretend-good-natured feminine jibes, had always made me uneasy.

When we reached Paris I was still undecided about going on to Moscow. I stayed around, happy to meet Gerald and Sara Murphy for the first time, Hemingway, who came up from Spain, and James Lardner, Ring Lardner's son, who was soon to enlist in the International Brigade and to lose his life in Spain a few months later.

I liked the Murphys. I was always to like and be interested in them, but they were not for me what they had been to an older generation. They were, possibly, all that Calvin Tomkins says in his biography: they had style, Gerald had wit, Sara grace and shrewdness, and that summer, soon after they had lost both their sons, they had a sweet dignity. But through the many years I was to see them after that I came to believe they were not as bonny as others thought them, or without troubles with each other, and long before the end — the end of my knowing them, I mean, a few years before Gerald died, when they saw very few of their old friends — I came to think that too much of their lives had been based on style. Style is mighty pleasant for those who benefit from it, but maybe not always rewarding for those who make and live by its necessarily strict rules.

There were many other people that summer in

102

Paris, famous and rich, who invited Dottie for dinners and country lunches and the tennis she didn't play and the pools she didn't swim in. It gave me pleasure then, and forever after, that people courted her. I was amused at her excessive good manners, a kind of put-on, often there to hide contempt and dislike for those who flattered her at the very minute she begged for the flattery. When she had enough to drink the good manners got so good they got silly, but then the words came funny and sharp to show herself, and me, I think, that nobody could buy her. She was wrong: they could and did buy her for years. But they only bought a limited ticket to her life and in the end she died on her own road.

It was a new world for me. I had been courted around New York and Hollywood, as is everybody who has been a success in the theatre and young enough not to have been too much on display. But my invitations were second-class stuff compared to Dottie's admirers that month in Paris. I had a fine time, one of the best of my life. But one day, after a heavy night's drinking, I didn't anymore. I was a child of the Depression, a kind of Puritan Socialist, I guess — although to give it a name is to give it a sharper outline than it had — and I was full of the strong feelings the early Roosevelt period brought to many people. Dottie had the same strong feelings about something we all thought of as society and the future, but the difference between us was more than generational — she was long accustomed to much I didn't want. It was true that she always turned against the famous and the rich who attracted her, but I never liked them well enough to bother that much.

I had several times that month spoken on the phone with my beloved childhood friend Julia, who was studying medicine in Vienna, and so the morning after the heavy drinking I called Julia to say I would come to Vienna the next day en route to Moscow. But that same night, very late, she called back.

She said, "I have something important for you to do. Maybe you'll do it, maybe you can't. But please stay in Paris for a few days and a friend will come to see you. If things work as I hope, you'll decide to go straight to Moscow by way of Berlin and I'll meet you on your way back."

When I said I didn't understand, who was the friend, why Berlin, she said, "I can't answer questions. Get a German visa tomorrow. You'll make your own choice, but don't talk about it now."

It would not have occurred to me to ignore what Julia told me to do because that's the way it had always been between us. So I went around the next morning to the German consulate for a visa. The consul said they'd give me a traveling permit, but would not allow me to stay in Berlin overnight, and the Russian consul said that wasn't unusual for people en route to Moscow.

I waited for two days and was about to call Julia again on the day of the morning I went down for an early breakfast in the dining room of the Hotel Meurice. (I had been avoiding Dottie and Alan, all invitations, and was troubled and annoyed by two snippy, suspicious notes from Alan about what was I up to, why was I locked in my room?) The concierge said the gentleman on the bench was waiting for me. A tall middle-aged man got up from the bench and said, "Madame Hellman? I come to deliver your tickets and to talk with you about your plans. Miss Julia asked me to call with the travel folders."

We went into the dining room, and when I asked him what he would like he said, in German, "Do you think I can have an egg, hot milk, a roll? I cannot pay for them."

When the waiter moved away, the tall man said, "You must not understand German again. I made a mistake."

I said I didn't understand enough German to worry anybody, but he didn't answer me and took to reading the travel folders until the food came. Then he ate very fast, smiling as he did it, as if he were remembering something pleasant from a long ago past. When he finished, he handed me a note. The note said, "This is my friend, Johann. He will tell you. But *I* tell you, don't push yourself. If you can't you can't, no dishonor. Whatever, I will meet you soon. Love, Julia."

Mr. Johann said, "I thank you for fine breakfast. Could we walk now in Tuileries?"

As we entered the gardens he asked me how much I knew about Benjamin Franklin, was I an expert? I said I knew almost nothing. He said he admired Franklin and perhaps someday I could find him a nice photograph of Franklin in America. He sat down suddenly on a bench and mopped his forehead on this cool, damp day.

"Have you procured a German visa?"

"A traveling visa. I cannot stay overnight. I can only change stations in Berlin for Moscow."

"Would you carry for us fifty thousand dollars? We think, we do not guarantee, you will be without trouble. You will be taking the money to enable us to bribe out many already in prison, many who soon will be. We are a small group, valuable workers against Hitler. We are of no common belief or religion. The people who will meet you for the money, if your consent is given, were once small publishers. We are of Catholic, Communist, many beliefs. Julia has said that I must remind you for her that you are afraid of being afraid, and so will do what sometimes you cannot do, and that could be dangerous to you and to us."

I took to fiddling with things in my pocketbook, lit a cigarette, fiddled some more. He sat back as if he were very tired, and stretched.

After a while I said, "Let's go and have a drink."

He said, "I repeat. We think all will go well, but much could go wrong. Julia says I must tell you that, but that if we should not hear from you by the time of Warsaw, Julia will use her family with the American ambassador there through Uncle John."

"I know her family. There was a time she didn't believe in them much."

"She said you would note that. And so to tell you that her Uncle John is now governor. He does not like her but did not refuse her money for his career. And that her mother's last divorce has made her mother dependent on Julia as well."

I laughed at this picture of Julia controlling members of her very rich family. I don't think we had seen each other more than ten or twelve times since we were eighteen years old and so the years had evidently brought changes I didn't know about. Julia had left college, gone to Oxford, moved on to medical school in Vienna, had become a patient-pupil of Freud's. We had once, in the last ten years, spent a Christmas holiday together, and one summer, off Massachusetts, we had sailed for a month on her small boat, but in the many letters we had written in those years neither of us knew much more than the bare terms of each other's life, nothing of the daily stuff that is the real truth, the importance.

I knew, for example, that she had become, maybe always was, a Socialist, and lived by it, in a one-room apartment in a slum district of Vienna, sharing her great fortune with whoever needed it. She allowed herself very little, wanted very little. Oddly, gifts to me did not come into the denial: they were many and extravagant. Through the years, whenever she saw anything I might like, it was sent to me: old Wedgwood pieces, a Toulouse-Lautrec drawing, a fur-lined coat we saw together in Paris, a set of Balzac that she put in a rare Empire desk, and a wonderful set of Georgian jewelry, I think the last thing she could have had time to buy.

I said to the gray man, "Could I think it over for a few hours? That's what Julia meant."

He said, "Do not think hard. It is best not to be too prepared for matters of this kind. I will be at the station tomorrow morning. If you agree to carry the money, you will say hello to me. If you have decided it is not right for you, pass by me. Do not worry whichever is decided by you." He held out his hand, bowed, and moved away from me across the gardens.

I spent the day in and around Sainte-Chapelle, tried to eat lunch and dinner, couldn't, and went back to the hotel to pack only after I was sure Dottie and Alan would have gone to dinner with the Murphys. I left a note for them saying I was leaving early in the morning and would find them again after Moscow. I knew I had spent the whole day in a mess of indecision. Now I lay down, determined that I would not sleep until I had taken stock of myself. But decisions, particularly important ones, have always made me sleepy, perhaps because I know that I will have to make them by instinct, and thinking things out is only what other people tell me I should do. In any case, I slept through the night and rose only in time to hurry for the early morning train.

I was not pleased to find Dottie and Alan in the lobby, waiting to take me to the station. My protests were so firm and so awkward that Alan, who had a remarkable nose for deception, asked if I had a reason for not wanting them to come with me. When he went to get a taxi, I said to Dottie, "Sorry if I sounded rude. Alan makes me nervous."

She smiled, "Dear Lilly, you'd be a psychotic if he didn't."

At the railroad station I urged them to leave me when my baggage was carried on, but something had excited Alan: perhaps my nervousness; certainly not his claim that they had never before known anybody who was en route to Moscow. He was full of bad jokes about what I must not say to Russian actors, how to smuggle out caviar, and all the junk people like Alan say when they want to say something else.

I saw the gray man come down the platform. As he came near us Alan said, "Isn't that the man I saw you with in the Tuileries yesterday?" And as I turned to say something to Alan, God knows what it would have been, the gray man went past me and was moving back into the station.

I ran toward him. "Mr. Johann. Please, Mr. Johann." As he turned, I lost my head and screamed, "Please don't go away. *Please*."

He stood still for what seemed like a long time, frowning. Then he moved slowly back toward me, as if he were coming with caution, hesitation.

Then I remembered: I said, "I only wanted to say hello. Hello to you, Mr. Johann, hello."

"Hello, Madame Hellman."

Alan had come to stand near us. Some warning had to be made. "This is Mr. Campbell and Miss Parker there. Mr. Campbell says he saw us yesterday and now he will ask me who you are and say that he didn't know we knew each other so well that you would come all this way to say goodbye to me."

Mr. Johann said, without hesitation, "I wish I could say that was true. But I have come to search for my nephew who is en route to Poland. He is not in his coach, he is late, as is his habit. His name is W. Franz, car 4, second class, and if I do not find him I would be most grateful if you say to him I came." He lifted his hat. "I am most glad, Madame Hellman, that we had this chance to say hello."

"Oh, yes," I said, "indeed. Hello. Hello."

When he was gone, Alan said, "What funny talk. You're talking like a foreigner."

"Sorry," I said, "sorry not to speak as well as you do in Virginia."

Dottie laughed, I kissed her and jumped for the train. I was nervous and went in the wrong direction. By the time a conductor told me where my compartment was, the train had left the station. On the connecting platform, before I reached my coach, a young man was standing holding a valise and packages. He said, "I am W. Franz, nephew, car 4, second class. This is a birthday present from Miss Julia." He handed me a box of candy and a hatbox marked "Madame Pauline." Then he bowed and moved off.

I carried the boxes to my compartment, where

two young women were sitting on the left bench. One girl was small and thin and carried a cane. The other was a big-boned woman of about twenty-eight, in a heavy coat, wrapped tight against this mild day. I smiled at them, they nodded, and I sat down. I put my packages next to me and only then noticed that there was a note pasted on the hatbox. I was frightened of it, thought about taking it to the ladies' room, decided that would look suspicious, and opened it. I had a good memory in those days for poems, for what people said, for the looks of things, but it has long since been blurred by time. But I still remember every word of that note: "At the border, leave the candy box on the seat. Open this box and wear the hat. There is no thanks for what you will do for them. No thanks from me either. But there is the love I have for you. Julia."

I sat for a long time holding the note. I was in a state that I have known since I was old enough to know myself, and that to this day frightens me and makes me unable even to move my hands. I do not mean to be foolishly modest about my intelligence: it is often high, but I have known since childhood that faced with a certain kind of simple problem, I sometimes make it so complex that there is no way out. I simply do not see what another mind grasps immediately. I was there now. Julia had not told me where to open the hatbox. To take it into the corridor or toilet might make the two ladies opposite me suspicious. And so I sat doing nothing for a long time until I realized that I didn't know when we crossed the border — a few minutes or a few hours. A decision had to be made but I could not make it.

Childhood is less clear to me than to many people: when it ended I turned my face away from it for no reason that I know about, certainly without the usual reason of unhappy memories. For many years that worried me, but then I discovered that the tales of former children are seldom to be trusted. Some people supply too many past victories or pleasures with which to comfort themselves, and other people cling to pains, real and imagined, to excuse what they have become.

I think I have always known about my memory: I know when it is to be trusted and when some dream or fantasy entered on the life, and the dream, the need of dream, led to distortion of what happened. And so I knew early that the rampage angers of an only child were distorted nightmares of reality. But I trust absolutely what I remember about Julia.

Now, so many years later, I could climb the steps without a light, move in the night through the crowded rooms of her grandparents' great Fifth Avenue house with the endless chic-shabby rooms, their walls covered with pictures, their tables crowded with objects whose value I didn't know. True, I cannot remember anything said or done in that house except for the first night I was allowed to sleep there. Julia and I were both twelve years old that New Year's Eve night, sitting at a late dinner, with courses of fish and meats, and sherbets in between to change the tastes, "clear the palate" is what her grandmother said, with watered wine for us, and red and white wine and champagne for the two old people. (Were they old? I don't know: they were her grandparents.) I cannot remember any talk at the table, but after dinner we were allowed to go with them to the music room. A servant had already set the phonograph for "So Sheep May Safely Graze," and all four of us listened until Julia rose, kissed the hand of her grandmother, the brow of her grandfather, and left the room, motioning for me to follow. It was an odd ritual, the whole thing, I thought, the life of the very rich, and beyond my understanding.

Each New Year's Eve of my life has brought back the memory of that night. Julia and I lay in twin beds and she recited odds and ends of poetry — every once in a while she would stop and ask me to recite, but I didn't know anything — Dante in Italian, Heine in German, and even though I could not understand either language, the sounds were so lovely that I felt a sweet sadness as if much was ahead in the world, much that was going to be fine and fulfilling if I could ever find my way. I did recite Mother Goose and she did Donne's "Julia," and laughed with pleasure "at his tribute to me." I was ashamed to ask if it was a joke.

Very late she turned her head away for sleep, but I said, "More, Julia, please. Do you know more?" And she turned on the light again and recited from Ovid and Catullus, names to me without countries.

I don't know when I stopped listening to look at the lovely face propped against the pillow — the lamp throwing fine lights on the thick dark hair. I cannot say now that I knew or had ever used the words gentle or delicate or strong, but I did think that night that it was the most beautiful face I had ever seen. In later years I never thought about how she looked, although when we were grown other people often said she was a "strange beauty," she "looked like nobody else," and one show-off said a "Burne-Jones face" when, of course, her face had nothing to do with Burne-Jones or fake spirituality.

There were many years, almost twenty, between that New Year's Eve and the train moving into Germany. In those years, and the years after Julia's death, I have had plenty of time to think about the love I had for her, too strong and too complicated to be defined as only the sexual yearnings of one girl for another. And yet certainly that was there. I don't know, I never cared, and it is now an aimless guessing game. It doesn't prove much that we never kissed each other; even when I leaned down in a London funeral parlor to kiss the battered face that had been so hideously put back together, it was not the awful scars that worried me: because I had never kissed her I thought perhaps she would not want it and so I touched the face instead.

A few years after that childhood New Year's Eve,
I was moved to a public school. (My father was having a bad time and couldn't afford to pay for me anymore.) But Julia and I saw each other almost every
day and every Saturday night I still slept in her grandparents' house. But, in time, our lives did change:
Julia began to travel all summer and in winter holi-
days, and when she returned all my questions about
the beauties of Europe would be shrugged off with
badly photographed snapshots of things that interested her: two blind children in Cairo — she explained that the filth carried by flies caused the blindness; people drinking from sewers in Teheran; no
St. Mark's but the miserable hovel of a gondolier in
Venice; no news of the glories of Vatican art but
stories about the poverty of Trastevere.

Once she returned with a framed photograph of a
beautiful woman who was her mother and an English-
man who was her mother's husband. I asked her what
she felt about seeing her mother — in all the years I
had never heard her mention her mother — and she
stared at me and said that her mother owned a "very
fancy castle" and the new husband poured drinks for
all the titles who liked the free stuff, but there was
also mention of Evelyn Waugh and H. G. Wells and
Nancy Cunard, and when I wanted news of them she
said she didn't know anything about them, they'd
said hello to her and that she had only wanted to get
out of the way and go to her room.

"But I didn't have a *room*," she said. "Everybody

has a suite, and there are fourteen servants somewhere below the earth, and only some of them have a window in the cell my mother calls their room, and there's only one stinking bath for all of them. My mother learns fast, wherever she is. She does not offend the host country."

Once, when we were about sixteen, we went with her grandparents at Easter time to their Adirondacks lodge, as large and shabby as was every place they lived in. Both old people drank a good deal — I think they always had, but I had only begun to notice it — and napped after every meal. But they stayed awake late into the night doing intricate picture puzzles imported from France, on two tables, and gave each other large checks for the one who finished first.

I don't remember that Julia asked their permission for our camping trips — several times we stayed away for weekends — on or near Lake Champlain. It wasn't proper camping, although we carried blankets and clean socks and dry shoes and canned food. We walked a great deal, often I fished for trout, and once, climbing a high hill, Julia threw a net over a rabbit, running with a grace and speed I had never before seen in a girl, and she showed me how to skin the rabbit. We cooked it that night wrapped in bacon and it is still among the best things I ever ate, maybe because *Robinson Crusoe* is one of the best books I ever read. Even now, seeing any island, I am busy with that rabbit and fantasies of how I would make do alone, without shelter or tools.

When we walked or fished we seldom did it side by side: that was her choice and I admired it because I believed she was thinking stuff I couldn't understand and mustn't interfere with, and maybe because I knew even then she didn't want to be side by side with any-body.

At night, wrapped in our blankets, the fire between us, we would talk. More accurately, I would ask questions and she would talk: she was one of the few people I have ever met who could give information without giving a lecture. How young it sounds now that although I had heard the name of Freud, I never knew exactly what he wrote until she told me; that Karl Marx and Engels became men with theories, instead of that one sentence in my school book which mentioned the Manifesto. But we also talked like all young people, of possible beaux and husbands and babies, and heredity versus environment, and can romantic love last, mixing stuff like that in speeches made only for the pleasure of girls on the edge of growing up.

One night, when we had been silent for a long time because she was leaning on an elbow, close to the fire, reading a German grammar, I laughed at the sounds coming from her mouth as she repeated the sentences.

She said, "No, you don't understand. People are either teachers or students. You are a student."

"Am I a good one?"

"When you find what you want, you will be very good."

I reached out and touched her hand. "I love you,

117

Julia." She stared at me and took my hand to her face.

It was in our nineteenth year that she went away to Oxford. The second year she was there I went to visit her. There are women who reach a perfect time of life, when the face will never again be as good, the body never as graceful or as powerful. It had happened that year to Julia, but she was no more conscious of it than she had been of being a beautiful child. Her clothes were ugly now, loose, tacky, and the shoes looked as if they had been stolen from an old man. Nobody came to her rooms because, as one smitten young Indian gentleman told me, she never asked anybody. She was invited everywhere in Oxford and in London, but the only names I remember her speaking of with respect were J. D. Bernal and J. B. S. Haldane. Once or twice we went up to the theatre in London, but she would sigh halfway through and say she had no feeling for the theatre, only Shakespeare on the page, and sometimes not even then.

The following year she wrote to tell me that she was leaving England for medical school in Vienna, with the probably vain hope that Freud would someday accept her as a student.

I wrote a number of letters that year, but the only time I heard from Julia was a cable on my birthday, followed by the Toulouse-Lautrec drawing that hangs today in my house. I was pleased that she thought I knew the excellence of Toulouse-Lautrec, because I didn't, and had to be told about him by a fellow student who used to buy me hamburgers in order, I think, to tell me about his homosexual experiences. (He was a very decorated hero during the Second World War and was killed a week before it ended.)

A few months later I had a letter from Anne-Marie Travers, a girl whom Julia and I had both known in school, but I knew better because we had gone to the same dreadful summer camp. Anne-Marie was an intelligent girl, flirtatious, good-mannered with that kind of outward early-learned passive quality that in women so often hides anger. Now, it seemed, she was in or near Vienna and her unexpected letter — I don't think we had seen each other for four or five years — said she had bumped into Julia on the street and been "snubbed," had heard from people that Julia was leading a strange life, very political, pretending not to be rich and living in the Floridsdorf district, the Socialist working-class "slums." Julia ranked second in the medical school, she had been told, the first candidate being an American also but of a German inheritance, a very remarkable boy from San Francisco, handsome in the Norwegian way, she, Anne-Marie, didn't like. It took knowing Anne-Marie to realize that German and Norwegian used in the same sentence was a combination of put-down and admiration. Anne-Marie added that her brother Sammy had recently tried to kill himself, and was I still torn between being a writer or an architect? There was something strange about the letter, some reason, some tone I didn't understand, didn't like. Then I forgot it for a month or so until her brother Sammy rang to ask me for dinner, saying that he had been living in Elba and thinking of me. He said it again at dinner, having had four whiskeys with beer chasers, and asked me if I was a virgin. This was not like Sammy, who had no interest in me, and I sensed something was to follow. At about four in the morning when we were sitting in Small's in Harlem, and there had been many more whiskeys and beers, he asked me why I had got a divorce, why hadn't I married his older brother Eliot, whose rich Detroit wife had lost all her money in the Depression, and so Eliot was again open to bids and would be right for me, although he himself thought Eliot a handsome bore. He said he rather liked his sister Anne-Marie, because he had slept with her when she was sixteen and he was eighteen. Then, perhaps because I made a sound, he said who the hell was I to talk, everybody knew about Julia and me.

It is one of the strange American changes in custom that the drunks of my day often hit each other, but never in the kind of bar fight that so often happens now with knives. In those days somebody hit somebody, and when that was finished one of them offered his hand and it would have been unheard of to refuse. (James Thurber had once thrown a glass of whiskey at me in the famous Tony's speakeasy, Hammett had pushed Thurber against a wall, Thurber had picked up a glass from another table and, in an attempt to throw it at Dash, missed and hit the waiter who was Tony's cousin. Tony called the police, saying over and over again that he had had enough of Thurber through the years. Almost everybody agreed with Tony, but when the police came we were shocked and went down to the police station to say nothing had happened except a drunken accident of a broken glass; and while I don't think Thurber liked me afterward, I don't think he had liked me before. In any case, none of us ever mentioned it again.) And so, at that minute at the table at Small's, there seemed to me nothing odd about what I did. I leaned across the table, slapped Sammy in the face, got up, turned over the table, and went home. The next day a girl called me to say that Sammy couldn't remember what he had said but he was sorry, anyway, and a large amount of flowers arrived that evening. The girl called again a few days later: I said there were no hard feelings, but Sammy was a bigger dope at twenty-five than he had been at seventeen. She said she'd tell him that.

I wrote to Anne-Marie saying that whatever Julia thought or did was bound to be interesting, and that I didn't want to hear attacks on her beliefs or her life. My letter was returned, unopened or resealed, and it was to be another year before I knew why.

Not long after, I had a letter from Julia suggesting that I come to Vienna for a visit, that Freud had accepted her, that there were things I ought to learn about "the holocaust that is on its way." I wrote back that I was living with Hammett, didn't want to leave, but would come maybe next year. Subsequent letters from her talked of Hitler, Jews, radicals, Mussolini.

We wrote a great deal that year, 1933–1934, and I told her that I was trying to write a play, hadn't much hope about it, but that Hammett was pulling me along. I asked her if she liked *The Children's Hour* as a title and was hurt when she forgot the question in her next letter, which was angry with news of the armed political groups in Austria, the threat of Hitler, "the criminal guilt of the English and French in not recognizing the dangers of Fascism, German style, the other one is a peacock." There was much in her letter I didn't understand, although all of us by that time knew that the Nazis would affect our lives.

I could not write a history of those years as it seemed to us then. Or, more accurately, I could not write my own: I have no records and I do not know when I understood what. I know that Hitler — Mussolini might have escaped our notice as no more than a big-talking man in silly uniforms — had shaken many of us into radicalism, or something we called radicalism, and that our raw, new convictions would, in time, bring schisms and ugly fights. But in the early Thirties I don't believe the people I knew had done much more than sign protests, listen to the shocking stories of the few German émigrés who had come to New York or Hollywood, and given money to one cause or another. We were disturbed by the anti-Semitism that was an old story in Germany and some of us had sense enough to see it as more than that. Many people thought of it as not much more than the ignorant rantings of a house painter and his low-down friends, who would certainly be rejected by the Germans, who were for my generation an "advanced," "cultivated" people.

But by 1935 or 1936 what had been only half understood, unsettling, distant stories turned horror-tragic and new assessments had to be made fast of what one believed and what one was going to do about it. The rebels of the Twenties, the generation before mine, now seemed rebels only in the Scott Fitzgerald sense: they had wasted their blood, blind to the future they could have smelled if the odor of booze hadn't been so strong. Scott knew this about himself, and understandably resented those old friends who had turned into the new radicals. But the 1920's rebels had always seemed strange to me: without charity I thought most of them were no more than a classy lot of brilliant comics, performing at low fees for the society rich. The new radicalism was what I had always been looking for.

In 1934, Hammett and I rented a charming house on Long Island and were throwing around the money from *The Thin Man*. It had been a year of heavy drinking for both of us: I drank almost as much as Hammett and our constant guests, but I was younger than most of them and didn't like myself when I drank. In any case, work on *The Children's Hour* was going bad and Hammett, who had a pleasant nature, had resolved on a new, lighter drinking program: nothing but sherry, port and beer. He was never drunker, never ate less, and was in a teasing, irritable mood. I wanted to get away from all of it. Hammett gave me the money to go to Europe.

Because I planned to stay away for a long time to

finish the play, the money had to last as long as possible. I went directly to Paris, to the small and
inexpensive Hotel Jacob, and decided to see nobody.
Once a day I went for a walk, twice a day I ate in
working-class restaurants, struggling through French
newspapers or magazines. They didn't teach me much
but I did know about the formation of the Popular
Front. There had been, there were to be, Fascist riots
in Paris that year. Like most Americans, now and
then, political troubles in Europe seemed far away
from my life and certainly far away from a play
about a little girl who ruined the lives of two women
in a New England private school.

But after a month of nobody, I was lonely and tired
of work. I telephoned Julia — we had talked several
times my first weeks in Paris — to say I'd like to
come to Vienna for a few days. She said that wasn't
a good idea at the minute, nor a good idea to talk on
a telephone that was tapped, but she'd meet me and
would send a message saying where and when. I
think that was the first time I ever knew a telephone
could be listened in on, a life could and would be
spied on. I was impressed and amused.

I waited but no word came from Julia. Then, two
weeks after my phone call, the newspaper headlines
said that Austrian government troops, aided by local
Nazis, had bombarded the Karl Marx Hof in the
Floridsdorf district of Vienna. Socialist workers, who
owned the district, had defended it, and two hundred
of them had been killed. I read the news in a little

restaurant called the Fourth Republic, and in the middle of my dinner ran back to the hotel for my address book. But Julia's address said nothing about the Karl Marx Hof or the Floridsdorf and so I went to bed telling myself not to imagine things. At five o'clock in the morning I had a telephone call from a man who said his name was Von Zimmer, he was calling from Vienna, Julia was in a hospital.

I have no memory of the trip to Vienna, no memory of a city I was never to see again, no memory of the name of the hospital, nor how I got to it or in what language. But I remember everything after that. It was a small hospital in a mean section of town. There were about forty people in the ward. Julia's bed was the first behind the door. The right side of her face was entirely in bandages, carried around the head and on to most of the left side, leaving only the left eye and the mouth exposed. Her right arm was lying outside the bed cover, her right leg was lying on an unseen platform. There were two or three people in uniform in the room, but most of the aides were in street clothes and it was a young boy, twelve or thirteen, who brought me a stool and said to Julia, in German, "Your friend has come," as he turned her head so that she could see me with her left eye. Neither the eye nor the hand moved as she looked at me and neither of us spoke. I have no loss of memory about that first visit: there was nothing to remember. After a while, she raised her right arm toward the center of the room and I saw the boy, who was carrying a pail, speak to a nurse. The nurse came to the bed and moved Julia's head away from me and told me she thought I should come back the next day. As I went past the desk, the young boy met me in the hall and told me to ask for a room at the Hotel Sacher. There was another note at the desk of the hotel, a place so much too expensive for me that I was about to take my bags and find another. The note said that the reservation had been made at the Sacher because I would be safe there, and that was best for Julia. It was signed John Von Zimmer.

I went back to the hospital later that evening and, as I got off the trolley car, I saw what I had not seen in the morning. The district was heavily ringed with police, and men in some other uniform. The hospital said I couldn't go into the ward, the patient was asleep after the operation. When I asked what operation, they asked how was I related to the patient, but my German, and much else, had given out. I tried to find out if the hospital desk knew John Von Zimmer's address, but they said they had never heard of him.

I was refused at the hospital the next day and the next. Three days later a handsome, pregnant lady, in a poor coat too small for her, took me into the ward. The same young boy brought me the same stool, and gently turned Julia's head toward me. Her right leg was no longer on a platform and that made me think everything was better. This time, after a few minutes, she raised her right arm and touched my hand. I stared at her hand: it had always been too large even for this tall girl, too blunt, too heavy, ugly. She took the hand away, as if she knew what I thought, and I reached back for it. We sat for a while that way and then she pointed to her mouth, meaning that she couldn't speak because of the bandages. Then she raised her hand to the window, pointed out, and made a pushing movement with her hand.

I said, "I don't know what you mean," and realized they were the first words I had spoken to her in years. She made the motion again and then shut her eye as if she couldn't go on. After a while I fell asleep on the stool with my head against the wall. Toward afternoon a nurse came and said I had to leave. Julia's bed had been wheeled out and I think the nurse was telling me that she was being "treated."

For the three days and nights I had been in Vienna I had gone nowhere, not even for a walk, only once a day to a cheap restaurant a block from the hospital where the old man who ran it talked in English and said he had once lived in Pittsburgh. I don't believe I understood where I was, or what had happened in this city, or why, and that I was too frightened of what I didn't understand to be anything more than quiet. (Fear has always made me unable to talk or to move much, almost drowsy.) I thought constantly about how to find the man called Von Zimmer, but it seemed to me each day that he would certainly come to me. On the fourth night, about ten o'clock, I had nothing more to read, was too restless and nervous for bed, and so I took the long walk back to the restaurant near the hospital. When I got there it was closed and so I walked again until it was long past midnight, thinking how little I knew about Julia's life, how seldom we had met in the last years, how little I knew of what was happening to her now.

When I got back to the hotel the young boy from the hospital ward was standing across the street. I saw him immediately and stood waiting for him. He handed me a folded slip of paper. Then he bowed and moved away.

In the lobby of the hotel, the note, written in a weak, thin handwriting, said, "Something else is needed. They will take me tomorrow to another place. Go back to Paris *fast* and leave your address at the Sacher. Love, Julia."

I was back in Paris before I remembered that when we were kids, doing our Latin together, we would take turns translating and then correcting. Often one of us would say to the other, "Something else is needed"; we said it so often that it got to be a family joke.

I waited in Paris for a month, but no word ever came. A German friend made a telephone call for me to the hospital in Vienna, but they said they didn't know Julia's name, had no record of her ever having been there. My German friend telephoned the university twice to ask for John Von Zimmer, but once somebody said he no longer was enrolled and once they had no information about his address.

And so I went back to New York, finished *The*

Children's Hour, and three nights after it was a success I telephoned Julia's grandmother. I think the
old lady was drunk — she often had been when we
were young — because it took a long time to explain
who I was, and then she said what difference did it
make who I was, she didn't know anything about
Julia, neither did the Morgan Bank, who had been
transmitting huge sums of money to her all over
Europe, and she thought Julia was plain crazy.

About a year later I had a letter from Julia, but it
is lost now and while I am sure of what it said, I am
not sure how it was said by a woman who wrote what
had become almost foreign English and was telling
me something she evidently thought I already knew.
The letter had to do with Nazism and Germany, the
necessity of a Socialist revolution throughout the
world, that she had had a baby, and the baby seemed
to like being called Lilly, but then she was a baby who
liked almost everything. She said she had no address,
but I should send letters to Paris, to 16 Rue de l'Uni-
versité, in care of apartment 3. I wrote immediately to
thank her about Lilly, then two more times, and finally
had a postcard from her with a Zurich stamp.

I can no longer remember how long after that Anne-
Marie telephoned to ask me for dinner. I think I was
about to say yes when Anne-Marie told me that a
friend of hers had seen Julia, that Julia was doing
something called anti-Fascist work, very dangerous,
and throwing away her money, did I know about the
baby and wasn't that nutty, a poor unwanted illegiti-

mate child? I said I was leaving town and couldn't
have dinner. Anne-Marie said that was too bad because they didn't often visit New York, but happened
to be here on the opening night of *Days to Come* and
had to say, frankly, that *they* hadn't liked my play.
I said that wasn't illegal, not many people had liked
it, and then there was more talk about Julia, something about her leg that I didn't understand, and
Anne-Marie said that she wanted me to meet her husband, who, as I certainly knew, had been a colleague
of Julia's in medical school in Vienna and was now a
surgeon, very successful, in San Francisco. She said
he was brilliant and a real beauty. I have never liked
women who talk about how men look — "so attractive" was a constant phrase of my time — and to hide
my irritation I said I knew she had married but I
didn't know his name. She said his name was John
Von Zimmer. I am sure she heard me take a deep
breath because she laughed and said the next time
they came to New York she would call me, and why
didn't I ever see Sammy, her brother, who was always
trying to commit suicide. I was never to see Sammy
again, but certainly he never committed suicide because I read about him in Suzy's society column a few
months ago.

In all the years that followed I only once again saw
Anne-Marie, with John Von Zimmer, in 1970, when I
was teaching in Berkeley. They were in a San Francisco restaurant with six or seven other stylish-looking
people, and Anne-Marie kissed me and bubbled and

we exchanged addresses. Von Zimmer was silent as he stared at a wall behind my head. Neither Anne-Marie nor I did the telephoning that we said we would do the next day, but I did want very much to see Von Zimmer: I had an old question to ask, and so a few days after the meeting in the restaurant I walked around to his office. But, standing near the great Victorian house, I changed my mind. I am glad now that I didn't ask the question that almost certainly would never have been answered.

But on that day in 1937, on the train moving toward the German border, I sat looking at the hatbox. The big girl was now reading the *Frankfurter Zeitung*, the thin girl had done nothing with the book that was lying on her lap. I suppose it was the announcement of the first lunch sitting that made me look up from the past, pick up my coat, and then put it down again.

The thin girl said, "Nice coat. Warm? Of what fur?"

"It's sealskin. Yes, it's warm."

She said, pointing to the hatbox, "Your hat is also fur?"

I started to say I didn't know, realized how paralyzed I had been, knew it couldn't continue, and opened the box. I took out a high, fluffy, hat of gray fox as both ladies murmured their admiration. I sat staring at it until the heavy girl said, "Put on. Nice with coat."

I suppose part of my worry, although I hadn't even

got there yet, was what to do with the knitted cap I was wearing. I took it off and rose to fix the fur hat in the long mirror between the windows. The top and sides of the hat were heavy and when I put my hand inside I felt a deep seam in the lining with heavy wads below and around the seam. It was uncomfortable and so I started to take it off when I remembered that the note said I should wear the hat.

Somewhere during my hesitations the heavy girl said she was going to lunch, could she bring me a sandwich? I said I'd rather go to lunch but I didn't know when we crossed the border, and immediately realized I had made a silly and possibly dangerous remark. The thin girl said we wouldn't be crossing until late afternoon — she had unpacked a small box and was eating a piece of meat — and if I was worried about my baggage she was staying in the compartment because she couldn't afford the prices in the dining car. The heavy girl said she couldn't afford them either, but the doctor had said she must have hot meals and a glass of wine with her medicine. So I went off with her to the dining car, leaving my coat thrown over the candy box. We sat at a table with two other people and she told me that she had been studying in Paris, had "contracted" a lung ailment, and was going home to Cologne. She said she didn't know what would happen to her Ph.D. dissertation because the lung ailment had affected her bones. She talked in a disjointed stream of words for the benefit, I thought, of the two men who sat next to us, but even when they left, the chatter went on as her head turned to watch everybody in a nervous tic between sentences. I was glad to be finished with lunch, so worried was I about the candy box, but it was there, untouched, when we got back to our compartment. The thin girl was asleep, but she woke up as we came in and said something in German to the heavy girl about a crowded train, and called her Louisa. It was the first indication I had that they knew each other, and I sat silent for a long time wondering why that made me uneasy. Then I told myself that if everything went on making me nervous, I'd be in a bad fix by the time it came to be nervous.

For the next few hours, the three of us dozed or read until the thin girl tapped me on the knee and said we would be crossing the border in five or ten minutes. I suppose everybody comes to fear in a different way, but I have always grown very hot or very cold, and neither has anything to do with the weather. Now, waiting, I was very hot. As the train pulled to a standstill, I got up to go outside — people were already leaving the train to pass through a check gate, and men were coming on the train to inspect baggage in the cars ahead of us — without my coat or my new hat. I was almost out the compartment door when the thin girl said, "You will need your coat and hat. It is of a windiness."

"Thank you. But I'm not cold."

Her voice changed sharply, "You will have need of your coat. Your hat is nice on your head."

I didn't ask questions because the tone in which she spoke was the answer. I turned back, put the coat around my shoulders, put on the hat that felt even heavier now with the wads of something that filled the lining, and let both girls go past me as I adjusted it in the mirror. Coming out on the platform, they were ahead of me, separated from me by several people who had come from other compartments. The heavy girl moved on. The thin girl dropped her purse and, as she picked it up, stepped to one side and moved directly behind me. We said nothing as we waited in line to reach the two uniformed men at the check gate. As the man in front of me was having his passport examined, the thin girl said, "If you have a temporary travel-through visa, it might take many minutes more than others. But that is nothing. Do not worry."

It didn't take many minutes more than others. I went through as fast as anybody else, turned in a neat line with the other travelers, went back to the train. The thin girl was directly behind me, but as we got to the steps of the train, she said, "Please," and pushed me aside to climb in first. When we reached our compartment, the fat girl was in her seat listening to two customs men in the compartment next to ours as they had some kind of good-natured discussion with a man who was opening his luggage.

The thin girl said, "They are taking great time with the luggage." As she spoke, she leaned over and picked up my candy box. She took off the ribbon and said, "Thank you. I am hungry for a chocolate. Most kind."

I said, "Please, please," and knew I was never meant for this kind of thing. "I am carrying it to a friend for a gift. Please do not open it." As the customs men came into our compartment, the thin girl was chewing on a candy, the box open on her lap. I did not know much about the next few minutes except that all baggage was dragged down from the racks, that my baggage took longer than the baggage of my companions. I remember the heavy girl chatting away, and something being said about my traveling visa, and how I was going to a theatre festival because I was a playwright. (It was two days later before I realized I had never mentioned the Moscow theatre festival or anything about myself.) And the name Hellman came into the conversation I could only half understand. One of the customs men said, "Jew," and the heavy girl said certainly the name was not always of a Jew and gave examples of people and places I couldn't follow. Then the men thanked us, replaced everything neatly, and bowed themselves out the door.

Somewhere in the next hours I stopped being hot or cold and was not to be frightened again that day. The thin girl had neatly retied my candy box, but I don't think any of us spoke again until the train pulled into the station. When the porters came on for the baggage, I told myself that now I should be nervous,

135

that if the money had been discovered at the border gate nothing much could have happened because I was still close to France. Now was the time, therefore, for caution, intelligence, reasonable fears. But it wasn't the time, and I laughed at that side of me that so often panics at a moment of no consequence, so often grows listless and sleepy near danger.

But there was to be no danger that day. The thin girl was right behind me on the long walk toward the station gate, people kissing and shaking hands all along the way. A man and a woman of about fifty came toward me, the woman holding out her arms and saying in English, "Lillian, how good it is to see you. How naughty of you not to stay more than a few hours, but even that will give us time for a nice visit — " as the thin girl, very close to me now, said, "Give her the candy box."

I said, "I am so glad to see you again. I have brought you a small gift, gifts — " but the box was now out of my hands and I was being moved toward the gate. Long before we reached the gate the woman and the thin girl had disappeared.

The man said, "Go through the gate. Ask the man at the gate if there is a restaurant near the station. If he says Albert's go to it. If he gives you another name, go to that one, look at it, and turn back to Albert's, which is directly opposite the door you are facing." As I asked the official at the gate about a restaurant, the man went past me. The official said please to step to one side, he was busy, would take care of me in a minute. I didn't like being in the station so I crossed the street to Albert's. I went through a revolving door and was so shocked at the sight of Julia at a table that I stopped at the door. She half rose, called softly, and I went toward her with tears that I couldn't stop because I saw two crutches lying next to her and now knew what I had never wanted to know before. Half out of her seat, holding to the table, she said, "Fine, fine. I have ordered caviar for us to celebrate, Albert had to send for it, it won't be long."

She held my hand for several minutes, and said, "Fine. Everything has gone fine. Nothing will happen now. Let's eat and drink and see each other. So many years."

I said, "How long have we got? How far is the other station, the one where I get the train to Moscow?"

"You have two hours, but we haven't that long together because you have to be followed to the station and the ones who follow you must have time to find the man who will be with you on the train until Warsaw in the morning."

I said, "You look like nobody else. You are more beautiful now."

She said, "Stop crying about my leg. It was amputated and the false leg is clumsily made so I am coming to New York in the next few months, as soon as I can, and get a good one. Lilly, don't cry for me. *Stop the tears*. We must finish the work now. Take off the hat the way you would if it was too hot for this place. Comb your hair, and put the hat on the seat between us."

Her coat was open, and the minute I put the hat on the bench she pinned it deep inside her coat with a safety pin that was ready for it.

She said, "Now I am going to the toilet. If the waiter tries to help me up, wave him aside and come with me. The toilet locks. If anybody should try to open it, knock on the door and call to me, but I don't think that will happen."

She got up, picked up one of the crutches, and waved me to the other arm. She spoke in German to a man I guess was Albert as we moved down the long room. She pulled the crutch too quickly into the toilet door, it caught at a wrong angle, and she made a gesture with the crutch, tearing at it in irritation.

When she came out of the toilet, she smiled at me. As we walked back to the table, she spoke in a loud voice, saying something in German about the toilet and then, in English, "I forget you don't know German. I was saying that German public toilets are always clean, much cleaner than ours, particularly under the new regime. The bastards, the murderers."

Caviar and wine were on the table when we sat down again and she was cheerful with the waiter. When he had gone away she said, "Ah, Lilly. Fine, fine. Nothing will happen now. But it is your right to know that it is my money you brought in and we can save five hundred, and maybe, if we can bargain right, a thousand people with it. So believe that you have been better than a good friend to me, you have done something important."

"Jews?"

"About half. And political people. Socialists, Communists, plain old Catholic dissenters. Jews aren't the only people who have suffered here." She sighed. "That's enough of that. We can only do today what we can do today and today you did it for us. Do you need something stronger than wine?"

I said I didn't and she said to talk fast now, there wasn't much time, to tell her as much as possible. I told her about my divorce, about the years with Hammett. She said she had read *The Children's Hour*, she was pleased with me, and what was I going to do next?

I said, "I did it. A second play, a failure. Tell me about your baby."

"She's fat and handsome. I've got over minding that she looks like my mother."

"I want very much to see her."

"You will," she said, "I'll bring her when I come home for the new leg and she can live with you, if you like."

I said, meaning no harm, "Couldn't I see her now?"

"Are you crazy? Do you think I would bring her here? Isn't it enough I took chances with your safety? I will pay for that tonight and tomorrow and . . ." Then she smiled. "The baby lives in Mulhouse, with some nice folks. I see her that way whenever I cross the border. Maybe, when I come back for the leg, I'll leave her with you. She shouldn't be in Europe. It ain't for babies now."

"I haven't a house or even an apartment of any permanence," I said, "but I'll get one if you bring the baby."

"Sure. But it wouldn't matter. You'd be good to her." Then she laughed. "Are you as angry a woman as you were a child?"

"I think so," I said. "I try not to be, but there it is."

"Why do you try not to be?"

"If you lived around me, you wouldn't ask."

"I've always liked your anger," she said, "trusted it."

"You're the only one, then, who has."

"Don't let people talk you out of it. It may be uncomfortable for them, but it's valuable to you. It's what made you bring the money in today. Yes, I'll leave the baby with you. Its father won't disturb you, he wants nothing to do with the baby or with me. He's O.K. Just an ordinary climber. I don't know why I did it, Freud told me not to, but I don't care. The baby's good."

She smiled and patted my hand. "Someday I will take you to meet Freud. What am I saying? I will probably never see him again — I have only so much longer to last in Europe. The crutches make me too noticeable. The man who will take care of you has just come into the street. Do you see him outside the window? Get up and go now. Walk across the street, get a taxi, take it to Bahnhof 200. Another man will be waiting there. He will make sure you get safely on the train and will stay with you until Warsaw tomorrow morning. He is in car A, compartment 13. Let me see your ticket."

I gave it to her. "I think that will be in the car to your left." She laughed. *"Left,* Lilly, *left.* Have you ever learned to tell left from right, south from north?"

"No. I don't want to leave you. The train doesn't go for over an hour. I want to stay with you a few more minutes."

"No," she said. "Something could still go wrong and we must have time to get help if that should happen. I'll be coming to New York in a few months. Write from Moscow to American Express in Paris. I have stuff picked up every few weeks." She took my hand and raised it to her lips. "My beloved friend."

Then she pushed me and I was on my feet. When I got to the door I turned and must have taken a step back because she shook her head and moved her face to look at another part of the room.

I did not see the man who followed me to the station. I did not see the other man on the train, although several times a youngish man passed my compartment and the same man took the vacant chair next to me at dinner, but didn't speak to me at all.

When I went back to my compartment from dinner the conductor asked if I wanted my two small valises put in the corridor for examination when we crossed the German-Polish border so that I wouldn't be awakened. I told him I had a wardrobe trunk in the baggage car, handed him the key for the customs people, and went to sleep on the first sleeping pill of my life, which may be why I didn't wake up until just before we pulled into the Warsaw station at seven in the morning. There was bustle in the station as I raised the curtain to look out. Standing below my window was the young man who had sat next to me at dinner. He made a gesture with his hand, but I didn't understand and shook my head. Then he looked around and pointed to his right. I shook my head again, bewildered, and he moved away from the window. In a minute there was a knock on my door and I rose to open it. An English accent said through the crack, "Good morning. Wanted to say goodbye to you, have a happy trip." And then, very, very softly, "Your trunk was removed by the Germans. You are in no danger because you are across the border. Do nothing for a few hours and then ask the Polish conductor about the trunk. Don't return from Moscow through Germany, travel another way." In a loud voice he said, "My best regards to your family," and disappeared.

For two hours I sat in bed, doubtful, frightened of the next move, worried about the loss of clothes in my trunk. When I got dressed, I asked the Polish conductor if the German conductor had left my trunk key with him. He was upset when he told me the German customs people had removed the trunk, that often happened, but he was sure it would be sent on to me in

Moscow after a few days, nothing unusual, the German swine often did it now.

The trunk did arrive in Moscow two weeks later. The lining was in shreds, the drawers were broken, but only a camera was missing and four or five books. I did not know then, and I do not know now, whether the trunk had anything to do with Julia because I was not to see Germany for thirty years and I was never to speak with Julia again.

I wrote to her from Moscow, again from Prague on my way back to Paris, and after I had returned to New York from Spain during the Civil War. Three or four months later I had a card with a Geneva postmark. It said, says, "Good girl to go to Spain. Did it convince you? We'll talk about that when I return to New York in March."

But March and April came and went and there was no word from Julia. I telephoned her grandmother, but I should have known better. The old lady said they hadn't heard from Julia in two years and why did I keep worrying her? I said I had seen Julia in October and she hung up the phone. Somewhere about that time I saw a magazine picture of Julia's mother, who had just married again, an Argentine, but I saw no reason for remembering his name.

On May 23, 1938, I had a cable, dated London two days before and sent to the wrong address. It said, "Julia has been killed stop please advise Moore's funeral home Whitechapel Road London what disposition stop my sorrow for you for all of us." It was signed John Watson but had no address.

It is never possible for me to cry at the time when it could do me some good, so, instead, I got very drunk for two days and don't remember anything about them. The third morning I went around to Julia's grandmother's house and was told by the butler, who came out on the street as if I were a danger to the house, that the old people were on a world cruise and wouldn't be back for eight weeks. I asked the name of the boat, was asked for my credentials, and by the time we batted all that around, I was screaming that their granddaughter was dead and that he and they could go fuck themselves. I was so sick that night that Dash, who never wanted me to go anywhere because he never wanted to, said he thought I should go to London right away.

I have no diary notes of that trip and now only the memory of standing over a body with a restored face that didn't hide the knife wound that ran down the left side. The funeral man explained that he had tried to cover the face slash but I should see the wounds on the body if I wanted to see a mess that couldn't be covered. I left the place and stood on the street for a while. When I went back in the funeral man handed me a note over the lunch he was eating. The note said, "Dear Miss Hellman. We have counted on your coming but perhaps it is not possible for you, so I will send a carbon of this to your New York address. None of us knows what disposition her family wishes to make, where they want what should be a hero's funeral. It is your right to know that the Nazis found her in Frankfurt, in the apartment of a colleague. We got her to London in the hope of saving her. Sorry that I cannot be here to help you. It is better that I take my sorrow for this wonderful woman into action and perhaps revenge. Yours, John Watson, who speaks here for many others. Salud."

I went away that day and toward evening telephoned the funeral man to ask if he had an address for John Watson. He said he had never heard the name John Watson, he had picked up the body at the house of a Dr. Chester Lowe at 30 Downshire Hill. When I got there it was a house that had been made into apartments, but there was no Dr. Lowe on the name plates, and for the first time it occurred to me that my investigations could be bad for people who were themselves in danger.

So I brought the body home with me on the old *De Grasse* and tried this time to reach Julia's mother. The same butler told me that he couldn't give me her mother's address, although he knew the mother had been informed of the death. I had the body cremated and the ashes are still where they were that day so long ago.

I should, of course, have gone to Mulhouse before I came home from London, but I didn't, didn't even think about it in those awful days in London or on the boat. After the cremation, I wrote to Julia's grandmother, told her about the baby and that I knew nothing more than that she lived with a family in Mulhouse, but Mulhouse couldn't be so big that they would have trouble finding an American child. I had no answer. I guess I knew I wouldn't, and so I wrote another letter, this time nasty, and got an answer from a fancy name in a fancy law firm saying that everything would be done "in this strange case" about a child only I believed existed and I would be kept informed of any "doubtful results."

In the next few months, I found I dreamed every night about Julia, who was almost always the age when I first met her. Hammett said I looked awful and if it worried me that much why didn't I find a lawyer or a detective in Mulhouse. William Wyler, the movie director, with whom I had made two pictures, had been born in Mulhouse and his family still owned a department store there. It is too long ago for me to be accurate about when and how he got me the name of a lawyer in Mulhouse, but he did, and after a while the lawyer wrote that the investigation was proving difficult, but he thought, in the end, they would certainly find the baby if she was still there.

Three months later the war broke out and I never heard again from anybody in Western Europe until I arrived in London from Russia in March 1944. My second day there — my reason for being there was to do a documentary film for the British government about people on the docksides during the V–2 bomb-

ings — I realized I was somewhere in the neighborhood of the funeral parlor. I found it, but it had been
bombed to pieces.

Nothing is left of all this except that sometime in
the early 1950's, I was sitting on a stone wall at a
Long Island picnic at Ruth and Marshall Field's. A
man next to me was talking about a man called Onassis — the first time I had heard his name — and a
lawsuit by the U.S. government against Onassis, and
when he was finished with that he turned to me and
said, "My father was the lawyer to whom you wrote
about Julia. I am Julia's third cousin."

After a while I said, "Yes."

He said, "My father died last year."

"Your father never wrote to me again."

He said, "You see, I'm not a lawyer, I'm a banker."

I said, "Whatever happened to her family?"

"The grandparents are dead. Julia senior lives in
Argentina — "

"The bastards," I said, "all of them."

He smiled at me. "They are my cousins."

"Did they ever find the baby they didn't want to
find? I don't care who you are."

"I never knew anything about a baby," he said.

I said, "I don't believe you," got off the stone fence,
left a note for Ruthie saying I didn't feel well, and
drove home.

THEATRE

IT is strange to me that so many people like to listen to so many other people talk about the theatre.
There are those who talk for large fees or give it away
at small dinner parties and often their stories are
charming and funny, but they are seldom people who
have done much solid work. You are there, you are
good in the theatre, you have written or directed or
acted or designed just because you have and there is
little that you can or should be certain about because
almost everything in the theatre contradicts something
else. People have come together, as much by accident
as by design, done the best they can and sometimes
the worst, profited or not, gone their way vowing to
see each other the next week, mean it, and wave across
a room a few years later.

The manuscript, the words on the page, was what

you started with and what you have left. The production is of great importance, has given the play the only life it will know, but it is gone, in the end, and the pages are the only wall against which to throw the future or measure the past.

How the pages got there, in their form, in their order, is more of a mystery than reason would hope for. That is why I have never wanted to write about the theatre and find the teaching of English literature more rewarding than teaching drama. (Drama usually means "the theatre," the stories about it, chatter of failure and success.) You are good in boats not alone from knowledge, but because water is a part of you, you are easy on it, fear it and like it in such equal parts that you work well in a boat without thinking about it and may be even safer because you don't need to think too much. That is what we mean by instinct and there is no way to explain an instinct for the theatre, although those who have it recognize each other and a bond is formed between them. The need of theatre instinct may be why so many good writers have been such inferior playwrights — the light that a natural dramatist can see on a dark road is simply not there.

There are, of course, other reasons why I have not written about the theatre: I have known for many years that part of me struggled too hard within it, and the reasons for that I do not know and they could not, in any case, be of interest to anybody but me. I always knew that I was seldom comfortable with theatre people although I am completely comfortable in a theatre; and I am now at an age when the cutting up of old touches must be carefully watched and any sentence that begins "I remember" lasts too long for my taste, even when I myself say it.

But I have certain pictures, portraits, mementos of my plays. They are what I have left of the long years, the pleasure in the work and the pains.

The Children's Hour was my first play. I don't remember very much about the writing or the casting, but I remember Lee Shubert, who owned the theatre, as he did many other theatres in New York, coming down the aisle to stare at me during a rehearsal day. I was sitting mid-theatre with my feet on the top of the chair in front of me. He came around to stand directly before me and said, "Take your dirty shoes off my chair."

I said, "My shoes aren't touching the chair, Mr. Shubert," but, after a pause, he pushed my right leg to the floor.

I said, "I don't like strange men fooling around with my right leg so don't do it again."

Mr. Shubert called out to Herman Shumlin, who was directing the play from the front row. They met in the aisle and I heard Herman say, "That girl, as you call her, is the author of the play," and went back to directing. About half an hour later, Mr. Shubert, who had been standing in the back watching the play for which he had put up the money, came down and sat behind me.

"This play," he said to the back of my head, "could land us all in jail." He had been watching the confession scene, the recognition of the love of one woman for another.

I said, "I am eating a frankfurter and I don't want to think about jail. Would you like a piece of it?"

"I forbid you to get mustard on my chairs," he said and I was never to see him again until the play had been running for about six months and then I heard him ask the doorman who I was.

I've always told myself that I was so drunk on the opening night of *The Children's Hour* because I had begun to drink two nights before. I had gone to have dinner with my mother and father, who had not read the play, had not seen the rehearsals, had asked no questions, but, obviously, had talked to each other when they were alone. Both of them were proud of me, but in my family you didn't show such things, and both of them, I think, were frightened for me in a world they didn't know.

In any case, my mother, who frequently made sentences that had nothing to do with what went before, said, in space, "Well, all I know is that you were considered the sweetest-smelling baby in New Orleans."

She had, through my life, told me this several times before, describing how two strange ladies had paused in front of our house to stare at me in the baby carriage and then to lean down and sniff me. One of them had said, "That's the sweetest-smelling baby in town." The other had said, "In all New Orleans," and when my mother told our neighbor about her pleasure in this exchange, the neighbor had said of course it was true, famously true, I always smelled fresh as a flower. I didn't know that my mother had never until that night told my father or, if she had, he was less nervous than he was two nights before the opening. Now, when she repeated it, he said, *"Who* was the sweetest-smelling baby in New Orleans?"

"Lillian," said my mother.

"Lillian? Lillian?" said my father. *"I* was the sweetest-smelling baby in New Orleans and you got that information from my mother and sisters and have stolen it."

"Stolen it?" said my shocked mother. "I never stole anything in my life and you know it. Lillian was the sweetest-smelling baby in New Orleans and I can prove it."

"It's disgraceful," said my father, "what you are doing. You have taken what people said about *me, always said about me,* and given it to your own child."

"Your child, too," said my mother.

"That's no reason for lying and stealing," said my father. "I must ask you now to take it back and not to repeat it again."

My mother was a gentle woman and would do almost anything to avoid a fight, but now she was aroused as I had never before seen her.

"I will take nothing back. You are depriving your own child of her rightful honor and I think it disgraceful."

My father rose from the table. "I will telephone Jenny and prove it to you," he said.

He was giving the phone operator the number of his sisters' house in New Orleans when my mother yelled, "Jenny and Hannah will say anything you tell them to. I won't have it. Lillian was the sweetest-smelling baby in New Orleans and that's that." She began to cry.

I said, "I think maybe you're both crazy." I went to the sideboard and poured myself a large straight whiskey. My father, holding the phone, said to me, "Sweet-smelling, are you? You've been drinking too much for years."

"Don't pay him any mind, baby," said my mother, "any man who would deny his own child."

I left before my father spoke to his sisters and only found out months later that although my mother and father came to the opening night together, and both of them kissed me, they didn't speak to each other for several days.

On the afternoon of the opening night of *The Children's Hour* I drowned the hangover with brandy. I think I saw the play from the back of the theatre, holding to the rail, but I am not sure: I do remember the final curtain and an audience yelling, "Author, author." It was not all modesty that kept me from the curtain call — I couldn't have made backstage with-

out falling. I wish I had understood and been happy
in all the excited noise that comes only when the author is unknown and will never come again in quite
so generous a fashion. I remember Robert Benchley
pressing my arm and nodding his head as he passed
me on his way out of the theatre. It was a nice thing
for a critic to do, but I don't think I knew what he
meant. I knew only half-things that happened that
night: I went to the Plaza Hotel, but I can't remember
who was at the table; I went to Tony's with some people who were at the Plaza; I went to Herman's apartment and he told me that the papers were very good
indeed and we would be a big hit and he had a bad
headache. For the next few hours I have no account.
Then I was in a strange bar, not unusual for me in
those days, and I was talking to a man and two women.
Or they were talking to me and the conversation had
to do with the metallic fringe that was on the bottom
of the younger woman's dress. Then I was asleep, sitting up, on my couch in the Elysée Hotel. When I
woke up one of the women was watering the plants on
the windowsill and the other woman was crying, standing against a wall. I said to the man, "Are these your
sisters?" and he laughed.

"What's funny about that?"

"Sez you," he said, "sez you."

"I'm going to marry him," said the one who was
standing against the wall, "and it's already shit.
Everybody has missed the boat, everywhere, everywhere, everywhere and somehow."

"Ssh," I said, "I owe this hotel a lot of money."

"The boat," she screamed, "everybody, every-where."

There was some more of that. I went to make coffee and when I came back the pair who were going to get married were sitting on the couch holding hands and the one who had been watering the plants was reading my first-night telegrams at the desk. (I was to meet her again a few years later. She was a handsome, boy-ish-looking woman at every society-literary cocktail party. Her name was Emily Vanderbilt and she was to marry Raoul Whitfield, a mystery story writer. A few years after the marriage she was murdered on a ranch they bought in New Mexico, and neither the mystery story expert nor the police ever found the murderer.) Nobody spoke until the potential bride suddenly pushed her fiancé off the couch, and the one reading the telegrams screamed, "Moxie! Moxie!"

I said — I think it was the sentence I most often used in those years — "Why don't you all go home?"

The man had picked himself up from the floor, was pouring himself a drink, Moxie and her friend were arguing about something or other, when I went in the bedroom shouting, "Why don't you all go home," and locked the door. It was still dark, maybe six o'clock, when I woke up with an awful headache and cramps in my legs, remembering that I should have tele-phoned Hammett, who was in Hollywood, to tell him the play was a hit. I wanted a cold beer and went through the living room to get it. I thought the room was empty, but as I was returning to bed with my beer, I saw the man sitting at the desk staring out of the window.

I coughed and he turned to me, raising his empty highball glass. "Want to get me a fresh drinkie?"

"What did you do with your ladies?"

"I certainly would like an eensy drink."

"I don't feel well. I have work to do. I have to make a phone call. I had a play open last night."

"You kept saying that," he said. "I'm a doctor."

"*You're* a doctor?"

"Opening an office next week, Park and 80th, going in with my uncle, the heart specialist. Come and see me."

I said I didn't think I'd do that and put a call through to Hammett in the rented house with the soda fountain in the Pacific Palisades. After a long time a woman answered the phone and said she was Mr. Hammett's secretary, what a strange hour to be calling. I sat on the couch thinking about that and feeling very dizzy from the beer.

The doctor said, "What's your name?"

I went back to the bedroom, closed the door, and knew the question had sobered me up. I had wasted what should have been the nicest night of my life. I disliked then and dislike now those who spoil pleasure or luck when it comes not so much because they refuse it — they are a different breed — but because they cannot see it or abandon it for blind nonsense. I had done just that and wanted now to find out about it.

159

The doctor opened the door. "Do you want to go out for breakfast or Atlantic City? What's your name?"

I said, "What's yours?"

"Peregrine Perry. From Lord Perry of long ago."

"Do they call you Perry Perry?"

"Oh, Christ," he said, "all you have to do is wait for it."

He closed the door, and when I woke up that afternoon the apartment was empty.

(Ten years later I bought a house on 82nd Street and somewhere in that first year I saw him come out of an office with a sign on it that said "Dr. P. John Perry" and get into a car driven by a chauffeur.)

But long before that, two days after the woman had told me she was Hammett's secretary, I realized that I had called Hammett at three A.M. California time and that he had no secretary. We had spoken on the phone a number of times in those days — he was very happy about *The Children's Hour*, proud that all his trouble with me had paid off — but on the day I understood about the secretary and three o'clock in the morning I took a plane to Los Angeles. By the time I got to the house in the Pacific Palisades it was night and I had had a good deal to drink. I went immediately to the soda fountain — Hammett had rented the house from Harold Lloyd — smashed it to pieces and flew back to New York on a late night plane.

The failure of a second work is, I think, more damaging to a writer than failure ever will be again. It is then that the success of the first work seems an accident and, if the fears you had as you wrote it were dissipated by the praise, now you remember that the praise did not always come from the best minds and even when it did it could have been that they were not telling the truth or that you had played good tricks. And you are probably too young, too young at writing, to have found out that you really only care what a few people think; only they, with the change in names that time brings about, will stand behind your chair for good or bad, forever. But failure in the theatre is more public, more brilliant, more unreal than in any other field. The praise is usually out of bounds: the photographs, interviews, "appearances," party invitations are so swift and dazzling that you go into the second work with confidence you will never have again if you have any sense.

Days to Come was written in Princeton, New Jersey. Hammett, who never wanted much to live in New York, had rented the lovely house of a rich professor who was a Napoleon expert. Its overformal Directoire furniture was filled each night with students who liked Hammett, but liked even better the free alcohol and the odd corners where they could sleep and bring their friends. That makes it sound like now, when students are often interesting, but it wasn't: they were a dull generation, but Dash never much examined the people to whom he was talking if he was drunk enough to talk at all.

Even now the pains I had on the opening night of

Days to Come puzzle me. Good theatre jokes are almost always based on survived disasters, and there were so many that night that they should, in time, have passed into comedy: the carefully rehearsed light cues worked as if they were meant for another play; the props, not too complicated, showed up where nobody had ever seen them before and broke, or didn't break, with the malice of animated beings; good actors knew by the first twenty minutes they had lost the audience and thus became bad actors; the audience, maybe friendly as it came in, was soon restless and uncomfortable. The air of a theatre is unmistakable: things go well or they do not. They did not. Standing in the back of the side aisle, I vomited without knowing it was going to happen and went home to change my clothes. I wanted, of course, to go to bed and stay there, but I was young enough to worry about cowardice and so I got back in time to see William Randolph Hearst lead his six guests out of the theatre, in the middle of the second act, talking very loud as they came up the aisle.

It is hard for me to believe these many years later in the guilt I felt for the failure of *Days to Come;* the threads of those threads have lasted to this day. Guilt is often an excuse for not thinking and maybe that's what happened to me. In any case, it was to be two years before I could write another play, *The Little Foxes,* and when I did get to it I was so scared that I wrote it nine times.

Up to a year ago I used to think of *Days to Come*

as the play that taught me not to vomit. (I have never vomited again.) Reading it then, for a book that includes all my plays, I liked it: it is crowded and over-wrought, but it is a good report of rich liberals in the 1930's, of a labor leader who saw through them, of a modern lost lady, and has in it a correct prediction of how conservative the American labor movement was to become.

Soon after *The Children's Hour* I had had an offer to write movies for Samuel Goldwyn. I think Mr. Goldwyn was in his early fifties when we first met, but he was so vigorous and springy that I was not conscious of his age for many years. He was, as were many of the bright, rough, tough lot that first saw the potential of the motion picture camera, a man of great power. Often the power would rise to an inexplicable pitch of panic anger when he was crossed or disappointed, and could then decline within minutes to the whispered, pained moral talk of a loony clergyman whimpering that God had betrayed him. What I liked best were not Mr. Goldwyn's changes of English speech, although some of them were mighty nice and often better than the original. Certainly "I took it all with a dose of salts" is just as good as a grain; the more famous "a verbal contract isn't worth the paper it is written on" makes sense; he meant to be courteous the day he called down "Bon voyage to all of you" to those of us on the dock, as he, a passenger, sailed away; and when, soon after the war, he was asked to make a toast to Field Marshal Montgomery, and rose, lifted his glass, and said, "A long life to Marshall Field Montgomery Ward," one knew exactly why. But I liked best his calculated eccentricities. When he needed a favor or had to make a difficult bargain and knew a first move was not the best position from which to deal, he was brilliant. I was in his office when he wanted an actor under contract to Darryl Zanuck and demanded that Zanuck's secretary call him out of a meeting. After a long wait, Mr. Goldwyn said into the phone, "Yes, Darryl? What can I do for you today?" And a few years after the McCarthy period, during which I was banned in Hollywood, my phone rang in Martha's Vineyard. Mr. Goldwyn's secretary and I had a pleasant reunion, she said he had been trying to reach me for two days to ask if I wanted to write *Porgy and Bess.* After a long wait Mr. Goldwyn's voice said, "Hello, Lillian, hello. Nice of you to call me after all these years. How can I help you?"

But I think our early days together worked well because I was a difficult young woman who didn't care as much about money as the people around me and so, by accident, I took a right step within the first months of working for Mr. Goldwyn. I had been hired to re-write an old silly, hoping I could make it O.K., to be directed by Sidney Franklin, a famous man who had done many of the Norma Shearer pictures. It was then, and often still is, the custom to talk for weeks and months before the writer is allowed to touch the typewriter. Such conferences were called breaking the

164

back of the story and that is, indeed, an accurate description. We, a nice English playwright called Mordaunt Shairp and I, would arrive at Franklin's house each morning at ten, have a refined health lunch a few hours later, and leave at five. The next day whatever we had decided would sometimes be altered and sometimes be scrapped because Franklin had consulted a friend the night before or discussed our decisions with his bridge partners. After six or seven weeks of this, Franklin said it was rude of me to lie all day on his couch with my back turned to him, napping. I left his house saying I was sorry, it was rude, but I couldn't go on that way. I took the night plane to New York, locked myself in with some books, and the first telephone call I answered two days later was from Mr. Goldwyn, who said if I came back immediately I could go to a room by myself, start writing, and he'd give me a raise. I said I'd think about it, didn't, and left for Paris. When he found me there a week later he offered a long-term contract with fine clauses about doing nothing but stories I liked and doing them where and when I liked. I had become valuable to Mr. Goldwyn because I had left him for reasons he didn't understand. For many years that made me an unattainable woman, as desirable as such women are, in another context, for men who like them that way.

They were good years and most of the time I enjoyed Mr. Goldwyn. The extraordinary conflicts in a man who wished to make "fine pictures" and climb into an educated or social world while grappling at the same time with a nature made rough by early poverty and tough by later big money amused me, and made him far more interesting than more "civilized" men like Irving Thalberg. (I never understood Scott Fitzgerald's *The Last Tycoon* version of Thalberg: the romanticism that went into that portrait had, in my mind, little to do with the obvious man who had once offered me a job by telling me how lucky I would be to work with him.) But, as in the theatre, I have few memories of the actual work I did in pictures, although I have sharp recollections of much that happened outside the work. And maybe, in the end, they are the same tale.

I had known George Haight in New York as a bright young man from Yale who had written *Goodbye Again*, a funny play. One of his friends, his ex-college roommate, I think, was a director, Henry C. Potter, and now all three of us were in Hollywood, George working as some kind of executive for Goldwyn. No two men, Haight and Potter, could have been more unalike: George was loose-limbed, sloppy, gay, wonderful at magicians' tricks, full of nice jokes; Potter was prep-school handsome, respectable, grandson of a bishop, an unexpected man for the world of the theatre or Hollywood. I was glad to find George working for Goldwyn: it was nice to wander into his office for an hour's exhibition of his newest card tricks or to have him wander into mine for a long afternoon's sleep.

I no longer remember what year I went to Cuba for

166

a vacation after the opening of what play and on my way to write what movie script. It was the custom then in some parts of Europe and most of Latin America to sell small boxes of wax matches with pictures of movie stars pasted to the box. I don't know what publicity department sent Henry C. Potter's picture out to what match factory — he did look like the cleanest of juveniles — but I came across two boxes and, to please George Haight, gave the head bellboy at the Hotel Nacional five dollars and the promise of a dollar a box for any more he could find. I arrived in Hollywood with nine Henry C. Potter matchboxes and for days George had them laid out on his desk brooding over them. Then he told me that Potter was giving a cocktail party in a few weeks and he thought he had the answer: we were to stamp twenty-seven condoms with the words "Compliments of Henry C. Potter," roll them three to a box, and he, Haight, would distribute them on tables at the cocktail party. Since George was very skillful with his hands and knew where all gadgets were to be bought, we did not foresee, that day of our pleasure, the awful work that was to come.

George bought the stamps, the delicate knives, a small stove to melt the wax that would be used to make the words and, during the first few days, the condoms in the drugstore opposite the studio. I was not skillful, but to my surprise he wasn't either. The carefully carved stamps broke the condoms because hot wax made holes and cool wax wouldn't take. After a time our drugstore ran out of condoms and one of

167

the lasting minutes my eyes will hold is the picture of the owner as he stared at George on his last request for twelve boxes.

When George was unable to persuade me that it was my turn to find a new place to buy condoms, we had a cool day of not talking to each other. But the following morning he showed up with a dozen more boxes, fresh stamps, a more delicate knife, and a new theory for the process. By the third or fourth day of our second week we had given up all other work. Haight's secretary had, from the first, been posted at the door to keep out visitors, but now I refused two conferences with Mr. Goldwyn on the grounds that I first had to try out my ideas on Haight, who had nothing to do with the picture I was writing. And by that time we were not in a good humor with each other — I thought he was not as skillful as he once was, and he said I was clumsy and that he should have known it. One day, in fact, miserable and tired, we raised our voices to the point where the music department, situated in the building directly behind, came to their windows to watch the waving about of ruined condoms, and I yelled at them to mind their business.

I can no longer remember how we solved the stamping, but we did, and there were twenty-seven perfect condoms laid out on a table, all reading in green "Compliments of Henry C. Potter." We quit work early that day, but after enough celebrating drinks we forgot why we had left the studio and went to gamble in the Clover Club and got back to the studio about five in the morning because George said we only had two more days before the cocktail party and I had wasted enough of Mr. Goldwyn's money. It was good we went back so early because a new and even more trying period was ahead: how to roll the things so that three, even two, could go neatly in the small boxes. We rolled them around toothpicks, we whittled sticks, we shaved down pencils, we straightened paper clips and hairpins, but it was obvious they were too wide for the matchboxes.

They were bad days, growing dangerous: Goldwyn's legal department wanted to see me about something or other and reported to Goldwyn that I said I was home with an abscessed tooth. That didn't fit with Goldwyn's having seen me arrive at the studio on William Wyler's motorcycle, so when he called to ask me why I didn't go immediately to a dentist, I forgot what I had told the legal department and said I didn't understand how a dentist could cure a badly sprained neck. Sam said that was odd, would I come immediately and talk to him, something strange was going on. George said I was a dope of a liar; I said I was not meant to spend my life on condoms and was ready to throw over the whole thing. He said I was a fink, and while we were being nasty to each other my elderly secretary, who knew nothing more through those days than that I was missing from my office, opened George's door to say *his* secretary wasn't feeling well and couldn't come to work, and stared down at the condoms. She was an unfriendly woman, but I heard George say to her,

"We have a problem. Have you ever rolled a condom?" I left his office to hide in the toilet and came back to find that she had solved the problem: we were not to roll the condoms, we were to fold them lengthwise, crosswise, and stack them.

George took them to the cocktail party, but either Potter never knew about the condoms or was smart enough not to give George the pleasure of his complaint. In any case, George and I never spoke about them again.

Ten of the twelve plays I have written are connected to Hammett — he was in the Army in the Aleutian Islands during the Second World War for one of them, and he was dead when I wrote the last — but *The Little Foxes* was the one that was most dependent on him. We were living together in the same house, he was not doing any work of his own, but after his death, when much became clear to me that had not been before, I knew that he was working so hard for me because *Days to Come* had scared me and scared him for my future.

If that is true — there is a chance I have made the dependency greater than it was — then it is the more remarkable because it was a strange time of our years together. I don't know if I was paying him back for his casual ladies of our early years — it takes a jealous nature a long time to understand that there can be casual ladies — but certainly I was serious or semi-serious about another man and Hammett knew it. Neither of us ever talked about it until I told Dash that I had decided not to marry the man.

He looked at me in surprise. *"Marry? You* decided? There was never a chance you'd marry him."

"It was about to happen," I said. "We had set the day and the place. I thought you knew that."

"I would never have allowed that. Never."

I laughed and he knew why I laughed because a few days later he said, "It was no good. It would never have been any good. The day it is good for you, I'll allow it."

"Thank you," I said, "but if that happens I won't ask your permission and therefore won't thank you for giving it."

"Without my permission you won't ever do it. And you ought to know that by now."

For years after I would say such things as, "May I have your permission this morning to go to the hairdresser, then to the library and on my way home buy an ice cream cone?" But he was not a vain man and, as time moved on, I knew he had been right.

The Little Foxes was the most difficult play I ever wrote. I was clumsy in the first drafts, putting in and taking out characters, ornamenting, decorating, growing more and more weary as the versions of scenes and then acts and then three whole plays had to be thrown away.

Some of the trouble came because the play has a distant connection to my mother's family and every-

171

thing that I had heard or seen or imagined had formed
a giant tangled time-jungle in which I could find no
space to walk without tripping over old roots, hearing
old voices speak about histories made long before my
day.

In the first three versions of the play, because it had
been true in life, Horace Giddens had syphilis. When
Regina, his wife, who had long refused him her bed,
found out about it she put fresh paint on a miserable
building that had once been used as slave quarters and
kept him there for the rest of his life because, she said,
he might infect his children. I had been told that the
real Regina would speak with outrage of her betrayal by a man she had never liked and then would
burst out laughing at what she said. On the day he
died, she dropped the moral complaints forever and
went horseback riding during his funeral. All that
seemed fine for the play. But it wasn't: life had been
too big, too muddled for writing. So the syphilis became heart trouble. I cut out the slave cabin and the
long explanations of Regina and Horace's early life
together.

I was on the eighth version of the play before Hammett gave a nod of approval and said he thought
maybe everything would be O.K. if only I'd cut out
the "blackamoor chitchat." Even then I knew that the
toughness of his criticism, the coldness of his praise,
gave him a certain pleasure. But even then I, who am
not a good-tempered woman, admired his refusal with

me, or with anybody else, to decorate or apologize or placate. It came from the most carefully guarded honesty I have ever known, as if one lie would muck up his world. If the honesty was mixed with harshness, I didn't much care, it didn't seem to me my business. The desire to take an occasional swipe is there in most of us, but most of us have no reason for it, it is as aimless as the pleasure of a piece of candy. When it is controlled by sense and balance, it is still not pretty, but it is not dangerous and often it is useful. It was useful to me and I knew it.

The casting of the play was difficult: we offered it to Ina Claire and to Judith Anderson. Each had a pleasant reason for refusing: each meant that the part was unsympathetic, a popular fear for actresses before that concept became outmoded. Herman Shumlin asked me what I thought of Tallulah Bankhead, but I had never seen her here or in her famous English days. She had returned to New York by 1939, had done a couple of flops, and was married to a nice, silly-handsome actor called John Emery. She was living in the same hotel I was, but I had fallen asleep by the time Herman rang my bell after six hours spent upstairs with Tallulah on their first meeting. He said he had a headache, was worn out by Miss Bankhead's vitality, but he thought she would do fine for us if he could, in the future, avoid the kind of scene he had just come from: she had been "wild" about the play, wild enough to insist the consultation take place while she was in bed with John Emery and a bottle. Shumlin

173

said he didn't think Emery liked that much, but he was certain that poor Emery was unprepared for Tallulah's saying to Herman as he rose to go, "Wait a minute, darling, just wait a minute. I have something to show you." She threw aside the sheets, pointed down at the naked, miserable Emery and said, "Just tell me, darling, if you've ever seen a prick that big." I don't know what Herman said, but it must have been pleasant because there was no fight that night, nothing to predict what was to come.

I still have a diary entry, written a few days later, asking myself whether talk about the size of the male organ isn't a homosexual preoccupation: if things aren't too bad in other ways I doubt if any woman cares very much. Almost certainly Tallulah didn't care about the size or the function: it was the stylish, *épater* palaver of her day.

It is a mark of many famous people that they cannot part with their brightest hour: what worked once must always work. Tallulah had been the nineteen-twenties' most daring girl, but what had been dashing, even brave, had become by 1939 shrill and tiring. The life of the special darlings in the world of art and society had been made old-fashioned by the economic miseries of those who had never been darlings. Nothing is displaced on a single day and much was left over during the Depression, but the train had made a sharp historical swing and the fashionable folk, their life and customs, had become loud and tacky.

174

Tallulah, in the first months of the play, gave a fine performance, had a well-deserved triumph. It was sad to watch it all decline into high-jinks on the stage and in life. Long before her death, beginning with my play, I think, she threw the talent around to amuse the campy boys who came each opening night to watch her vindicate their view of women. I didn't clearly understand all that when I first met her, but I knew that while there was probably not more than five years' difference in our ages, and a bond in our Southern background — her family came from an Alabama town close to my mother's — we were a generation apart. I first realized it when we were still in rehearsal, about a week before the play was to open in Baltimore.

Tallulah, Herman and I were having dinner in the old Artists and Writers Club, a hangout for newspapermen. Tallulah took two small bottles from her pocketbook, put them on the table, and seemed to forget about them. As we were about to go back to rehearsal, she picked up one bottle and tipped it to put drops in her eyes. She rose from the table, repacked the bottles, led the way to the door, and let out a shriek that brought the restaurant to its feet. Herman rushed to her, she pushed him aside, other people pushed toward her, she turned for the door, changed her mind, and whispered to nobody, "I have put the wrong drops in my eyes." Herman ran to a phone booth, she shouted after him, he called out that he was getting a doctor, she said he was to mind his business, and

175

suddenly, in the shouting and running, she grabbed my arm, pulled me into the toilet and said, "Get Herman off that phone. I put the cocaine in my eyes and I don't tell that to doctors or to anybody else. Tell him to shut up about it or I won't go back to the theatre." She sat down at a table, grinned at everybody, and ordered herself a shot of whiskey. I squeezed my way into the phone booth, told Herman about the cocaine. He moved slowly toward her and said, "Put down the whiskey and come outside."

On the sidewalk he said, "I don't like what just happened. This play is going to open on time and I want you to cut the nonsense."

Tallulah said, in controlled stage-anger, "I'm a professional. It's none of your damn business what I do. I warn you never to talk to me this way again."

As she hailed a taxi, Herman said, "If you don't come back to rehearsals in half an hour, don't come back at all." She slammed the door of the taxi, he and I walked back to the theatre, and ten minutes later Tallulah appeared on the stage.

Cocaine was not mentioned again until the opening night party she gave in her Baltimore hotel rooms. It was, indeed, quite a night. Her father, the Speaker of the House of Representatives, and her uncle, the Senator, had come down from Washington. Hammett had arrived a few days before, then Dorothy Parker and her husband Alan Campbell, with Sara and Gerald Murphy. We were a mixed bag, the cast and guests, trying to circulate in a room too small for us.

With time and booze things got loud and the Senator took to singing "Dixie," spirituals, and a Civil War song, until the fastidious Gerald Murphy said to him, "Lovely. But now you must rest your fine vocal cords."

Tallulah was sitting in a large group giving the monologue she always thought was conversation. I was tired, waiting to go to my room, and I guess I yawned once too often because she began to tease me, in the kind of nagging fashion she used when she knew somebody wanted to leave her. A young Negro waiter moved back and forth, passing drinks, and as he came near us she asked him if he wanted to sleep with her or me. He stood still, frightened. She pulled him toward her and kissed him.

I said to the waiter, "Better get out of here now. She's probably not up to much, but this is Maryland."

He went rapidly toward the door, Tallulah went after him, offering to hit me along the way, and Hammett moved behind her. When things had settled down, she put her arms around Hammett and promised that she'd forgive him because she was a sucker for a handsome man. He thanked her and said he didn't much like to be around people who took dope, in his Pinkerton days he had been more afraid of them than of murderers. They talked that over for a while but I lost track until I heard her shout at him, "You don't know what you are talking about. I tell you cocaine isn't habit-forming and I know because I've been taking it for years."

When I laughed too long she got upset with me

177

again and Gerald Murphy said he thought I'd be safer in bed.

Unfortunately my bedroom was next door and I lay sleepless until five in the morning. Then I fell asleep to be awakened by a fight that was going on behind my bed. Tallulah and a woman I had met at the party — an assistant or an ex-secretary — were arguing about an income tax claim and what the woman had done with Tallulah's money. (I think that several years later there was a lawsuit between them.) I yelled through the door that I wanted to sleep. Insults came back and then a demand to join them for a drink. When I said I didn't want a drink and why didn't they go knock each other off the hotel roof, one of them began to pound on my door with what sounded like a bottle and, in time, the pounding became, with giggles, the rhythm of "America the Beautiful." I got dressed and decided to go sit in the park, but before I left the room I broke a desk chair against their door.

Tallulah sent commands the next day for me to appear at rehearsals and apologize, but I was with Dottie, Alan and the Murphys in the hotel dining room from ten in the morning until they closed the place at midnight. It was one of the most pleasant days of my life. I was sleepy and content: the play had gotten fine reviews, we all had a lot to drink, and nobody talked about the play or the theatre. I remember dozing on the table for a while and waking to hear Gerald say, "It's not an easy business, the theatre," and Dottie's saying, "Lilly does things the hard way. Why didn't

178

she have sense enough to get Harpo Marx instead of Tallulah?" and then a long discussion about General Sherman, who was Sara Murphy's grandfather.

There are not many good critics for any art, but there have been almost none for the modern theatre. The intellectuals among them know little about an operating theatre and the middlebrows look at plays as if they were at a race track for the morning line-up. It is a mixed-up picture in many ways. One critic who wrote that *The Little Foxes* was a febrile play later called it an American classic without explaining why he changed his mind.

The *New York Times*, for many years, has been the only newspaper that mattered to the success of a play. That is not the fault of the paper, but it is not a good state for a struggling art form. Now, with Mr. Clive Barnes, even that has changed for the worse: a good review by him no longer makes a hit, but a bad review does damage. The *Times* has had a long list of earnest, honest, undistinguished critics. Walter Kerr is the only one, I think, who learned and thrived. Mr. Barnes is the first fashion-swinger in the list but, like most, he can't quite find where the swing is located for the new season.

I knew many of the virtues and the mistakes of *The Little Foxes* before the play opened. I wanted, I needed an interesting critical mind to tell what I had done beyond the limited amount I could see for myself. But the high praise and the reservations seemed

to me stale stuff and I think were one of the reasons
the great success of the play sent me into a wasteful,
ridiculous depression. I sat drinking for months
after the play opened trying to figure out what I had
wanted to say and why some of it got lost.

I grew restless, sickish, digging around the random
memories that had been the conscious, semiconscious
material for the play. I had meant to half-mock my
own youthful high-class innocence in Alexandra, the
young girl in the play; I had meant people to smile
at, and to sympathize with, the sad, weak Birdie, certainly I had not meant them to cry; I had meant the
audience to recognize some part of themselves in the
money-dominated Hubbards; I had not meant people
to think of them as villains to whom they had no
connection.

I belonged, on my mother's side, to a banking,
storekeeping family from Alabama and Sunday dinners were large, with four sisters and three brothers
of my grandmother's generation, their children, and a
few cousins of my age. These dinners were long, with
high-spirited talk and laughter from the older people
of who did what to whom, what good nigger had con-
sented to thirty percent interest on his cotton crop and
what bad nigger had made a timid protest, what new
white partner had been outwitted, what benefits the
year had brought from the Southern business interests
they had left behind for the Northern profits they had
had sense enough to move toward.

When I was fourteen, in one of my many religious

periods, I yelled across that Sunday's dinner table at a great-aunt, "You have a spatulate face made to dig in the mud for money. May God forgive you."

My aunt rose, came around the table and slapped me with her napkin. I said, "Someday I'll pay you back unless the dear God helps me conquer the evil spirit of revenge," and ran from the room as my gentle mother started to cry. But later that night, she knocked on my locked door and said that if I came out I could have a squab for dinner. My father was out of New York but, evidently informed of the drama by my mother, wrote to me saying that he hoped I had sense enough not to revenge myself until I was as tall and as heavy as my great-aunt.

But a few years after I had stopped being pleased with the word spatulate, a change occurred for which even now I have no explanation: I began to think that greed and the cheating that is its usual companion were comic as well as evil and I began to like the family dinners with the talk of who did what to whom. I particularly looked forward to the biannual dinner when the sisters and brothers assembled to draw lots for "the diamond" that had been left, almost thirty years before, in my great-grandmother's estate. Sometimes they would use the length of a strip of paper to designate the winner, sometimes the flip of a coin, and once I was allowed to choose a number up to eight and the correct guesser was to get the diamond. But nobody, as far as I knew, ever did get it. No sooner was the winner declared than one or the other would sulk and, by prearrangement, another loser would console the sulker, and a third would start the real event of the afternoon: an open charge of cheating. The paper, the coin, my number, all had been fixed or tampered with. That was wild and funny. Funnier because my mother's generation would sit white-faced, sometimes tearful, appalled at what was happening, all of them envying the vigor of their parents, half knowing that they were broken spirits who wished the world was nicer, but who were still so anxious to inherit the money that they made no protest.

I was about eighteen when my great-uncle Jake took the dinner hours to describe how he and a new partner had bought a street of slum houses in downtown New York. He, Jake, during a lunch break in the signing of the partnership, removed all the toilet seats from the buildings and sold them for fifty dollars. But, asked my mother's cousin, what will the poor people who live there do without toilet seats? "Let us," said Jake, "approach your question in a practical manner. I ask you to accompany me now to the bathroom, where I will explode my bowels in the manner of the impoverished and you will see for yourself how it is done." As he reached for her hand to lead her to the exhibition, my constantly ailing cousin began to cry in high, long sounds. Her mother said to her, "Go along immediately with your Uncle Jake. You are being disrespectful to him."

I guess all that was the angry comedy I wanted to mix with the drama.

Angry comedy came another way. I was to get my first taste during *The Little Foxes* of the red-baiting that later turned my life into disorder and financial disaster.

The Spanish Civil War — I had been in Spain during the war — had reached the sad day of Franco's victory and many Republicans were trapped on what was known as the International Bridge. Some of them were my friends, some of them I only knew about. Their lives were at stake. Many of us sent all the money we could give or collect and looked around to find other money fast. Herman Shumlin and I decided to ask the cast of *The Little Foxes* if they would do a benefit for the Spanish refugees. Tallulah and the rest of the cast were courteous but well within their rights when they refused, and nothing more was said about benefits until the week after Russia moved into Finland.

I had been in Helsinki in 1937 for two weeks and had turned my head each day from the giant posters of Hitler pasted to the side wall of my hotel. One night a member of our Olympic team, a man of Finnish descent, had taken me to a large rally of Hitler sympathizers and translated for me their admiring speeches. I needed no translator for the raised arms, the cheers, the Wessel song.

Finland's ambassador to Washington was a handsome and charming man who met Tallulah at a dinner party. The day following Tallulah's meeting with the ambassador she announced that *The Little Foxes*

would give a benefit for the Finnish refugees. The day
following that Shumlin and I announced that *The
Little Foxes* would not give a benefit. I can't remember now whether we explained that we had been refused a benefit for Spain, but I do remember that
suddenly what had been no more than a theatre fight
turned into a political attack: it was made to seem
that we agreed with the invasion of Finland, refused
aid to true democrats, were, ourselves, dangerous
Communists. It was my first experience of such
goings-on and I didn't have sense enough to know that
Tallulah's press statements, so much better than ours,
or more in tune with the times, were being guided by
the expert ambassador. Although her anger — she
often had the righteousness that belongs to a certain
kind of aging sinner — once aroused needed no guidance and stood up well against all reason. And nobody
has ever been able to control me when I feel that I
have been treated unjustly. I am, in fact, bewildered
by all injustice, at first certain that it cannot be, then
shocked into rigidity, then obsessed, and finally as
certain as a Grand Inquisitor that God wishes me to
move ahead, correct and holy. Through those days
Tallulah and I were, indeed, a pair.

And so we never spoke again for almost thirty
years. Then I met her at a party and heard myself
say, "Maybe it's time we said hello." The face that
looked up from years of physical and spiritual beat-
ings was blank. I said, "I'm Lillian Hellman," and
Tallulah flew toward me in a scream of good-natured

greetings and a holiday of kisses. I was pleased for the first half-hour. But reconciliations can be as noisy as the fights that caused them.

Only two diaries written at the end of 1938 could convince me now that *Watch on the Rhine* came out of Henry James, although, of course, seeds in the wind, the long journey they make, their crosses and mutations, is not a new story for writers and even make you hope that your seeds may scatter for those to come.

I was driving back to the farm trying not to listen to the noise that came from two crates of Pekin ducks when I began to think of James's *The American* and *The Europeans.* In the short time since James, the United States had become the dominant country not alone in money and power, but in imposing on other people a morality which was designed in part to hide its self-interest. Was that a new American game or had we learned it from the English who invented it to hold down their lower classes? We still spoke as nineteenth-century Cromwellians in church, home, and university, but increasingly, the more we recognized disorder and corruption at home the more insistent we grew about national purity.

Many Europeans had moved here with the triumph of Hitler in the 1930's. Few of us asked questions about their past or present convictions because we took for granted that they had left either in fear of persecution or to make a brave protest. They were our kind of folks. It took me a long time to find out that many of them had strange histories and that their hosts, or the people who vouched for them, knew all about their past. Two of the perhaps eight or nine that I met turned out to have unexpected reasons for emigration: both had been Nazi sympathizers; in one case, the grandfather wanted to preserve his remarkable art collection from the threatening sounds the "new barbarians" made about modern painting; in the other, bribe money had not been able to suppress a nineteenth-century conversion from Judaism to Luther. I was vaguely related to that family, and when I asked about the truth of the rumor, the son of the family never spoke to me again. But a few weeks later I had a note from his mother saying that she was surprised to find that certain Jews in America claimed a blood connection to her family, when, in fact, they had "no legal or moral right" to do so. I had no right, from my safe place, to feel bitter about such people, but I did and, of course, by 1938 I had been through the life and death of my friend Julia, and had been to Spain during the Civil War, and had been moved by men willing to die for what they believed in.

I wanted to write a play about nice, liberal Americans whose lives would be shaken up by Europeans, by a world the new Fascists had won because the old values had long been dead. I put the play in a small Ohio town. That didn't work at all. Then one night, coming out of a long dream about the streets of London, I knew that I had stubbornly returned to the peo-

ple and the place of *Days to Come.* I was obsessed
with my dream, stopped writing for a month or so,
and only started again when I found the root of the
dream; then I moved the play to Washington, placed
it in the house of a rich, liberal family who were about
to meet their anti-fascist son-in-law, a German, who
had fought in Spain. He was, of course, a form of
Julia.

The dream had taken me back to an evening in
1936 when, on a visit to London, I had a phone call
from the famous Margot Asquith. I had never met
Lady Asquith, but I remembered Dorothy Parker
writing of her *Autobiography*, "The affair between
Margot Asquith and Margot Asquith will live as one
of the prettiest love stories in all literature." Lady
Asquith told me that the novelist Charles Morgan
wanted to meet me, would I come to dinner? It was a
strange evening: from the minute the butler opened
the Baker Street door and said, "Oh, you're bloody
young," I felt as if I had gone swimming in strong
waters and would have to struggle hard to reach land
again.

The dinner party was Lady Asquith, her son An-
thony, a movie director, her daughter Elizabeth,
Princess Bibesco, and the Romanian Prince Antoine
Bibesco, her husband. Princess Bibesco had written a
number of books and I would have liked to talk to
her, being at that point in my life most respectful of
lady-books that carried delicate overtones of sadness.
There was no Charles Morgan and Lady Asquith was

surprised that I thought there would be, but halfway through the dinner a very tall young man sat down next to me and, although I never heard his name through the marshmallow English syllables, there was some reference to his royal cousins.

Tony Asquith was most pleasant, but his mother frowned at me down the table as if she didn't understand why I was there and, as far as I remember, Prince Bibesco said no word. The butlers were plentiful, the conversation so faltering that one had the impression that everybody was ill, and when Bibesco rose, pushed aside his plate, said he'd meet us upstairs, I thought only that he was a sensible man to refuse the bad food.

When we left the savories — that upper-class English habit of drowning the bad with the worse — we joined the prince in a small room off the drawing room. It was filled by a large poker table, the chips already racked, and Bibesco didn't look up from his game of solitaire. Lady Asquith said she was due at a Parliamentary committee, called me Mrs. Dillman as she said goodbye, and left the rest of us to watch the prince play solitaire. When his third game came out fine, he patted me on the arm and asked if I played poker. I said yes, I liked it; he said he did, too, but didn't play much anymore and was out of practice. The semiroyal gentleman coughed, but I thought that was because a Mr. and Mrs. Something-or-Other came into the room.

In a few minutes we were all in a poker game. Elizabeth Bibesco didn't play but sat reading in a room off our room. In the first half-hour of the game her husband made jokes about how you cut cards, in what direction you started dealing, did a straight come before a full house, and by midnight I had lost almost three hundred pounds and semiroyalty had lost over five hundred pounds. I have no memory of what happened to the two strangers: I think they lost or won very little, although the man sneezed a lot through the evening. By the time I decided that my losses were far more than I could afford, I had learned that Bibesco had been the Romanian ambassador to Washington and a regular at the games of Vice-President Charles Curtis, a famous poker player. And I had heard enough to understand that it was not my literary reputation that had gone ahead of me, but a piece in the *New York Herald Tribune* saying that the boys in the famous New York Thanatopsis poker game had thought of inviting me to join them, but finally decided a woman would set a bad precedent. This was verified by the royal cousin, who drove me to my hotel in a high-powered racing car. He was a charming mixture of glum and glee as he said that he knew he was a bad player, always vowed he'd never go back to that particular high-stake game, and went back whenever he was asked. I thought about that poker game for years afterward and came to feel that the evening, the dinner, Bibesco, and Lady Asquith herself were characters sitting in a second-act drawing room because the stagehands had forgotten to tell them

189

that the scenery had changed to the edge of a volcano.

It was a pleasant experience, *Watch on the Rhine*. There are plays that, whatever their worth, come along at the right time, and the right time is the essence of the theatre and the cinema. From the first day of rehearsal things went well. It was a hardworking cast of nice people, with the exception of Paul Lukas, the best actor among them; but his capers were open and comic. (He told me that he had been a trusted follower of the Hungarian Communist Béla Kun, but that the week before Kun fell he had joined Kun's enemies. He saw nothing contradictory in now playing a self-sacrificing anti-Fascist.) But not everybody thought Paul was funny. John Lodge, then an actor and later to be our ambassador to Spain — when Dorothy Parker heard about his diplomatic appointment she said, "Lilly, let us, as patriots, join hands and walk into the water" — was shocked when Paul cheated him at tennis, and Eric Roberts, who played Paul's twelve-year-old son, disliked him so much that some nights he ate garlic before he climbed into Paul's lap and other nights he rubbed his hair with foul-smelling whale oil. I remember all that with pleasure, although a diary tells me that Herman Shumlin and I were having our usual fights.

The Baltimore opening of *Watch on the Rhine* went just fine and gave me a chance to see the medical historian Dr. Henry Sigerist. Sigerist was one of the heroes of my life: a learned man in medicine who read in many other fields; a political radical who was an

expert cook and on whose judgment professional tea
and wine tasters often depended; a tough man who
was gentle; a sad man who did not complain. And
he was a wise political observer: he had left the University of Leipzig, guessing two years before Hitler
came to power what was to come, and several years
before the full flower of Joe McCarthy, during a time
when the rest of us thought McCarthy a clown, he resigned from Johns Hopkins University and moved
back to his native Switzerland.

The week before he left America he came to visit
us at the Pleasantville farm and cooked a great and
complicated meal with our friend Gregory Zilboorg,
and all of us were happy with food and wine and
affection.

I was to see him only once again after that dinner,
in 1953, when, because he believed that McCarthy
might use him against me — I had the year before
been called before the House Un-American Activities
Committee and that year been subpoenaed by a summons that was never served by the McCarthy committee — if I came to visit him and his wife in Switzerland, we arranged to meet in Milan.

It was fine that day in Milan. Henry had gone to
school there and now had pleasure in showing it to
me. We drove a long way to a monastery that had
remarkable early wall paintings and the abbot and
two old priests were openly admiring of this Marxist
unbeliever; we drove further to a small castle on a
hill where the owner, a young woman, had a Cana-

letto he wanted to see again and they talked together of her grandparents; we had lunch and dinner in small, fine restaurants where the owners knew Sigerist and one of them asked for his opinion of a new wine and neither would allow him to pay a bill; we toured the ugly Milan Cathedral and he told me of the difference in the history of the Northern and Southern Catholic Churches; and when we said goodbye he told me he was ill and that I must come back soon because he would have only a few years more to see his friends.

He died on time, as he did everything else.

It is the lifelong problem of only children that they doubt all affection that is offered, even that which has been proved, and so, as the years passed, I told myself that Sigerist had been polite and kind to me, but that I had not gone back to see him because I was not needed or wanted. I only recognized the vanity behind my lack of vanity when his daughter published a part of his diary in which there is proof of what he felt for me. We all have been spared some nonsense and I have been spared caring very much what most people thought about me. But I cared so much for what this distinguished man thought that I cut the words from the book, put them in a frame, and locked the frame in a safe.

Yesterday, nineteen years later, standing in a pretty Wellfleet cemetery at Edmund Wilson's funeral, I thought of Henry Sigerist and knew why. These two men, so different in temperament, in interests, in belief, one so European, one so American, were alike in the kind of wide-ranging mind rare in a time of specialists, alike in the nineteenth-century conviction that culture was applied curiosity. I remembered once telling Edmund that I had asked Sigerist if it was true that he knew thirteen languages and he had said, "No, no. I know only nine. I can read in three others but I cannot say more than a sentence and that not well." Edmund had smiled at that, but a few minutes later told me that he was studying Hungarian and I knew my story had started a charming competitiveness in him and a counting on his fingers.

Watch on the Rhine is the only play I have ever written that came out in one piece, as if I had seen a landscape and never altered the trees or the seasons of their colors. All other work for me had been fragmented, hunting in an open field with shot from several guns, following the course but unable to see clearly, recovering the shot hands full, then hands empty from stumbling and spilling. But here, for the first and last time, the work I did, the actors, the rehearsals, the success of the play, even the troubles that I have forgotten, make a pleasant oneness and have been lost to the past. The real memories of that time are not for the play but for the people who passed through the time of it. President Roosevelt was one of them.

In those days it was a yearly custom for a play to be chosen to give a kind of command performance before the President for the benefit of the Infantile Paralysis Fund. When *Watch on the Rhine* was invited to Washington for a Sunday night early in 1942, it was the first public appearance of President Roosevelt since war had been declared.

John Lodge was a Naval Reserve officer about to be called up, and a good deal of the train ride from New York to Washington was taken up with the question of what he should wear to the White House for a supper party after the performance. A Navy uniform seemed premature; others of us argued that plain dinner clothes were not quite right for a man of distinguished family about to serve his country, perhaps to die. I suggested a sword and red ribbon as being neither too little nor too much, but John, who seemed to like that idea, said it would be impossible because nobody could find such stuff on a Sunday.

While the cast rehearsed light cues and tried the acoustics of the theatre, I talked an idle assistant manager into phoning a friend who worked at a theatre warehouse and offering him fifty bucks if he could come up with sword and wide ribbon. In a few hours I was backstage ironing the old crushed ribbon and clanking around with the sword. I guess people laughed too much because John, who had seemed most pleased about the idea, now refused the sword in peevish, stiff terms. I felt bad about that, it would have been nice, and only came around to feeling better when Mr. Roosevelt entered the theatre. The bold, handsome head had so much intelligence and confidence that the wheelchair in which he sat seemed not a handicap but an interesting way to move about.

At supper Roosevelt remembered that I had once visited him at Warm Springs, coming, by accident, on the same day as Huey Long. We talked about Long and my native Louisiana, but he was more interested — he asked me several times — in when I had written *Watch on the Rhine*. When I told him I started it a year and a half before the war, he shook his head and said in that case he didn't understand why Morris Ernst, the lawyer, had told him that I was so opposed to the war that I had paid for the "Communist" war protesters who kept a continuous picket line around the White House before Germany attacked the Soviet Union. I said I didn't know Mr. Ernst's reasons for that nonsense story, but Ernst's family had been in business with my Alabama family long ago and that wasn't a good mark on any man. Mr. Roosevelt laughed and said he'd enjoy passing that message on to Mr. Ernst.

But the story about my connection with the picket line was there to stay, often repeated when the red-baiting days reached hurricane force. But by that time, some of the pleasant memories of *Watch on the Rhine* had also disappeared: Lukas, once so loud in gratitude for the play, put in his frightened, blunted knife for a newspaper interviewer, and Lucille Watson, a remarkable actress, changed her written affection for me when she came to work in *The Autumn Garden* almost ten years later. She rehearsed with us then for three days. On the fourth day she did not return. She told another actor that perhaps she could put up with me because I was "a toilet-trained Jew," but she couldn't put up with Harold Clurman, the director, because he was "just plain Jew." The hardest lesson to learn in the theatre is to take nobody too seriously.

It is possible that because the war so drastically changed the world, the small, less observed things changed without being recognized. Now, looking back, I think that after *Watch on the Rhine* much of the pleasant high-jinks of the theatre were never to be seen again because the theatre, like the rest of the country, became expensive, earnest and conservative. The Tallulahs and the Lukases were not easy to take, but they belonged to a time I liked better. Whatever the reason, the theatre pictures behind my eyes for the period after that are fragmented and it would be useless and untruthful for me to order them up from scrapbooks or other people's memories. About the plays that followed that period, the pictures are there, but not many are much more than a camera angle that was part of a whole, of course, but is now seen only by itself.

Of *The Searching Wind* I have very little now except the memory of a wonderful old actor, Dudley Digges, arriving at seven-thirty each night during the run of the play to meet Montgomery Clift, a gifted, inexperienced young actor in his first large part. To-

gether they would sit on the stage until the second curtain call and go through a scene from Shakespeare or
Ibsen or Chekhov, or a series of poems, anything that
Digges had chosen to teach Monty. It was mighty nice,
the two of them, and I took to going to the theatre
several times a week just to stand in the wings and
watch the delicate relationship between the dedicated
old and the dedicated young. I was never to see much
of Clift after the closing of the play, but in the years
that followed, mostly unhappy ones for him, I am told,
I would often get a long-distance call from him, we
would arrange to meet, never manage it, but always
we would talk of Dudley Digges, who died a few years
after *The Searching Wind*.

I had always planned *The Little Foxes* as a trilogy,
knowing that I had jumped into the middle of the life
of the Hubbards and would want to go forward in
time. But in 1946 it seemed right to go back to their
youth, their father and mother, to the period of the
Civil War. I believed that I could now make clear
that I had meant the first play as a kind of satire. I
tried to do that in *Another Part of The Forest*, but
what I thought funny or outrageous the critics thought
straight stuff; what I thought was bite they thought
sad, touching, or plotty and melodramatic. Perhaps,
as one critic said, I blow a stage to pieces without
knowing it. In any case, I had a good time directing
the play, not because I wanted to, but because I was
tired of arguments and knew no director I thought
was right for me. I did a good job, I think, so good

that I fooled myself into thinking I was a director, a mistake that I was to discover a few years later. But then and now it gives me pleasure that I found an unknown girl, Patricia Neal, and watched her develop into a good actress and a remarkable woman.

With *Montserrat,* an adaptation I made from the French play by Emmanuel Roblès, I not only cast the play with a kind of abandoned belief that good actors can play anything, but I directed it in a fumbling, frightened way, intimidated by Emlyn Williams, the British actor and writer, who was playing the leading part. I do not blame Mr. Williams for his disapproval of me, although the way he showed it had a bad effect on the actors and thus on the play. He must have known from the first days of rehearsal that fear infects and corrupts what it touches. It is best in the theatre to act with confidence no matter how little right you have to it. It is a special and valuable gift, directing, but it has come to its present power mostly in comedies or musicals. Few dramas can stand up against another assertive talent, even if it is more distinguished than the original creator. Movies have come close to solving that problem: the director and writer are now often the same person, or two people who seen to function as one. But in the theatre, drama, even plain, dull seriousness, is still a business of unsolved delicacy between the writer, the director and the actors.

*   *   *

Many writers work best in time of trouble: no money, the cold outside and in, even sickness and the end in view. But I have always known that when trouble comes I must face it fast and move with speed, even though the speed is thoughtless and sometimes damaging. For such impatient people, calm is necessary for hard work — long days, months of fiddling is the best way of life.

I wrote *The Autumn Garden* in such a period. I was at a good age; I lived on a farm that was, finally, running fine and I knew I had found the right place to live for the rest of my life. Hammett and I were both making a lot of money, and not caring about where it went was fun. We had been together almost twenty years, some of them bad, a few of them shabby, but now we had both stopped drinking and the early excited years together had settled into a passionate affection so unexpected to both of us that we were as shy and careful with each other as courting children. Without words, we knew that we had survived for the best of all reasons, the pleasure of each other.

I could not wait to hear what he thought about the news in the morning paper, about a book, a departing guest, a day's hunt for birds and rabbits, an hour's walk in the woods. And nobody in my life has ever been as anxious to have me stay in a room, talk late into the night, get up in the morning. I guess it was the best time for me, certainly the best time of our life together. Now, I think, that somewhere we both knew — the signs were already there, Joe McCarthy was

over the land — that we had to make it good because
it had to end. One year later Hammett was in jail;
two years later the place where I intended to live the
rest of my life had to be sold; three or four years
later neither of us had any money and, more important than any of that, all of which can be borne
without too much trouble, we were to face Hammett's
death around every corner. If we did smell the future,
I am glad we had sense enough never to mention it.

I have many times written about Dash's pleasure
in *The Autumn Garden*. Now, this minute, I can hear
myself laugh at the fierce, angry manner in which he
spoke his praise, as if he hated the words, was embarrassed by them. He was forever after defensive — he
had never been about my work or his — if anybody
had any reservations about the play. A short time
after the play opened, I came home very pleased to
tell him that Norman Mailer had told me how good
he thought the play. Norman had said it was very
good, could have been great, but I had lost my nerve.

Dash said, "Almost everybody loses their nerve.
You almost didn't, and that's what counts, and what
he should have said."

By 1955 I needed money. I wish I could tell myself
that was why I adapted Jean Anouilh's *The Lark*.
But my reason was not money: I was feeling mischievous and the reasons for the mischief still exist as
they were written on a Ritz Hotel menu in London.

My producer, Kermit Bloomgarden, had bought the

play and wanted me to make a new adaptation. I flew to London to see Christopher Fry's version, didn't like it, cabled Kermit that it wasn't up my alley. Then I had lunch at the Ritz with Dr. Van Loewen, Anouilh's agent. I was pleased to meet a doctor-agent having only once before heard of one, Milton Bender, a former dentist, who perhaps had a better right to the title. So I said, "I am sorry, Doctor, but I do not believe this play is right for me. I . . ."

The doctor said, "We, Mr. Anouilh and I, have the greatest respect for your gifts, Mrs. Hellman, but *L'Alouette* comes from the mind of a poet and must, therefore, be adapted by a poet."

"Poet," I said, *"poet?"*

"We have the greatest respect for your gifts, Mrs. Hellman, but . . ."

"You are right. I am not a poet."

"There," he said. "You are a lady of honesty for whose gifts we have . . ."

"You don't need a poet. You need George Bernard Shaw, but he's dead."

The doctor said, "Shaw was not a poet. I do not think he would have been the right adaptor, either."

After I made that note on my menu and thought about foreigners, I said, "Mr. Shaw wrote a fine play about Joan of Arc, without all of Mr. Anouilh's bubble glory stuff."

"Mr. Anouilh is a poet," said the doctor.

"Perhaps," I said, "but not in French," laughed, and felt ashamed of myself.

I don't remember how long it took Bloomgarden to talk me out of the conversation with the doctor, but by the time I agreed to do the play I was convinced that Joan was history's first modern career girl, wise, unattractive in what she knew about the handling of men, straight out of a woman's magazine. The wonderful story lay, as Shaw had seen it, in the miraculous self-confidence that carried defeated men into battle against all sense and reason, forced a pious girl into a refusal of her church, caused the terrible death that still has to do with the rest of us, forever, wherever her name is heard.

And so for good or bad, I scaled down the play, cut the comparisons to the World War II German invasion of France and the tributes to the French spirit. I had doubts about the French spirit and, if the gossip about Mr. Anouilh has any truth, he had doubts; and I didn't like fake doves flying out over the audience to show the soaring spirit of Joan, the victory of idealism, or just to indicate the end of a play. And the fine, straightforward performance of Julie Harris helped make the play the first success Mr. Anouilh had in America, which is possibly why we never again heard from him or from the doctor, although all profits, quite properly, have been accepted by them.

Some kind of confidence, even fake, is needed for any work, but it is particularly required in the theatre, where ordinary timidity and stumbling seem like disintegration, and are infectious and corruptive to other frightened people. I think now that I began to leave the theatre with the production of *Candide,* an operetta with music by Leonard Bernstein, lyrics by Richard Wilbur. (I was not to leave for another two plays, but I am slow at leaving anything.)

I can account for the deterioration of my script from what I think was good to what I know is not good, but any such account would be confused, full of those miserable, small complaints and blames that mean nothing except to the person making them. I was not used to collaboration, I had become, with time, too anxious to stay out of fights, and because I was working with people who knew more about the musical theatre than I did, I took suggestions and made changes that I didn't believe in, tried making them with speed I cannot manage.

All that, I could and did put aside. The confidence went for another reason: I knew we were in bad trouble the day the cast first read and sang the play. I knew it, I said it, and yet I sat scared, inwardly raging, outwardly petty passive before the great talents of Leonard Bernstein, who knew about music, and Tyrone Guthrie, the director, who knew about the theatre. The lady producer knew nothing about either.

All of it, after the nice, hopeful period of work with Lennie and Richard Wilbur, through rehearsals to the closing night of *Candide* — and again, years later, the 1972 Kennedy Center revival with which I refused any connection — was sad and wasteful and did not need to be.

Several months after the play closed in New York, Tony Guthrie said, "Lennie, Wilbur, Oliver Smith, Irene Sharaff, Miss Hellman and Mr. Guthrie were too much talent for a good brew." That is hard for me to believe. Vanity, which I think is what he meant, can be of great use: it was dangerous during *Candide* because it was on a blind rampage.

I think now that Guthrie was as frightened as I was. I should have recognized that the night of the Boston dress rehearsal when Marc Blitzstein, an old friend of Lennie's and mine, walked me back to the hotel. We were depressed, neither of us talked the long way across the Boston Common. At the door of my room Marc said, "You're cooked, kid, and so is the show. I was sitting near Guthrie. He grinned at me once, his mouth full of sandwich and wine, and said, 'Well, Marc, that's that. Lillian is often right, but Lennie is so charming.'"

Guthrie was an imaginative man, bold in a timid business, uncaring about money in a world that cared about little else. It is true that the imagination led to tinkering: he reinterpreted almost every play he directed, but he did it with brilliance.

I turn my head now, look out at a jetty in front of my house, and see again this giant-tall man sitting on the end rock, telling me of his childhood, his university days, and then, as if he had talked more than he meant, suddenly pitching himself into the water at a dangerous angle. In the years after *Candide,* we sometimes saw each other, more often wrote letters. In one letter, I told him that *Candide* had done bad things to me, I wasn't working. He did not answer that letter, but a few months later he was in New York and we met for lunch. As I came in the restaurant door, a voice on my right side said, "Stop the nonsense. Get on with new work, get on with it today."

It was a valuable accident that a few days after that, or so I thought until a week ago, I spent the evening with Elena and Edmund Wilson. During the evening we talked of a man we both knew and Edmund asked why he didn't write anymore. I mumbled something about writing blocks, I had one myself, all of us, and so on.

Edmund said, "Foolishness. A writer writes. That's all there is to it."

For anybody of my generation, so eager for the neurosis, yours if you could manage it, if desperate somebody else's, the hardheaded sense of that was good stuff. But it did not happen a few days after I saw Guthrie. Last week I came back from Edmund's funeral and sat thinking about him most of the night. The next morning I went through old diaries of the many times I had spent with the Wilsons and found that "A writer writes. That's all there is to it," came almost two years after my lunch with Guthrie. But it is true that the next day after Edmund said it I went to work on *Toys in the Attic.*

Months before that day, Hammett and I had walked down from the house into the beach grass to look at a quail nest and see how things were going. I had known about the emphysema since Dash got out of the Army in 1945, known it had grown worse when he went to jail in 1951, knew that we could go less and less to the beach or any place else. But I don't think I had ever heard the heavy panting breath until that day as we climbed the steps back to the house. He stopped and lowered his head. I held out a hand.

He looked away from my hand and said, "I've been meaning to tell you. There's this man. Other people, people who say they love him, want him to make good, be rich. So he does it for them and finds they don't like him that way, so he fucks it up, and comes out worse than before. Think about it."

I wrote an act and a half and gave it to Hammett to read. When he had finished with it, he said, "Take the boat and go fishing. Forget the play for today. Maybe by night I'll . . ."

"No," I said. "This time you don't have to tell me what's wrong. I can write about men, but I can't write a play that centers on a man. I've got to tear it up, make it about the women around him, his sisters, his bride, her mother and — "

"Well," he said, "then my idea's out the window. Never mind. I'll use it myself someday."

He never lived to use it. But he lived long enough to have great pleasure from the play, and the last trip he ever made was to Boston for the opening. We had fun together, very like the old, first days of jokes, and wanting to be together, resenting the times we weren't. I skipped rehearsals for a couple of days and we went once more to see Paul Revere's house, Faneuil Hall, the Old South Meeting House, drove out to the Old Manse in Concord and had an argument about Emerson as if we had never had it before. I realized that in the pleasure of those days I had forgotten how sick he was and was worried that he would pay for the tramping about. But for the first time in years he seemed better for it, and we had late, cheerful dinners in our rooms.

I said, "The Ritz Hotel has the best thermoses. I wish I could just up and take one home."

"For years you've thought you were stealing what hotels mean for you to take, washrags, shoeshine cloths, soap, and then patting yourself on the back for the nerve of doing it. Take the thermos. You'll feel better."

"I can't. And you've never stolen anything."

"I never wanted anything enough."

"That isn't the reason. You think it isn't dignified."

The next day, coming back from a shopping trip with Maureen Stapleton during which I persuaded her into two expensive dresses and an alligator bag about which to this day, whenever there is too much of what she calls wine, she says I bankrupted her forever, Hammett was waiting for me with his suitcase packed.

I said, "You didn't tell me you were leaving today."

He said, "Did we ever tell each other?"

207

(This morning, twelve years later, I poured myself a cup of coffee from a Ritz Hotel thermos bottle. Dash had put it on top of his clothes, sent for a bell-boy to close the valise, and winked at me when the bellboy showed no sign of seeing the thermos. No, I told myself this morning, we had never told each other, never made a plan, and yet we had moved a number of times from West Coast to East Coast, bought and sold three houses, been well-heeled and broke, parted, come together, and never had plans or even words for the future. In my case, I think, the mixture of commitment with no-commitment came from Bohemia as it bumped into Calvin: in Hammett's it came from never believing in any kind of permanence and a mind that rejected absolutes.)

Toys in the Attic, with a splendid cast, was a success. The money came at the right time, because for a year I had known that death was on Hammett's face and I had worried about how we could manage what I thought would be the long last days.

It had been my habit to set the alarm clock for every two hours of the night: I would stumble down the hall to sit with him for a few minutes because he could sleep so little as he panted to breathe. Now it was possible to have a nurse and I looked forward to a whole night's sleep. But it didn't work that way: I didn't like a stranger in his room, I didn't want the night's sleep.

In 1962 I began an adaptation of Bert Blechman's novel *How Much.* The play was called *My Mother,*

My Father and Me and, by the time I finished, was half Blechman, half me. I thought, I think now, that it is a funny play, but we did not produce it well and it was not well directed. More important, I found that I had made some of the same mistakes I had made with *Candide:* I changed the tone midway from farce to drama and that, for reasons I still do not understand, cannot be done in the theatre.

The play waited in Boston for the New York newspaper strike to end. Once again I sat bewildered in a hotel room, making changes I did not believe in, this time under the pressure of how much money was about to go down the drain.

The playwright is almost always held accountable for failure and that is almost always a just verdict. But this time I told myself that justice doesn't have much to do with writing and that I didn't want to feel that way again. For most people in the theatre whatever happens is worth it for the fun, the excitement, the possible rewards. It was once that way for me and maybe it will be again. But I don't think so.

Arthur W. A. Cowan

THEODORE ROETHKE and I stood in the back of the auditorium until the poet Babette Deutsch finished reading. I am a noisy audience in a theatre, moving my body and feet without knowing it, cracking the knuckles of my hands, coughing. But I had been quiet that night because Ted had been tap-dancing in the back aisle to music only he could hear and several people in the last row had objected.

When Babette finished, somebody whose name I do not remember came onstage and said things I wanted to hear but couldn't because Ted said, very loudly, "I have just made up a poem. It begins 'Isn't it thrilling.' Now you write the next line. Go on, write the next line." I smiled because that's usually safe with drunks, but it didn't work.

"You don't want to write a poem with me. I don't

think you want to write a poem at all. O.K. We'll
write a play together, just the two of us. What you say
to that?"

He said it again and poked me in the ribs. "Sure,
Ted. A play," and hoped he wouldn't poke me again.

"You say sure, anything, sure, because no matter
how much work *I* do on our play people will think
you wrote it and I won't get any credit. So we'll sign
an agreement to have one name for both of us. What
name would you like?"

I said, "Let's go sit down. My feet hurt."

"Not until we find a name. I know, I know, I've
got it. We'll sign it with the salmon. How about
Irving K. Salmon? I like that, Irving K. Salmon, a
good name."

All through dinner there had been talk of a
salmon but I didn't know if he was talking about a
particular salmon or all salmon because sometimes
he talked about their spawning habits, sometimes he
talked of one or two or eight fishing trips he had
made, and once he told me about a nun he knew in
Seattle who had caught a giant fish and given it to
him.

Then another man came onstage, Roethke gave a
whoop, pulled me by the hand and dragged me down
the aisle. "Now stop talking about our play. That can
wait. I want to hear Cal."

We started into aisles that were already filled,
backed out, crossed a number of annoyed people in
the front row, and by this time had the full attention

of our side of the house. Robert Lowell had started to read in a rather low voice by the time we finally sat down and I wondered how he would make out if Ted kept on talking. But he didn't. He sat hunched forward, moving his lips to the poems, smiling, applauding occasionally at the end of a line. After a long silence he said in a new, piping, child's voice that carried through our section, "The kid's good." I am sure the kid was good but I hadn't been listening: I was tired after hours of being moved around New York, the pounding, often incoherent talk, the energy that had made us sprint into the zoo, running from monkey house to bird house, and then amble through lunch only to sprint again to visit a friend of Ted's who turned out to have moved from New York two years before.

When the Lowell reading was over, Ted made for backstage. He was ahead of me, forgetting me I think. But I decided not to follow him and walked slowly home, not expecting to see him again until the next time he came East.

In front of my house were Lowell, Ted, Babette, and three other people. Ted lifted me from the ground and said, "I told 'em you'd be right along after you had finished your secret pint."

To this day I do not know who two of the strangers were, but I came to know the third and he is the reason for my writing now about that night. I came to know his face as well as my own, but I have no memory of it that first time, nor did I then know his name.

I remember only that I found myself yawning into the face of a man sitting near me, yawned in another direction, and a few minutes later became conscious that the man had been staring at me for a long time, not with a flirting look, but as if he were trying to understand something.

He said, "Where do you keep your books?"

"Upstairs. There is a kind of library."

"Thank you," he said, "I am glad to know that." And then I was too tired to care that neither of us said anything else. A little while later everybody went home except Ted, who was weaving back and forth in a kind of shuffle, his lips forming words I couldn't hear.

I said, "Ted, I'm sleepy."

He said, "Ssh. I've got it. I've got it. The best poem written in our time. Now listen carefully: 'Isn't it thrilling there's another Trilling?' Got it? 'Isn't it thrilling there's another Trilling?' Got it? 'Isn't it thrilling there's another Trilling?' "

The second time he poked me in the ribs with his pleasure in creation I said, sure, the poem was fine, but why didn't he go home. He gave me a sad, hurt look, fell on me from his side of the couch and went to sleep immediately. I got from under his dangerous weight without waking him, but the next morning when I came down for breakfast he was gone. There was a note on the table: "I tell you it *is* thrilling, the Trilling. And just you remember about Irving K. Salmon."

I don't know how I came to mix up the salmon with the flowers, but four or five days later, Helen, a black woman who had worked for me for many years, suddenly appeared in the reading room of the Society Library. When something important had happened, or she was disturbed, she made military gestures. Now she hit me on the shoulder, made a sign meaning I should follow her, and while we walked the few blocks to our house she said, "Mary is down with it again. This time she got her good reasons."

Mary and her husband Ed had been the janitors of the house for the many years I owned it. They were Irish, feckless, kind, and often drunk, at which time they scattered into excitable pieces over nothing more than the mail being late or a light bulb wearing out.

"What's the matter this time?"

"I tell you this time she got her good reasons. A child's coffin. A child's coffin has come to the house."

"A child's coffin?"

"In a pine box. Dripping."

Indeed there was a pine box in the hall, it was the size of a small child, it was dripping, and most of the red lettering of the sender had been washed away. One could still read, "Mother Joa — " and numbers that still had two eights in them. Mary and Ed were too upset for me to know or care whether they had been drinking, but when I said, "It smells of fish," Mary shrieked, went out into the street and was followed by Ed, who took her arm and led her off, I guess, toward their favorite Lexington Avenue bar.

Helen went to get the handyman from the apartment house next door and when he pried off the lid there was a large salmon lying on what had been a bed of ice. The fish was turning, not enough to make us sick, but enough to make us carry it out to the street and close it up again.

In time, it turned out that Roethke had sent the salmon, and we exchanged a number of letters about it, although it was never clear about "Mother Joa — " A further mix-up came about because while we were opening the salmon box a large basket of flowers arrived, Helen put them on the floor, and somehow they got thrown out in the salmon excitement. I don't know why I thought Roethke had sent the flowers, but I thanked him, and long after I knew he had not sent them, he wrote that they came as a tribute because I liked his greenhouse poems.

A few weeks later another basket arrived. There were two enclosed cards: one from the lady florist who wanted to know if I had received a basket sent a few weeks before, and a second card on which was printed "Arthur W. A. Cowan, Esquire" and then a designation I have long forgotten that meant he had something to do with the State of Pennsylvania. I did not recognize the name Cowan, had never before known an Esquire, wondered when you were entitled to use it. Later that day I tried to phone the lady florist to find out about Esquire, but the phone was busy and I forgot about the whole thing until a third, even fancier arrangement arrived, with the same card and a scribbled sentence that thanked me for a nice evening.

I don't know when or how I connected the name with the man who had asked me about the books. It may have been because Lowell told me that he had never met Cowan before the night of the poetry reading but that he knew his name because Cowan had been a large financial contributor to *Poetry*. Nor do I have any memory of how Cowan and I first came to have dinner together, and then to have another, and then to find ourselves good friends.

It is hard, indeed, to construct any history of Arthur, in part because he traveled so much, but mostly because he talked of his own past and present in so disjointed a fashion, often taking for granted that you knew what you could not have known, certain that you were pretending ignorance only to annoy him. He is the only person I have ever known who had no sense of time: he did not know whether he had met people last week or many years before, and once he told me he had been divorced for three years when, in fact, he had been divorced for fourteen. And so, in the first few months I knew him, I could follow very little of the mishmash of what he said, and knew only that he had gone to Harvard Law School, moved on to the Philippines, been poor and grown rich, now practiced law in Philadelphia, had a large number of brothers and sisters, three houses, and expensive motor cars which he was constantly exchanging to buy others.

His no sense of time was tied up with no sense of

place, yours or his, so that he was bewildered and angered if you didn't know the names of his friends or
the kind of work he did, even though nothing had ever
been said about them. For example, the third time we
had dinner he told me that he had spent much of his
childhood in a Philadelphia orphan asylum.

I said, "But you're not an orphan. You just spoke
of seeing your mother yesterday."

He was at that minute, as at so many other minutes,
complaining about the steak he was eating, joking
with the waiter about taking it back.

The good humor turned immediately to anger.
"God damn it. That's the silliest stuff I ever heard
anybody talk. You don't have to be an orphan to get
into an orphan asylum. We were poor. We didn't have
enough to eat. So they put two of us in the joint. Then
sometimes when my father got a job they'd come and
get us for a while and then bring us back again. I've
told you all that a hundred times before."

In those early days of knowing him, I still believed
in reasonability and so I tried to say he could not have
told me a hundred times before, we had only known
each other a few months. But before I could say that,
he was telling the waiter that the steak was fine, but
his dinner companion wasn't. I would have been angry, as I was to be many such times in the future, but
that night I put down his sharpness with me to painful memories of the orphanage years.

I said, "I'm sorry. It must have been a bad time for
you."

"What the hell are you talking about?" he said for the next four tables. "It was the best God-damned time of my life. It was clean, and there was meat every day. They had books and it was there I learned to read. It was the best part of my life and you're an ass. Even you. All women. Every God-damned woman is an ass."

He shouted for the check, left the waiter an enormous tip, put me in a taxi and marched off. The next day almost the same arrangement of flowers arrived and I threw them out.

A few weeks went by, perhaps a month, and then I had a telephone call. He said, very cheerfully, "What's the weather like?"

"It's a sunny day, but not for you and me. How is it in Philadelphia?"

"I'm in London and I called to say that I don't bear any grudge against you. I'll be back tomorrow and will take you to dinner."

I said I didn't intend to eat dinner the next night and he laughed and hung up.

The following night I was having a tray in bed and listening to the phonograph when Helen came in, turned off the phonograph and said, "Can you hear it now?"

"Hear what?"

"There's something bad going on in the elevator."

The house had a small self-service elevator, but once inside you needed a key to get out or somebody to open the door on our side. It was an old elevator, and although nothing much had ever happened to it, we were always conscious that it might stick or fall, or that, without care, we could admit intruders. I got out of bed, went to the elevator door, and when I asked who was there the rhythmic pounding ceased.

A voice said, "Who wants to know?"

"I want to know."

"Who are you?" a second, high voice said.

Helen said, "Tell them to go out the way they came."

The first voice said, "Who said that? How many thieves are in my house?"

The elevator began to move upward. Helen whispered, "Don't open the door. There's more than one." The elevator went past us and continued up to the floor of my tenant.

The high voice said, "Open up or I'll shoot the place down."

My tenants, above me, had an elderly Japanese cook, and after a minute we could hear him running down the service stairs.

Helen said, "There goes the Jap. You can't blame the poor soul."

Like most people my age, I had a hard time believing in city crime, perhaps in any kind of danger. So I said to Helen, as I would not say today, "Let the Jap in our service door and tell him there's nothing to be afraid of."

Then, very loudly, I shouted into the elevator door, "Please leave the house immediately."

"What'll you do if we don't?"

"Call the police. So go immediately."

"I've got a better idea," said a voice, now undisguised. "Get dressed and I'll buy you a decent steak."

A few hours later, sitting next to him in his newest Aston-Martin, having just had a bad steak in a restaurant somebody had told him about — somebody was always telling him about a restaurant; in the years I knew him I don't think we ever went twice to the same place — I said, "Arthur, you're too young for me."

"Without question. How old are you?"

"Forty-eight. Too old for your high-jinks. How old are you?"

He said he was forty-two, and I didn't know that night why he coughed so much after he said it, nor why he stared at me so hard when we reached my door.

I was to find out a few weeks later. It started when the mail brought an engraved invitation for a dinner party to be given in Philadelphia by Arthur W. A. Cowan, Esquire, in honor of Miss Lillian Hellman. Although the engraving proved that the party must have been planned weeks before, I had had on the Sunday before the arrival of the card a most disturbing time with Arthur.

On that bad Sunday, driving to the country on the first, lovely spring day, as the Saw Mill River Parkway went by the turnoff, I said that the farm I had owned for so many years was just around the bend, over the bridge. This was the first time since I had sold it that I found myself so close to it, and if I was silent for a long time it was because I was trying not to cry. After a while, he stared at me and asked irritably why, if I liked the place so much, I had sold it. He knew why, because I had told him, and so I didn't answer until the question was repeated.

"The House Un-American Activities Committee. The Joe McCarthy period. I went broke. I've told you all that, Arthur."

"Yeah," he said, "but I never understood it."

"O.K."

But he was not a man to leave things alone when the toothache of blind contention was upon him and so, after a while, he said again that he didn't understand what Joe McCarthy had to do with the sale of a farm and he thought I was just blaming my mistake on somebody else. I knew, of course, before that day that his politics were eccentric, going in one direction on some days, in another the next. He was solidly conservative, sympathetic to every piece of legislation that benefited the rich, was the attorney for millionaires like Del Webb, and yet was a close friend of Mark De Wolfe Howe of Harvard and the Philadelphia liberal lawyer Thomas McBride. We had had no previous political arguments, in part because the mishmash he talked was too hard to follow, but mostly because I had already learned that I could not, did not wish to explain, or be wise about, or handle the bitter storm that the McCarthy period caused, causes, in me, and knew even then that the reason for the storm was not due to McCarthy, McCarran, Nixon and all the rest, but was a kind of tribal turn against friends, half-friends, or people I didn't know but had previously respected. Some of them, called before the investigating committees, had sprinted to demean themselves, apologizing for sins they never committed, making vivid and lively for the committees and the press what had never existed; others, almost all American intellectuals, had stood watching that game, giving no aid to the weak or the troubled, resting on their own fancy reasons. Years later, in the 1960's, when another generation didn't like them for it, they claimed they had always been anti-McCarthy when they meant only they were sorry he was not a gentleman, had made a fool of himself, and thus betrayed them. That was, that is, to me the importance of the period — the McCarthys came, will come again, and will be forgotten — and the only time I ever heard all that properly analyzed was by Richard Crossman in London, and although I have never seen Mr. Crossman again, I have often wished that he had written it down. It is eccentric, I suppose, not to care much about the persecutors and to care so much about those who allowed the persecution, but it was as if I had been deprived of a child's belief in tribal safety. I was never again to believe in it and resent to this day that it has been taken from me. I had only one way out, and that I took: to shut up about the whole period.

And so on that day, driving in the country, I had

225

no words. But by the time we returned to New York I was so shocked at the insensibility that forced Arthur to make fun of what had harmed me and had sent Hammett to jail, that I felt nothing more than weariness and that I must not ever listen to such stuff again.

A few days later, I wrote Arthur a note saying that, found the note incoherent, tore it up, telephoned to say that I couldn't come to my party. The operator said he was in Paris. I telephoned him in Paris, the hotel said he was in London. I got him in London, and before I was able to say much of anything he told me that he had just taken a woman to dinner who had on a red coat, he hated red coats, would never see the woman again, didn't know what I was talking about but was in the middle of a meeting and had just bought me a bracelet. He hung up, and when I called him the next day I heard him tell the operator that Mr. Cowan was not available.

Somewhere in the next few weeks, I had dinner with Mark and Molly Howe in Boston. I told them about Cowan's defense of McCarthy. Mark got up from the table and didn't come back for a while. Molly said of course they had heard the same kind of thing, and when Mark came back in the room he said, "Arthur is unbearable, unbearable." He was so disturbed that we ate our dinner almost in silence, only speaking when the Howe children came in and out of the room. Mark and Molly walked me back to my hotel and, as we stood in front of it, Mark's fine face was obviously getting ready for something difficult. He said "He is unbearable. He is unbearable. But it is only fair to tell you that his opinions often have nothing to do with his actions. I once told him about a Communist who had no money for legal defense. He paid the total bill and sent the wife a thousand dollars. I don't know his friend Tom McBride, but I am told he has another form of the same story." Molly said she thought maybe Arthur was just plain crazy, but I think both of them were saying they would understand if I wrote him off, but they hoped I wouldn't. I didn't.

*   *   *

Thinking about that night a few weeks ago, I wrote to Molly Howe, who has moved to Dublin since the death of Mark Howe. She does not refer to that night, perhaps she doesn't remember it. But she understood Arthur:

Dear Lillian: What can I say of Arthur? It's like roaming through a churchyard and picking out the names of old friends on the tombstones. Mark, Johnny Ames, Arthur Cowan, Bunny Lang, my old father-in-law, Felix Frankfurter, McBride, Joe Wall, all of them strung together by one name — Arthur's.

Arthur becomes a game of true or false. What did you or I *really* know about him?

I first met him a few years after the war. We had dinner, Mark, Johnny Ames and I at the Athens Olympia. He was then triumphing over the winning of some case in New Jersey, I think, and I think it was connected with aspirin, which indeed one was inclined to need after a few hours in his rather fevered company.

And after that . . . flying visits into the law school. Everyone knocked out of their legal torpor. Griswold actually took to hiding. Always with a new sports car, wearing frightfully expensive rather gaudy clothes, driving like a madman; off to the Ritz; bursting into the Poets Theatre. You almost knew by the weather when Arthur was coming. Something threatening about those clouds massing in the north. And you never knew he was coming until he was there. And the letters from Paris, from London, from Rome, from Hawaii, from the desk of Arthur Cowan. It must have been a flying desk.

I've never had such a curious relationship with a man before or since. It was purely friendly, almost fraternal. I really confided in him. I wrote him constantly, and the things he told me as well — true or false? To this day I do not know which. Brought up in an orphanage, number 58. That's why the number of our house 58 Highland Street was so important. He was convinced he would die when he was 58! Father killed himself during the Depression. Worked his way through college by professional boxing. Belonged to a delightful club in New York called the Bucket of Blood. Was married once to some girl in Philadelphia who played too much tennis. It broke up. He had girls everywhere. Two of them in London, and he had great difficulty keeping them apart. A girl in Paris — very special. Never liked actresses. Never liked models.

All lesbians at heart and everywhere else. Once caught them in the very act.

Arthur as a houseguest was not good. Stayed with us four days on the Cape in 1954. Would only eat steak and lettuce three times a day. Insisted on going round three-quarters naked with shaven chest. This last revolted Mark. We had some stuffy neighbors to cocktails and Arthur sat in a stately manner (this was six P.M.) naked except for a slight pair of pants, reading a life of Byron. "Arthur," I hissed in passing, "this man is a brother-in-law of the Rockefellers." When I looked round again he had vanished, went upstairs, came down twenty minutes later in an immaculate white linen suit. Unfortunately the Rockefeller contingent had gone. The next night we all went to dinner in Provincetown with Isabella Gardner and her brother Bob. Sudden outbreak from Arthur, who had been curiously quiet all evening. Shouted at Bob Gardner, "You're stupid! Phony! Numb! Ridiculous!" All heads turned in his direction. Nobody could understand it. Belle G. was furious and would never meet him again. A year or two later during the summer he suddenly shouted at Perry Miller — we were having cocktails on the porch, Perry as I remember was offering some learned information on Cotton Mather — "You're posturing. Why are you always posturing?" I don't believe Arthur knew whether Cotton Mather was a textile or a boll weevil, but suddenly something infuriated him. As he was always in very good trim and looked, with that broken nose, like

229

an aging but powerful boxer, nobody cared to take things up with him.

And his health. He was always having mysterious operations. He went through a period of having someone come in and give him an enema every day. He took royal jelly. Some great man in New York took care of his teeth. A splendid fellow in Switzerland for the eyes. Somebody in Philadelphia for the gallbladder and he told Mark he had himself sterilized in Paris. He didn't want any trouble of that kind. Paternity suits. Can't be too careful. And the diets. I never knew anyone go through such rigorous and varied diets. Do you remember the time he had to have raw parsley and carrots? Then there was the tablespoon of vinegar and all red meat phase and the exercises.

Every time he arrived there was a new and expensive camera. Color Polaroid long before anyone else and the constant taking of photographs was a ritual which had to be gone through on arrival and the camera was usually so new, so expensive, so complicated he didn't know how to use it. The cursing and swearing was heartrending.

Johnny Ames, for instance. Why did Arthur like such a New England Henry Jamesian old bachelor with very little money, of no importance in the world, because let's face it Arthur did like the Big Names. Why? And Johnny was fascinated by Arthur. They always had to meet when Arthur was in Cambridge. And they always talked about money. Do you remember Arthur talking about money? He talked about it the way some people talk about poetry. The voice was low and reverent, the face radiated a beautiful joy, and Johnny listened as if Arthur was the oracle, and Arthur advised Johnny on how to invest his little bit of capital. Advised him so well that by the time Johnny died he had almost doubled it. They conversed a great deal in French which was another bond and Johnny made the best martinis in Boston.

Why did he like V. R. Lang? A way-out blonde girl who wrote two good plays and some poetry and died of cancer aged thirty — a year after her very happy marriage. He met Bunny at the Poets Theatre, was fascinated by her play and fascinated by her world of Frank O'Hara, Bob Bly, Ted Gorey. It was through Bunny, in some way, he met you, Lillian, and moved into the Big World of Brains and never was happier. It all culminated for me at that wonderful house party, Birthday Party, weekend in Vineyard Haven that you gave for Arthur. How old was he then? It must have been twelve years ago. McBride was there and the Bernsteins and the Warburgs for dinner. Before Mark and I left that Monday morning, Arthur said to me, in that curious falsetto whisper: "It's not often you spend a weekend with all the people you like best. I have a feeling it only happens once." I have often thought of that since. Was it prescience?

He *was* a good friend. When Mark had a bad go of flu from overwork I told Arthur that Mark simply could not go on with the second volume of the Holmes and carry on a full teaching schedule at the law

231

school. It took Arthur only a few weeks to manage that. Mark was relieved of half the law school load and Arthur paid the half of his salary on a grant basis. In fact, if it hadn't been for Arthur, vol. II would never have been written, and if it hadn't been for vol. II, Mark might have lived longer.

Then there was the episode of Little Hel. Do you remember our youngest daughter was always known by Arthur as Little Hel? One afternoon he and Mark went for a walk round Eagle Pond on the Cape and unknown to them Little Hel took it into her head to follow them through bush and through briar a good mile on her own wobbly legs. She caught up with them eventually and Arthur couldn't get over it. The courage! The guts! The determination! He carried her back the rest of the way on his shoulders. He was almost crying. Of course he was going to mention her in his will. That well-known will of Arthur's that you and so many others were going to benefit by.

Did you ever read his poems? He brought out a book of poems I think in the late Forties. I had a copy once. God knows where it went. They were, of course, very bad.

And then those books inscribed to us by authors who had never heard of us, with Arthur standing over them with a gun. "To my dear friends Mark and Mollie Howe from André Maurois, with the compliments of Arthur Cowan." *You* must have several shelves of them.

He was a James Bond character. You remember

the sudden sinking of the voice to a whisper and the shifty look around and quick glance over the shoulder? What *was* he up to?

Well, he died alone on a dusty road in Spain, our friend, and we don't even know the truth about that.

*   *   *

And so I went to the party. I was taken first to what he called the guesthouse — Cowan owned two houses in Philadelphia — and then hustled around to where he lived in the few weeks of the year when he lived in any one place. It was a handsome old house in Rittenhouse Square, the windows spoiled with ugly draperies, the furniture heavy expensive copies of what the movies think is an English greathouse library. I dislike dark rooms and so, without plan, I went to one of the windows and pushed aside the draperies to see the view. Arthur dashed for the draperies, closed them and shrieked at me: "My books! My books! Don't do that."

"Don't do what?"

"Don't let in any light. It will harm the bindings. Why don't you know such things? I'll tell you why — because you don't have a fine binding in the world."

"I don't like them," I said. "If I had the courage, I'd throw out all my books, buy nothing but paperbacks, replace them — "

"I can't stand what you're saying, I can't stand it. You're not fit to touch a book in this house. I forbid you to *touch my books*."

The first guest came in on the shouting. Arthur immediately put an arm around me, his voice low, immensely loving. "This, I am proud to say, is my friend Lillian Hellman."

It was the usual cocktail stuff before dinner, but I was uneasy at being shown off and uncomfortable under the almost constant stare of a pretty girl across the room. At dinner I sat next to Tom McBride, whom I liked immediately. I knew that he had defended two radicals during the McCarthy period, and when I spoke of it and said there weren't many lawyers, certainly not successful ones, who had such courage, McBride pointed down the table to Cowan.

"That nut made it possible. I couldn't afford to take the cases, with a family and growing children, couldn't have involved my law partners. Cowan gave me all I needed through that time even though he hated what I was doing. He's a nut, but you'll get used to him, if you can stay with the nuttiness without wearing out. God knows what goes on in his head, if anything, but he'll kick through every time, without questions, and without wanting thanks, for the few people he has any respect for, and you're already one of them, the only woman it's ever happened with, and you must remember that."

I did remember it a few years later. Cowan said, "What's the matter with you? You haven't said a word for an hour." I said nothing was the matter, not wishing to hear his lecture about what was. After an hour of nagging, by the repetition of "Spit it out," "Spit it out," I told him about a German who had

fought in the International Brigade in the Spanish
Civil War, been badly wounded, and was now very ill
in Paris without any money and that I had sent some,
but not enough.

Arthur screamed, "Since when do you have enough
money to send anybody a can to piss in? Hereafter, I
handle all your money and you send nobody anything.
And a man who fought in Spain has to be an ass Com-
mie and should take his punishment."

I said, "Oh shut up, Arthur."

And he did, but that night as he paid the dinner
check, he wrote out another check and handed it to
me. It was for a thousand dollars.

I said, "What's this for?"

"Anybody you want."

I handed it back.

He said, "Oh, for Christ sake take it and tell yourself it's for putting up with me."

"Then it's not enough money."

He laughed. "I like you sometimes. Give it to the
stinking German and don't say where it comes from
because no man wants money from a stranger."

I sent the money to Gustav and a few months later
had a letter from his wife asking if I knew anything
about an American who had appeared at the hospital,
left an envelope for Gustav with five hundred dollars,
refused his name, spoke fine French, and had asked
the nun at the desk if she fucked around very much.

But that day after the Philadelphia dinner party,
the day he shoved in my pocket the largest and most
vulgar topaz pin I have ever seen, and was strangely

235

silent and thoughtful, was the day that marked our relationship for the rest of his life. We were driving back to New York — it is strange that almost every memory of Arthur is connected to a restaurant or to a car — and I had not talked to him very much because I sensed that he was on the verge of a temper. (I was to realize in the years to come that sadness often looked like temper, often turned into it, as if he were rejecting despair for something healthier.) As Arthur slowed down from his usual speed of a hundred miles an hour to avoid hitting two other cars, he said, "I'm the only good driver in America. Sons of bitches." Then he sighed. "Well, I might as well tell you, that's that. All my friends last night think you're too old for me."

I laughed. "Too old for what?"

"For me. They think that wouldn't be any good. I'm five or six years younger than you are." This was to be accepted throughout the years I knew him.

"What wouldn't be any good?"

He shifted around. He was uneasy, embarrassed, and that was always one step in front of irrationality. I should have been ready.

"You know what I'm talking about. Stop pretending."

"I don't know what you're talking about, Arthur."

"You know damn well. You're a combination of shyster lawyer and Jesuit. I mean you are too old for me to marry. That's what I mean and you made me say it."

I said, "That's not the way it is or ever could be."

236

"It's always the way it is. For every Goddamn broad that ever lived. Marriage, marriage, marriage."

"Not for me. Twice in my life, maybe, but not about you. I wouldn't marry you, Arthur, I never even thought about it."

"Like hell you wouldn't, like hell." He stopped the car in the middle of the Pennsylvania Turnpike. "You're lying. You'd marry me in a minute. Maybe not for anything but my money, but I'm not marrying you, see?"

I opened the door of the car and got out, getting home late that night by walking a long way to a place that suggested I call another place for a taxi.

But this time, the next day, in fact, I called him. I had not slept much that night, waking up to read, and to think about Arthur. I was what he wanted to want, did not want, could not ever want, and that must have put an end to an old dream about the kind of life that he would never have because he didn't really want it. We have all done that about somebody, or place, or work, and it's a sad day when you find out that it's not accident or time or fortune but just yourself that kept things from you. Years later, when Arthur was telling me about "a beautiful model who double-crossed me when I'd have given her the money without the double-cross," I told him what I had thought that night when he blamed my age and his friends for not wanting to marry me. He patted my arm and said, "Aah. Aah. Sometimes you're not an ass. Why don't I buy you a pound of caviar?"

But when I say years later and things like that, I

237

am not sure they are accurate. I did sometimes make notes in a diary, I have a large number of letters from Arthur, I remember more about him than I do about most people, and I know I can put together the order of his words with accuracy, but time, in his case, skips about for me, and I often mix up the places where we met, so that something that might have happened in Paris I have possibly transferred to Martha's Vineyard or Beverly Hills. The passing of time, the failure of memory, did not cause those confusions: they were always there. Perhaps because we never shared ordinary days together, more probably because everything about his life, the present and the past, was in jumpbites: he would tell a story about friends but he would start the story in the middle; he would ask you to regret a building he had just sold when he had not told you he had ever owned it; if he told a joke he would start with the last line and go backward; if he wanted to talk about a woman he was tired of, he started to tell you about another woman he had been tired of twenty years before.

I did piece together a kind of history, but I am not sure how much of it happened before I met him or after I knew him, since there was no way of sorting the past from the present. I knew that he didn't practice law much anymore, but that he himself was always suing somebody or some organization, and since that happened at least four or five times a year, I would get the details and the results mixed up. I knew that he had made a lot of money, before I met him, as counsel for a large drug company in a patent suit

and that he took stock instead of a legal fee. (It is in-
dicative that Molly Howe remembers the legal fight as
having to do with aspirin and I remember it as ben-
zedrine, and it was probably neither.) I knew that he
was a large investor in the stock market and a brilliant one. But I only knew that because sometime in
the first two years I knew him, he said, "Where is
your money invested?"

"I don't have much anymore. I have the house on
82nd Street, but — "

"What the hell did you do with all you earned?"

I said we were on a sensitive subject, the Joe Mc-
Carthy period and no work in Hollywood and the In-
ternal Revenue Department's refusal to let Hammett
have a nickel of his royalties, and thought we better
not get into an argument.

He said, "Don't tell me the reasons. Just go upstairs and get me all your records. Checkbooks, mort-
gages, everything. You'll starve in the streets without
me, that's where you'll end."

The following day I telephoned to say I needed my
checkbook because I forgot I was leaving in a few
days for London. Arthur said, "I'll give it to you in
the airport." Of course I thought he meant the airport
in New York and tried to reach him when he wasn't
there. He was waiting for me in the London airport
and swore that he had told me that. He had a new
Rolls-Royce, his third in about two years, and drove
me to the hotel. As I was signing, and the manager
came to greet me, Arthur said, "One room, not two,
and make it a cheap one. Miss Hellman has wasted

more money than anybody since Hubert Delahantey."

It was many references later, and many years, before I asked about Hubert Delahantey. It turned out he never existed in life: he was a rich American drunk who threw away all his money and died in a Paris garret in a novel Arthur had once bought at a French railroad bookstand but whose title he couldn't remember.

The following night, when the *Candide* rehearsals were over, Arthur came around to the theatre to take me to a new restaurant somebody had just told him about. After he had gone through his usual denunciation of the steak, he put my checkbook on the table.

"From now on you can have fifty percent of what you earn. I will invest the rest. You know nothing about money and are a disgrace. You'll end in a charity hospital and die without a pot to piss in or a bone to chew."

I said, "You talk too much about my death. And if that's the way it's going to be then I won't die much different from the rest of the world."

"You're the kind of fool who has forgotten more than you ever learned," he said so loudly that the next table of six upper-class English ladies and gentlemen looked down at their plates.

I said, "The English don't raise their voices, Arthur, although they may have other vulgarities."

"Fuck the British. I think they were in collusion with the Germans all through the war."

At the next table one man spoke to another man and the second man got up and came to our table. Arthur rose, grinning with pleasure.

He said, "My dear, good sir. During my attendance at Harvard, a university situated in Boston, the Athens of America, I was middleweight intercollegiate boxing champion and I am flattered that you recognize me. Let me buy you a drink."

The man, who was a tall, good-looking example of Empire, said he did not wish a drink, but he felt impelled to say that he thought insults to the English in their homeland were totally inappropriate for a foreign guest. Arthur gave a mirthless bad-actor laugh and said he wasn't anybody's guest: his hotel and this restaurant were gyp joints, what the hell did guest mean when you paid your way and the billions we spent with the Marshall Plan?

I got up and said, "I'm going to the toilet. Leave a note what jail you're in or what hospital."

When I came back Arthur had joined the English table and was sitting with his arm around the tall gentleman. After he had introduced me he whispered that Sir Francis was a distinguished barrister, they had many friends in common. After half an hour I said I was tired and wanted to go to bed.

Sir Francis said, "You're not going back to the toilet?"

I didn't much understand that or the giggles that went round the table until Arthur, walking me to the hotel, said, "They didn't like your saying toilet. I don't either and have always meant to tell you. Why can't you say ladies' room like other people? Sir Francis didn't like it for his wife. He said, 'I've heard of Hellman. But even an actress needn't say toilet.' "

"And what did you say, Arthur?"

"I said Miss Hellman is a playwright, most distinguished, and they made me name the plays. Anyway, we're invited to dine in the country with them tomorrow. Don't wear that tweed coat. Wear something quiet, black."

When we got to the hotel I said, "I am now going upstairs to the toilet and so I won't be able to go to the country with you tomorrow. If you don't tell them you are a Jew they'll think you're charming, but you can even tell them that if you also tell them how rich you are and very possibly good business for them."

We did not mention Sir Francis again until many months after we had both returned to New York and after somebody told me that Arthur had appointed him his representative in London.

I said, "Nice about you and Sir Francis. Have you given him enough business to install a toilet?"

"So you've heard about her," he said. "Want to see her picture?"

He took out of his wallet one of the many snapshots he was always taking with the most expensive of cameras he had just broken. A youngish woman was standing against a very large house, her entire body and face shaded by giant trees.

242

"Admit that she's a beauty," Arthur said.

"I can't see her. You can never see anybody in your pictures."

"I should tell you that I may decide to marry her."

"Who is she?"

"She is the niece of Sir Francis. A great beauty. I call her Lady Sarah."

(He did not lie, I guess. He did call her Lady Sarah but it was only last year that I discovered her name was not Sarah, she had no title, and neither, for that matter, did Sir Francis. Arthur had bestowed the titles upon them as a sign of the esteem he then felt.)

It is a strange side of many women that they are jealous even when they do not want the man, but I was old enough to watch for that and wait it out. I suppose I waited it out without speaking because after a while he said, "Don't worry."

I said I wouldn't and he said he thought I should and I asked him why and he said I was hiding things and he didn't like me when I did that. After we had batted that around for a long time, he said, "Don't you, don't you, well?"

"Don't I what?"

It is hard now to believe that I didn't know what he wanted me to feel and say and certainly the stumbling words, so unlike him, the sadness in the face, should have told me. But even if I had known in time I am not sure I could have said it.

"Don't I what?"

The sadness disappeared. He clipped out the words, "Worry about my money. You don't have to. Marry or not I'll take care of you."

I said I was having more trouble than usual finding out what he was talking about, and when he shouted, "My will. After I die. That's what I'm talking about," I thought it wiser to be off in another direction. So I asked him what had happened to the lady in Philadelphia and the one in Paris, had he told them about Lady Sarah?

"I'm through with them. If you ever listened you'd have known that months ago. Tomorrow morning I am flying to Hollywood for a vasectomy. Between that shit orthodontist and the abortions I spent fifteen thousand six hundred dollars last year."

The complaints about the orthodontist were old stuff but the vasectomy was new. I said, "If you're getting married why do you want a vasectomy?"

"Who wants children in this stinking world? I spent my life wondering why they ever had me. Who wants to throw out five thousand six hundred dollars on abortions?"

"You," I said, "for ladies who pocket four thousand of it."

We were at my front door. I said, "Arthur, you know that Hammett lives here now, is very sick, that means I don't get much sleep and am tired most of the time. Good night."

"So you don't want to talk about my marriage? If it worried you, you were going to miss me, that would

244

be something else. But you're just afraid the marriage will cut you out of my will, no money for you. I've told you, and I'll keep my word, I'll take care of you."

And he pushed me through my door and went down the street. I stood in the kind of anger I hadn't known for many years but which, even as a young child, I knew was uncaring of consequence, without control, murderous. I ran down the street and caught him as he was stepping into a taxi. I grabbed his arm and spun him around and spoke in the tones of quiet reasonability which have always been for me the marks of greatest anger. "Stop trying to buy me. You've been doing it too long. Not you or my mother's family or anybody else and just maybe because I am frightened it could happen. So skip me and have your vasectomy and your teeth fixed and your face operated on again and leave me alone and don't mention money or your Goddamn will again."

I stopped in pain at what I had let slip. For two years I had pretended that I didn't know that this interesting-looking man didn't like his face, had had two operations in Hollywood to correct what he didn't like, and neither had corrected anything except to make him look assembled and had taken away the lively brightness, the amusing crinkles of time, all that had been good.

He said quietly, "You don't think the operations made me look better?" Then he turned and took a long time to pay off the taxi driver and when I saw

245

his face the tears in his eyes had stopped. He took my arm and we walked up and down the same Madison Avenue block for an hour or so, neither of us speaking. Then, from the corner, I saw the light in Hammett's room go on, which meant that the night was over for him. We turned down to the house.

I said, "There would be no meaning to any apology, no sense saying I didn't mean to hurt you because I did. When I get like this it's better to be rid of me." We shook hands and I went upstairs.

One likes to think that words are understood, that what has been painful or forbidden will not happen again. But a few weeks later I had a note from Arthur: "I canceled the vasectomy, although I'll probably have it another time. If then I die on the operating table, you'll be a very rich woman."

I can no longer remember how long after that night we let each other rest in a kind of unplanned moratorium, but long after his death, one of his many stockbrokers told me that during that time the market had fallen sharply and that Arthur had put up a good deal of his own money to carry the margin account he had insisted I have; and sometime during that period a puzzling letter arrived from Barclays Bank in London telling me that Mr. Arthur W. A. Cowan had instructed them to notify me that in the event of his death securities had been placed in their vaults for me, although, of course, they could not reveal the nature or the amount. It was with that letter that I knew he had understood nothing of what we had said on our long walk up and down Madison Avenue and that there would never again be any point in telling him that what was proof of friendship to him wasn't, necessarily, for me. I felt self-righteous about that, as I frequently have about other people's money stuff, until Helen, a few days after Christmas, showed me a hundred-dollar bill Arthur had sent her.

"My," she said.

"If you want to send it back, don't worry about me."

"He means no harm," she said. "You never understood that."

Helen was a fine cook, the best I've ever known, and the nicest times we had together were in the kitchen. It had long been our habit, if we were alone, to make each other a gift dinner: she cooked me something I liked and I made her something she had come to like, my "foreign stuff," which she pretended she could never learn. That night I was making her saffron rice.

"Buy yourself a new coat with the hundred. You need it."

"No, I don't. The hundred dollars came pinned to a new coat. It's too small, of course."

Helen was a very big woman and the picture of Arthur trying to guess her size made me laugh.

"The coat be good for my niece. He means well. Men are different. You ain't ever learned that."

"Better than we are, worse?"

"Different. Where is Mr. Cowan?"

I thought I knew what she meant. She could barely

write the alphabet and could spell very few words.

"You can thank him on the phone."

"I ain't worried about thanks and neither is he. *You* ought to write him, it's a shame. He's doing what we all must do, come soon, come late, getting ready for the summons, and you ought to put out a hand."

That kind of talk was a part of her Catholic convert nature: it had happened before. If I argued with her there was a chance of depriving her of what she needed, but to be silent made hypocrisy between us and she had often played at seeing which she could catch me at. But now, although I only half understood, I was disturbed.

"Getting ready for the summons? What do you mean?"

When she didn't answer me, I said, "You talk too much about death. And he's a Jew. We don't get ready for the summons."

"Jew, not Jew. Nobody's anything. We all lost sheep."

I had heard this many times before and I knew I could annoy her by quoting the Reverend Whittier, a famous Negro backwoods preacher of her childhood and my mother's. "Sheep? The Reverend Whittier didn't like sheep. He said, 'Rise up and make yourself in the image of the lion. Throw off the shackles, grab away the whip, cut the chains of your oppressors as the lion would spring from —' "

"Oh, sure," she said, "sure enough. If we took away

the whip and cut the chains the white man would atom us out."

I laughed because I knew she wouldn't like it. She said, "I ain't talking about black nor white. I'm talking Bible, the summons to the Lord. The horn's over the hill and Mr. Cowan's been hearing it for years."

"Mr. Cowan's been hearing nothing but the sizzling of steaks, the crackle of money and airplane engines. What are you talking about?"

"Write him," she said. "Tell him my coat's fine and the money too."

All my life, beginning at birth, I have taken orders from black women, wanting them and resenting them, being superstitious the few times I disobeyed. So I did write about the money and the coat and for months received no answer. But in June of that year, a few months after Helen, Hammett and I moved to Martha's Vineyard, I had a note from him saying he'd like to come up for my birthday. I postponed telling Dash that he was coming. He had never met Arthur but he didn't like visitors, didn't like their seeing how sick he was, and would disappear into his part of the house during any visit. In any case, I didn't expect Cowan until the 20th, and so on the 17th of June, returning from market with a good many packages, I was surprised and nervous when I saw a Rolls-Royce parked in the drive.

Dash was sitting in the living room. Before I spoke he put up a warning hand and pointed outside to the

249

terrace. The local chief of police was there watching a figure in the distance running up and down the beach.

"What's happened? Cowan was coming in a few days. I forget to tell you — "

Dash said, "He came in here all done up in a motorcycle helmet, carrying a gun. He pointed the gun at me and said, 'Put 'em up, sir, and hand over the jewelry.' It didn't worry me because I know a toy gun when I see it, but it worries the police because he did the same thing at the gas station, where they don't know a toy gun."

Dash was a good-natured man, but in the last, bad, suffering years almost anything was too much for him.

I said, "Sorry. What should I do?"

"Cowan is down on the beach doing push-ups or something. Go upstairs and bring down the toy gun."

When I came back with it — it had been sitting on top of the collected works of Yeats — Hammett went out to the terrace and from the window I could see him and the police chief looking at the gun and speaking words I couldn't hear. The policeman took the gun, waved at me through the window, and climbed the steps to his car.

Hammett went to his end of the house and I followed him up the stairs, bracing myself against the fall I always thought he would have. He put himself on the bed and stared at me as he always did when the years had done nothing to convince him that he knew much about me.

I said, "I didn't know he was coming today."

He closed his eyes. I said, "Is something the matter? Can I get you something?"

"No. I'm just thinking that for the first time in my life I've met a crazy man who is pretending that he is crazy and wondering why you never see danger. Maybe it's what saves you. Let me know when he leaves."

Arthur stayed for three days. He never asked about Hammett, Hammett never asked about him. On the last day of the visit, we took a picnic lunch to an ocean beach. After he had done his push-ups, taken his mile run, we had a nice day, full of disconnected talk about people and places, an occasional passing reference to Lady Sarah. On the ride home Arthur fished out a folded check from the glove compartment. It was made out to me for ten thousand dollars.

"What's this about?"

"It's not a birthday present. You earned it. Remember the Soloway case, the lawsuit I told you about? You said maybe I should just tell the truth because I'd get anything else mixed up."

He laughed with pleasure at the memory and I tried to remember which of the many lawsuits was called Soloway. "Well, only a first-rate shyster mind like yours could have thought that up. I won the case and that's your part. You'll need it when I die."

"Are you going to die again?"

"You're not to ask questions because they've forbidden me to answer."

"They?"

"Yes, this time, *they*. I have taken an important job with the government and an oath not to reveal what it's about. I am telling you that much because my travels may seem odd to you from now on."

"Odder than usual?"

"Odder than usual. That's why I want you to have the check. If I am killed, of course, there will be more for you, the securities at Barclays Bank."

I waited until that night, always his choice for driving because he could reach higher speeds, and put his check in the glove compartment of his car. As he came up the steps with his bags and got into his car, I said, "I don't like CIA spy stuff anywhere, Arthur, and I am too old to waste time talking about how such people are needed, I guess, in every country. I don't ever want another fight with you, so this will be the last time — "

He said, quietly, "Mark Howe said the same thing a few days ago. He believed that I don't lie. Do you?"

"Yes."

"I don't work for the CIA. I never even heard about them until Mark explained. I don't like people who spy on other people, either. It's not the CIA I am working for and I swear to it. But I owe you and Mark the truth. My new bosses did question me about both of you. I said you were about as radical as rice and Mark was the most distinguished man at Harvard and if I had to listen to one word against either of you, then to hell with the whole thing. They're gentlemen, my new bosses, and they apologized."

I said I was glad they were gentlemen and then,

somehow touched, I said I didn't have to know what foolishness he was up to and I didn't want to part with him ever.

He said, "We're never going to part. I always knew that," and the car roared out of the driveway.

I telephoned Mark the next morning and asked him who he thought "they" were. He said he didn't know, couldn't believe the job was of any importance because he was going on the assumption that nobody with any sense would allow Arthur to make decisions, except in the field of law, and he wasn't even sure about that.

About a year later, on the opening night of Simone Signoret's production of *The Little Foxes* in Paris, I made the guess that the job had something to do with the Common Market, although there was never anything to prove that true. Arthur had ordered twenty tickets for the opening night and was sitting next to Jean Monnet, who in the few minutes I spoke to him after the play told me that he found Arthur "a brilliant financier" and so did "other countries." I was too sad about the evening to ask the questions that probably wouldn't have been answered anyway. I wanted only to get out of the Théâtre Sarah Bernhardt.

I had arrived for the last two weeks of rehearsals. Arthur met me at Orly Airport and we had a good evening. His love of Paris was always a pleasant thing to watch, but it was the last good evening I was to have until I left Paris the day after the opening of the play.

Much in the theatre always goes wrong, it's as if

from the beginning it was intended that way, but I had never before seen so much go bad so early: it was an awkward, too literal translation of the play; it was in a theatre meant for a pageant or an ice show; the set, which was intended only to show the middle-class indifference of a woman who had all her life been on her way to another house, was cluttered and decorated with the largest and most demanding objects I had ever seen on a stage; and the Texas sombreros chosen for Alabama bankers became a large and dangerous argument between Simone and me when, of course, they were only a small symbol of our irritation with each other.

Simone Signoret is an intelligent, charming woman, as remarkable in front of a camera as she is bewildered by a stage. Not knowing much makes many people in the theatre turn natural sense and humility into nonsense and pretense. It is understandable, it is sad, but it is also difficult and tiresome. And I am often no good with actors or directors. I do not speak when I should, speak out when I shouldn't; I praise in order to hide complaints and that is recognized; and my manners grow excessively good to hide anger that can't be hidden. I thus offend more than if I had had an open fight.

Every evening, after rehearsals, Arthur came to the theatre to take me to dinner, bewildered, he told me later, at a side of me he had never seen before. I would sit silent, unable to eat the good food, drinking too much of the wine, smiling at the wrong places in his complicated stories, shaking my head when I should have laughed. The night before the official opening his patience was coming to an end: why did I worry about an old play when he had made me enough money to live well for the next few years? Why did I make faces about his newest diet, buttermilk with melted butter and cheese? Did I want to see a picture of Lady Sarah in a sable coat he had bought her? Why was there a copy of Büchner on my bed table when I knew how he hated Germans? Had I read *Candy* in the French edition he had given me? I must say immediately what I thought of *Candy*. There was justice in his impatience, but the questions were provocative. I was tired and so, trying not to answer him, I wrote on the back of the menu, "Arthur is a man of unnecessary things. That's sad, but there's no cure. Did I make that up or have I read it?"

He said, "I've asked you three times. What do you think of *Candy?*"

"A nasty way to make a buck." And waited for the trouble.

I don't think he heard me because he said, "Roscoe Pound saved me. At the end of my first year in Harvard Law School I didn't have enough money to come back for the second. Pound called me in and said he'd find the money for me to get through. That was before I married the tennis player whose family had never read a book. They wouldn't have liked *Candy*, either. The ignorant bastards."

"O.K., Arthur, I see what's coming."

"I only started out to say I have been faithful to you in my fashion, Cynara, you and the Harvard Law School, and not much else."

(As I write these words I would not believe them, but I have a letter, written about a week later, in which they are repeated exactly as they came that night.)

"I get tired of other women."

"What's happened to Lady Sarah and the marriage?"

"So Pound got the law school to make me the loan and when he called me in to tell me I could stay, well, I can't tell you — Anyway, I cried so hard afterward that I hit a guy in the cafeteria who asked me why my eyes were red. When I die, I will take good care of my sister, I hate the rest of my family, but I'll leave her enough so she can support them, and then the rest is for the Harvard Law School and you."

I said, "Why don't you do things while you're alive and then not so many people would look forward to your death, which may be the longest in history?"

"O.K.," he said, "I'll buy you a house."

"I have a house."

"Then you'll have two houses. You're no problem, but what should I do for Harvard Law School?"

I started to say fuck the Harvard Law School, I've got other problems, but I said, without interest, "Maybe a scholarship as a thank you to Pound?"

He got to his feet, pulled me up, embraced me until I lost my breath. "Wonderful. When it comes to

the clinches, you're not such an ass. That's just what
I'll do. Now stop being so sad about *Foxes*, I promise
you I am never going to marry Lady Sarah."

A few months later he told me something about the
scholarship and I think he remembered to tell me because we were on our way to dine with Ben Kaplan, a
member of the Harvard Law faculty. Arthur was in a
gay, charming good humor that night — he liked lawyer academics, respected them — until a man sitting
next to him spoke of Goethe. Then one of the storms
that came across the ocean of his years broke with
tornado force, more out of control than I had ever
seen before, without sense or reason, from depths so
unknown and frightening that even these strangers
turned aside in pity or embarrassment. Arthur was
shouting to a silent table that Goethe was an old
German ass, like all Germans, past and present. Then
a woman, maybe the bravest or the silliest, asked
about Bach and Beethoven and I knew immediately
that would make things worse because Arthur didn't
like women to speak when he was angry, maybe because middle- and upper-class men had convinced him
against his will that women' shouldn't be shouted at
or knocked to the floor. He suddenly grew dangerous
quiet as he told her that nobody was sure Bach and
Beethoven were Germans, and anyway they were
musicians and what did that have to do with thinking? I was, as I had been many times before, torn
with shame that he was my friend and a strong desire
not to deny or desert him. So I made the wrong,

257

nervous remark: I said it all came back to Arthur's never having forgiven the Germans for producing Karl Marx. The quiet tone was gone again: Arthur told the table that my ancestors were German, that I had, therefore, inherited the national villainies, that my grandmother's name was Marx and therefore I was related to Karl Marx, and was even numbskull enough to like Heine. Still mistakenly intent on diverting him — it sometimes could be done and then he was grateful for the extended hand — I said that I had always liked Heine's remark that when the Germans made a revolution they would first have to ask permission. Arthur shouted at me that even I should know that Heine meant the *Nazi* revolution because Heine was an early Nazi and he wouldn't any longer sit at a table with me or anybody else who had an ounce of German blood.

It was that night, at that table, as I watched him leave the Kaplan house and move down toward the beach, that I knew something had gone wrong with Arthur, now forever: the inside lines that hold most of us together had slackened or broken and bad trouble was ahead. The early deprivations, the lost belief that money solved the problems of his life, the wild traveling about, the women, perhaps even the mysterious new job, maybe all of it or only some, certainly much I didn't know about, had made the life into a line on a fishing reel that tangled and couldn't be untangled, held by a hand that didn't have the sense or the courage to cut the line and tie it together in another place. But I had to cut the line of me where it crossed and tangled with his, and that night I did it, although, I am glad to say, he never knew it happened.

I was not angry that night, I was never to be angry with him again. It was no longer possible to pay him the compliment of anger, and I think he knew it and was worried about it. We saw less of each other, but in that next year and a half I had more affectionate letters than ever before, and once he arrived late at night, directly off a European plane, with a charming gold pin, and once he told me he had used the securities in my name at Barclays Bank but not to worry because he had increased my inheritance in his will, and once he told me that I was his best friend and that he loved me, and a number of times we had pleasant evenings and he became, for the first time, almost a suitor, as if he was looking for the affection he felt he had lost. He had not lost it. The truth was more important to us both: he had become to me a man of unnecessary things and often I felt that he knew what he was, was gallant about the pain it caused him and tried to hide it from himself with new cars, new houses, new friends, new women half forgotten at the minute they were half loved, new faces for himself, teeth set and reset, even new writers, here and in France, sub-sidized too long for their always shabby talents, new banks, new stocks, a new city or village or ocean that

259

he liked so much one year and disliked so much the next.

The last time I ever saw him was an August week he came to stay with me in Martha's Vineyard. An old friend of mine was there, he liked her, and the three of us had a pleasant time. We raced to many beaches in his newest Rolls-Royce, the old having been bought a year before, we walked, we climbed cliffs where he would be waiting for me at the top to say that even if I was six years older than he I was still in bad shape, and he would prove that further by running down the cliff and for a mile stretch on the beach, the fine powerful body no heavier, he said, than when he had been young. And for once there were no boring lectures about new diets: he ate the delicious stuff that Helen cooked and kissed her after each meal.

I said to her, "Mr. Cowan looks fine, doesn't he?"

She stared at me and fished out of her pocket a piece of paper. It read, "Before I fly tonight to Paris, Air France, Flight 972, I wish to bequeath to Helen Anderson in case of my demise the sum of ten thousand dollars in repayment for her kindness during these years."

I laughed. "He does that often, with all the ladies he likes."

"It's not nice," she said.

A few hours later, Helen and I walked with him as he carried his luggage to the car. I said, "Have a good trip."

Behind me, Helen said, "It's not nice, this piece of paper about the money."

I said, "Oh, what difference does it make?"

He kissed us both, said something about coming to visit his new apartment in Torremolinos about which I had not previously heard, and started the engine. I don't think he heard Helen say, "Drive slow, Mr. Cowan. Pray the summons back."

On November 11, 1964, I came into a hotel in Mexico City to hear myself paged. The voice said that Cowan was dead, killed instantly when the Rolls-Royce was smashed in Seville. But the accident was not in Seville and he had not died instantly and he had not been driving the Rolls-Royce. No will was ever found, but Lady Sarah and the pretty lady from the Philadelphia party of so long ago came up with old letters, almost exactly like Helen's, and collected large sums of money. In time, I asked Helen if she didn't want to present her note for collection, the going was good, and for a while she pretended not to know what I was talking about. Then one day she told me she had torn up the note as we stood saying good-bye to him that last day at the car door. The conflicting details of the accident, why a will disappeared that he certainly wrote and rewrote through the years, the failure even to find out what job he had been doing for what agency, all are to this day unexplained. If his life was puzzling, he entrusted the memory of it to people who have kept it that way. He has disappeared. I do not believe he would have wanted it that

261

way. And he was not six years younger than I, he was two years older, and there was a girl with him when he died. She was unharmed in the accident, she was nineteen years old, and she was German.

"Turtle"

I HAD awakened at five and decided to fish for a few hours. I rowed the dinghy out to the boat on that lovely foggy morning and then headed around my side of Martha's Vineyard into the heavy waters of West Chop. Up toward Lake Tashmoo I found the quiet rip where the flounders had been running, put out two lines, and made myself some coffee. I am always child-happy when I am alone in a boat, no other boat to be seen until the light breaks through. In an hour I had caught nine flounders and a couple of tautogs that Helen would like for chowder and decided to swim before going home to work. The boat had drifted out, down toward the heavy chop, but there was nothing new in this, and I was never careless: I tied my two-pound stone to a long rope, carried it down the boat ladder with me, and took it out to where I would swim near it. I don't know how long it took me to know that I wasn't swimming but was moving with incredible swiftness, carried by a tide I had never seen before. The boat had, of course, moved with me, but the high offshore wind was carrying it out of the rip into deep water. There was no decision to make: I could not swim to the boat, I could not force myself against the heavy tide. I have very little knowledge of the next period of time except that I turned on my back and knew that panic was not always as it has been described. For a time I was rigid, my face washed with water; then I wasn't rigid and I tried to see where the tide would take me. But when I turned to raise my head, I went down, and when I came up again I didn't care that I couldn't see the shore, thinking that water had been me, all my life, and this wasn't a bad way to die if only I had sense enough to go quietly and not make myself miserable with struggle. And then — I do not know when — I bumped my head against the pilings of the West Chop pier, threw my arms around a post, and remembered all three of us, and the conversation that took place four days after the turtle died when I said to Hammett, "You understood each other. He was a survivor and so are you. But what about me?"

He hadn't answered and so I repeated the question that night. "I don't know," he said, "maybe you are, maybe not. What good is my opinion?"

Holding to the piling, I was having a conversation

with a man who had been dead five years about a turtle who had been dead for twenty-six.

Even in those days, 1940, it was one of the last large places in that part of Westchester County. I had seen it on a Tuesday, bought it on Thursday with royalties from *The Little Foxes,* knowing and not caring that I didn't have enough money left to buy food for a week. It was called an estate, but the house was so disproportionately modest compared to the great formal nineteenth-century gardens that one was immediately interested in the family who had owned it for a hundred and twenty years but who had, according to the agent, disappeared. (This was not true: eight or nine years later a young man of about sixteen or seventeen came by and asked if he could see the house and picnic at the lake. He said he had been born in the house and he took with him a giant branch of the hawthorn tree he said his mother had planted to celebrate his birth.)

In the first weeks, I closed the two guesthouses, decided to forget about the boxwood and rare plants and bridle paths, and as soon as Hammett sold two short stories we painted the house, made a room for me to work in, and fixed up the barn. I wanted to use the land and would not listen to those who warned me against the caked, rock-filled soil. I hired Fred Herrmann, a young German farmer, because I had an immediate instinct that his nature was close to mine, and together, through the years, we drove ourselves to the ends of weariness by work that began at six in the morning and ended at night. Many of our plans failed, but some of them worked fine: we raised and sold poodles, very fashionable then, until we had enough profit to buy chickens; I took the money I got from the movie script of *The Little Foxes* and bought cattle and three thousand plants of asparagus we bleached white and sold at great prices. We crossbred ducks that nobody liked but me, stocked the lake with bass and pickerel, raised good pigs and made good money with them and lost that money on pheasants; made some of it back with the first giant tomatoes, the sale of young lambs and rich unpasteurized milk. But all that was in the good years before the place had to be sold because Hammett went to jail in the McCarthy period and I was banned in Hollywood after I was called before the House Un-American Activities Committee. The time of doing what I liked was over in 1952.

I have a jungle of memories about those days: things learned and forgotten, or half remembered, which is worse than forgetting. It seems to me I once knew a lot about trees, birds, wildflowers, vegetables and some animals; about how to make butter and cheese and sausages; how to get the muddy taste out of large-mouth bass, how to make people sick with the weeds I would dig and boil up according to all those books that say you can. The elegant Gerald and Sara Murphy grew very ill on skunk cabbage I had disguised according to an eighteenth-century recipe.

But the day I remember best was in the first spring

I owned the place. The snow had gone on the bridle paths and, having finished with the morning's work at the barns, I took Salud, the large poodle, and four of his puppies on an early morning walk to the lake. As we reached the heavily wooded small hill opposite the lake, Salud stopped, wheeled sharply, ran into the woods, and then slowly backed down to the road. The puppies and I went past him to the lake and I whistled for him, sure that he had been attracted by a woodchuck. But when I looked back he was immobile on the road, as if he had taken a deep breath and had not let it out. I called to him but he did not move. I called again in a command tone that he had never before disobeyed. He made an obedient movement of his head and front legs, stared at me, and turned back. I had never seen a dog stand paralyzed and, as I went back toward him, I remembered old tales of snakes and the spell they cast. I stopped to pick up a heavy stick and a rock, frightened of seeing the snake. As I heard Salud make a strange bark, I threw the rock over his head and into the woods, yelling at him to follow me. As the rock hit the ground, there was a heavy movement straight in front of the dog. Sure now that it was a snake about to strike, I ran toward Salud, grabbed his collar, and stumbled with the weight of him. He pulled away from me and moved slowly toward the sound. As I picked myself up, I saw a large, possibly three-foot round shell move past him and go slowly toward the water. It was a large turtle.

Salud moved with caution behind the turtle and as

I stood, amazed at the picture of the dog and the slowly moving shell, the dog jumped in front of the turtle, threw out a paw, and the jaws of the turtle clamped down on the leg. Salud was silent, then he reared back and a howl of pain came from him that was like nothing I had ever heard before. I don't know how long it took me to act, but I came down hard with my stick on the turtle's tail, and he was gone into the water. Salud's leg was a mess but he was too big for me to carry, so I ran back to the house for Fred and together we carried him to a vet. A week later, he was well enough to limp for the rest of his life.

Hammett was in California for a few weeks and so I went alone almost every day to the lake in an attempt to see the turtle again, remembering that when I was a child in New Orleans I had gone each Saturday with my aunt to the French market to buy supplies for her boarding house. There had been two butchers in the market who had no thumbs, the thumbs having been taken off as they handled snapping turtles.

Hammett came back to the farm upset and angry to find his favorite dog was crippled. He said he had always known there were snappers in the lake, and snakes as well, but now he thought we ought to do something, and so he began his usual thorough research. The next few weeks brought books and government publications on how to trap turtles and strange packages began to arrive: large wire-mesh cages, meant for something else but stared at for days until Hammett decided how to alter them; giant fishhooks;

extra heavy, finely made rope; and a book on tying knots. We both read about the origin of snapping turtles, but it didn't seem to me the accounts said very much: a guess that they were the oldest living species that had remained unchanged, that their jaws were powerful and of great danger to an enemy, that they could do nothing if turned on their backs, and the explanation of why my turtle had come out of the woods — each spring the female laid eggs on land, sat on them each day, and took the chance that the hatched babies would find their way to water.

One day, a month later perhaps — there was never any hurrying Hammett when he had made up his mind to learn about something — we went to the lake carrying the wire cages, the giant fishhooks, fish heads and smelly pieces of meat that he had put in the sun a few days before. I grew bored, as I often did, with the slow precision which was part of Dash's doing anything, and walked along the banks of the lake as he tied the bait inside the traps, baited the hooks, and rowed out with them to find heavy overhanging branches to attach them to.

He had finished with one side of the lake, and had rowed himself beyond my view to the south side, when I decided on a swim. As I swam slowly toward the raft, I saw that one limb of a sassafras tree was swinging wildly over the water, some distance from me. Sitting on the raft, I watched it until I saw that the movement was caused by the guyline that held one of the hooks Hammett had tied to the branch. I shouted at Hammett that he had caught a turtle and he called back that couldn't be true so fast, and I called back that he was to come for me quick because I was frightened and not to argue.

As he came around the bend of the lake, he grinned at me.

"Drunk this early?"

I pointed to the swinging branch. He forgot about me and rowed over very fast. I saw him haul at the line, have trouble lifting it, stand up in the boat, haul again, and then slowly drop the line. He rowed back to the raft.

"It's a turtle all right. Get in. I need help."

I took the oars as he stood up to take the line from the tree. The line was so heavy that as he moved to attach it to the stern of the rowboat he toppled backward. I put an oar into the center of his back.

He stared at me, rubbing his back. "Remind me," he said and tied the line to the stern. Then he took the oars from me.

"Remind you of what?"

"Never to save me. I've been meaning to tell you for a long time."

When we beached the boat, he detached the rope and began to pull the rope on land. A turtle, larger than the one I had seen with Salud, was hauled up and I jumped back as the head came shooting out. Dash leaned down, grabbed the tail, and threw the turtle on its back.

"The hook is in fine. It'll hold. Go back and get the car for me."

I said, "I don't like to leave you alone, you shouldn't be handling that thing — "

"Go on," he said. "A turtle isn't a woman. I'll be safe."

We took the turtle home tied to the back bumper, dragging it through the dirt of the mile to the house. Dash went to the toolhouse for an axe, came back with it and a long heavy stick. He turned the turtle on its stomach, handed me the stick, and said, "Stand far back, hold the stick out, and wait until he snaps at it."

I did that, the turtle did snap, and the axe came down. But Dash missed because the turtle, seeing his arm, quickly withdrew his head. We tried five or six times. It was a hot day and that's why I thought I was sweating and, anyway, I never was comfortable with Hammett when he was doing something that didn't work.

He said, "Try once more."

I put the stick out, the turtle didn't take it, then did, and as he did, I moved my hand down the stick thinking that I could hold it better. The turtle dropped the stick and made the fastest move I had ever seen for my hand. I jumped back and the stick bruised my leg. Hammett put down the axe, took the stick from me, shook his head and said, "Go lie down."

I said I wasn't going to and he said I was to go somewhere and get out of his way. I said I wasn't going to do that either, that he was in a bad temper with me only because he couldn't kill the turtle with the axe.

"I am going to shoot it. But that's not my reason

273

for bad temper. We've got some talking to do, you and I, it's been a long time."

"Talk now."

"No. I'm busy. I want you out of the way."

He took my arm, moved me to the kitchen steps, pushed me down and went into the house for a rifle. When he came out he put a piece of meat in front of the turtle's head and got behind it. We waited for a long time. Finally, the head did come out to stare at the meat and Hammett's gun went off. The shot was a beauty, just slightly behind the eyes. As I ran toward them the turtle's head convulsed in a forward movement, the feet carried the shell forward in a kind of heavy leap. I leaned down close and Hammett said, "Don't go too near. He isn't dead."

Then he picked up the axe and came down very hard on the neck, severing the head to the skin.

"That's odd" he said. "The shot didn't kill it, and yet it went through the brain. Very odd."

He grabbed the turtle by the tail and carried it up the long flight of steps to the kitchen. We found some newspapers and put the turtle on top of the coal stove that wasn't used much anymore except in the sausage-making season.

I said, "Now we'll have to learn about cutting it for soup."

Dash nodded. "O.K. But it's a long job. Let's wait until tomorrow."

I left a note under Helen's door — it was her day off and she had gone to New York — warning her

274

there was a turtle sitting on the stove and not to be frightened. Then I telephoned my Aunt Jenny in New Orleans to get the recipe for the good soup of my childhood and she said I was to stay away from live turtles and go back to fine embroidery like a nice lady.

The next morning, coming down at six to help Fred milk the cows, I forgot about the turtle until I started down the kitchen steps and saw blood. Then, thinking it was the blood that we had spilled carrying the turtle into the house the evening before, I went on toward the barns. When I came back at eight, Helen asked me what I wanted for breakfast, she had made corn bread, and what had I meant by a turtle on the stove?

Going up to have a bath, I called back, "Just what I said. It's a turtle on the stove and you must know about snappers from your childhood."

After a few minutes she came upstairs to stare at me in the bathtub. "There ain't no turtle. But there's a mess of blood."

"On top of the coal stove," I said. "Just go have a look."

"I had a lot of looks. There ain't no turtle on top a stove in this house."

"Go wake Mr. Hammett," I said, "right away."

"I wouldn't like to do that," she said. "I don't like to wake men."

I went running down to the kitchen, and then fast back upstairs to Hammett's room, and shook him hard.

"Get up right away. The turtle's gone."

275

He turned over to stare at me. "You drink too much in the morning."

I said, *"The turtle's gone."*

He came down to the kitchen in a few minutes, stared at the stove, and turned to Helen. "Did you clean the floor?"

"Yes," she said, "it was all nasty. Look at the steps."

He stared at the steps that led to the cellar and out to the lawn. Then he moved slowly down the steps, following the path of blood spots, and out into the orchard. Near the orchard, planted many years before I owned the house, was a large rock garden, over half an acre of rare trees and plants, rising steep above the house entrance. Hammett turned toward it, following a path around the orchard. He said, "Once, when I worked for Pinkerton, I found a stolen ferris wheel for a traveling country fair. Then I lost the ferris wheel and, as far as I know, nobody ever found it again."

I said, "A turtle is not a ferris wheel. Somebody took the turtle."

"Who?"

"I don't know. Got a theory?"

"The turtle moved himself."

"I don't like what you're saying. He was dead last night. Stone dead."

"Look," he said.

He was pointing into the rock garden. Salud and three poodle puppies were sitting on a large rock, staring at something in a bush. We ran toward the garden. Hammett told the puppies to go away and parted the branches of the bush. The turtle sidling in an effort at movement, was trying to leave the bush, its head dangling from one piece of neck skin.

"My God," we both said at the same time and stood watching the turtle for the very long time it took to move a foot away from us. Then it stopped and its back legs stiffened. Salud, quiet until now, immediately leaped on it and his two puppies, yapping, leaped after him. Salud licked the blood from the head and the turtle moved his front legs. I grabbed Salud's collar and threw him too hard against a rock.

Hammett said, "The turtle can't bite him now. He's dead."

I said, "How do you know?" He picked up the turtle by the tail. "What are you going to do?"

"Take it back to the kitchen."

I said, "Let's take it to the lake. It's earned its life."

"It's dead. It's been dead since yesterday."

"No. Or maybe it was dead and now it isn't."

"The resurrection? You're a hard woman for an ex-Catholic," he said, moving off.

I was behind him as he came into the kitchen, threw the turtle on a marble slab. I heard Helen say, "My goodness, the good Lord help us all."

Hammett took down one of the butcher knives. He moved his lips as if rehearsing what he had read. Then he separated the leg meat from the shell, cutting expertly around the joints. The other leg moved as the knife went in.

Helen went out of the kitchen and I said, "You know very well that I help with the butchering of the animals here and don't like talk about how distasteful killing is by people who are willing to eat what is killed for them. But this is different. This is something else. We shouldn't touch it. It has earned its life."

He put down the knife. "O.K. Whatever you want."

We both went into the living room and he picked up a book. After an hour I said, "Then how does one define life?"

He said, "Lilly, I'm too old for that stuff."

Toward afternoon I telephoned the New York Zoological Society of which I was a member. I had a hard time being transferred to somebody who knew about turtles. When I finished, the young voice said, "Yes, the *Chelydra serpentina*. A ferocious foe. Where did you meet it?"

"Meet it?"

"Encounter it."

"At a literary cocktail party by a lake."

He coughed. "On land or water? Particularly ferocious when encountered on land. Bites with such speed that the naked human eye often cannot follow the movement. The limbs are powerful and a narrow projection from each side connects them to the carapace — "

"Yes," I said. "You are reading from the same

278

book I read. I want to know how it managed to get down a staircase and up into a garden with its head hanging only by a piece of skin."

"An average snapper weighs between twenty and thirty pounds, but many have weighed twice that amount. The eggs are very interesting, hard of shell, often compared with ping-pong balls — "

"Please tell me what you think of, of, of its *life*."

After a while he said, "I don't understand."

"Is it, was it, alive when we found it in the garden? Is it alive now?"

"I don't know what you mean," he said.

"I'm asking about life. What is *life?*"

"I guess what comes before death. Please put its heart in a small amount of salted water and be kind enough to send us a note reporting how long the heart beats. Our records show ten hours."

"Then it isn't dead."

There was a pause. "In our sense."

"What is our sense?"

There was talk in the background noise and I heard him whisper to somebody. Then he said, "The snapping turtle is a very low, possibly the lowest, form of life."

I said, *"Is it alive or is it dead?* That's all I want to know, please."

There was more whispering. "You asked me for a scientific opinion, Miss Hellernan. I am not qualified to give you a theological one. Thank you for calling."

Ten or twelve years later, at the end of a dinner

party, a large lady crossed the room to sit beside me. She said she was engaged in doing a book on Madame de Staël, and when I had finished with the sounds I have for what I don't know about she said, "My brother used to be a zoologist. You once called him about a snapping turtle." I said to give him my regards and apologies and she said, "Oh, that's not necessary. He practices in Calcutta."

But the day of the phone call I went to tell Hammett about my conversation. He listened, smiled when I came to the theological part, went back to reading an old book called *The Animal Kingdom*. My notation in the front of this book, picked up again on a July afternoon in 1972, is what brought me to this memory of the turtle.

Toward dinnertime, Helen came into the room and said, "That turtle. I can't cook with it sitting around me."

I said to Hammett, "What will we do?"

"Make soup."

"The next time. The next turtle. Let's bury this one."

"*You* bury it."

"You're punishing me," I said. "Why?"

"I'm trying to understand you."

"It's that it moved so far. It's that I've never before thought about *life*, if you know what I mean."

"No, I don't," he said.

"Well, what is life and stuff like that."

280

"Stuff like that. At your age."

I said, "You are much older than I am."

"That still makes you thirty-four and too old for stuff like that."

"You're making fun of me."

"Cut it out, Lilly. I know all the signs."

"Signs of what?"

He got up and left the room. I carried up a martini an hour later and said, "Just this turtle, the next I'll be O.K."

"Fine with me," he said, "either way."

"No, it isn't fine with you. You're saying something else."

"I'm saying cut it out."

"And *I'm* saying — "

"I don't want any dinner," he said.

I left the room and slammed the door. At dinner-time I sent Helen up to tell him to come down immediately and she came back and said he said he wasn't hungry immediately.

During dinner she said she didn't want the turtle around when she came down for breakfast.

About ten, when Helen had gone to bed, I went upstairs and threw a book against Hammett's door.

"Yes?" he said.

"Please come and help me bury the turtle."

"I don't bury turtles."

"Will you bury me?"

"When the times comes, I'll do my best," he said.

"Open the door."

"No. Get Fred Herrmann to help you bury the turtle. And borrow Helen's prayer book."

But by the time I had had three more drinks, it was too late to wake Fred. I went to look at the turtle and saw that its blood was dripping to the floor. For many years, and for many years to come, I had been frightened of Helen and so, toward midnight, I tied a rope around the turtle's tail, took a flashlight, dragged it down the kitchen steps to the garage, and tied the rope to the bumper of the car. Then I went back to stand under Hammett's window.

I shouted up. "I'm weak. I can't dig a hole big enough. Come help me."

After I had said it twice, he called down, "I wish I could help you, but I'm asleep."

I spent the next hour digging a hole on the high ground above the lake, and by the time I covered the turtle the whiskey in the bottle was gone and I was dizzy and feeling sick. I put a stick over the grave, drove the car back towards the house, and when I was halfway there evidently fell asleep because I woke up at dawn in a heavy rain with the right wheels of the car turned into a tree stump. I walked home to bed and neither Hammett nor I mentioned the turtle for four or five days. That was no accident because we didn't speak to each other for three of those days, eating our meals at separate times.

Then he came back from a late afternoon walk and

said, "I've caught two turtles. What would you like to do with them?"

"Kill them. Make soup."

"You're sure?'

"The first of anything is hard," I said. "You know that."

"I didn't know that until I met you," he said.

"I hurt my back digging the grave and I've a cold, but I had to bury that turtle and I don't want to talk about it again."

"You didn't do it very well. Some animal's been at your grave and eaten the turtle, but God will bless you anyway. I gathered the bones, put them back in the hole, and painted a tombstone sign for you."

For all the years we lived on the place, and maybe even now, there was a small wooden sign, neatly painted: "My first turtle is buried here. Miss Religious L.H."

PENTIMENTO

IN 1961, a few weeks after Hammett's death, I moved to Cambridge to teach a writing seminar at Harvard. I had thought Hammett would be coming with me and had arranged with the help of Harry and Elena Levin for a room in a nursing home, a pleasant, sprawling nineteenth century house a few blocks away. Now, living with Helen on the top floor of Leverett Towers, a new student building, I could look down on the nursing home from the window and one night, when I couldn't sleep, I went to stand in front of it. That got to be a habit, and two or three times a week I would walk to the house Hammett had never seen, stand until I was too cold to stand any longer, and go back to bed.

The fifth or sixth time I took my late night walk — Helen was a heavy sleeper and I didn't think there was a chance that I could wake her as I dressed quietly in the next room — there had been a snow-storm during the day that made the few blocks hard going and slippery. But I never reached the nursing home that night, turning back for a reason I didn't as yet know, into Athens Street. Long before I reached our corner I saw Helen, looking very black in her useless summer white raincoat, standing with a tall boy who was holding a motorcycle. I felt the combination of gratitude and resentment I had so often felt for her through the years, but I didn't wish to waste time with it that night.

"Bad night," I said as I went past them.

I heard them behind me as I reached the court-yard of the building, and then I heard a misstep and a sound. As I turned, Helen had slipped, but the boy had caught the great weight and was holding to her, sensibly waiting for her to straighten herself. I knew she would not like me to see this, and so I went on into the building, took one elevator, waited until I heard her take another, heard the boy say some-thing outside our door, and closed my own door against whatever she might say to me.

A few days later I saw her cross the courtyard, the tall boy behind her carrying two large bags of groceries. As she opened our door she took the bags from him and said, "Thank you, son. Come when-ever you want your good dinner."

That night I said to her, "You've got a good-looking beau."

She had very little humor, but she liked that kind

288

of simple stuff. Now she didn't answer me and I realized that for the last few days she had said almost nothing to me. She gave me my dinner in silence. After dinner I read for a while, felt restless, and went to get my coat. She came out of her room.

"Death ain't what you think," she said.

"I don't know what it is, do you?"

"A rest. Not for us to understand."

I was used to this palaver, but that night I was ill-humored and made a restless movement.

"I don't want to talk about death."

As I stood waiting for the elevator, she watched me from the doorway.

"You go stand in front of that place because you think you can bring him back. Maybe he don't want to come back, and maybe you don't — " she shrugged, always a sign that she had caught herself at something she considered unwise or useless to continue with.

It was a long time before I knew what she had been about to say, and it was at least a year later, after I had moved back to New York, before I knew that she had discussed me with the tall boy. I thought that was disloyal of her and struggled for months about telling her that, and then knew it wasn't disloyal, and didn't care any more because I had come to like the boy and to understand she had needed him at a lonely time in her own life, in a strange city, living with a woman who did odd things at night.

Soon after the night we had talked about death I

came into the apartment to change my clothes for a dinner with friends. The boy was sitting at the table, Helen opposite him. He got up when I came into the room. We shook hands and Helen said to him, "Sit you down and eat your soufflé before it falls." As I went to my room I heard him say to her, "I never ate a soufflé before. It's wonderful."

"You can have one every night," she said, "a different kind."

When I came out of the bath I could see the boy from the hall mopping the kitchen floor. Helen came into my room.

"He eats nice. Two steaks."

I laughed. "*Two* steaks?"

"He asked what you'd think about that. I told him you got some strange sides, getting stranger, but you don't think about things like that."

"Thank you."

"He is taking me for a drive Thursday."

"On that motorcycle?"

"His rich roommate got a car. He says his roommate's on the stuff."

This then new way of saying dope, the only modern phrase I had ever heard Helen use, was no surprise. Years before she had told me her son was on the stuff and she would have to take him back to South Carolina to the farm her family still owned.

That Thursday, her day off, she got ready early in the morning and looked mighty handsome and big in a suit and a great coat.

"This early?" I said. "Doesn't he go to classes?"

"Jimsie is very, very bright," she said.

"What is Jimsie's last name?"

"I don't know," she said, "he's poor."

Jimsie was not as young as his classmates. He was twenty when we met him in his sophomore year. He told me he had had to wait to save a little money and win a scholarship, and when I asked him what his father did he laughed and said that nobody in his family had earned a living for three generations. He came from Oregon and one night he told funny stories about his mother and father, his five sisters and brothers.

I said, "You like them. That's unusual."

"Like them? I don't know."

"You don't know?"

"I don't know what they mean when they use words like that. I like to be around some people, or my motorcycle, and chemistry. I like one thing more than another. But that's all. Is that bad?"

I said I didn't know, I wasn't that kind of teacher. Then he went back to talking about his family and read me a letter from his father. His father wrote that a doctor in Portland had diagnosed stomach cancer but that he himself had cured it with a mixture of hot beer, cloves, and a sweet onion.

Through that first year I spent at Harvard, Jimsie would drop in at least three or four times a week to see Helen, carry her packages from the market, borrow his roommate's car to take her on small trips.

291

Often he would stay to eat dinner with her and sometimes with me.

It was the period of the early student movement and there was a time when he disappeared into Mississippi and came back beaten up around the kidneys, a favorite place, then and now, for a police beating since it doesn't show. Helen moved him in with us for a week, saying that a roommate who was on the stuff would be no good as a nurse. Jimsie was puzzled, uneasy about the fuss she made over him. And her lack of response to the state of the Negro in the South made him stubborn and nagging. It took years for him to know that it had to do with her age and time: her anger was so great, hidden so deep for so long, that it frightened her and she couldn't face it. He didn't understand her at all, in fact, and there was a funny, nice night in which his attempt to explain to her the reasons for the insanity of the Bay of Pigs was hilarious to hear. She didn't like talk like that: she liked best the times when he played his harmonica, and once she told me with pride that while she had not seen his "report card" another boy in the building had told her he was the most brilliant man in the class who played a harmonica.

In May of that year, about a week before we were to leave Cambridge, I woke up, knocked over an ashtray, and lay sweating with the mess I had been dreaming. After a while I got up, put on a coat and walked to the nursing home, certain that I would never go again. I stood in front of it for a long time, and when I turned to go back, Jimsie was directly behind me. I knew, of course, that Helen had telephoned him, but now, as we walked together, I had no concern for either of them. We didn't speak until I heard myself say, "Pentimento."

"What's that mean?" he said.

I said, "Don't follow me again, Jimsie, I don't like it."

But I don't wish to write about Jimsie; that isn't the point here and he wouldn't like it. Everybody else in this book is dead. We have become good friends, although now, twelve years after I met him, I don't understand him, or why he has decided on a life so different from the one he planned the year I met him. He was a chemistry student then and stayed on, after graduation, to work with Robert Woodward, the Nobel laureate, and spoke of the beauties and mysteries of chemistry with an emotion he showed for nothing else. Then he suddenly switched to astrophysics, and the night he tried to tell Helen what that meant she said he gave her a headache for a week, and because she came down with a bad cold after the headache and died from pneumonia a month later, I have always thought of astrophysics as having to do with her last days.

Jimsie was at the funeral in the ugly Harlem funeral place and I saw him standing in the rear, talking to her son. But by the time I reached the back of the place, through the mass of incompetent relatives she had been supporting for years, he had disappeared, and it was only last year that I found out it was he, not her son, who had taken the coffin by train to Camden, South Carolina, and waited with it on the station platform for a night and a day until her sister and brothers came a long distance over country roads to take it from him.

Somewhere in the years before or after that, I can no longer remember, Jimsie won a Marshall Scholarship, harder to earn than a Rhodes or a Fulbright, and went off to study in Cambridge, England. A friend of mine, an old Cambridge graduate, sent me a letter: "He has dazzled them here. I took him out for a drink, less because you wrote than because he is so interesting. But something has gone awry: I don't think he wants astrophysics, I think the world puzzles him."

I guess that was true, because he returned to Harvard, although I am no longer clear about when or why, except that he was there when I went back to teach in 1968, the year of the student riots. I remember that one day, at the height of the protests, we walked together in the Harvard Yard. George Wald, who had been a hero, and may be again, was not doing well that day as he stood before students making a conciliatory speech, too sure that his audience was with him, he with them. There were angry boos and the boy in front of us took an apple from his pocket and raised his arm for the pitch. Jimsie caught his arm and said, "Put it down, kiddie, a fine way of saying no to an old man." The boy pulled away angrily until he turned and recognized Jimsie, and then he said, "Oh, it's you," and patted him on the shoulder.

I guess he went back to England, because some-time in 1970 I had a short letter: "Do you think I can write? Of course not. But I'm through with astro-physics. I don't intend to work for the bastards and there is no other place to take it." I wrote back to say I didn't think he should try writing and didn't hear again until I had a card with an Albanian post-mark that says, "I like these folks. They're willing to fight everybody and they know the reason why. See you soon."

But it wasn't soon, not until last year during the summer, when I had a letter from Oregon saying he was back there, his father had given him forty acres of ruined land, the way everything his family touched was ruined, things were agreeable, but he was sick of communal life except for Carrie, who was clean and hard-working. A few days before this Christmas he called me, said he was in New York, could he take me to dinner?

It was good to see him again. The too bony face and body had grown now into power and full mascu-line good looks. We ate in a Greenwich Village fancy joint one of his friends had told him about and he whistled when he saw the prices on the menu.

He said, "I can't buy you dinner. I thought I could, but I can't at these prices."

"I'll buy it for you. It doesn't matter."

"Yes, it does, but never mind. You look tired. Is something wrong?"

"I am tired."

"Come to Oregon. I'll take care of you. Carrie has learned to cook and she scrubs around. I can't stand dirt. My mother is such a slob. A pretty, nice lady, but a slob."

"You like Carrie?"

"She's O.K."

"That's all?"

"Isn't that enough?"

"No," I said, "I don't think so."

"Not for you," he said. "For me."

"Do you farm the land?"

He laughed. "I have a good vegetable garden and I had a hundred chickens, but my father killed the chickens for a neighborhood celebration. I earn a living as a carpenter and now, *now*, I'm getting rich. Some ass in Portland, a woman decorator, sells what she calls rosettes des bois and I carve them for her. Got that? I make *rosettes des bois*."

"Somewhere I know those words," I said, "but I can't remember —"

"They're rosettes of wood and you stick them on headboards of beds or old armoires, mostly new junk you fix to make old. She started out paying me five bucks apiece but now she pays me twenty-five. I'll get more when I get around to telling her I want it. Good?"

When I didn't answer, he put down his fork. "Good?"

"Stop it," I said. "You know what I think. Do you want another steak?"

He laughed. "If you've got the money, yes. Helen told you about the two steaks she used to cook me?"

"Yes."

"That great, big, fine lady, doing her best in this world. Do you know she gave me this coat?" He pointed to a sheepskin coat, expensive but old, lying on the chair next to him. "And when I brought it to her, said it cost too much, couldn't take presents from a working lady, know what she did? She slapped my face."

"You once told me you didn't understand about like or dislike."

He said, "I loved Helen."

"Too bad you never told her so. Too late now."

"I told it to her," he said, "the night I looked up your word, pentimento."